# A SUMMER AFFAIR

# A SUMMER AFFAIR

Book 2: The Hotel Baron Series

MARY OLDHAM

Kindle ISBN: 978-1-7377839-7-8
ePub ISBN: 978-1-73778398-5
Paperback ISBN: 978-1-7377839-9-2

Any references to historical events, real people, or real places are used fictiously. Names, characters, and places are products of the author's imagination.

Story Editor
Edits by Sue, Sue Grimshaw

Cover Art by Lynn Andreozzi

Book design by Tamara Cribley at The Deliberate Page

Author Photo by Tanith Yates

Printed in the United States of America.

By-Creek-Ity Publishing
Portland, Oregon

First printing, 2021.

www.maryoldham.com

*To Suzie Rollow, my sister from another mister. You are Kat to my Laura. I'm so lucky to have you in my life. Much love to you, sister.*

# CHAPTER ONE

Adam Stark would never allow himself to fall in love again. Since he'd made the decision several months earlier, he'd felt better. The weight in his chest, where his heart once resided, seemed to lessen.

It was easy to be unemotional about his future when he'd been sent away from every place that held memories of his once happy life. He loved his cousin, Alex, for making the suggestion to get out of town, but he also hated his cousin for making sure that he might forget everything through hard work—as in the most strenuous, hard, physical labor he'd ever done in his life. He'd traded an office for a spade and dirt.

Did he miss an office where everyone called him Mr. Stark? No, he missed his family. Nothing was going to change that. He was lonely. Lonelier than he'd ever been in his life. He needed something to believe in again. He wanted to be close to another person; he wanted to be needed and not just to Stark International Hotels. But falling in love wasn't an option.

One quick glance to the shoulder of the road silenced every desolate thought, as his jaded heart fluttered wildly to life and issued a warning that couldn't be ignored. Be careful what you ask for, you just might get it. Happily, his brain and his heart were momentarily not working together.

He laughed. How long had it been since he'd laughed? At least a year. What he saw made him forget, momentarily, all those haunting and sad memories.

The woman was breathtaking as she kicked the bumper of an old, silver BMW with a flat tire and luggage piled next to the open trunk. And by the dent she'd created, he suspected she'd been at it for a while. With one last kick, she gave up, and turned to look down at the ocean raging in the notoriously evil cove known as Devil's Punchbowl. Her shoulder-length blonde hair whipped around her face in the warm wind, but she did nothing to stop it—she just stared, perhaps mesmerized by the crashing waves as they hit the rocks below.

Or maybe she'd just broken her foot.

Either way, he had to stop. Damn it.

Pulling off the road, he coasted the old pickup with a faded The Bay Shore logo to a stop a safe distance away.

Glancing toward him, she lowered her big, black sunglasses, her expression a mix of curiosity and apprehension. She was crying. Not a few tears, he realized, but a torrent. He surmised that this was about a lot more than a simple flat tire.

"Aw, hell," he muttered, getting out of the pickup, and lifting his hand in a friendly greeting. He knew how he looked. He'd spent the better part of the day digging up dead pine trees. A once clean white t-shirt and jeans were covered with a mixture of dirt and debris. She, on the other hand, was elegant in a crisp white blouse and black wraparound skirt, which alluded to a lush, curvaceous figure.

"Hello," he greeted, above the roar of the ocean. "Do you need some help with your tire?"

She nodded and held up a cell phone. Her voice cracked as she said, "I can't get cell service in this fucking vortex and the fucking tire won't come off the fucking car because the fucking tire guy used an air wrench to put the lug nuts on and I can't fucking get them off because they are so tight. Fuck! Fuck! Fuck!"

"Wow, okay. Are you okay?" She was not okay, and he knew he probably should not have asked her.

"I'm fine can't you fucking tell! I'm just peachy," she replied, with a sob she'd tried to stifle.

Adam's chest automatically tightened in empathy. "I can tell you're upset."

Bright blue eyes, rimmed in red, stared at him as her lower lip quivered.

Articulate by nature, he faltered. Best to get on with the business at hand. "I think I can help you. I'm stronger than I look. Do you know if you have a spare?"

"Of course, I have a spare. I tossed it over there," she said, lifting her hand and pointing. The spare was leaning against a railing, a good hundred feet away. A little more spin and it would be swimming in the Pacific Ocean.

Adam walked slowly toward the tire. She must have been angry. The momentum wouldn't have sent it this far unless she had kicked it…hard.

He got to the tire, picked it up, and carried it back to where she was leaning against the disabled car.

"I hate that tire, put it down and I'll kick it some more," she murmured as she started crying again.

Adam set the tire down and gently laid his palm on her bare arm, just below the cuff of her white blouse.

"I think the tire has had enough for today. Now please, don't worry, I'm here and I'll take care of this for you," he said, then added, "I've changed many flats and I'm quite good at it." Well, changed a few but no need to worry her at this point.

She lifted her gaze to meet his. Beautiful cornflower blue irises seemed to glow as they searched his face. She'd been crying for a long time, her lids swollen, and he guessed, burning from the irritation.

He didn't expect what happened next. She fell forward and he opened his arms, her body basically supported by his own. He didn't judge, but he did understand. How many times in the last year had he wished for someone, anyone to just hug him and offer comfort? He missed the touch of a woman.

Trying not to think about the acutely feminine body in his arms, or the subtle perfume reminiscent of roses that infused the air between them, masking his own scent of working male, he asked, "Would you like to talk about it?"

She blurted out, "My bastard husband left me for another woman, and the latest rumor is that she is pregnant. Didn't the

3

wedding ring on his finger mean anything to either one of them? She's an idiot and I hate him."

Adam said the first thing that entered his mind. "Your husband is the idiot."

She stepped away from him and he felt the loss of her. He could have stayed the way they were for a very long time.

"Thank you. Thank you for saying that. He'd vacillate between wanting children and not wanting children. I've always wanted a baby and he finally agreed. And then I couldn't get pregnant and now he is having a baby with someone else. What the hell? Do you know what it feels like to gain weight and give yourself hormone shots to get pregnant? It sucks and it hurts. And that bastard told me I was gaining weight while he was having an affair with his legal assistant…meanwhile I'm giving myself shots! *Shots.* I'm scared of needles, but I did it even though Dr. Mallory showed my husband how, but he was scared to do it, so I injected myself. In the stomach. Every fucking day. It was all for his baby and she's the one who gets pregnant, I hate him," she answered softly.

"I'm sorry?" Adam said, not sure what to say. Apparently, she needed to get it all out, it had obviously pent up inside of her for a long time and he just happened to be there.

The woman was lovely despite the grief and smeared makeup. He sighed, placing his hands on her shoulders, hoping she would believe him when he said, "If your husband were here, right now, I'd punch him for making you feel so bad, for not being a man and giving you the shots, for messing around with someone else. You're beautiful and he is an ass."

"Thank you, thank you for listening," she said and smiled, but he could tell she didn't quite believe him. Her gaze fell to the gold band he still wore on his left hand. "Your wife is a very lucky woman. You'd help her with the shots."

"Absolutely, and I was the lucky one to have found her," he corrected. "Let me help you with this tire."

"You're very kind, I'm sorry about falling apart, I usually have my shit together, but this tire, this fucking tire, and all the hormones. The doctor said it would take a while for them to get out of my system," she said, smiling a little and stepping aside as he reached for her trunk latch. "I don't think they are out yet."

"Don't worry about it. Let me have a look in the trunk."

"The jack and lug wrench are over there," she said. It was obvious that she'd thrown them in frustration as they were a good ten feet away from her car.

He retrieved them and said, "Don't go back to him, whatever he says. You deserve someone who adores you. He sounds like a real bastard." His tone conveyed it was more of an order than a suggestion, as he began to loosen the nuts on her wheel. He had no respect for men who cheated on their wives. In fact, he and his cousin, Alex, had disowned one of their closest friends from school after he forgot his marriage vows and hit on Alex's now wife.

"I'll never, *ever* talk to him again. As of ten this morning, I'm divorced," she said, and he thought she might start crying again.

"Good. He wasn't worthy of you, and life is too short." He jacked up the car, removing the nuts and hefted on the new tire, then tightened the nuts back on again. He opened the spare tire well and placed the damaged tire in the open space, replacing her luggage.

Looking down at her white blouse, he cringed. He couldn't help but notice the dirt smudged on the once pristine fabric.

Guiltily, he stepped back and apologized, "I'm sorry, but it seems I've covered you in dirt."

"It's a fair trade. You're covered in my tears and lipstick," she said, pointing to his t-shirt where a perfect red lip print was emblazoned next to several damp spots.

They both smiled tentatively, and she reached out, her small hand gently touching his arm. "Thank you," she said with heartfelt sincerity. "I'm so glad you stopped, not only for the tire, but what you said. Thank you. I'd like to pay you for fixing my tire."

Placing his hand on hers, he shook his head and said, "It was no trouble. I won't accept anything from you, but will you be okay?"

"Yes," she replied. "I'm not far from home."

He smiled one last time and turned away, walking swiftly back to his pickup. It was harder than he thought, leaving this woman he'd only known for a few minutes, but he'd served his purpose and it was time to move on. The pain he usually felt thinking about his family and what he'd lost subsided for those few minutes and all because of her. Getting back in the truck, he gave her one last smile and was rewarded with a wave, which he returned, before driving away.

The lacy wrought iron gates of Tranquility, which guarded admittance to the large seaside estate, swung open to welcome Laura. The journey had taken several, painful months. In as much time, she'd divorced her cheating husband, moved out of their beautiful home, and—adding insult to injury—come to terms with the harsh reality that she would never be able to conceive a child of her own. If she ever needed the solace Tranquility and its occupants could offer, it was this lovely day in June.

For the first time, she noticed the trees. What were they? Alder? Green and lush, they were top heavy, but leaning to the east. Over the years, they had become bent by the west wind that came in off the Pacific Ocean, but they were sturdier than they looked. She could relate.

The two-story, Mediterranean palace in butter yellow and white rose to greet her as she pulled her eight-year-old silver BMW into the circular drive. The seaside estate, Tranquility, was lovelier than she could describe and would be her oasis for as long as she needed it. How lucky was she to be close friends with Hollywood power couple, Katrina and William Russell? Damn lucky.

When they bought Tranquility five years earlier, it had been a big financial stretch. They had not only purchased several additional parcels of land around them. They also renovated their estate down to the studs. They had upgraded it in a way that made it an Italian architectural dream: part fabulous beach house, part five-star hotel, and part hidden oasis.

Several months earlier, after discovering the depth of her husband's deception, Laura had packed her bags and filed for divorce. Had it not been for her teaching position, she would have driven to the security of Tranquility then. Instead, she'd put her belongings in storage, slept on a fellow teacher's couch, and continued to teach as her world fell apart around her, each new day revealing another one of Leland's deceptions.

Today, she'd turned in her final grades minutes before a messenger delivered the last documents for her ultra-smooth, ultra-fast divorce. Fast was the only perk, Laura conceded, of being married to a divorce attorney. Red tape in the form of mandatory waiting periods simply disappeared. For as much as she enjoyed the speed of the termination of her marriage, she also realized it signaled how much her ex-husband wanted to move on with his life as well. He had a new life waiting with Amber, his assistant. What kind of life did Laura have? She had her teaching and the shattered pieces of her life. That was it. Their friends had taken sides. His friends were mainly people from the firm he worked at, and over time, many of their wives had become her friends. She'd lost them in the divorce, too. They were probably just happy Amber wasn't the third woman in their marriages. Laura had been the sacrificial lamb and they wanted nothing to do with her once she'd been slaughtered.

Picking up the large envelope containing the documents of her freedom, she'd locked her classroom and left San Francisco, vowing not to return until the week before school started in September. After a week or two with William and Kat, she would hit the road.

Where she would go, what she would do, she did not know. Maybe she'd buy a tent and camp along the Pacific coastline. Heck, maybe she'd drive to Yellowstone and watch bison. Maybe she'd go from town to town sleeping in youth hostels and living on $25 a day. She had three months to fill before she moved into her new apartment in an old Victorian brownstone near the high school where she taught in the Buena Vista neighborhood of San Francisco. It was an amazing find, and barely affordable on her salary, but it would be hers and not have any connection to her ex-husband or her previous life. At the end of the summer, she wanted to be a different person. She wanted to be whole again.

Driving along the coastline, she'd counted down the miles, wanting and needing to get to the welcoming arms of her friends.

For months she'd held her emotions together, never allowing the pain to overtake her. She'd suffered a double blow; the demise of her marriage and the knowledge she'd never have the one thing she wanted more than anything else, *children*. She was a teacher because she liked children. The sweet torture was that was as close as she was going to get. Which thing made her cry more? Leland's betrayal and the demise of her marriage, or the knowledge she would never hold her own child in her arms? The answer was a bit shocking to her. She had loved Leland, but she loved the idea of being a mother more.

Laura still could hardly believe she told a stranger of her woes. *My God girl, you cannot cry a river to people like that—it's just not cool.* Boundaries: she needed them. She knew she put the poor guy, her *tire knight*, into an uncomfortable position. Sigh. *Why did he have to be so kind and caring? And married? Why hadn't she married a man like that instead of Leland?*

Turning off the engine, she caught a glimpse of her reflection in the rearview mirror. Dark circles and puffy lids surrounded her large blue eyes, telling the story of pain so deep that it was hard to remember when she hadn't seen sadness looking back. This was her new personal low.

Beautiful Kat appeared at a set of large, open, French doors like some sort of magical siren of the sunset. Seeing Laura, she gracefully glided down the travertine front steps, waving as she did so. A tall, raven-haired beauty in a wild multicolored outfit of red, orange, and yellow silk, Kat was every inch the glamorous movie star. Laura felt dowdy and inadequate just at the sight of her. It had been this way since they were kids. They were exact physical opposites. Kat was willowy and trim, while Laura was short and curvy. Most of all, Kat was startlingly beautiful, while Laura's beauty was uncomplicated, so uncomplicated as to be bordering on nonexistent. Superficial qualities aside, their friendship endured. She loved Kat like a sister and the feeling was mutual.

Jumping from the car, Laura ran to the waiting arms of her best friend. Kat held her in a tight embrace and then put an arm around her shoulders and led her inside, handing her car keys to a khaki-attired member of her staff who had appeared out of the shadows.

"Thank you," Kat offered softly and then turned to her friend, concern in her voice. "You're covered in dirt. My god, did you and Leland sling mud at each other? I hope you won."

Leave it to Kat to find a way to make her laugh when she'd wanted to cry. "No, but it's a long story, strange and surreal...Kind of the best part of the otherwise horrible day."

"Oh, that sounds delicious, I can't wait!"

They went to Kat's favorite room, a small, cozy alcove overlooking the sea and decorated in soft colors of aqua and sand. Kat kicked her shoes off, curling her feet beneath her as she sat across from Laura on one of the sand-colored overstuffed couches, settling in for a long heart-to-heart talk. Laura similarly kicked off her shoes and sat on the other sand-colored couch across from her best friend.

"Start at the beginning and don't leave anything out," Kat ordered softly.

"I still can't believe it," Laura said, shaking her head. "I wake up each morning thinking I had a nightmare, but it's real. I'm sorry I didn't tell you everything. I wasn't dealing with it very well."

"I would have been there in a heartbeat if I could have been." Kat had been filming a movie in a remote location in China. "But then, I didn't know," she added, sounding a little hurt.

"There was nothing you could have done. I just had to get through it. Besides, you were half a world away."

"When did you know?"

"When he started complaining about my weight. It was just strange," she said in barely a whisper. It embarrassed her to discuss her weight issues, but her need to confide in her best friend overcame the awkwardness. After all, Kat was all too familiar with Laura's fertility challenges, even offering to fly her anywhere she could to get help. She was the one person who knew how important it was to Laura to have a baby. They had laughed together, confided in each other, and most of all, they shared in each other's successes as well as failures.

"One evening he told me that until I lost the twenty-five pounds I'd put on with the fertility meds or 'baby weight' as he called it, he wouldn't make love to me." Laura waited, watching Kat's eyes grow wide with fury. "I lost ten pounds by starving myself. Then he told me he was upping the number to thirty more pounds because the ten didn't show. I wondered why the lack of sex didn't bother him. Then I wondered if he was getting it from another source. I was right, of course."

"You should have left him then."

"I thought about it, but the very next day I found his Visa statement with all these strange charges. He didn't even try to deny the affair. He just told me that until I lost the weight and he felt attracted to me again, he'd keep doing it because he shouldn't suffer through my issues. That was the day I left."

"If I'd been here, I would have driven to San Francisco and helped you pack. I'll never forget that I wasn't there for you when you needed me. When I called your house and Leland answered, telling me you'd left, I couldn't believe it," Kat said, leaning forward.

"Up until last week, he was telling me I behaved like a child. He's the one having an affair with his twenty-six-year-old assistant who rumor has it is now pregnant." She shook her head and stared at one of the smudges of dirt on her sleeve. "I'm officially divorced as of today."

"Oh, Laura," Kat said, sadly. "I'm sorry, but good riddance. That pregnancy is purely salt in the wounds, what an ass!"

"He fell out of love with me because I wanted a baby. Okay, so I didn't feel pretty, and I haven't for a long time, maybe ever. I don't know if I blame him for not liking me. I don't know if I like me anymore. I've lost my identity. I don't want to be just a teacher. I want to be a mother."

"Okay, what the hell? Where is this crap coming from? Leland is the ugly one, you're pretty, Laura," Kat insisted, interrupting Laura's thoughts. "Even when you cry, your eyes sparkle. My own husband thinks of you as some sweet little reincarnated Scandinavian goddess."

"Hardly, Kat," Laura protested, dabbing at the tears leaking from her eyes.

"Truth, if I wasn't married to him and having fantastic sex and I mean mind-blowing multiple orgasm sex, I'd worry a little, but I've got him trapped in my sexual web, so I think I'm good."

Laura laughed, "William is totally under your spell."

"Exactly, and that is the kind of man I want for you. One who trips over his own feet thinking about you."

"Leland wasn't it," Laura admitted.

"I know the kid thing is big for you, especially since you lost your parents so young. You're not fat. You're curvy. You look healthy," she announced. "I'm really jealous of your boobs. They are pretty fantastic. The uplift is amazing."

"I do like to think they have nice uplift," Laura muttered, "But Leland told me I've let myself go. He said my body was ugly." As she said these last words, tears started leaking from her eyes.

Kat handed her tissue. "You've had round after round of fertility treatments. It's taken a mild toll on your body that only you notice. If the situation were reversed and Leland couldn't have children, would you have slept with another man and put him on a crazy diet? And what if you had a child? He abused you verbally, what would have happened to the child?"

"I fear that you know the answer." Laura hated that Kat was right. In no time at all she had cut through Leland's twisted logic and dramatic bullshit. Kat always took her side, told her the truth, and loved her for her faults. It was exactly why she'd come to Tranquility.

"But he did sleep with someone else. And what makes me want to kill him is that he tried to make his unforgivable acts your fault."

"To him, I'm a middle-aged, overweight, dumpy, high school math teacher," Laura replied, as a small sob escaped her throat.

"Leland only loves himself. You're well rid of him. I hope the knocked-up assistant trades him in for a new model in a couple of years, trust me, she will," Kat sighed, glancing at Laura, and shook her head. "Remember when we were eleven and Patrick Willis was throwing rocks at that sweet stray dog, who was all hurt and wounded?"

She nodded, and said sarcastically, "Of course I remember the dog."

"Laura, you beat up Patrick Willis, the biggest bully in the fifth grade. When you were finished, he was crying and bleeding. You took that sweet dog home and told your parents you were keeping him no matter what. I think you might have beaten them up if they had argued with you. You were passionately in love with the dog from the moment you saw him."

"Scooter was a beloved member of our family for eleven years," she retorted. "I loved that dog."

"He loved you. Laura, you were his hero. He would have done anything for you."

"Damn it, Kat! Thinking about the best dog that ever lived isn't stopping my tears," Laura said, smiling a little as she remembered her pet. Scooter had helped her through the death of her parents, then he too, died. The memory still hurt.

"Well, kiddo, you married the guy who likes to throw rocks. You married Patrick Willis all grown up. And Laura, you deserve much better than that." Kat pointed her finger to emphasize the point.

"Am I the dog in this scenario?" she asked with a sad chuckle as a tall silhouette filled the doorway. The dark-haired stranger, the one who'd held her in his arms along the side of the road, stuck his head inside the room, trying to catch Kat's attention, but catching Laura's instead. Recognition hit him at the same instant, his eyes growing wide with surprise as a quick smile graced his face.

"Hello again," he managed.

"Adam?" Kat asked, then glanced toward Laura. "Laura? You two know each other?"

# CHAPTER TWO

"Hello," Laura answered, her voice uneven as she took in the ruggedly handsome man with the strong jaw and chiseled features. He was clean and freshly shaven. His thick, blue-black hair was still wet presumably from a shower. She tried not to stare, but something about him made it hard to look away.

"Wow, what a surprise…I didn't know you were coming to Tranquility." His gaze ran over her body, and he frowned. "Again, I'm sorry about the dirt."

"It's okay, thank you for helping with the tire, I just wish you'd let me pay for it," she said, feeling warm. When he'd walked away, she'd felt oddly cheated, wanting something more from him, but not sure what. She didn't even know his name. Now she did. *Adam.*

"Well, Adam, I think you'd better come in," Kat announced with a small laugh. "It sounds like you've already met my oldest and dearest friend."

"No, not formally," he replied. "I'm sorry, I don't even know your name."

"Laura…Laura Daniels…I mean Laura Hokensen as of today," she announced holding up her empty left hand. Why did she need to keep sharing that she was divorced? She'd told him earlier. He probably thought she was out of her mind.

He elegantly stepped toward Laura and extended his hand. She took it, her fingers feeling small in his grasp as she shyly met his warm, brown gaze. She got a whiff of his cologne, an exotic mix of cedar and something faintly sweet that was intoxicating.

"So, you're responsible for the dirt," Kat surmised with a coquettish smile. "How very interesting."

"Long story, Kat," he said, and dismissed her with a smile. Turning to Laura, he said, "I'm Adam."

"Excuse my manners, Laura. Adam is a family friend of William's. He's doing some business down at the old Bay Shore Hotel this summer. In exchange for room and board, he's volunteered to give us some advice on running Tranquility. Our house has become large enough and sophisticated enough that it is self-aware, and we need guidance to help it run smoothly. We're delighted to have him."

Adam smiled politely, but his eyes continued to inspect her as he said, "Trust me, I got the better end of the deal. It's nice to meet you, Laura."

"Nice to meet you, Adam," Laura said, and without any thought, she unburdened her soul for the second time that day to the handsome stranger. "I'm Kat and William's parasitical friend. They've graciously taken pity on me, inviting me for a week or two while I lick my wounds. You know the rest of the story."

"Laura!" scolded Kat, sitting up in surprise. "You are most certainly not a parasite. William and I are delighted to have you. You are my best friend, you are like a sister to me, and have been since second grade."

Laura held up her tissue in apology and said, "Tears seem to bring out my honesty. I think Kat is horrified. I thought you were a landscape architect or something…"

"You probably thought I was a landscaper, I was so filthy," Adam said as the corners of his mouth curved into a smile, amusement dancing in his warm eyes. "I'm kind of a jack of all trades at the moment. If it makes you feel any better, I'm the parasite who needed a break before I cracked up at my job in New York. My boss, —who is my cousin—strongly suggested I take a little time off to refocus. Since the company recently bought The Bay Shore, it all worked out. I'm helping with the initial renovation, while I work on my personal renovation."

"I feel like I'm running some sort of celebrity rehab," Kat said to no one in particular, shaking her head. "Laura's my oldest friend and you, Adam, well," she turned to Laura, "every female member of the staff is literally swooning over this man. I'd love to keep him forever."

Adam shook his head, his attention on Laura. "Does she ever stop acting?"

"Darling," Kat scolded. "I might be happily married, but I'm not dead."

Laura laughed for the first time in weeks, admitting to Adam, "She's not acting. This is who she is."

He smiled, his cheeks crinkling with dimples fully aimed at her. Blushing and needing to look away, she reached for another tissue, but realized too late the box was empty.

Reaching into the breast pocket of his suit coat, he pulled out a silk handkerchief and offered it to her.

"Oh, I couldn't…" she protested, but he pushed it into her hand, the fabric sliding between her fingertips. Staring at the obviously expensive item, she said, "I might ruin it with my mascara."

"Don't worry about it. It's much gentler on your eyes than tissue."

Before she could thank him, Kat asked, "Can you join us? We were about to have several large cocktails, then a little dinner of something wonderful Chef Marco is putting together. I can't pronounce it, but it is Italian for cheese and cream with pasta."

Meeting Laura's eyes, he said, "That sounds great, but I've got a dinner with the interior decorator, who's here from San Francisco with some ideas about tile for the pool." With a glance to his watch, he added, "And I'm afraid I'm late. Another time." He smiled at Laura. "It was nice to meet you again, Laura. Glad you're here. I hope you like your cottage. We'll see each other again soon, I hope."

"Thank you, I'd enjoy that," she said, smiling genuinely for the first time in weeks.

Before he was entirely out of earshot, Kat teased, "I get the feeling Adam doesn't think of you as a dumpy high school math teacher."

"I get the feeling he is observant. You're out of tissues," Laura announced, shaking the empty box.

Ignoring her, Kat asked, "Okay, part of the story is coming together, but how exactly did you get dirt smears on your blouse?"

"I…I well…"

"Go on…" Kat prodded.

"It sounds bad," Laura started, "I pulled off at a viewpoint because I was crying and couldn't see to drive. So, I got out for a bit of fresh air and noticed my tire was flat. I tried to change it myself, but the tire guys used electric wrenches to tighten the lug nuts when they put on my summer tires last month and I couldn't get them loose. It made me mad, so I threw the jack and the wrench thing, and the tire. I tried to call for help on my cell, but I didn't have service. That's when I got really upset and started saying fuck, a lot. The next thing I knew, this old pickup pulled up, a man got out and started walking toward me. A minute later, I think I kind of fell into his arms, telling him about what an ass Leland was, and he was holding me, telling me everything would be all right. We chatted for a few minutes, he fixed my tire, and then he left…"

"Laura Hokensen! You let a total stranger hug you on the side of the road? Do you have any idea how dangerous that is?"

"Kat, it was just Adam."

"You didn't know that. You've got to be more careful," she scolded. "We have a lot of wacky people in California, and you could have met one."

Laura wasn't listening, she was watching the direction Adam had left. She replied, "He was so kind. What a wonderful man. His wife is so lucky…"

Kat grimaced at Laura's words, then said, "Um, about that. Adam's wife, Melinda, and little boy, Adam Jr., died last summer."

Laura's head jerked up. "What?"

"They were killed by a drunk driver."

"How absolutely horrible," Laura replied quietly, absently rubbing her fingers against the silk handkerchief as she thought of what he must be going through.

"His cousin, Alex Stark, called William a few weeks ago and said Adam needed to get away from New York. Alex is the head of Stark International Hotels, and Adam works in New York for the company. Alex had recently purchased The Bay Shore, which is in need of serious renovation, and it seemed like a natural fit.

He'd asked if we had a guesthouse Adam could rent, but when we insisted he come as our guest, Alex suggested that Adam had excellent architectural vision and could give us a consultation on Tranquility. William jumped at the chance."

She put her hand on Laura's and said softly, "Tranquility is a good place to come when you need time to think."

"Thank you for inviting me, Kat."

"This is your home. I just hope it's helping Adam." With a flirtatious wink, she added, "All the ladies are enjoying the eye candy."

"Ah-ha," Laura agreed with a nod of her head. Kat could be outrageous. It was what she liked most about her friend. But she could admit, Adam was a good-looking man.

"You two certainly seemed to have hit it off."

Laura shook her head, "I don't know what happened. He just appeared. It was crazy. And I knew he understood what I was going through."

"He's had personal experience."

"Sounds like it. What a tragic story."

"It is, but we hope Tranquility is helping him. You should see what he has suggested, and we've already completed the work on the guest cottage, which you will see since that is where you are staying. It is closest to the ocean, and it is spectacular. I thought you might like to have it be your home for the summer."

Laura smiled. "You're a good friend. I don't deserve you, but I'll only stay at most a week or two."

"Laura, you're our family. It is important to both William and me to have you here."

"Fish and houseguests go bad after three days, Kat. Even with this big house, I'd feel like I was imposing."

"You're my family. You're not imposing. Wasn't it always a nice escape when you were married?"

"It was," Laura said sincerely. "Thank you."

"You deserve the opportunity to have a summer to yourself, relaxing and enjoying. William and I want to do this for you. Besides we just got the new infinity pool that looks like it disappears into the ocean. It is fabulous! You should try it."

"Thank you, but aside from the pool what would I do for three months?"

"Nothing but relax," Kat purred.

"I can't lay around for the next couple of months and do nothing," Laura protested.

"You should, you can, and you will."

"I'll drive you crazy. Besides, I couldn't let you pay all my expenses for the summer."

"Consider it a happy divorce present," Kat said, offering a wicked smile. "Besides, I'm family and family does for family. You do know how much money I have, don't you?"

"That's too generous."

"Laura, please," Kat said thoughtfully, changing the tone of the conversation. "Remember when five figures in my bank account became six and I was so excited we opened champagne? Well, honey, I'm at eight figures now. Hell, William predicts nine by next year."

"Damn! Congratulations!"

"I know! Can you believe it?"

"You've worked hard," Laura said admiringly.

"Here's a thought. Why don't you pick up your watercolors again? You were always so good. I never thought you fully realized your talent. If you stay, you'll have the time, not to mention the scenery. You could be our artist in residence!"

"I'll think about it," she relented.

"You will stay. You can read a book, lay by the pool, walk along the beach, or sleep until noon. Try your best to drain the liquor cabinet. Take the next couple of months to decide what you want to do with your life. I'm going to say this once, Laura. William and I never liked Leland. He wasn't good enough for you. Life is short."

Laura crossed the distance between them and hugged her friend, the lump in her throat making her unable to speak.

"Okay, I've said enough. Let's have some dinner," Kat said, smoothing Laura's hair and giving her another quick hug back. Then she stood and ran to the doorway.

"Marco!" Kat yelled, using what Laura liked to think of as her real voice, not the Hollywood voice she'd perfected, down the long hall, "We are hungry now! Feed us, damn it, before we starve! What the fuck!"

Kat was a down-home type of woman that enjoyed fine things, but she was real. Her staff adored her and the way they bantered with one another was fun and respectful, and Kat paid them very well. After a wonderful sunset dinner with much cheese, cream, pasta, and wine, they stepped into the cool evening air which hinted at the warm summer that was coming. They picked up a small, winding, brick path lit with tiny dome lights that started at the south end of the new infinity pool and wound to a small, darling structure at the south end of the estate. It was built on a small bluff that overlooked the Pacific. Laura had heard the term "enchanted cottage," and this fit the bill. It even had window boxes full of nasturtiums with dark red flowers. Even though it was dark, Laura could see the waves breaking on the rocks below. The ocean, in fact, looked iridescent in the evening light. She inhaled the salty sea air and yawned.

"How have you been sleeping?"

"Badly, if at all," Laura answered as she stepped inside the warmly lit cottage. Soft, floral prints perfectly coordinated with the cozy, overstuffed furniture against whitewashed woodwork.

"Kat, this place is beautiful."

"Well, I can't take all the credit. Adam finished the cottage and got it ready for you yesterday."

"Adam did all this?" It was hard to think the same man who'd been covered in dirt could have the sophistication to decorate a cottage. She thought of how he looked in the suit and realized she'd underestimated him.

"He wanted to show me how they decorated their suites for special guests at the hotel." Fingering the petal on a rose in a large bouquet, Kat murmured, "I do believe he knows his stuff."

"Look at this place," Laura said in awe. "It's gorgeous."

"I decorated in Laura Ashley, only the good English stuff, not that American décor, in your honor. We're calling it 'Laura's Cottage'."

"You flatter me, but then you're a good actress. When do you start filming your new movie?"

"We changed the filming schedule. Now it's the middle of July, after our Fourth of July party. Speaking of the party, if you would like something to do, you can help me plan the menu. I've also got to double-check the guest list. I don't want any reality television types sneaking in like they did last year. They got one of my bartenders stoned on acid, the little assholes."

"I'd love to help. I need as many distractions as possible. Where's your first movie location?" She hoped Kat wouldn't be too far away.

"This is the best part! We'll be in the south of Italy, near Positano, where we spent our honeymoon. They've settled on the title: *The Italian Affair*. William's in Italy, checking out set locations right now. I miss him like crazy. I'm counting the days until he gets back next week and I can bang his brains out. I crave that man and his body. I'm married, I can say that," she said with a wink.

Laura was already missing her. She was happy Kat would be filming, but she didn't think she could stay at Tranquility without her. It would be too lonely.

After Kat said goodnight, Laura walked around the cottage picturing Adam arranging the space for her. Fresh flowers, of different sizes and varieties, were arranged artfully and placed in each room. Even the bed was turned down, exposing luxurious satin sheets. Had Adam done that? And why did the thought of him touching her sheets make her feel strange? She sank into the plush mattress and closed her eyes. Reaching into the pocket of her skirt, she pulled out the cream-colored silk handkerchief and rubbed it against her cheek. The silk carried with it the slight scent of his cologne.

When she realized what she was doing, she dropped the handkerchief as if it were on fire. A few hours earlier, she was crying over her ex-husband. Now she was mooning over some man she'd just met? A man who'd held her while she cried. A perfect stranger. What was wrong with her? She'd practically told him her life story. Blaming her behavior on fatigue, she got ready for bed and tried not to cringe at the memory. Her luggage had not only been brought to the guesthouse, but it had also been unpacked.

Pulling a pale peach and cream patterned silk nightgown and matching robe from the neatly folded pile; she stepped into the bathroom and looked in the mirror. She was a mess; her face was puffy and red. Makeup had run down her cheeks and settled in wrinkles she didn't know she had. Her blouse and skirt had smudges of dirt from where she'd rubbed against Adam as she'd clung to him. Groaning, she decided on a warm shower.

By the time she was sliding between cool silk sheets on her four-poster bed, she was exhausted. She sank into the deep mattress and sighed with pleasure. It had been almost three months since she'd slept in a real bed. As exhaustion gave way to sleep, her last thoughts were of the soft brown eyes that had looked at her with quiet compassion.

# Chapter Three

The dream was vivid. Laura watched silently from the end of the large bed where red satin sheets shimmered in the candlelight as two pale bodies swam on a sea of crimson. The woman's red hair splayed on the mattress as a well-muscled blond man pumped rhythmically into her. The look of ecstasy on the woman's face was mesmerizing as she moaned with each thrust. Their bodies were tangled together, entwined in primitive mating. When the passion reached a frenzy, the redhead screamed in a howl of pure rapture. The sound of the man's release mingled with hers, the muscles straining painfully in his neck. At last sated, the redhead smiled, a cat having enjoyed a bowl of cream. The man looked over his shoulder and smiled cruelly at Laura. Her ex-husband had taken great pleasure in making love to another woman, while she watched.

Laura awakened in the dark, struggling in the unfamiliar bed. The images of the dream were raw, colorful, and intensely erotic. At first, she wanted to be the woman consumed by passion, her body aching with the need of a man. She wanted to be taken in the same way, possessed with the same carnality. The color of the man's hair and the well-defined muscles in his shoulders were familiar. She recognized the smile, which turned from benevolent to malicious in an instant. *Leland.* Her erotic dream was her worst nightmare, her husband making love to another woman in her bed. The satin sheets were a new addition, probably because of the satin sheets on her bed now.

"Ex-husband," she said aloud and pushed free of the tangled sheets. Wrapping herself in her robe, she walked through the unfamiliar cottage trying to clear her mind. Thirsty, she opened the refrigerator and sighed. It was fully stocked. Had Kat seen to this or was it Adam's doing? Grabbing some water, she leaned against the granite countertop and drank thirstily from the bottle, no doubt needing to replenish what the tears had taken away. Glancing out the open window, she watched the moon illuminate the breaking waves.

When a shadow, just beyond the window, moved, she dropped the bottle, the cold water splashing her, as the plastic container bounced noisily on the counter and rolled into the sink. The shadow was the figure of a man sitting on a low wall a few yards in front of the cottage. Sensing he was being watched, he turned and looked at her.

A moment passed, then another. Laura's heart raced as her skin prickled in fear. Who was out in the dark watching her? When he raised a hand in silent greeting, she recognized the tall, strong frame. Self-consciously she waved back and tightened the belt of her robe before opening the front door and stepping into the mild evening air.

Adam greeted her with an apology, "I'm sorry, I hope I didn't scare you."

"You did, until I recognized you. What are you doing here?"

"I found this spot when I first arrived. It's where I come when I can't sleep. But there are a lot of other places I can go." Adam stood, ready to walk away.

"Please don't go. I don't mind the company."

"Are you all right?"

"Not really," she answered honestly.

He sighed, sat, and patted the space next to him on the low wall that separated her yard from the rest of the estate. "Care to join me?"

"Sure, you don't mind listening to me for the third time in one day?" she replied, sitting gingerly next to him, feeling the cool stone through her thin robe.

"No, I was hoping I might see you."

Surprised, she asked, "Why?"

"I'll let you know when I figure it out."

She pondered his words before asking, "You couldn't sleep either?"

"No. Never more than two or three hours a night," he admitted, sounding tense.

"That's not enough," she chided, wishing she'd thought to grab a blanket.

"I'll survive."

She thought about that afternoon, the way he'd held her. Who held him when he needed someone?

"Did I wake you?" He asked, Laura sensed his eyes lazily taking her in.

"No, I had a nightmare."

"Want to tell me about it?"

Turning to look at his profile in the moonlight, she said, "I don't want to bore you."

"Did you ever think you might be distracting me from my own demons?"

"No, I didn't." She rubbed her hands over her silk clad thighs to warm them. "Okay, remember you asked. I occasionally have the same dream, a dream about my ex-husband and his girlfriend... together...in my bed...fills my head."

He raised his hand and slowly placed it on the stone next to her, close, but not touching, "I'm sorry, I don't think I'd care for that either."

Something about the way he said the words, this man who'd lost his family, broke her heart. Her body shaking from a mix of emotions and cool evening air prompted Adam to move closer. Tentatively, he put an arm around her shoulders. She leaned into him, attracted to his warmth. Breathing in the same hint of cologne that lingered in the silk handkerchief, she burrowed against his neck as her arms gently reached for him. He was solid, but he leaned against her, appearing to need her as much as she needed him.

Eventually, she heard the breakers crashing on the rocks her body gently rocking in his arms as his hands rubbed the length of her spine. His lips brushed her forehead, placing a gentle kiss to her temple.

"Laura, When I saw you today…I…"

"Adam…" she said, her cheek brushing against his chin. "It was the kindest, most wonderful thing that you could have done for me…You hugged me, thank you…"

"I didn't want to walk away…it was the first time since my wife…"

She gently pulled back, her body fighting her with every inch. "You were there when I needed you, nothing more, nothing less. Just like tonight."

"You were there for me too, in more ways than you could know," he said.

"Friends then, okay?"

"I'd like that. Come on," he said, standing and holding out his hand, "I'll walk you back."

He led her up the slate path to the cottage. At the doorstep she paused, not knowing what to say.

"Get some rest. Tomorrow will be better, I promise," he said, stepping away from her.

"Liar."

Even in the moonlight, she could see his smile. "It's what I tell myself every day and today it was the truth."

"Then what was keeping you awake?"

"Tonight, it was you." Before she could say another word, he kissed her, a warm, fleeting contact, that fluttered on her lips like the wings of a butterfly and then he was gone.

Kat distracted Laura her first week at Tranquility, with double and triple-checking the guest list and consulting on the menu for the upcoming Fourth of July party. Exciting and fun, the parties were always fabulous and something Laura looked forward to for the entire year. Kat's guest list was extensive. Old friends and family, to some of the most famous names in Hollywood were invited. Even more impressive, they all attended.

Staring down at the menu, not thinking at all about the list of hors d'oeuvres she was supposed to be overseeing, Laura's gaze wandered to the window and beyond. She was in Kat's elaborately decorated red office with a magnificent view of the Pacific. Adam's kiss still lingered on her mind. Five days had passed since she'd seen him. Kat had commented that things at The Bay Shore were heating up and Adam was spending most of his time on site. As time passed, she was able to think of the kiss as more of a dream that hadn't happened.

Occasionally, her thoughts drifted to Leland. In the four months since she'd discovered his betrayal, she'd learned to live without him and found she didn't miss him, not as she'd once feared.

"Laura? Earth to Laura…Come back."

"What?" she asked, looking at a broadly smiling Kat.

"Welcome back."

"I'm sorry. I was thinking…"

"You were on another planet. I think it's time for a break. Come on, let's get out of here."

Laura watched curiously as Kat opened the little refrigerator built into the wall, pulled out a bottle of Perrier Jouët champagne and two glasses. She handed the bottle and glasses to Laura, forced open the nearest window and stepped through to the large terrace that ran the entire length of the backside of Tranquility. Reaching back, she grabbed the bottle and glasses from Laura's hands.

Leaning through the open window, she frowned. "Well, what are you waiting for?"

"Do you often leave your house through the window?"

"Only when I don't want to be found. Come on!"

Laura did as she was told, following her friend through the open window frame, onto the veranda and down white marble steps. Despite her gold, four-inch, high-heeled sandals, Kat ran gracefully across the lawn, her aqua silk outfit flowing in the breeze, the champagne bottle, and glasses in tow. She ran right into the laurel hedge in front of her, completely disappearing from view.

Laura stopped twenty feet behind Kat, placing hands on her hips. "What the hell?"

Kat had literally disappeared into the hedge.

Kat yelled cheerfully, "Come on Laura, look for the cut in the hedge!"

She walked closer; looking for the place Kat had stepped through. Seeing a three-dimensional illusion, she stepped through the hedge to be faced with another wall of laurel.

"Kat, is this one of those scary mazes like in The Shining?"

"No," Kat said disappearing around a corner. "Stop being a chicken and get in here."

Laura walked down a narrow path between two columns of green and rounded another corner, which opened into a large, laurel walled garden. The green oasis was filled with meticulously manicured plants and colorful flowers in large pots on a slate tile floor all of which were perfectly maintained.

"Isn't it beautiful?" Kat asked.

"It's gorgeous." Laura's eyes lingered on a large chaise lounge the size of a double bed with overstuffed green and white striped cushions. "Has this been here the whole time?"

"Only two months. William gave it to me as an anniversary present," Kat said, popping the cork on the champagne. "Try it out, we sure did."

Laura sat, lost her balance, and fell backward ungracefully as the cushion moved. "Wow! What is this?"

"Part hammock, part couch and all-around swing! Isn't it fun?"

"Until it makes me sick."

"What do you think of my little secret garden?"

"That sounds so decadent...I love it. It's exactly what you need. Your own private place."

"Our private place. I want you to enjoy it while you're here," she said, handing her a glass.

"Thank you, Kat...for everything."

"I love having you here, especially with William away. I'm lonely for my family..."

They sat on the chaise and drank champagne watching the clouds and chatting about everything and nothing.

"Do you think he'll marry her?" Laura asked, as her thoughts drifted to the woman who'd broken up her marriage.

"Maybe, but after the baby is born, if there is a baby, reality is going to hit him in the face. Lactating women who love their baby more than their husband or baby daddy and no longer like sex as much because they are tired have a way of doing that. And from her perspective, he's going to look like what he is, an old man who wanted a little fun with a young thing and ruined her by making her a mother at a young age. She'll dump his sorry old ass like you did. Then, watch out sister, he'll come back for you."

"Oh Kat, I don't believe all that. Let's change the subject please."

"Okay," she said, reaching into the pocket of her bright silk lounging pajamas. "I found this the other day. I thought you might enjoy it." She handed Laura a photo of the two of them riding in the backseat of Laura's father's convertible Mustang, with Scooter between them. They were very alike then, with their bad spiral perms and silver barbed wire braces.

Speechless, Laura took in every detail of the photo, focusing on her parents in the front seat.

Kat exclaimed, "Look at us! We thought we looked so cool in the back of your dad's car. Even the dog is smiling."

Laura swallowed down the thick emotion seizing the muscles in her throat. She remembered the photo, had committed to memory the day their neighbor decided to try out his new camera. It was the summer after her twelfth birthday. For Kat, the best was yet to come, her life about to rocket to stardom. Laura hadn't known she had less than ten years left with her parents. She hadn't known she should savor every moment, because they would be gone by her twenty-first birthday. She hadn't known when she saw the photo again she would be a sad, barren, divorced schoolteacher feeling every one of her thirty-seven years.

She looked up just as Adam entered the private enclave. Dressed in jeans and a white button-down shirt, the hard outline of his broad shoulders tapered gracefully down to a narrow waist. Perfectly proportioned, he was powerful, yet lean. His smile of triumph quickly faded when his met Laura's eyes, her expression giving away her pain.

"Adam, how did you find us?" Kat asked, unaware of Laura's discomfort.

"I heard you talking, but that hedge is deceiving. Very clever, Kat."

"Well, now that you're here, you'll have to try out the swing," she teased.

Laura placed the photo on the little table near the chaise, her heart beating double time.

"Thanks, maybe another time. William's been trying to get you on your cell and the house phone. No one could find you, so he called me. He suggested I look in the hedge. All the way out here, I thought he was crazy."

"Damn, I left my cell in my bedroom." Kat left the chaise making it rock from side to side. "He probably wants to talk dirty or let me know when he is going to be home."

"Here," he said, holding out his own phone to her.

"Thank you. Stay, keep Laura company and try out the swing." She left the garden to talk to her husband, leaving Adam and Laura alone. Laura reclined on the chaise, watching Adam. He walked to the side Kat had vacated and not waiting for an invitation, joined her, setting the rocker into motion as he stretched out next to her.

"Damn!"

"I should have warned you," she said, as the chaise moved wildly pushing their bodies toward the center.

Ignoring her, he asked, "Why are you upset?"

There was no point in denying it. "Kat showed me an old photo. It triggered some memories, happy times…"

"Your ex?" he asked, little wrinkles forming around his eyes. Their faces were just inches apart. When Kat lay in the same space, the distance hadn't bothered Laura, but with Adam so close, she became acutely aware of her body in relation to his. His warm eyes continued to watch her, waiting for her answer.

"No, not my ex, my parents." Handing him the photo, she swallowed uncomfortably and said, "My parents died right before I turned twenty-one. They were my only living relatives, so I was orphaned in more ways than one at an early age."

"What happened?"

"My dad always wanted to be a pilot. When I was away at college, my mother agreed to let him go for his license. About six months before the accident, she started going up with him. The sad part was, she was scared to fly, but she trusted my dad. The medical examiner thinks he had a heart attack. My mother experienced her worse nightmare. It's been hard for me to come to terms with that knowledge. Kat surprised me with the photo. She didn't mean to upset me. In fact, she doesn't know she did."

"I'm sorry," he said, studying the photo. "Your parents were nice looking people."

"They were the best people in the world."

Handing her the photo, he said, "Kat wouldn't want to think she upset you."

"No." Clearing her throat, she asked, "Is William okay?"

"He's just worried. He's been trying to get her all morning. Kat always has her cell with her. I think there's been a change of plans."

Before Leland's affair, before they'd found out she couldn't have children, he was never crazy with worry if he couldn't get a hold of her. Pushing Leland from her mind and remembering the kiss she'd shared with the virtual stranger lying next to her, she said, "You must be sleeping well."

"Why do you say that?" His hand absently brushed hers.

"I haven't seen you." She wouldn't admit how many times she'd gone to the window and looked for him.

"I didn't want to scare you again."

"You didn't scare me the first time." It had thrilled her. She wanted him to kiss her again. At least give her a chance to participate.

"Good." As if he could read her mind, he smiled ruefully, "I predict insomnia any night now."

Her lips curved into a smile she didn't try to hide. Not quite making eye contact, she managed, "If my light's on, I'm awake and open to company."

"So noted."

Heat was lapping up her neck, consuming her face in a scarlet blush. She had a crush on this handsome man and wasn't doing a very good job of hiding it. It had been years since her last crush, probably about the same time the photo was taken. He'd simply provided a shoulder to lean on during a lonely moment. The fact he was dazzlingly gorgeous and years younger, made the possibility of mutual attraction impossible. The kiss was more for comfort than anything else. Men didn't find her attractive. They didn't look to her, not the way they looked at Kat. Leland always said Laura was pixie cute. She hated pixies. Besides, she had to be almost foot shorter than Adam, who had to be at least six foot tall.

He was staring at her, his chocolaty eyes warm pools. "Laura, are you okay?"

She was anything but. "I'm fine, just nervous about Kat's call." Quickly changing the subject, she asked, "What have you been up to?"

"I've been working on my hotel. I had a meeting with the county yesterday. They aren't keen on our remodeling plans and the delays will be expensive."

She wondered how many women were in attendance. No woman with a pulse would be able to deny him anything. She was living proof of that.

"What is that look for?" He reached over and pulled a wayward petal from her hair. They were on their sides, facing each other on the swinging bed. The sun warmed their skin, the sound of the ocean played gentle background music. It was pure heaven.

When she didn't answer, he drew his hand up and gently stroked her cheek, running a finger over her lips, which opened slightly in invitation. He bent toward her, hesitated for a second and then kissed her. She leaned into him, her hand gently resting on his arm as the kiss deepened. He pushed her back into the cushion and she wrapped her arms around him, feeling the muscles in his back flex as the weight of his body settled on top of her. Their mouths touched and tasted breathlessly, giving, and taking pleasure Laura felt all the way to her toes. Her fingers got tangled in his thick, dark hair as his palm ran along her side pausing to squeeze the mound of her breast.

Too soon Kat's voice could be heard calling from just beyond the hedge. Immediately, they broke apart, Adam rolling off her ungracefully as she straightened her rumpled blouse. Kat rounded the corner a moment later, smiling and whooping loudly. She was breathless, her face glowing with beauty no camera would ever adequately capture.

"William is flying home tomorrow! He's got to arrange a couple of things here. Then, oh damn! I can't believe it! We leave for Italy in *three* days! He's going to start filming next week! The damn sunlight is perfect or something...Thank goodness, I hate sleeping alone. I like to curl up to his naked body—"

They looked at her; two children caught red handed in the cookie jar. She put her hands on her hips as Laura held her breath and waited, but what came next surprised her.

"What? I love my husband. I love playing with him while naked. We're married, we can do that. Now come on people, don't just lay there...we need to *move!*"

With a regretful, guilty glance mirroring Adam's, she jumped off the chaise and wondered how Kat had missed their obvious guilt.

The rest of the day was a whirlwind but did little to distract Laura from thoughts of Adam. She would absently touch her lips, remembering the heat from his touch, the slight burn of his whiskers against her skin.

Half listening to Kat, she missed something important.

"Well, why not?"

"What?" Laura asked, from where she sat in the oversized chair in Kat's office, once again going over the menu for the party.

"Why don't you come to Italy with us?" Kat asked, enunciating each word carefully.

For more reasons than Laura could list, she didn't want to go. She didn't want to be the third wheel. She didn't want Kat to pay for the trip after everything she had done. Eventually, she needed to go back to San Francisco and set up the empty apartment waiting for her. Kat had offered to furnish it, bringing tears of gratitude to Laura's eyes, but it was too much. She graciously declined the offer. Spending the entire summer at Tranquility or going to Italy fit into the same category of generosity as far as Laura was concerned.

"It doesn't feel right for me to go."

"Laura, is this a money thing again? I want to take care of everything and trust me, I can. Money isn't an issue." Kat tossed down a stack of papers in her hand. "In fact, I negotiated the highest salary I've ever made for this picture and if I can't share it enjoying time with my best friend, why am I even making money in the first place?"

"Kat," she said slowly, drawing her friend's full attention. "I know you want to spend gobs of money on me, and I appreciate it, really. You're too generous. I'll never be able to repay you, but besides that very basic thing…the timing isn't right. I appreciate your offer, but I don't even have a passport."

Stonewalled, Kat relented, "Damn, well…given the choice between Italy and this place with all its current amenities…" She winked conspiratorially. "I can't say I'd blame you."

"Current amenities?"

"Adam," Kat drew out with a shrug.

"What?"

"Sweetie, do you think I'm naïve? Give me credit, I did announce myself." Laura's mouth fell open as Kat smiled the grin of a Cheshire cat. "I think it's great, just don't give your heart away."

"Kat!"

"Do not 'Kat' me," she scolded. "He kissed you and I bet it was more than once."

"Did you see him kiss me?"

"No, but your lips were puffy, your face was bright red, and you looked guilty. You still do. He just looked sexy as hell." She leaned toward Laura as if she were about to tell her a secret, "For your information, sexy is better than guilty any day. Enjoy it."

"Nothing happened. Nothing will happen. He's at least five years younger than me…"

Kat held up a perfectly manicured red nail and pointed it at Laura. "Something happened. Something more will happen, probably the moment we leave for Italy."

"Kat, it was innocent. He doesn't want me…he was just comforting me…"

"Uh-huh," Kat muttered. Pointing the finger again, she said, "In three days, William and I will be gone until the Fourth of July. You and Adam will have the run of the place. I guarantee you one night with Adam, and you'll forget Leland ever existed."

"How would you know?"

"I wouldn't, because I adore my husband, but if I didn't, Adam would be a sweet temptation and you know how I feel about dessert."

"Kat!" Thoughts of Adam naked on the swinging chaise flooded her mind.

"Nothing to stop you," she offered nonchalantly. "And I think it would be good for both of you. A little friends with benefits, if you get my drift."

Laura pointed back at her and said, "It's like you're practically telling me to have a fling."

"I'd never tell you what to do. I'm merely pointing out the obvious."

"You're out in left field on this one, Kat," Laura protested, but in her heart she hoped Kat was right.

"Just don't fall in love," she warned. "That could get messy."

"Adam's hurting. He lost his family."

Kat sighed and tossed her pen on the desk. "After what you've both been through, I think if you can find a little mutual happiness humping each other's brains out…you should go for it."

"This is the most ridiculous conversation. I can't believe…He's just…I don't know!"

"He's staying in your old room upstairs. I've had it completely remodeled, so it won't remind you of staying here with Leland."

"Why are you telling me this?"

"So, you'll know where to find him."

"Are you forgetting I just got divorced? I'm broken hearted." Laura stood, placing her hand to her chest. "Not only did my husband have an affair the rumor is that he got her pregnant. I'm a mess. No man in their right mind would want me."

"Third door on the right."

"Fine," Laura said, walking toward the door. "I'm going to take a walk and clear my head of this nonsense of yours."

Kat called after her, "I'll expect a full report when we get back."

That night, Laura was restless, re-reading the same page in her novel over and over again. She hadn't lied to Adam. She wasn't sleeping, hadn't since she'd left Leland. Truth be told, from the moment she'd sensed something was wrong between them, sleep was elusive. Now at Tranquility, she stayed up later and later each night, reading and distracting herself until exhaustion took over. Often, she awoke to look out her window hoping to see Adam. Despite the stolen kisses they'd shared and Kat's words of encouragement, Laura knew the truth. He might have enjoyed kissing her, but he was either still too hurt or more than likely, uninterested to move forward. She should be thankful nothing had happened. But part of her wanted to believe that Adam would appear and make love to her as if they were the last two people on the planet.

# CHAPTER FOUR

William returned, bringing a new vitality to Tranquility and Kat. Laura helped her get ready for the shoot in Italy, reading lines, packing, and making hundreds of last-minute arrangements. On William and Kat's last night, they put together an impromptu dinner party.

Laura was seated at a long table with the dozen other Tranquility staff while the host and hostess took up positions at the ends of the table. Laura knew Kat had seen to it she was across from Adam. He was polite; greeting her warmly, but quickly appeared more interested in the company seated next to him, Kat's red-haired secretary, Jackie. The woman, in a low-cut green wrap dress, drew Adam into conversation, making sure he got a good glimpse of her ample breasts.

Watching the two interact, their heads lowered as they spoke intently, Laura felt ridiculous. She wasn't right for Adam and obviously he'd come to the same conclusion. To think she had entertained ideas to the contrary seemed immature and slightly embarrassing. Adding insult to injury, he hadn't glanced her way or even tried to engage her in conversation since they'd sat down.

Kat's husband, a tall, salt and pepper haired man with a generous smile and kind eyes, turned his attention to her as he opened the wine for the second course. "I want to make sure you all know Laura. She and Kat grew up together and she is Kat's bestest friend. Don't be fooled by how cute she is. Laura, sweetie, tell everyone what the students in your class like to call you."

The others at the table paused, Adam and Jackie both looking at her for the first time as she answered, "The Danulator."

"What does that even mean?" Jackie asked, scrunching up her nose.

"My last name, up until a couple of weeks ago, was Daniels and I have a reputation for lots of homework. But, if you fail a test, I might let you retake it and average the scores. I believe in challenges and hard work."

"What do you teach?" Mrs. Johnston, a grandmotherly cook asked.

"High school math, specifically higher levels, geometry and calculus."

"I never had a math teacher who looked like you…I feel extremely cheated," William teased, bringing a round of chuckles from everyone at the table. Everyone, that was, but Adam. Watching her, his expression wasn't hard to read. His cool, casual indifference appeared to border on annoyance. Fine, she got it, he regretted the kisses they'd shared. Okay, it was over, and she needed to stop thinking of him.

"We're trying to convince Laura to spend her entire summer vacation at Tranquility. She is an extremely talented watercolorist, and it would be a great opportunity for her to work on her portfolio. In fact, we'd love to have more of her art to hang here. Marco, you'll have to make her some of your house specialties to entice her while we are away," Kat said wickedly, winking at Laura.

"My pleasure," the small Italian man said, his dark eyes leering in her direction.

Great, all she needed was a little toad cook trying to get close to her. Did he want to feed her or eat her? She couldn't tell, but either wasn't going to happen.

After dinner, Kat and Laura stood out by the pool, leaning against a small retaining wall, drinking a glass of warmed amaretto, and watching the ocean.

"See? You were wrong," Laura said in a low tone. "I almost made a complete fool of myself. I guess that will have to be a new moniker for this year."

"About what was I wrong?" Kat asked.

"You know what. He was talking to Jackie and staring at her cleavage. He didn't even look my way. The only person who paid any attention to me was that chef who gives me the creepy vibe, Marco."

"Were we at the same dinner?" Kat asked, pausing to take a long sip of her amaretto. "From my vantage point, Adam couldn't keep his eyes off you. He looked like he wanted to kill Marco with his bare hands. I'd pay to see that fight, yummy."

Before she could argue the point, William joined them, wrapping an arm around each of them. "Well, if it isn't the two most beautiful women in the world."

"Flattery will get you everywhere darling," Kat offered saucily, turning to her husband, and kissing him softly on the lips.

"Hey, you taste sweet," he said and kissed her again. Laura looked away feeling like a third wheel.

"You see Laura, you need a man like this," Kat announced, looking up at her husband as her hand ran possessively over his chest.

William slapped his wife on the rump and pulled her close, then reached up and gave Kat's breast a little squeeze eliciting a happy squeal from Kat and making Laura envious of their easy affection.

"Can I talk to you about something, Laura?"

"Sure," she replied uneasily, meeting William's suddenly serious eyes. What now?

"You're our family, so I need to tell you—," he paused, "I have a bad feeling when Leland realizes how much he misses you, he'll come looking for you."

"He's with someone else, who he has impregnated," she said bitterly.

"I hope he'll stay away, but I've asked Adam to check in on you. You can call him if you need anything," he announced and then, misunderstanding the look that passed between Laura and Kat, asked, "What? You don't like Adam? Have you *seen* Adam? Every woman within five miles is drooling over the guy. You know, if I didn't keep my wife so happy, I'd worry about her trying to seduce him."

"Well, someone should," Kat replied, winking at Laura.

"I like Adam just fine, but I don't think there will be any need to bother him."

"You wouldn't be bothering him. I think he is bored stiff. The hotel conversion isn't going well, and he could use the distraction. I'd appreciate it if you'd invite him over for drinks or have him take you to dinner in town. I don't want him to be alone for too long."

"Listen to William, Laura." Kat added, "We wouldn't want either one of you to be lonely."

"Kat," she scolded.

"Is something going on that I don't know about?"

"Nothing," both women answered in unison.

William grew serious, "I'm worried about Adam. He hasn't been the same since the accident."

"What exactly happened?" Laura asked, feeding the curiosity that kept her up at night.

"A drunk driver hit them when they were driving home one night. It was raining. Adam was driving, and he was injured, you can see it sometimes when he walks. He broke his femur, and on some days it is still a bit stiff. His wife was killed on impact, but his son died in his arms before the paramedics arrived. It was absolutely horrific. He's going to testify at the trial of the driver this fall. We've tried to be careful, respecting his privacy, giving him space, but he could use a friend."

Laura was picturing the scene in her mind, trying to comprehend what Adam went through. She looked up to find William watching her. "I'll invite him over, make sure he eats, talk to him so he isn't lonely."

"I'd appreciate it," William replied, grabbing her hand, and giving it a squeeze.

Adam stared down at the photos on his dresser, the images of his Melinda and A.J. blurring before his eyes. He saw their faces in his nightmares. The images that used to bring comfort now caused unbearable pain. His son was laughing, his wife giving him a teasing smile he loved, and then everything stopped. He felt the impact, metal hitting metal and then he heard their screams. It was a horror film that played in his head each and every night.

It might have been a mistake to bring as many framed photos as he had. It wasn't like he'd ever forget what either one of them looked like. Their pictures only acted as a reminder on nights like this, a trigger for his guilt. And in the last several days, he had a lot to feel guilty about.

*Laura.* He'd made a fool of himself with the woman right from the start. What on earth had compelled him to stop by the side of the road? She needed a tire repair guy, but he'd hugged her. *A hug for god's sake!* But that wasn't what initially made him stop. She had. The way her long golden hair moved in the breeze, the way she looked, as she leaned against her car and gazed out at the ocean. She'd captivated his every thought and for a moment, one brief oasis in his tortured existence, he'd looked at her and known happiness again. But when he'd held her, he'd felt contentment. It had overwhelmed him. So much so that he'd walked away.

Driving back to Tranquility, he'd almost turned around and gone back, needing another fix. He'd fought the urge and told himself it was for the best. Washing off the dirt and grime with a hot shower, he'd tried to forget how it felt to hold her in his arms. He'd dressed for dinner with the interior design team to look at swatches and color schemes, something to do with the outdoor pool, which would do little to distract him, but he was determined to try.

Walking along the main hall, he'd almost made it to the front door of the large mansion when he heard her voice. At first, he'd thought he was dreaming. You couldn't memorize someone's voice having only heard it once, but he had, he'd done just that, memorized the soft, sexy quality that set Laura apart from every other human being on the planet.

Fate had given him a second chance.

She'd looked just as pleasantly surprised to see him, as he was to see her. When he couldn't sleep that night he went to his favorite place on the estate, which happened to be right in front of her cottage. When she'd appeared in her robe and nightgown, he'd wanted to peel away the garments and see if every inch of her skin was just as smooth and flawless as the peach silk she wore.

For the first time in almost ten years, he'd enjoyed kissing a woman not his wife. He hated to think of what might have happened if Kat hadn't returned that afternoon in the private garden. Would he have stopped with kisses? He didn't think he'd have stopped for anything less than total immersion. He'd never felt such lack of control. Maybe he just missed the feel of a woman, who could blame him

Thinking of control, his thoughts traveled to his wife's sister, Tess. He groaned, shaking his head. *Tess.* She had decided to be her sister's replacement in his life whether he wanted her or not. A couple months after Melinda's death, she tried to convince him that she could be there for him.

He was still embarrassed to think of what happened between them. She'd shown up at the New York townhouse he'd shared with her sister and thrown herself at him. Not bothering to knock, she'd used her key and suddenly appeared before him in high heels and nothing else. He'd had to fight her off. She'd assumed he would be in favor of the idea, but in the end she almost begged him to make love to her. He'd turned her down, sickened by the very idea of any kind of intimacy with his wife's sister. It not only felt incestuous, it felt wrong on many levels. She'd not taken 'no' for an answer and the entire episode had turned distasteful and unpleasant before she'd grabbed her clothing and stalked out calling him every name in the book before slamming the door. The spoiled little girl inside of her, showing her true colors.

His mind hated to go to the real reason for Tess's sudden attention. Her family knew that he was one of the stockholders in Stark International. It hadn't mattered to Melinda, but it was always something that mattered a lot to her parents, especially when he and Melinda were dating and first married. Melinda once said her parents knew they'd never have to worry about money with him in the family. The admission and what it said about her parents bothered her, it bothered him. They had discussed it many times. It made them distance from her family, especially the parents and Tess.

He wasn't ready for another relationship with anyone, even if he'd have an opportunity to be with Laura. He couldn't be the kind of man she, or any woman for that matter, deserved. He was damaged, broken. If he wanted something casual without the emotional commitment, he could get it. Kat's secretary, Jackie, had made that quite clear and all but put her hand on his crotch in invitation. The trouble was that he wasn't remotely attracted to her. And he was never big on screwing Kat and William's hired help. *Not cool.*

He thought of his beautiful wife. For what seemed like the millionth time, he tried to make sense of senselessness. Glancing at a photo of his son holding a plush green dinosaur and then toward his own bed where the dinosaur now sat, Adam made one of the hardest decisions of his life. He turned his family's photos over, one by one, until just one remained. Picking it up, he placed it gently on the nightstand next to his bed. It would be the first image he saw in the morning and last image he saw at night.

# CHAPTER FIVE

The days after William and Kat left were marked with the nastiest June weather on record. Laura stayed in her cottage, listening to the rain, reading novel after novel. She kept up with her friends on Instagram and Facebook, avoiding mention of Leland and Amber, who had announced they were in a relationship on Facebook. She had at least a half a dozen messages from mutual friends. More rumors about Amber being pregnant were circulating.

*How did she feel about the news?* Like she wanted to punch Leland and tell Amber to run for her life. But mainly, it depressed her and made her want to hide, which was ridiculous. She realized she was jealous of Amber, but not for having Leland. She was jealous of the baby she was carrying. Why had this happened to her? Why did her life have to be so hard? Would anything ever come easy to her?

When she wasn't reading, she spent long moments looking out the window trying to answer questions for which there would never be an answer.

Food held little appeal. She picked at the gourmet contents of her refrigerator with little interest. Without any distractions, she replayed the last few months of her life over and over in her mind, feeling worse about herself. She'd been at Tranquility for two weeks and despite the pain she was experiencing, she was sure Leland hadn't thought about her at all. He was off with his new girlfriend, making plans. The same kind of plans she'd once made with him.

The reality of her new life was taking shape. She no longer had another person to help with the expenses. As a high school teacher, she would have to adjust her lifestyle considerably, not that she had ever been extravagant. Maybe she would start tutoring. With all the online and zoom options, this could be a good revenue source for her. Leland had been firmly against it when they were together, but now it might help make ends meet. She had a small checking account, which Leland condescendingly had thought was 'cute', for her own splurges and special purchases. It was enough for the deposit on her new apartment and several pieces of furniture.

When she'd moved out of their home, which she'd painstakingly decorated, Leland reminded her of the prenuptial agreement he'd surprised her with on their wedding day. She was only entitled to her personal belongings. Even her engagement ring stayed with her ex-husband, not that she'd have wanted to keep the garish thing, but it did have pawn value. Maybe he'd have it resized for Amber. Refusing to dwell on the things she'd left behind, she tried to embrace the idea of a fresh start.

She would take up painting again. When the weather let up, she'd drive the twenty miles to Seaside and buy the necessary supplies. Working in watercolor, she would focus on the different landscapes Tranquility offered. Maybe it was time to pursue her dream of finding a gallery to handle her work. She would find her way and persevere. It would just take time.

After four days, there was a break in the weather, fog replacing rain. Suffering from a bad case of cabin fever, Laura put on her jeans, which felt roomier—well that was a nice side effect of not eating—and a sweater and left the cottage for an early morning walk. The cool, gray mist matched her mood. Meandering along the beach, she could barely make out the horizon. A figure moved toward her at a steady pace, an early morning jogger, who was limping slightly. As the figure grew closer, she recognized Adam. She'd missed him, thought a lot about the promise she'd made to William, but something stopped her from trying to find him. Memories of the dinner she'd endured watching him in action with Jackie were never far from her mind. As far as she was concerned, he'd made his position clear and that was probably for the best.

When he saw her, he offered a curt smile and slowed.

She greeted him first. "Good morning."

"Good morning. I've been meaning to drop by and check on you," he said, panting, as he bent to catch his breath.

Did he feel an obligation to see her? Had William laid the same speech on him? 'Poor rejected Laura....'

"I'm fine," she replied cautiously.

"Well, William and Kat wouldn't be happy with me if they knew I was neglecting my duties."

"I'm a duty?" It appeared William had been a busy boy before he left. She'd put a stop to this immediately.

"No, on the contrary, I meant watching out for you."

"I'm fine, Adam. Really fine. You aren't responsible for me."

"Come on Laura, you know William and Kat are worried about you…you're going through something very difficult. I was asked to keep an eye on you…"

"I understand that, but consider yourself relieved of the duty," she said, putting her hands on her hips. "I'm just fine."

"Laura…" He began but she cut him off quickly.

"You can stop worrying about me. And, after all, I'm the one who's supposed to be watching out for you. You look fine too, so we are done watching one another, okay?" Not waiting for a response, she turned away, walking briskly until Adam disappeared into the fog behind her.

Back at the cottage, she regretted her choice of words immediately. She debated about whether or not she should apologize. There was no reason not to be civil. Just because Adam wasn't interested in her didn't mean she had to act like the scorned lover. Knowing what needed to be done, she walked toward the door, with the intention of going back to the main house to find Adam so she could apologize. Her cell phone buzzed just as she placed her hand on the knob. Distracted, not looking at the caller ID, she grabbed it, answering, "Hello."

"Laura?" It was Leland.

"What do you want?"

"We need to talk."

"About what?"

"Are you over your little tantrum yet?"

"Divorcing you? That, in your opinion, was a tantrum?" She had to give him some credit; he always managed to surprise her. Once an asshole, always an asshole. Was he really trying to rewrite history? He'd cheated.

"Laura, we've been over this," he sounded like he was explaining a simple concept to someone too stupid to understand, "I said I was sorry, but you have to take responsibility for your actions."

"Congratulations on your new girlfriend, asshole." Immediately, she hung up on him. The phone rang again, and she threw it against the wall. Smacking loudly, it hit the whitewashed wainscoting leaving a mark. Grimacing, she felt guilty for marring the perfection of the paint. The resulting crack in the phone screen was very noticeable. That would cost a bunch of money she couldn't afford. She tested it by calling her own number, it still worked, she'd live with the crack.

She decided to take a shower to calm down. The routine relaxed her as she dressed in a floral cotton skirt and white blouse and applied a small amount of makeup. She paced the length of the cottage, the heels of her sandals clicking noisily on the floor. What a crap day—First Adam let her know what she was to him and then Leland had called. The irony was that she was more upset with Adam.

She wondered if Adam had been 'keeping an eye' on her that first night in front of her cottage. Maybe Kat asked him to provide a strong, handsome shoulder to lean on. If that were true, it was humiliating. She continued to pace, gritting her teeth. Before she could talk herself out of it, she stormed from the cottage and headed to the main house. The fog had burned off, the sun now high in the sky and warm. She ignored the blue sky, the glistening infinity pool, and beautiful gardens. Climbing the marble steps with purpose, she yanked open a terrace door, stepped inside the main house and searched for Adam.

Hearing his voice from the corner office William and Kat set up for him, she waited in the open doorway, watching him stand by the desk dressed immaculately in a black suit with Jackie by his side scrutinizing paperwork. Jackie was staring intently at him, hanging on his every word. Basking in the glow of the amorous attention, he gave her instructions for the Fourth of July party. Kat had said he would be helping, and it appeared he'd found an assistant.

"May I have a word?" Laura interrupted formally, stepping into the well-appointed space.

Adam slowly raised his eyes to hers, "Yes, of course Laura."

"Privately."

"I'll be with you in a minute. I'm in the middle of something and should be done shortly."

"I can wait." Laura folded her arms, raised an eyebrow, and looked pointedly at the redhead.

"Jackie, please organize Mrs. Russell's notes for the caterer. I'll be a moment with Mrs. Daniels." Laura's head jerked in surprise. Had he done that on purpose? Using her former title was a slap on the face.

Jackie looked uncomfortably between them and replied, "Sure Adam."

"Please close the door as you leave," he instructed, his eyes focusing on Laura.

Laura glanced at the other woman as she passed, smelling her perfume, a too sweet aroma reminiscent of sugar and frosting.

Adam dropped the papers on his desk and crossed the distance between them. "What can I do for you?" he asked, spreading his arms wide in false sincerity.

"I'm sorry for the things I said," Laura blurted out, "But I have to know...did Kat send you to the cottage that first night?"

"What?"

"Did Kat ask you to watch me the night you came to the cottage?"

"No one tells me what to do."

"They didn't ask you to babysit me?"

"No," he said, looking irritated and added, "of course not."

"Then what happened? You kissed me then you acted like a stranger. Maybe I'm confused, but you did kiss me, right?" She couldn't believe what she'd said. One minute she was going to apologize and the next she was baring her soul. As her voice trailed, he shut his eyes and dipped his head. Placing his hand to the bridge of his nose, he squeezed painfully.

Glancing at his arm, she noticed a strand of long coppery hair catching the light from where it had landed on his dark sleeve. Jackie's hair. Seeing a hair from another woman on his coat filled her with jealousy. The desire to reach out and touch Adam removing the hair in the process was overwhelming. She had no right to even exercise such thoughts. It was ridiculous. The whole idea that she should be standing in front of him now and asking him to define their relationship was crazy. If she had any respect for herself, she would apologize for the intrusion and leave. Maybe leave Tranquility.

Adam interrupted her quiet revere. "I don't know what to say...I was out of line."

With a slight hitch in her voice, she said, "Don't worry about it. We can forget it happened." Tears threatened. She didn't want to forget a single detail about the way he kissed her.

"Damn it, Laura, I couldn't keep seeing you and not have something happen, something we both might regret. I've stayed away on purpose."

She reached out, touching his sleeve. "I'm sorry I've put you in this position."

His eyes followed her hand as she removed the long red hair. "I've enjoyed every moment from the first time I saw you at Devil's Punchbowl."

"Thank you for that. Look, I'll leave you alone. We can just avoid each other for the rest of our time here. Maybe I'll even leave. Goodbye Adam," she whispered, looking away. Taking long strides toward the door, she hoped the tears would wait until she made it back to the cottage where she could deal privately with her complete embarrassment.

After three steps, a strong hand caught her from behind and spun her around. She was in his arms, and he was staring down at her. In those warm brown eyes, she didn't see pity or anger, only passion he was trying hard to fight. Opening her mouth to protest, she was stopped by his kiss. She sank against him as he kissed her again and again, her body yielding to him. He grasped her hips, his fingers digging into her flesh. Pulling the cotton blouse from the waistband of her skirt, he ran his hands under the fabric seeking her bare skin and finding her silk covered breast.

As quickly as it started, he stopped and stepped back.

"I'm so sorry, I know I shouldn't be doing this," he said, the shock filling his voice, his hands coming up, his body stepping further away from hers. Adam faced her then, his eyes downcast as he asked, "Are you all right?"

"I'm fine, I didn't mind it," she repeated. Walking quickly to the door before he could say anything more, she lingered in the doorway and said, "In fact, I'm bereft that it ended. In fact, I might have let you make love to me on that couch. I'm sure you would've thought that was a mistake too, but I'm not sure it would have been."

She quickly stepped outside and walked back to the cottage on quivering legs.

That night, she lay awake thinking. What happened with Adam was frenzied and passionate, but obviously he thought it was a mistake. She relived the scene over and over in her mind. Her only regrets lay in the knowledge that he would never touch her again. They'd run into each other again and it would be awkward. He'd tell her why he wasn't ready for that kind of relationship, and she'd agree, because that is what adults did. They accepted what they could not change, and they moved on. But, if she had her choice, instead of talking, she'd invite him into her bed. Making love with Adam was exactly what she needed.

Her cell awakened her the next morning. Groggily, she managed to grab it on the fifth ring, but checked the caller ID, still leery of Leland. Then she saw that it was an international call.

"How is Italy?" she asked, by way of greeting.

"Are you still asleep?"

"No," she replied, sitting up and forcing her eyes open.

"Well Italy is fine, I'm all over William and he seems to like it, what's new there?"

She wanted to say, *Adam kissed me like a man who hadn't seen a woman in a couple of years*. It would delight Kat, but since she didn't think it would happen again, or go any further, so she chose to keep it to herself.

"Leland called and I hung up on him after calling him an asshole." Laura hoped the tidbit would keep Kat occupied and it did. She wanted to know all of the details and when Laura was finished, she said, "Good for you. I'm proud of you, honey!"

Kat told her about one of her new co-stars, who was working his way through every available woman on the set. It seemed he'd sleep with any willing female. Feeling oddly sensitive about the comment, Laura didn't ask for any of the tawdry details. Half an hour later, they hung up and she felt horrible for lying by omission to her best friend.

For the rest of the day, she hid in the cottage. If Adam wanted to find her to talk, he knew where to look. But he didn't look for her and it hurt a little.

Unable to sleep for a second night in a row, her insecurities got the better of her. She would have let Adam make love to her, in his office, nonetheless. She barely knew him! The next time she saw him wouldn't be easy. It would be terrible. He'd take one look at her and realize that he'd almost been with her, an overweight schoolteacher. She didn't think she could face him. The thought of leaving Tranquility started to sound like a prudent idea.

She'd pack her bags, call her new landlord and ask if she could take possession of the rental early. Maybe she'd go check out the bison in Yellowstone after all. If she couldn't afford that, she'd find a cheap hotel, one of those extended stay or pay by the week jobs.

Unable to go back to sleep, she got out of bed and decided to start packing. Before turning on the light, she looked out the window.

Adam was there, sitting on the short wall, staring out at the iridescent water.

Before she lost her nerve, she grabbed her robe and stepped into the humid night.

"Hello Laura."

It was a sad, wary greeting.

Maybe she should have stayed inside. "Hi Adam, couldn't sleep?"

"No. You?"

"No," she answered and wondered where they went from here.

"I should have come to see you today," he began.

She cut in before he said something she didn't want to hear. "I know you're busy with the party and the hotel. We don't need to talk about what happened."

"Yes, we do," his voice cut through the darkness.

"I don't want to hear that you're sorry. That might just push me over a very fine emotional edge, so I'd rather not talk about it."

"I'm not sorry it happened. I don't regret it. I'm just sorry I was so…damn it, Laura! I want you, but I'm not sure of my reasons. I'm not sure it is fair to you."

She took a deep breath, inhaling the scent of his aftershave, placing her hand on his leg she said, "I repeat and please believe me this time…I enjoyed our kisses. Maybe we just need to be there for each other."

His hand tentatively touched hers, weaving their fingers together. "It's been a long time since, well, it's been a long time."

"It's been a long time since for me too…"

"Laura…"

His hand slipped from hers. "Laura…I…I'm still in love with my wife. I don't want to replace her, not now, maybe not ever. What happened between us was a very physical reaction. I can't offer you more and you've been through so much…"

"I'm still dealing with my own feelings about my marriage. You provided a very pleasant distraction."

Ignoring her, he continued, "I've never been the kind of man who has casual sex, has hookups, that isn't me.…I have relation-ships, which I'm not capable of having right now." Closing his eyes, he rubbed his hands over his face. "I lost the only woman I've ever loved, maybe ever will love, yet I'm fighting the urge to drag you to the ground and have you. What does that say about me?"

"I'm in no position to be in a new relationship. Maybe we are just friends who help each other through a hard time, maybe we should try it."

"What if the friendship ends badly?"

"Then we weren't very good friends to begin with." She sounded braver than she was. She was kidding herself if she thought saying goodbye to him would be easy.

"Is there any chance you might go back to your ex?"

"No, no never," she said defiantly. "I'm not going back."

"You're not the kind of woman who has casual sex."

"How would you know?"

"I know."

Mustering all her courage, she held her hand out to him and waited, hoping he wouldn't notice that her hand was shaking. After a moment of hesitation, that had her rethinking her bravado, he placed his hand in hers. Then she led him back to her cottage.

Once inside the cottage, they fumbled in the darkness, not saying a word as they made their way into the bedroom. Leaving the lights off, they quickly shed their clothing.

Adam pulled back the covers and waited for her, murmuring, "I wondered how these sheets would feel against my skin."

"So, it was you who turned back the covers my first night."

"Yes, and I'm the one who picked the satin. They arrived the same day you did."

"Good timing," she mused, sliding between the cool sheets. The mattress dipped as he joined her, his body warm and solid next to her. Closing the distance, he pulled her to him, kissing her as his hands roamed, exploring every inch. She trembled as much from the warmth of his body as the knowledge he was naked and in her bed.

"You're shaking," he announced, kissing a pathway along her neck, "Are you cold?"

"Do I feel cold?"

"You feel lush...sexy," he murmured, taking his time learning every curve and nuance. Tentatively, she explored him in the same way, running her fingers through the soft hair that dusted his chest and tracing it down to the patch of coarse hair framing his erection.

"You're already wet," he murmured as his fingers explored her dampening sex.

"For you…"

When his fingers found her clit and began to stroke, she shut her eyes and moaned. Cupping him and caressing his smooth, warm penis in the same way, she made him falter. He kissed his way down her body, sucking her nipples making them tighten as he increased the pressure on the finger exploring the area between her legs. Her body tightened, coiling in the anticipation of orgasm.

"I want to be inside you when you come."

She managed a wispy, "What are you waiting for?"

"I don't have a condom."

"Don't worry about it, I can't have children or even get pregnant. As part of some recent medical procedures, I was tested for every known thing, I'm clean and healthy otherwise."

"I had sex with the same person for over ten years, and I don't think there is any issue."

"I'm fine with no condom if you are," she said.

"As long as I can't get you pregnant, I'm fine."

With his knee nudging between her legs, she spread open to welcome him. With finite patience, he entered her slowly, taking possession of her inch by slow inch. When she was filled, he held her, suspended on his thick shaft. Her body pulsed, her muscles encasing his thickness, but he remained still. He suckled her breasts with the tip of his tongue making her writhe beneath him. Pulling out slowly, he drove back in with the same constrained desire that coursed through every nerve in her body.

Laura thought of nothing but how he felt. Joined with him she felt complete. Trying to say as much without words, she raised her hips, wrapped her arms and legs around him, and willed him to go deeper, faster. As her moans turned to quick pants, he sped up, until he was thrusting powerfully, driving into her with all his strength.

Every nerve in her body electrified and released wave after wave of pleasure, she heard Adam's cries of release mix with hers, a primal melody of cresting passion.

Seconds stretched into minutes, Laura aware of her own labored breathing and that of Adam's, as they lay in the warm satin, their bodies entangled and damp.

Kissing her temple and then her cheek, he mumbled, "Well, if that wasn't a total loss of control…"

"It was good, intense, I liked it," she agreed, not willing to admit it might have been the best orgasm of her life, her body still throbbing with aftershocks.

Adam held her for a few moments and then said, "I should probably go."

He couldn't leave her, not yet. Surprising herself, she said, "Stay, because I want you again, that is…if you think you'd be up for it."

"I'll be up for it." He kissed her, tasting her with the tip of his tongue and then stroking the inside of her mouth thoroughly. Quicker than she would have thought possible, he was hard, and they were making love again. Her body, already primed from their earlier lovemaking, reawakened quickly.

Afterward, they spooned, his arm draped protectively around her middle, gently cupping the mound of her breast. He rested his cheek against her temple, his breathing growing heavy as he fell asleep. She lay awake listening to the steady rise and fall of his chest. She couldn't believe she was in his arms. Laura Hokensen, an overweight and recently divorced high school math teacher, had taken a younger, sexy man to her bed.

# Chapter Six

A patch of bright sunlight illuminated the spot Adam had occupied in her bed. Laura was alone, not having heard Adam leave. Every muscle in her body was languid and sore in a very satisfying good way. She hadn't expected him to stay but was still disappointed he'd gone.

During a long, hot shower, memories of the night before filled her mind. Adam was an amazing lover. She'd never been more attracted to a man, including her ex-husband. Thinking of Leland, she cringed. In the last year of their marriage, their sex life had been unsatisfying and in the last few months, nonexistent. When they had been trying to get pregnant, sex had become mechanical. Laura brushed off the clinical nature of their lovemaking to a combination of fertility meds and the disappointment of not being able to conceive. What she couldn't ignore were the ugly comments about her weight. As the medications wreaked havoc with her hormones, she gained weight and Leland's comments became crueler. Before long she could not stomach the thought of him touching her. When they did make love, she wasn't able to achieve orgasm. Leland didn't notice or care. His lack of sensitivity about her satisfaction hurt deeply. Never quite finding the words to express her pain, she suffered silently, but Leland simply found someone else.

Wrapping herself in a large, fluffy towel, she stepped from the shower, facing the harsh realities of her failed marriage. Even when things were good between them, before all the fertility issues, her orgasms weren't anything like she'd experienced with Adam. In his arms, desire sparked to life and quickly spread through her body with little or no conscious thought. Just as she thought she might die from the pleasure of it, her body had released tension from not only the past few months, but possibly years of frustration. She still felt relaxed, and very, very lush, and sexy.

While brushing her hair, she paused to smile at her glowing reflection in the mirror. Dressing in a pair of white shorts and a soft pink linen shirt, noticing the zipper went up a little easier feeling a little looser around her hips, she walked barefoot across the hardwood floor into the kitchen, gazing leisurely around the tidy space for something to eat. Despite her growling stomach, she had no appetite.

Deciding on a banana, she unpeeled it casually and meandered to the front door intent on letting in some fresh air. On her doorstep, lay a single white rose tied with a white satin ribbon. She loved roses. They were, by far, her favorite flower. Picking up the plump blossom, she inhaled the rich fragrance. The heady aroma matched her mood. Finding a vase in the kitchen, she placed the fragrant blossom next to her bed, wondering what had possessed Adam to leave it. But then, his attraction to her came as a surprise. Her voluptuous curves had crossed the invisible line to Rubenesque long ago. Despite all the self-deprecation, picturing him leaving a flower on her doorstep made her smile. And although he'd made resolute comments about not being able to offer anything but a few moments of passion, he was sentimental enough to leave the rose.

Needing to collect her thoughts, she got in her car and drove south to Seaside. Passing The Bay Shore, a glorious ghost of a once elegant beachside resort, she saw a Tranquility estate car, a black Escalade parked among the contractors' trucks. Fighting the urge to swing into the parking lot to visit Adam, she continued on her way. It was too soon after what they had shared. She hoped in time he would show her what he was doing with the old hotel, but until then, a little time away would clear her mind and help her digest what was happening between them.

She parked in the sleepy tourist town and walked along the sidewalks window-shopping until she found the art supply store where she stocked up on supplies. Returning to Tranquility in the early afternoon with a book of watercolor paper, an easel, and a set of watercolors, she felt dreamy, all thoughts of fleeing Tranquility gone from her mind. After a quick nap on one of the oversized chaise lounges with a view of the ocean, she would try her hand at painting.

Lying by the pool, she stretched like a cat in the sun. Life was complicated, but she had found a little happiness. Refusing to have any regrets for enjoying the passion Adam brought to her, she hoped he would come to her again soon. Her body was already craving him, tingling at the thought of his muscular body filling hers.

When a shadow fell over her, she opened her eyes. *Adam.*

"Good afternoon."

"It is now," she smiled lazily and stretched. "Hello there."

"I've been looking for you," he said seriously.

"Really?" she asked saucily, flashing him a smile.

"I'd like to go over the appetizer list for the party around three if you're available."

Opening her eyes a little wider, she took in the rest of his appearance. He was in a suit, looking hot and uncomfortable in the afternoon sun. Giving nothing away with his expression, he looked handsome, but hard, small wrinkles formed around his eyes against the bright sky. It unnerved her.

"Sure," she said, sitting up a little taller. "Where would you like to meet?"

"How about the cottage?"

"Okay."

"I'll see you at three." Without another word, he winked, turned, and walked swiftly away.

By three, she was a nervous wreck. He knocked on her door five minutes later, clutching a large black notebook in his hand and looking impatient. Stepping out of the way, she let him in, deflated and hurt by his stiff, formal appearance.

"Can I get you an iced tea or soda?" she asked, hiding her disappointment. "It's a warm afternoon…" This good-looking man had been in her bed the night before making love to her. Now, he was acting different, was he acting shy? Was he about to tell her why he couldn't see her again? She watched him carefully set the notebook on her small dining room table and reached up to loosen his silk tie, then remove it. Next came his suit coat, which he draped over a dining room chair. His face broke into a wicked grin as he sauntered toward her. Oh goody. The night had an effect on him too.

"It is a warm afternoon and maybe later on the soda," he said, his face inches from hers, his arms closing around her.

"I thought you were serious about the damn appetizers!" she scolded, as his lips brushed hers.

"Well, I couldn't very well tell Kat's staff to leave me alone this afternoon so I could have sex at three, could I?"

"You could have told me," she offered defiantly, pushing him away with a playful shove.

"I'm sorry. I was sure you could see through my little farce." Not waiting for a reply, he said, "How about we get you out of your clothes." His voice was low and husky as he herded her toward the bedroom.

Smiling, she shed her shirt and shorts, but by the time she got down to her bra and panties, she hesitated. If he picked up on it or chose to ignore it, he never let on. As he concentrated on carefully folding his trousers to maintain the crease, she slipped under the covers, hiding her body.

He joined her, pulling her into his arms. Kissing her, his hands stroked delicious patterns over her skin and just like the night before, their need took over. Within minutes they were a tangle of limbs, their bodies sweaty and spent.

Laying gently on her, kissing her, despite the heat, he ordered softly, "Open your eyes."

Her body was throbbing, flushed from their coupling, more powerful in the light of day. She cautiously opened one eye, then the other. His eyes smoldered with undeniable passion. He placed soft kisses to her lips and rubbed seductively against her. Before long, he was ready for her again.

"This time I want you to keep your eyes open," he murmured as he slid into her.

Doing as he asked, she looked into those soft brown pools, while he caressed her. Everything blurred, but the eyes watching her. The closeness, matched with such intimacy, was foreign to her. Interlocking their fingers, they held steadily to each other as they climbed the same peak together. Laura was mesmerized by the subtle changes as he read her body, adjusting his with small movements to intensify her pleasure.

Afterward, his hands gently cupped her face, then traced along the curve of her chin before moving to her breast and its taunt, rosy tip. She ran her foot along his leg and arched her back, wanting him to put his lips where his hands played.

"I have to ask you something," he said, looking at the breast under his palm.

She stilled. His tone set off alarm bells. She thought of her body, the rounded curves under his scrutiny. Had she disappointed him? She wanted to cry and kick herself for every time she hadn't been able to do just ten more minutes on the treadmill or chosen to eat something even slightly unhealthy. Why had she thought he would see through her inadequacies?

"Stop worrying," he scolded, running his hand playfully through her hair. "I felt your whole-body tense. It's nothing bad, well, I think it is…"

"You're not upsetting me. You're scaring me."

"I'm sorry," he said, caressing her cheek with the tip of his finger. "I just need to know if there is any chance that you could get pregnant. I know we talked about it, but I guess I need reassurance because it is a bit of a sensitive subject for me."

Swallowing back some emotion, she said, "Sadly, not a chance. My doctor said it would take a miracle for me to ever have a baby. It just isn't possible."

"Did you try a specialist?" he asked, continuing to stroke her cheek.

"Of course, I consulted several. I did everything. I tried every fertility treatment. I'm as barren as you can get." Relief over questions about her body was replaced by the deep sadness she always fought to hide when discussing her inability to have children.

"I'm sorry."

"It's okay. I'm dealing with it. Well, some days, not as much as others, but I've found a way. If you can't have children, you accept what you cannot change."

He slid closer, pulling her into the crook of his arm so he could spoon her from behind, the sensual mood replaced with a different kind of intimacy.

"I miss my son every minute of every day," he said sadly, placing a protecting arm around her, his hand resting on top of hers.

"Now I'm the one who's sorry."

"I don't want to diminish what you've been through."

"You didn't. You're relating," she said, turning to meet his eyes.

Holding her a little tighter he said, "We're very ironic, you and me. You want a baby and can't have one. I'm thinking about having a vasectomy because I don't want to be a father again."

His voice was so cool and resolute she couldn't help wanting to dig deeper. "Why?"

"I never want to lose a child again. I watched my son die. That's enough for one lifetime."

"I think I understand," she replied, feeling a vice grab hold of her heart and squeeze.

"We're two peas in one messed up pod."

Hiding the flood of emotion welling up inside of her, she cleared her throat and said, "Think before you have a vasectomy, Adam. You're young. A few years from now you might see things a little differently."

"I'm not that young."

"Younger than me," she admitted. "Even if I could have a baby, I'm almost too old."

"How old are you? Thirty, thirty-two?"

"I'm thirty-seven. How old are you? Twenty-five?" she asked, forcing a playful tone into her voice.

"I'm thirty-four," he replied, giving her rump a playful swat.

"I knew I was older."

"My first older, more experienced woman. I can't wait to see what you'll teach me," he chuckled, nuzzling her neck until she laughed.

Eventually he said he should leave and asked if he could take a shower. When he came out of the bath with a towel wrapped around his middle, Laura's mouth dropped opened in admiration of his beautiful, toned body. He had a wonderful tan and she felt privileged to see every line. When he was fully dressed, his tie perfect, he turned back to her and bent for a kiss. "I don't want to leave, but I have some work to do."

"I don't want you to leave either."

"Can I come again?"

"I'd be hurt if you didn't."

He kissed her again and turned to leave.

"Adam?"

"Yes?"

"Make it sooner than later."

"Would you mind if it was tonight, maybe most nights? I sleep better after we make love."

"I hope to see you tonight."

A pattern quickly developed between them. Most nights, Adam was there, and if he couldn't make it, she felt uneasy, lost without his body next to hers. Several times he came in the early afternoon, but most of the time he appeared late in the evening just as the summer sun set and she was getting ready for bed. He'd stay the night but leave before she awakened.

In the first week and a half, they were together every night, Laura less shy each time. Although he never said anything to her, she knew he sensed her reluctance to be completely nude in front of him. Early one evening, when he came straight from a day at The Bay Shore, they were in the middle of a particularly frenzied session of lovemaking when he threw off the sheet and rolled her in one quick motion, placing her on top of him. Part of her always took comfort in the protection of the satin sheet. A torrent of past emotion, every fear and doubt she had ever stifled, raised its ugly head. Instead of continuing, she stiffened and stopped moving ignoring the rhythm of his body.

"What's wrong?" he asked, his voice thick with passion and worry.

"I…I…" To her horror she began to cry, tears leaking from her eyes as her face compressed into sobs. "I don't want you to see me like this."

Adam put a gentle hand on her cheek, whispering, "I don't understand."

"My horrible, squishy body dipping toward you," she blurted out, shutting her eyes.

He sighed, but she kept her eyes closed not wanting to see pity where not so long ago there was passion. Sliding off him, she sat on the edge of the mattress, protectively pulling the sheet around herself before getting up.

Grabbing her wrist, he said, "You're not going anywhere." His voice was strong as he tightened his hold and pulled her back to him. She didn't go willingly. Sitting up, he wrapped his arms around her and pulled her back to him. Voice softening, he said, "Now listen, this is ridiculous. Your body is beautiful. Everything you said is complete crap. I really, really like having your beautiful breasts dipping toward me."

"You don't have to do this…"

"I'm telling you the truth. Do you understand?" he asked as he cupped her breast and groaned happily.

Shutting her eyes against falling tears, she felt his lips on her temple, then her cheek, kissing away her tears. "You're beautiful."

"I'm not beautiful. Just ask my ex-husband. He'll tell you how hard it was to even look at me."

"Well, he's a jerk. I especially don't want him in your mind when you're in bed with me."

Eyes jerking open in surprise, she protested, "He's never on my mind when I'm with you. Never."

"Good. Now look, I don't want to wrap my arms around some bony woman. I want to hold someone with curves."

"I'm not just curvy. I'm girthy."

Sad eyes stared at her. She was responsible for the tension between them now. Aside from her body issues, now he thought she was missing Leland. Why had she ruined everything?

"Laura, damn it," he said, his lips tensing into a straight line. "I don't want you to be self-conscious around me. I love every sexy inch of you. Now, ride me, straddle me like I'm your favorite horse."

She shook her head feeling his hands tighten around her wrists. He must have seen the confusion in her eyes when he pulled her close and whispered, "I wouldn't be here if I wasn't enjoying myself. I think about you, about being with you…all the damn time."

"I think about you, too."

"Don't ever second guess yourself around me," he ordered and leaned back against the pillows, watching her. It was a pivotal moment. She had to believe his words, had to push past the self-imposed barrier she had erected.

Slowly, she approached him, letting the sheet fall away. He lay back and held out his arms. Carefully, she sat astride him. Picking up her hand, he pressed a kiss to her palm, giving a gentle tug to her arm. She lowered her face placing a small kiss to his lips, then his cheek and along the hollow of his neck as he slid his hands over her bottom, up her back, a gentle gliding motion as if she were delicate, making her feel adored. The velvety tip of his erection nudged at her, seeking her entrance. Parting her legs, she slid onto his thickness.

Strong hands reached up and cupped her face.

"You're beautiful," he said as his hands slid down to grasp her hips. With a sly smile that accompanied a twinkle in his eye, he ordered, "Now, throw your head back and ride me."

She blushed, heat enveloping her cheeks. "You're wicked," she said, shutting her eyes to concentrate on the feel of his deep penetration, her muscled walls tightening around him. Rotating her hips in tight circles she increased the tempo between them as he groaned. She was in control, finding her own power, a new freedom she'd never experienced before. Every move of her clenching muscles brought a new reaction from him. Opening her eyes, she looked down and saw his carnal smile. She rode harder, changing his pleasure to exquisite pain.

He swore loudly as she moved faster taking them both over the edge at the same time. His hands grabbed hold of her hips, and he rolled, taking her with him. The world spun and then she was looking up at him, his body on top of hers as he took control moving faster and faster within her, their bodies slapping against each other, drawing out every drop of pleasure.

Her muscles felt heavy as she laid her head on his chest, her eyes half closed. His hand lazily stroked her hair, a smile in his voice, as he mumbled, "That was hot."

Lifting her head just enough to meet his gaze, she asked, "Was it good for you?"

Their earlier tension now gone, he tossed her onto her back and smiled down at her. "Now who's being wicked?"

She laughed as he dipped his head and rolled her nipple between his lips and began to suck, tasting her greedily.

The buzzing cell phone interrupted them just as Adam was kissing a trail down her belly pausing to tickle the small dimple of her belly button.

"Don't answer it," he requested, splaying his hands over her belly in an effort to keep her from moving.

"What if it's important?" she asked, sinking her hand carelessly into his thick blue-black hair.

"Nothing is as important as this," he said, spreading her knees and dipping his head to place a kiss into the moist heat between her legs.

Gasping at the feel of his warm tongue making contact with her most sensitive flesh, she tried to pull away.

"Easy," he murmured, crooning to her as he would a scared animal. "You've come a long way, don't get shy now."

"Adam, I…please…" She tried to pull away, but he wouldn't let her. His hands held her tighter, intent on his task, his tongue making small circles on her small, hard nub. Lifting his head, his eyes half closed, he said, "You taste sweet…relax and let me have my fun."

She shut her eyes and sank back into the soft satin, the ringing phone forgotten.

His tongue lodged a soft assault as his hands slid under her hips, lifting her to give him better access. He feasted on her, but when he slipped a finger inside her and then a second and began to rotate them mirroring the action of his tongue, she screamed and bucked. Her body thrashed with pleasure. When the last tremor had passed and he'd kissed his way up her body, she was lost, unable to form any words, her breath coming out in short gasps.

He kissed her shoulder, pulled her into his arms. "Shhh…don't try to talk. You're almost hyperventilating. Don't forget who did that to you, or what I did to get you feeling this good. I sure as hell won't forget it."

She was finding it hard to catch her breath. The rise and fall of her chest was not without effort. The climax he'd given her had gone on and on. She'd never experienced such intense, raw pleasure.

"Adam," she murmured as a single tear slid lazily down her cheek.

"Shhh…" he silenced her with his lips and tongue, which tasted of their lovemaking. This man, this wonderful man was hers, if not forever, for at least the summer. For the moment, that had to be enough.

He glanced at the clock on her nightstand. "Damn, we've been at it for almost three hours. How about taking a shower with me before I go?"

She'd hoped he might stay for dinner, but he'd come early so it was a good guess he wouldn't be spending the night.

He got out of bed and stretched, his body was perfection in the golden glow of the early evening light.

"Would you like to stay? I could make dinner."

"It sounds wonderful, but I'm going to San Francisco tomorrow morning to see my parents. They're in town for the weekend. I've got a few things to do yet tonight, so I've got to head out. That's why I came early, I didn't think I'd end up sleeping here tonight."

"I understand," she managed, grabbing the hand he held out to her.

She led the way to the bathroom and tried not to feel disappointed. Of course, he wouldn't invite her to go with him. Grabbing a rubber band, she impatiently pulled her hair up, off her shoulders. Reaching into the shower, she adjusted the water, holding her hand under the stream as soft kisses touched her neck removing every thread of tension from her body. Stepping inside the stall, she arched her back as his hands moved up to cup her breasts, his lips nuzzling at her ear.

He had distracted her, but her mind was still on his family. What his parents would think of her, she could only guess, but then, they would never meet her. She was merely his summer friend and lover, not even reaching the rank of girlfriend. Shaking the sad thoughts from her mind, she turned to him wanting to shut out each and every fear. He indulged her, hungrily running his hands over her skin, reawakening their passion. Lifting her, he wrapped her legs around his waist and leaned her against the tiled shower wall.

Overwhelmed with the different textures, she fell back against the cool tile as his body, hot and wet with the cascade of water pulsating between them, held hers firmly in place.

Minutes later, he pulled back, panting, leaning his forehead against hers. "I'm sorry baby, but I have to get going. If I don't stop now, I'll never leave."

"I understand," she said, not letting her voice betray her. Leaving was the last thing she wanted him to do.

Wrapped in a pale pink terrycloth robe, she stretched out on rumpled bed and watched him dress.

Looking at his watch, he cursed, "Damn it. I have to go."

She wondered if he was telling her or convincing himself. Not moving, she let her eyes drink in every detail of him from his thick, luscious hair to fit of his trousers, which only enhanced his masculine form. He was the sexiest man she'd ever known.

"You really don't want to go, do you?" she asked, for the first time in her life, allowing herself to believe a man could want her as much as she wanted him.

He reached for her hands, "Hell no."

"Good."

"You're beautiful," he said, bending to kiss her.

After he was gone, Laura poured herself a glass of wine and sat in front of her television, not even sure what she was watching. She felt drunk but had yet to try her wine. Her mind was consumed with the man who'd spent the afternoon making love to her. Every time she thought of Adam, pictured him naked and pressing into her, her body trembled.

The intrusive noise of her cell phone interrupted her dreamy state. Grabbing it, she answered sleepily, "Hello?"

"Laura?"

"Leland?" In the aftermath of her afternoon with Adam, she had no tolerance for her ex-husband. "What do you want, asshole?"

"Nice. Laura, we need to talk…"

"No, we don't." The small place in her heart she thought would always belong to him had been invaded and completely taken over by her feelings for Adam.

"It's important Laura. We need to talk about us."

"There is no us, get that through your fucking head. Goodbye Leland." She pushed a button to terminate the call.

# CHAPTER SEVEN

Saturday afternoon lasted forever. Laura lay on her couch, the novel she'd been intent on reading now discarded, as her thoughts drifted to the previous afternoon she'd shared with Adam. The things he'd done to her. The way he'd touched her.

Adam would do every forbidden thing she could imagine. And when she imagined all the things she wanted to do to him, a sinful little thought burst inside her mind. What Adam had done to her, tasting her with his tongue was only the beginning.

She needed a distraction. She looked up Yoga online and started doing some of the basic stretches. If anything, these would help to make her more flexible for Adam. More ways to make love. The thought filled her mind with dirty ideas.

While making an elaborate and time-consuming early dinner, meant to occupy her and her thoughts, she heard her cell phone and paused. Wiping her hands on a dishcloth as she ran to answer it.

Let it be Adam. With a smile in her voice, she said, "Hello."

"Laura?"

It was that fucking asshole, Leland. It might be time to block his number. As it was, she'd changed his incoming notification on the cell to read, "Fucking Ex-Husband, & Asshole."

"Why did you have to do this, Laura? I thought if I called your bluff you wouldn't go through with it."

If she lived to be a hundred years old, she'd never understand her ex-husband. Just when she thought she knew how to play the game, he changed the rules. "Are you actually talking about our divorce?"

"Of course, what the hell did you think I was talking about?"

"Let's be clear. I asked for a divorce because you cheated on me. You slept with another woman. And then you drew up the fucking papers!"

She heard him sigh, the same sigh he used when he wanted her to know he thought she had said or done something he found to be incredibly stupid. "It's off with Amber, okay? I didn't love her, not like I love you."

She laughed into the phone. "I don't care. Don't you remember? We're divorced. Now, go away and leave me alone."

"Just wait a minute. We were married for nine years. I deserve the right to discuss this with you."

"No, you don't. I've moved on."

"Laura, damn it, the affair didn't mean anything."

"It meant something to me," she said, her heart beating double time.

"Listen, why don't you come back home so we can discuss this in person? I'll take you someplace nice…like Aqua. I understand you're mad, but we can get past this and get on with our lives."

"Oh, hell no," she said bitterly through clenched teeth.

"Think of the other partners in the law firm. Think of how this looks to them and our clients…"

"You're a divorce attorney and now we're divorced. Wow, how did I miss that?"

After a pause, he announced with his firm lawyer's tone, "I want to reconcile Laura. I never wanted the divorce. We have too many years together to just give up."

"Did she lose the baby?"

"There was no baby, thank God. And, that's in the past and none of your business. If you must know, I've decided to end it when I found out there was no baby. It's done."

Gripping the phone hard enough to break it, she replied sarcastically, "Makes no difference to me, I know who you are."

"Laura, we went through a rough patch, I'm willing to make the concession. I'm willing to admit my failings. Now, if you'd offer some concessions of your own, we could be happy again. People do it all the time."

"Not me. I'm done, you abusive son of a bitch."

"What's it going to take?" He completely ignored her comment like days of old. The man hasn't changed one iota.

"All I've ever wanted was a baby of my own. You knew that. I'm a schoolteacher because I love children. You never once considered my pain. You didn't care. You were just angry that I wanted to have a baby. I deserved to try to have one if I wanted one. You never understood how important it was to me. Instead, you berated me, you were mean to me. You never knew me, Leland, and I'm not about to waste any more time trying to figure you out. Get out of my life. We are done."

"We aren't finished, Laura."

Instead of saying goodbye, she simply hit the red X on her cell. Let him have the last word, she didn't care anymore. Gently, she placed the phone on the table, sat on the couch. It took a full thirty seconds before she put her face in her hands and cried. Thoughts of Adam trickled into her mind.

If she hadn't gotten divorced, she wouldn't have met Adam. Adam was the key that unlocked every sensual nerve in her body. Filled with passion for Adam, she'd been able to stand up to Leland and tell him exactly what she thought of him. She had loved Leland, been in love with him. Now all that was left was cold, angry pain.

Walking into her bedroom, she lay down on the bed and let the pain consume her. Curling into a ball, she clutched a pillow and sobbed. How many times had she wanted to tell Leland how unfair and cruel he'd been to her? The old, deep feelings of pain came back in a rush.

As the sun lowered in the horizon, turning her bedroom to soft hues of pink and orange, she sat up, feeling a little dizzy, a little nauseous. Leaving the cottage, she walked down to the beach and kicked off her sandals. She sat, watching the iridescent waves crash on the beach, digging her toes into the cool sand as the sun became a runny yoke and melted into the ocean. She practiced some of the Yoga moves she'd learned earlier and let the setting sun warm her.

Nothing Leland could say would make her go back. Adam had swung the pendulum, showing her what it was like to be if not loved, adored by a man. He'd brought her pleasure she hadn't thought possible, putting her desire above his own. There were no ultimatums or conditions. They were just together. Even after all he had been through, he was the most passionate, kindest lover she'd ever met. She wanted to know more, she wanted to know everything, but she wasn't sure she'd get the chance.

Leland had fallen out of love with her along the way. He enjoyed telling her in a thousand different ways. Death by a thousand verbal cuts. Focusing on her weight was just one small, constant jab he could use over and over again. One little verbal disparaging comment that added to the rest of the abuse. Refusing to make love to her or criticizing her when he did was another. She thought of how bad she felt every time she undressed in front of him; the way his eyes scanned her body, not with the adoring eyes of a lover, but the critical eyes of an enemy. She had stayed too long sharing an unhappy existence with Leland. He'd repeated his words until they had gotten under her skin. She had forgotten who she was, becoming a puppet for the master. Cutting the strings that bound them together hurt, but freedom was priceless. No way would she ever go back to that kind of abuse again. No way could she ever survive that again. She'd rather be alone for the rest of her life than be subjected to that hatefulness.

It was really quite simple. Being with Adam made her incredibly happy. They were lovers, nothing more, nothing less. She knew thoughts of his wife and child consumed him especially at night. When he came to her in the evening hours, he was sadder and quieter. It was in those hours that he held her more tenderly.

The air turned cool, making her shiver. She uncoiled from the position she'd assumed, stood, and brushed sand from her legs and feet. Adam would be back tomorrow. She hoped he would come to her, the thought of his touch caused heat to pool between her legs.

That night she slept restfully, cradling the pillow to her, thinking of Adam, no longer haunted by dreams of Leland for the first time in months.

The next afternoon, a lazy, warm Sunday, she lay by the pool and watched the clouds float overhead. She wanted to see Adam.

She needed to see him. If he came to her early, they could have dinner. She had yet to cook for him and wanted the chance. That was something she knew she did well and thought he was the type of guy to enjoy a home cooked meal. Then, he could take her to bed and they could enjoy each other intimately.

When her cell phone buzzed, she glanced at the caller ID before answering. Not Adam, but a friendly voice nonetheless.

"Kat!"

"Laura? How are you darling?"

Voice cracking with emotion, she admitted, "I'm hanging in there. Leland called. He wants to reconcile. There is no baby. I told him no, called him a few bad names."

"Oh god," Kat sounded disgusted. "Are you okay?"

"I'm better today, but he is such a jerk, it bothered me a little. I'm so thankful I got away from him."

"If I was there, we'd drink until we were stinking drunk."

"You're a good friend. I'll have a glass of wine in your honor."

"Find Adam and make him drink with you. I know you and I can only imagine what is going through your head. I don't want you to be alone right now."

"I'm not alone, I'm talking to you and I'm not suicidal for goodness sake. I'm just a little emotional," Laura said, watching a butterfly dance from flower to flower in one of the large, sculpted cement planters of bright red geraniums that outlined the perimeter of the pool area.

"Find Adam. He could probably use a drink, too."

"Well, I would…"

"But?"

"It's just that he's not here. He went to San Francisco for the weekend."

"Damn, he didn't go to meet some woman, did he?"

"I don't think so." He better not be. "He said he was meeting his parents."

"William says they're nice. Too bad they didn't come to the house."

Leave it to Kat to call a large palatial estate by the ocean, "the house."

"He'll be back tomorrow. I'll hit him up for a drink then." After several rounds of mind-blowing sex.

"Good. Get him drunk and have your way with him."

Laura grinned but didn't share the news of her relationship with Kat. For some reason, it was sacred and private.

Kat interrupted her reverie, "I wish you were here. Positano is so beautiful but filled with rich American tourists."

"Like you?"

Kat laughed, "Darling, I'm here on business, but I have to admit, William is turning this into a second honeymoon. It must be all the Prosecco we are drinking."

"I love Prosecco."

"I know you do, so I'm bringing you a case. We will be home in a couple of days and then we are going to celebrate your personal Independence Day in style."

Laura didn't feel like celebrating the demise of her marriage, but she knew Kat was trying her best. From thousands of miles away, camaraderie wasn't easy.

"Now promise me, as soon as Adam gets back, you'll have a drink with him."

"We will get stinking drunk." She and Adam rarely drank. They usually ended up in bed before they made it through a glass of anything.

After they hung up, Laura wondered if she should have told Kat the truth about being Adam's no strings friend with benefits. If she knew Kat, the other woman would figure it out as soon as she returned to Tranquility and saw them together.

Pulling the black Tranquility Escalade under the breezeway of the San Francisco Stark Hotel, Adam stopped next to the two men awaiting his arrival.

A short man in a black business suit shooed away the valet with a raised eyebrow, opening the car door personally, "Good afternoon, Mr. Stark."

"Hello Griffin, how are you?"

"I'm well, sir. And you?"

"About the same. Have Mr. and Mrs. Radcliff checked in?"

Griffin removed an envelope from his pocket as he spoke. "Yes sir. They're in suite 3030. You're down the hall and around the corner in 3072 as instructed." Handing Adam the envelope containing a key card, he announced, "Mr. Alexander Stark has sent a package for your attention. It's waiting on the desk in your suite. He asked that you call at your earliest convenience. Also, I've made reservations at Spruce for this evening at seven. I've informed Mr. and Mrs. Radcliff and they have requested that you join them in their suite at six for drinks."

Adam grimaced, but managed, "Thank you, Griffin. When do they think I'm arriving?"

"In about four hours, sir."

"Good. Let's keep it that way." The last thing he wanted was to spend any more time with Brian and Lillian Radcliff than absolutely necessary. He had loved Melinda, but there was no love for her family.

Taking a private elevator to his suite, Adam arrived in the luxury space without encountering another living soul. He could grudgingly admit, Brian and Lillian, his mother and father-in-law, had been good to him, especially when he unknowingly adhered to their agenda, marrying their eldest daughter, Melinda, ten years earlier. Lucky for him, they'd been in love. She was nothing like the rest of her family. It sickened him to think the remaining Radcliffs might garner hopes of him marrying someone else in their family. Lillian and Brian Radcliff had been subtly encouraging him to seek out their youngest daughter, Tess, to help him through his grief. Tess was a far too willing participant. Memories of their last, awkward encounter were still fresh in his mind. What really resonated was the knowledge it had nothing to do with him as a person and a lot more to do with all the zeros after other numbers in his bank account.

A valet silently brought in his luggage and received a generous tip. Adam noticed the large envelope on the desk as he picked up the phone and dialed his cousin, Alexander Stark, in Portland, Oregon, Stark International headquarters.

Obviously anticipating his call, Alex answered on the first ring, "Homesick yet?"

"Hell no, but my back is sore from the physical labor," Adam replied, gazing out the window at his view of Union Square. Laura made it better, but that was none of Alex's business.

"Still going back in September?"

"I've got to, I've got the trial. I'm still waiting for the official start date." It was a ticking time bomb. He couldn't wait to have it behind him.

"I know, but after that..."

Playing with the tassel of a curtain tieback, he groaned. "I haven't decided. And, to put your mind at ease, The Bay Shore will be ready for a May 1st opening."

"I have no doubt about The Bay Shore. I'm concerned about you, Runt." Alex had called Adam 'Runt' since they were little kids. In Alex's opinion, Adam was the runt of their family litter. When they'd grown up, Adam was exactly one inch shorter than Alex, so the nickname stuck.

"Thank you, Alex for letting me do this. I just need some time. New York has a lot of memories, bittersweet." It was where he'd fallen in love with Melinda, and they'd started their life together. A.J. had almost been born in a cab on Lexington Avenue. "And New York has The Radcliffs. They're a different problem altogether. I'm concerned it won't end well for my former relatives."

"Tess is on high alert, I bet," Alex teased. Adam had told him of her attempted seduction.

"Well, no matter what they hope might happen, nothing will. Tess isn't at all like Melinda. I'm not going to let them push her on me like a consolation prize. I find her repulsive."

"Look, if keeping you away from the Radcliffs' clutches means sending you to manage the new hotel in Dubai, I'm not opposed to doing it. Tess not only wants you, but she also wants your name and your money. Women of that kind are very, very dangerous and I'm not a fan."

"I agree. How is your little sandcastle in the middle of the desert?"

"It's a damn palace. It is our most opulent, gorgeous, spare no expense, over the top..."

"You sound like a carny hawking a flea circus," Adam interrupted.

"Well, it is our crown jewel. And there isn't a flea or bedbug within five miles of the place."

"I know what it looks like, I helped you with the plans, remember? My brain is still quite functional, despite what you might think." Well, except when he was with Laura. He sometimes forgot his name when he was making love with her.

"I remember. I'll expect you at the party on New Year's Eve. In fact, I'm taking the jet over on the 29th. I'll save you a seat. And Adam, think about what I said. I'll give it to you. You would have complete freedom to operate it how you saw fit. Hell, I'll even pay you, not that you need the money, but you can name your price."

Adam knew he would. He could name any price and his cousin would simply shrug in agreement. "How about more company stock taken from your holdings?"

Alex sighed, then said, "You're killing me."

"Tell you what, I'll think about it, but I'm partial to rain and occasional snow. You'd better keep looking for someone else. I thought Spencer wanted to get in the game." Spencer Whitlow was a silent partner, Alex's likeable cousin on his mother's side. Their three fathers had all started the business together, but now the next generation had stepped in. Ironically, Spencer had always been willing to help out but had preferred ranching at his place in Texas to running hotels.

"Fine, I won't push right now. I know you'll think about it...at least you'd better, Spencer is showing a certain fondness for Italy," Alex replied sarcastically. "He wants to remodel the hotel."

"Maria Medici might have something to say about that. Or is he trying his luck at her?" Adam asked. Maria was the manager of their Rome operation and Alex's half-sister, a product of his father's affair, a fact only few people knew. Alex had only just told Spencer.

"She could do worse, but she doesn't know yet. When she does, I'm more concerned that she will try to kill him, and I'll be called upon to hide his body. Besides, the idea of my paternal half-sister and my maternal cousin getting together romantically makes me a little sick even if they aren't technically related."

"Don't call me," Adam said, "I want no part of it, and someone will have to run things if you all go to jail."

"Yeah, yeah," Alex said, then in a softer tone, "Okay, so tell me, how are you? You sound pretty good. Are Kat and William keeping you entertained?"

"They're filming a movie in Italy, but I'm keeping busy."

"Who is she?"

"What?" Adam froze, looking away from the window.

"Adam, please…I can tell. There is a glimmer of the old Adam… you're either dating someone or you're getting laid or both."

"No comment." His relationship with Laura was private.

"Well, is she nice at least?"

Alex had always been able to read his mind. They'd been best friends since the age of five, growing up next door to each other. Giving up, Adam blurted out, "She is and don't ask about her, because the relationship has an expiration date."

"What? Is she going bad? How bad does she get?" Alex asked, chuckling.

"No, but I'm not staying around, and she knows it." Already feeling like a jerk, he changed the subject. "Look, I don't want to talk about her. Not today. You've sent this very intriguing envelope. What the hell do you want me to do with the damn thing?"

"Fine, I won't harass you, because I know the Radcliffs will do it for me. I don't envy you, just stay strong and watch your drink. I wouldn't put it past them to slip you a roofie, and the next thing you know you'll wake up in bed with Tess and she'll be pregnant."

"Shut up, you dumb motherfucker. You are scaring me!"

"Okay, why don't you open the damn envelope and I'll tell you what you're looking at?"

They talked for another half hour going over the documents Adam needed to sign. After he got off the phone, he stretched out on the oversized king bed and tried to relax. Alex was trying to help in his way. Adam wouldn't have made it through the last year if it weren't for his cousin, but in the last month there had been moments when his pain hadn't held him hostage. Being with Laura was his escape. If he were at Tranquility right now, he would have meandered over to her cottage, taken her straight into the bedroom, and made love to her until he was physically exhausted. He took it for granted that she would be open to the idea, but then she was always a willing, if not shy, participant. She was one of the sexiest women he'd ever known and yet she had no idea the power she held over him. When she looked at him with those big, innocent, blue eyes, he wanted to hold her and love her, convince her that she was amazing.

His wife Melinda had been amazing. Beautiful and sophisticated, she turned heads the minute she walked into any room. Raven-haired and tall, she'd made his head turn the first day of freshman chemistry class and he'd been lost. Luckily, she ran in Alex and his sister Rebecca's crowd, and they'd been able to introduce Adam to her. Up to then, Adam usually liked blondes, but there was something about Melinda that was exotic. They would have shared a lifetime together if it hadn't been for the drunk driver that took her and A.J. from him.

He wondered if Melinda would approve of what he was doing with Laura. Melinda would have liked her. But it was unlikely she would approve of his summer romance. He wasn't using Laura, he justified to himself. They were using each other. Laura was an adult and knew what they were doing, just as he did.

Angry for thinking of Laura when he should be thinking about his beloved wife, he got off the bed and went into the large marble bath intent on a cold shower.

Standing under the frigid water, he swore loudly. Today was the year anniversary of his wife and son's deaths. He was about to have dinner with his wife's parents. Thinking about being with another woman and wondering what his deceased wife might think about it was the height of disrespect to her memory, not to mention their child's. After the shower, he stood before the mirror, unable to look at his reflection.

"Asshole," he murmured.

Deciding one drink would take the edge off, he settled for vodka on the rocks. Downing it quickly, he had a second cocktail before brushing his teeth again and using mouthwash. Swearing again, he realized he'd almost forgotten the most important thing. Reaching into his shaving kit, he pulled out a small box. Extracting the simple gold band, he put it on the ring finger of his left hand. Taking it off after the first time he and Laura made love had been a hard decision but seeing it and feeling guilty over his wife while he was with another woman was worse. The Radcliffs would consider it an act of betrayal should they ever catch him without it. They wouldn't understand that taking it off had been the act of a husband still reeling with grief.

Knocking on the Radcliffs' door at five minutes past six, he shouldn't have been surprised when Tess flung it open and jumped into his arms. There had been no mention of Tess when her parents had asked him to join them in San Francisco, but he knew she'd be there, and she had a fuzzy memory of their past bad encounter.

Now in her late twenties, she was tall and lithe, a blonde with cold gray eyes and finishing school manners. Working in a department store as an haute couture fashion buyer, a job her father's investment firm connection had arranged, had given her even more confidence in her own sophistication and beauty. Comparing her to the other blonde in his life, he had to stop from shaking his head. Laura was a natural beauty. She just didn't know it. Tess wasn't, but she tried hard to be, too hard.

"Adam, oh Adam," she gushed, "I've missed you so much. Come in, come in." Dressed in a powder-puff pink Chanel suit with matching gold Chanel earrings and large, noisy, gold coin bracelets, she resembled a human wedding cake. Any shyness, embarrassment, or chagrin she should feel after her display at his home right before he left for The Bay Shore wasn't evident.

He followed her down a long hallway, ignoring the way she provocatively sauntered her hips, gyrating from side to side, to a large sitting area where Brian and Lillian Radcliff waited. Shaking Brian's hand, he hugged Lillian delicately as if she were made of bone china. They were just as elegant and dignified as they had been when he'd seen them in New York two months earlier. In their early sixties, they were still technically young, but the loss of their eldest daughter and only grandchild had taken the light from their eyes.

Sitting in one of the plush chairs, he accepted a drink from Brian and waited for the questions to begin. It had been this way since he was a college student dating their eldest daughter. It was a form of intimidation, and Adam had to admit the technique still held some power.

"So, Adam, how is this little hiatus working out?" asked Brian, as he looked down his nose at Adam with an air of disgust.

Brian hadn't approved of Adam's decision to leave his position as the manager of the Stark International Hotel New York.

"It's wonderful," he replied, taking a long sip of the whiskey Brian had placed in his hand. "I love the west coast and William and Kat are spoiling me."

"I still don't understand. Are you, like, working for them on the side?" Tess asked, scrunching up her face.

"I'm advising them on Tranquility, finding ways to get the estate to run smoother, like a hotel."

Tess scowled, "From what I heard it almost sounded like you were some kind of like, butler."

"Glorified," Adam replied gleefully, hoping the thought would terrify her.

"That's kind of, like, beneath you," she added. "Melinda used to say you were worth millions."

Melinda did nothing of the kind. Their finances were private.

"I thought you were doing something with an old, dilapidated hotel," Brian stated, his eyebrows coming together in a frown.

"The Bay Shore. It's an elegant old place a few miles down the road from Tranquility. I'm overseeing the renovation for Alex. It's a lot of fun. Like nothing I've ever done before."

Lillian looked disapprovingly at him as she spoke up. "Adam, you didn't need to do this. Why didn't you just take the house in Aruba for a few months? It would have relaxed you before the trial."

"Of course, the offer will always remain open," said Brian.

"I could join you for the summer," Tess added. That would be a terrifying idea.

"Or even after the trial," Brian offered with a calculating smile.

*The trial.* Since the man who'd hit their car had been arrested, all his wife's parents had been able to think about was the trial. They wanted revenge in the worst way and Adam couldn't say he blamed them. But the outcome of the trial wouldn't change the outcome of his life. He'd lost the two people he loved most in the world. The trial would never fix that. Nothing would fix that.

"Thank you, Brian, but I need something to do...away from New York, away from my memories of Melinda and A.J."

"We miss you, Adam. You're part of our connection to them," Lillian stated and dabbed at her eyes. "You were with them...when..."

She began to remind him as she always did...as if he would ever forget.

"I know and no matter how hard I try, I relive the accident every day of my life."

Lillian began to sob delicately as Brian placed an arm around her, explaining, "It's been hard with the year anniversary."

"I understand." Shutting his eyes and bowing his head, Adam relived memories too horrible to describe. Hearing his wife's final screams echo in his head, he wished he'd had a third drink in his suite. He wished he'd refused to meet these people today. If the Radcliffs hadn't requested this meeting, he would have spent the day at Tranquility, doing anything he could to distract himself. But he knew, over the next few hours, they would go to dinner and discuss Melinda and A.J.'s lives and deaths in detail. Dinner would settle like a rock and with any luck, he'd be just drunk enough to pass out at the end of the evening. He didn't need other people to help him keep their memories alive; not the way his in-laws did. He had his family in his heart every minute of every day.

Feeling arms wrap around him, he opened his eyes. Tess's face with her pink glossy lipstick and thick eyelashes coated with mascara were inches from his, smiling coquettishly. "I'm here anytime you need me. In fact, if you get bored in your little Tranquility place, I could join you for a few weeks."

But in her eyes, he didn't see compassion or sorrow. He saw lust and it scared the hell out of him.

# CHAPTER EIGHT

E arly Monday morning, Laura jumped in her car and left Tranquility for a spur-of-the-moment drive. Opening the sunroof, she let the wind whip through her hair. Adam had returned the night before. She'd seen him walk to the main house as she meandered along the beach at sunset. No doubt, he'd seen her as well, but made no effort to come to her. If he missed her, he wasn't showing it. She contemplated going to him, but what if he turned her down? She couldn't handle his rejection. What if something had changed in San Francisco? She didn't want to think about it, so she had jumped in the car and run away.

Having only been off the main grounds a few times, she was unfamiliar with her surroundings, but it didn't matter which direction she went, she just needed to clear her mind. And if she got really lost, she had her GPS to help her find her way back. She drove north thinking of how her life had turned upside down in a few short months, her thoughts drifting to her divorce. Since her phone call with Leland, she'd been unsettled. They were done. She hadn't fought the prenuptial she'd signed. Having returned her engagement and wedding rings, she would be the first to admit freedom had come at a stiff price.

Even if she'd had the money to fight him, she wasn't certain she'd have waged the battle. Kat and William would gladly have written a check for any amount to hire an attorney, but she wouldn't let them. When Leland made her an offer, giving her a modest settlement that allowed her to expedite the divorce, she'd accepted. After the final papers were signed and she'd deposited the small check, she thought they'd make a clean break and go their separate ways. Now, he was calling again. What did he expect her to do? Go back? Not before and certainly not now. Not after Adam.

A few hours later, having exorcised several of her demons, she drove through the gates and past the main house. She planned to change her clothes and find Adam. If he were following his usual routine, he would be back from a morning at The Bay Shore. She was in the mood for sex, and she hoped he was, too.

Skidding to a stop on the loose gravel drive, she swore as her mouth twisted into a snarl of anger. Leland's black Porsche Boxster was parked in the circular drive directly in front of the main doors. Son-of-a-bitch, what the hell was he doing here?

Stepping on the gas pedal, she peeled out, scattering gravel as she went straight for the garage. Eyes alert for Leland, she walked back to her cottage. She knew he had to be close, prowling around, looking for her, filled with self-righteous impatience.

Her relief that he wasn't waiting on the cottage's front porch was short lived. As she got closer, she saw a note tacked to the front door.

*9:30 am*

*Laura,*

*Leland Daniels is waiting at the main house to speak with you. He is outside my office.*

*Adam*

Spewing a list of expletives usually foreign to her gentle nature, she glanced at her watch. It was past one o'clock. With a sinking feeling, she realized it was Monday. Leland was missing work… billable hours. Adam had been there for Leland's arrival, not at The Bay Shore. She could only imagine what Leland had said to him. Damn cell phone! It never worked when she left the estate, and now, glancing at it, she saw all the text messages waiting for her, much in line with the note on her door.

Adam and Leland were two people she hoped would never, ever meet. Taking a deep breath, she pulled herself together as she changed into a simple summer dress. Noticing the fabric was loose as she walked to the main house, she couldn't help but smile a little. She'd lost weight, which gave her the exact boost of confidence she needed to face her ex-husband.

Hoping to find Adam first, she stepped inside the French doors cautiously. Leland wasn't waiting by Adam's office. Looking around each corner before proceeding, she heard Adam's voice as he talked to someone. She made a beeline for his office.

"Laura!"

Turning, she raised her chin and offered a defiant, "Why are you here?"

Leland's face was red with anger. She'd seen the look many times before. He was trying hard to contain himself, typical of his controlled demeanor. The suit he wore looked wrinkled and tired. He looked older; his taught, tanned face puffy, jowls beginning to droop from his checks. When had he gotten so old?

"Where the hell were you? That guy," he pointed at Adam's office, "had people looking all over for you. Since when did you stop answering your cell?"

Regardless of the fact her cell didn't work outside the grounds of Tranquility, he couldn't talk to her like that. "That is none of your business. We're divorced. I come and go as I please."

"Laura, you've been my wife for nine years." His nose wrinkled, making him resemble a pink skinned pig.

"Stop referring to me as your wife. I stopped being your wife the day I found out about your affair." She no longer cared about trying to be nice and keep peace. It was too late for pleasantries.

"Laura…"

"I don't know why you're here, but unless you've had a change of heart about the settlement and would like to give me a fair offer, you're wasting your time and mine."

"Why the hell are you being so defensive? I drove all this way to see you and talk."

"I'm sure that was hard on you," she said as she folded her arms stubbornly.

"Laura, damn it, I needed time to think. I've missed you," he said, stepping toward her.

Taking a step back, she asked, "Why did you come?"

"I just told you…I missed you."

"Sure. Maybe you missed my cooking and laundry services. Sorry, I never made it to the dry cleaner after I found the Visa statement in your pocket. I went and spoiled all your illicit fun." Not quite believing her own ears, she couldn't stop, "The idea that you miss me is appalling, even for you Leland. You miss abusing me."

"Think what you want. I didn't enjoy our last verbal intercourse. Since you don't think enough of our marriage to want to meet me in San Francisco to discuss it, I came to you." He held up his arms in frustration. His thick blond hair and tan linen suit made him look like a monochromatic hustler. With his pink face and sleazy aura, it was hard to believe she'd once found him handsome.

"Your girlfriend dumped you, so you've come here hoping I'll make you feel better. I'm sorry, but you've wasted your time or shall I say billable hours. We're done. I will never, ever go back to you. Leave. Get out!"

"This is very unlike you Laura, but after our years together you still surprise me."

Their tenth anniversary would have been in November. She'd hoped for a second honeymoon to Paris. In retrospect that dream seemed childish and naïve. She couldn't believe she'd once enjoyed his touch. He was a living, breathing, human serpent.

"When I think of how I listened to you tell me how unattractive I was and how you couldn't bear to touch me…" She broke off, shaking her head, "Well guess what? Now I can't bear to have you touch me either."

"Ah, so Katrina's been poisoning you against me. What else is new?"

"Don't blame her. She's not even here. You poisoned me all by yourself with your cruel words and actions."

Surprising her, his eyes softened, and he smiled, "Look, can't we just both admit we've done a few things we aren't proud of? Can't we get past this?"

"We don't have a relationship anymore. We haven't for a long time."

"Come on Laura…You're starting to look good. You've lost some of your baby fat if you'll excuse the pun."

Her mouth opened, but she was unable to speak. The depth of his cruelty knew no boundaries. When she thought he couldn't hurt her anymore, he managed to find a way.

"What have you lost? Fifteen, twenty pounds?" Smiling, he was checking her out lecherously, his gaze lingering on her breasts, oblivious to her anger.

Narrowing her eyes, she pointed toward the door. "Fuck you! Get out of here and stay out of my life."

"So, this is the way you want it, huh Laura? I'm going to have to beg you to get you to come back to me…" Leaning close, he reached out his hand, trying to rest it on her arm. Pulling away in disgust she fought the urge to pick up the nearest vase of flowers and break it over his head.

"I will never go back to you and don't ever touch me again!"

Adam stepped up behind her. She didn't even need to turn to sense his presence or his anger. Wondering how long he'd been listening, she glanced at him; saw the fire in his eyes and the firm set of his jaw. He was a volcano ready to erupt.

"Mr. Daniels, I think you should leave, before this gets any uglier," Adam said to the other man.

"This is a private discussion between my wife and me." Leland took a threatening step toward Adam, who held his ground.

Laura's hands balled into fists. "You're not my husband. We're done. It's over. I don't love you. I don't know if I ever did. Just leave me alone."

Leland looked at her and shook his head, "And you wonder why I cheated on you. Lady, you're one cold bitch."

Stepping back from the verbal attack, Laura bumped into Adam. He hands encircled her middle, picked her up, and moved her out of the way in one fluid movement, his body now completely blocking her view of Leland. It was predatory male positioning and she loved him for it.

"I believe the lady asked you to leave. You're on private property. If you say one more word to her, I'll throw you out myself."

"Are you screwing her?"

"That works," Adam replied, and charged Leland, by dropping his shoulder and plowing into the other man's stomach. Laura watched Leland's pained expression as the air left his lungs, both men sailing to the floor in a heap. Adam stood quickly, pulling Leland up with him, twisting Leland's arm behind his back and heading for the nearest set of doors.

Marco, the cook, was conveniently walking by with a flat of strawberries. He dropped the flat on the nearest table, ran to the French doors, and opened them with a flourish. Adam pushed Leland, who was spewing obscenities and threats, through the open doors and down the steps toward his Porsche. Marco hurried before them to open the car door and help Adam push Leland inside.

Laura bit her thumbnail as she heard Adam's last words, "Stay the fuck away from her. If I see you again, I'll have you arrested for trespassing after I beat the shit out of you."

Gone was the consummate gentleman in the suit. She knew he was passionate, but in a matter of moments Adam had turned into a foul-mouthed street fighter. She was proud, but embarrassed, wanting to cheer and cry at the same time.

Adam thanked Marco for his assistance. The other staff members, who'd gathered from the noise and witnessed the commotion clapped, drowning out the Porsche's noisy departure.

"Break it up," Adam warned, turning his attention back to Laura.

She couldn't quite meet his eyes.

"Why don't you step into my office, where we can discuss this privately?" Holding the door open for her, he ushered her inside.

Once they were alone and the door was shut, she was in his arms, her tears turning to sobs.

"I'm sorry," he said sitting on the couch and pulling her into his lap.

"Thank you…"

"I should've handled it differently. Here I'm trying to set an example for the staff, and I completely lost my cool."

Pulling back, she met his eyes, "You were wonderful."

"He's a bastard, but that doesn't mean I should lose my temper."

"Did you hear what he said to me?"

"Every damn word."

"He has a certain knack for cruelty," she admitted.

"No one will ever speak to you that way again. I won't allow it. Never." He reached up and stroked her hair, trying to comfort her.

"Why is he coming after me? We're divorced."

"I'm sure he's been kicking himself for ever letting you go. That doesn't make him any less of an asshole."

She nodded as he soothed her with a benign declaration, "It will be fine."

Putting a hand on either side of her face, he made her look into his eyes. Then, he leaned in and kissed her. Relaxing a little, she kissed him back, needing to feel his reassurance. She readjusted her body to straddle him provocatively. His hands grasped her hips, moving her against the erection now straining against the fabric of his trousers. She wanted him inside her, needed to have the event with Leland forgotten. As they kissed, she reached for his belt buckle, but his hand closed over hers, stopping her.

"We can't, Laura. Not here. Not in the office."

"I'm sorry…" she apologized, quickly moving off him, her face blazing with embarrassment.

"It's me who's sorry. I don't need you to thank me for dealing with your husband. Not like that."

"I didn't know I was," she answered, wiping away fresh tears.

"Can either one of us be sure?"

"I guess not." Straightening her skirt, she retreated toward the door, flushed with humiliation.

"Laura?"

She stopped but didn't turn around. Coming up behind her, he whispered, "You're too good for a romp on some office couch."

"I'm sorry, I didn't mean for you to think I'd use you."

"I didn't think that. Everything is fine."

But as she walked back to the cottage, nothing felt fine. She thought of all the reasons they shouldn't be together. They were both going through huge life changes. Adam was grieving. What exactly had happened in San Francisco? Maybe he was seeing a woman. It wasn't as if she had any claims on him. They hadn't discussed exclusivity. Then again, after what they'd shared the afternoon before he'd left, how could he be with another woman?

If he came that evening, she would know everything was good between them. But he didn't come. She curled up in her satin sheets, hugging her pillow, trying to sleep, but her mind replayed the scene between Leland and Adam over and over in her mind.

Waking the next morning after a restless night, her first thought was of Adam. Today, he would come to her, and they would make amends. She tried to make it easy for him, staying visible throughout the day, walking along the beach, sauntering around the gardens, and setting up her easel next to the pool. From Adam's office, she would be right in his sight line, but if he was at The Bay Shore, her entire effort was wasted.

What had started off as an attention seeking game turned into something much more. Her sketch of the main house, from her perspective at the pool, was breathtaking. Within an hour she was engrossed, barely noticing the people that moved past her to set up for the impending Fourth of July party. In her own world, she found peace. Four hours later, she was looking at the first piece of art she had completed in over nine years, and it gave her greater satisfaction than anything she had done in about as long.

It wasn't until she was sliding between the cool satin sheets that night that she focused on Adam. He hadn't sought her out. In fact, she hadn't seen him all day. She wondered if he had looked out his office window and seen her, engrossed in her art. If he had, he hadn't wanted her to know. It hurt a little. Actually, it hurt a lot.

She could text him, but she wasn't that person who ran after men. If he wanted her, he knew where to look. She wasn't that needy— okay, she was, but she'd be damned if he knew just how needy.

He was busy, she reasoned. Besides The Bay Shore, he was helping with the party. Kat and William would be home the next day and the party was happening the day after. But she hadn't been with Adam in five days. It was the longest they had ever gone, and it felt wrong. Maybe their affair was over. She had only herself to blame for trying to jump him in his own office minutes after he had an altercation with her ex-husband. The more she replayed it in her mind the worse she felt.

Kat and William arrived at Tranquility amid the buzzing party excitement. Laura met them in the main sitting room, running into Kat's open arms. Over Kat's shoulder, she noticed Adam talking to William quietly in the corner. He glanced her way and unlike the heat that usually accompanied his gaze, today there was only awkwardness.

"Laura! You look great! How are you darling?"

"I'm okay. But you...Kat, you look fabulous."

"William and I were like bunnies in Italy. What you are seeing is my sex flush."

"You are so bad..."

Kat lowered her voice, her face concerned. "I've only been home a few minutes and several people have told me about a scuffle between Adam and a man bearing a striking resemblance to your ex-husband."

Glancing toward the corner, Laura asked in an equally quiet tone, "Have you talked to Adam?"

"Not yet," Kat replied, following Laura's gaze to where Adam and her husband continued their hushed conversation. "I think I want to hear it from you first."

Laura sighed as the other woman grinned. "It wasn't at all funny, Kat."

"If the rumors are true, I'm sad I missed the show."

She bent close, lowering her voice. "Leland showed up. I asked him to leave, he said something lewd, and then Adam escorted him to the door and shoved him into his car."

"That's not a very detailed account," Kat said, shaking her finger at Laura.

"That's what you get. Take it or leave it."

"If you don't tell me more, I'll make Adam tell me."

"I'd prefer you didn't remind Adam."

Kat nodded and glanced at her husband and Adam. "Then, you'd better tell me more. Did Adam comfort you in your time of need?"

Laura shook her head and lowered her voice. "Adam is right over there. It was horrible. Leland called me a cold bitch. Said I'd lost some of my baby weight. Adam walked up, got between us. I thought they were going to start hitting each other."

"I bet that was sexy to watch."

"It was horrible, Kat," Laura repeated. "Very, very embarrassing…"

"Try not to let your eyes sparkle when you talk about it. It's an obvious tell."

Before Laura could argue, Kat called out to her husband, "William, Adam's a hero. Wait until you hear what he did to protect our resident damsel in distress."

Laura groaned, biting her lip, but Kat grabbed her wrist, pulling her off the sofa to lead her to where the men stood. William grabbed her for a tight hug as Kat hugged Adam.

"Anyone who kicks Leland's ass is a hero in my book," Kat exclaimed. "Thank you for taking care of my best friend." Then, she gave him a loud kiss on the cheek that left a red lipstick print.

"It was nothing," Adam replied nonchalantly, his eyes meeting Laura's.

"It was wonderful," Laura admitted.

"Family honor was at stake. I'm glad you were there for her," William said, thanking Adam with a firm handshake. "I think a bottle of Dom is in order."

"No, thank you…" Adam and Laura answered in unison. Adam made his apologies and left, glancing one last time at Laura before he stepped from the room.

"How interesting," Kat murmured. Laura ignored the comment and made her own apologies, needing the familiar comfort of her cottage.

# Chapter Nine

The Fourth of July dawned warm and clear. The Pacific was calm, more lake than ocean. Laura helped Kat with the last-minute party details and tried not to think about Adam. She saw him directing a steady stream of caterers, party planners, and wait staff, which had organized like an army. Hearing him give orders on etiquette and the importance of not asking any of the celebrities for autographs, she had to stifle a smile. He looked uncharacteristically frazzled and when their eyes met across the large expanse of lawn, now decorated with tables and Chinese lanterns, he gave a quick smile and her heart fluttered in response.

By late afternoon, as the pyrotechnic specialists set up a large bunker down on the beach, Laura stood by the pool and watched. Kat walked quietly up behind her and placed an arm around her shoulders, offering a friendly, "Hey there."

Startled, she jumped, "I'm sorry, I didn't hear you…Do you need my help?" Even stressed, Kat still managed to look beautiful, making Laura doubly envious.

"No, no darling. Everything is perfect. Having a houseguest familiar with hotels and large banquets is fabulous. I just sit back and let Adam do all the work. I don't know what I'd have done without him. I'm going to see if I can entice him back next year."

"He looks unusually stressed."

"So, you've been watching?" Kat asked, her voice smooth, yet prying.

"There's a lot to see and not just with Adam. Are you sure I can't help with something?" She wanted to confide in her friend, but with the way Adam was treating her, there might not be anything to tell.

"No, just amuse yourself by watching Adam."

"I can't help it. He's everywhere."

"Well, now that's settled, I'm off for a quick nap to get rid of this jet lag. The guests are arriving at six and fireworks begin at ten. I just wanted to check in and make sure you had an outfit for tonight."

"Yes, I have an outfit!" Laura exclaimed sarcastically but was secretly happy for the change of subject.

"What is it?" Kat asked skeptically and added a crooked smile.

"A lovely floral cotton sundress. Very Fourth of July."

"That white number with the big red poppies?"

"With matching red sandals. How is it possible that you can remember my wardrobe?" Laura asked, thinking of all the beautiful clothing Kat had in her closet.

"It's strange, I admit. Maybe it's my overwhelming desire to chop off about five inches from the hem of every dress and skirt you own. Not to mention cutting a big chunk of fabric out of the front, you know where your cleavage goes?"

"No one wants to see that," Laura replied, sarcastically.

"I won't argue the point today. I will just tell you I brought you a little present from Milan on the way home. It isn't a cotton sundress so don't get your hopes up. It's laid out on your bed. I hope you like it. I wanted it to be special. I spent a lot of time picking it out, boring William out of his mind, so you must wear it tonight."

"You didn't! Are you sure it will fit me?"

"Of course, the damn thing will fit you. You'll love the matching shoes and earrings."

"I…Kat it's too much. Letting me stay here is too much."

"Consider it your happy divorce present. This gift you can't return, so I suggest you just enjoy it. Now, I'm off to find my husband for a little afternoon delight…" she offered with a wink. "Why don't you see what's waiting for you?"

"Thank you, thank you!" Laura exclaimed, giving her friend a quick hug.

A deep red, silk sheath dress was laid out on her bed with a stack of neatly arranged packages on a nearby chair. Reaching out to touch it, Laura pulled her hand back not wanting to mar the perfection of the silk in any way. Smiling from ear to ear, she opened each box slowly, savoring the treasure within. She found the matching wrap first. It was a long, narrow piece of lace in the same shade of red, beautiful and sexy. The matching shoes were strappy high-heeled silk sandals with red beading, made by a famous designer she had always lusted after but never been able to afford, even with Leland's salary. Another package contained a red silk clutch and assortment of makeup including the perfect shade of matching lipstick.

The last box was the smallest and contained the most wonderful gift yet; garnet and diamond teardrop earrings. The generous diamonds sleeved into a pair of garnet drops that were the exact shade of her dress. The note in the box said it all: *Wear these with our love, Kat and William.* They loved to spoil her and always had. She had never been able to keep up.

Delighted, she put on the earrings and spent the rest of the afternoon lying by the pool watching Adam from a distance. He was aware of her, every now and then looking her way. Eventually, he would have to speak to her, and she doubted she'd enjoy what he had to say. They had shared several exciting and unforgettable moments of passion. If the few evenings they'd been together weren't meant to continue, she would simply enjoy the sweet memories and move on. The freedom in letting go allowed her mind to still. She dozed off, not thinking of anything and when she awoke, she had just enough time to shower and get ready for the party.

Standing before the full-length mirror, she toyed with her reflection. She had to admit, she looked better than she had in years. The dress was stunning, dipping to a vee in the front and back, exposing just the right amount of cleavage. A subtle slit up one side added a sexy accent. Leland had been right about one thing: she had lost weight. Her new tan made her skin glow against the gorgeous red silk. Turning from side to side, she delighted in how perfectly the dress fit. She applied the red lipstick and admired the sparkle and flash of her new earrings.

Just as she was ready to leave, something caught her eye. A white rose lay on her pillow. She walked over and picked up the plump blossom. As before, it was tied with a white ribbon. Happiness flooded through her. Adam had been here. He still cared.

With a beaming smile, she walked through the warm air toward the noisy festivities feeling better than she had in a week. She moved from room to room in the main house, stargazing and chatting with the few people she knew. Picking at sumptuous morsels from the buffet tables, she was careful not to drop or spill anything on her dress. The staff nodded and smiled as she spoke to them, but Adam was nowhere to be seen.

Kat, dressed in a low-cut blue satin cocktail dress studded with sequins and with William at her side, was busy with hosting duties. Laura carefully avoided both of them, not wanting them to feel they had to keep her entertained. An actor she recognized as the one Kat had mentioned for bedding any woman that moved, Thad Sterling, worked the room moving from one woman to another like a disease. She knew the instant she was in the tall and rugged playboy's sights. His eyes drifted over her, scanning every curve. He hesitated for a moment and then honed in. She had to stifle a laugh. Obviously, he'd had to think about approaching the over-weight middle-aged woman.

"Well, hello there," he offered, handing her a glass of champagne.

"Hello, Mr. Sterling," she said as she accepted the drink.

"You know me?" he asked, feigning surprise. Not waiting for an answer, he said, "Call me Thad."

"Hello Thad, of course I know you. I've seen several of your movies," she said, thinking that somewhere, in an alternate reality, a ski slope was missing its bum.

"And who might you be?"

Oh, nobody, Laura thought as the familiar self-doubt awakened. "I grew up with Kat. We've been best friends since second grade. I'm Laura Hokensen. It is nice to meet you, Thad."

"Katrina? Really? You've known each other that long?" Yes, really. We're the same age and yes, she looks wonderful. "But you're not an actress," he stated, an observation, not a question.

"No, I teach."

"Acting?" he asked, suddenly interested.

"Math," she replied, knowing with certainty if he'd been one of her students, she'd have flunked him.

"Oh, I see…"

She saw Adam chatting with Kat's secretary, Jackie, the one who liked to leave her long strands of hair on everything, including Adam. Laura and the redhead had given each other a wide birth since that fateful day in Adam's office. She no doubt knew about Adam and Laura's affair. Laura had no reason or right to be jealous, but she couldn't help it. Adam was walking with Jackie, giving her his full attention.

He looked up just in time to see Laura with the hunky actor. Their eyes met and she said absently to Thad, "If you'll excuse me, Thad, I need a little fresh air." Walking away from the shocked actor, whom she'd dismissed, she fled out the open doors. Resuming her favorite perch next to the pool, she looked out at the setting summer sun and tried to calm down. Had Adam moved on to Jackie? She remembered the dinner party when Jackie was in the green dress, snaring Adam's complete attention. She sighed, but it sounded more like a growl. Watching the deep blue ocean turn lavender as the sun dipped below the horizon, she stayed at her perch until the light faded and the carefully placed Chinese lanterns softly illuminated the darkening sky. In the distance, she heard the laughter and chatter of other guests and felt like an outsider. She'd been through too much in the last few months to celebrate anything, including Independence Day.

Last year she'd been at this party with Leland. It was the only party of Katrina's she could get him to attend because he liked to be able to brag that he had been at a party full of celebrities. It had bothered her to no end when he asked her to carry his extra business cards in her handbag. For Leland, a party wasn't just a party, it was a business opportunity. She hoped he was aware of the date, at home and brooding.

She was brooding herself. What did the rose mean? What if Adam hadn't left it? It could have been someone else, but the possibility hadn't dawned on her until now. It could be the maid, who against Laura's protests, still came to the guesthouse each day and replaced her linens, putting fresh sheets on her bed. There was always Marco. He'd been attentive since the dinner party, delivering dinners to her several nights a week. If she were out painting anywhere on the estate, he would deliver a panini at lunchtime.

Of course, it was Marco. It had to be Marco. She'd been crazy to ever think Adam would be moonstruck enough to leave roses on her pillow.

She'd had enough of the party, of Tranquility…of the whole damn place. It was time to go home, wherever that was. Well, she thought, home was yet to be defined. She would make it. She would be okay. With her mind feeling a little more peaceful, she decided that it was time to go back to the cottage and think about her new home. She would need to pick colors and decorate. On her budget, it wouldn't be easy, but she was creative. In fact, maybe she should be painting a few landscapes with design in mind. It would be nice to have a few of her paintings on the walls. Leland would be horrified. His taste went toward the stuffy traditional. He'd have hated her watercolors.

Just as she was about to turn to leave, a warm hand touched her bare back.

Adam.

She knew the touch of her lover as clearly as if he had spoken her name. Looking into his eyes, she didn't know what to say. The dark sky conspired with his chocolaty eyes, giving away none of his thoughts. Dipping his head, he touched his lips to hers, a soft tentative kiss, which asked a question. How she kissed him back would choreograph their next move. Leaning up on her tiptoes, she pressed into him, kissing him with a week's worth of pent-up need. Her hands trailed up the front of his jacket, encircling his neck to pull him closer.

When they came up for air, he kissed her ear, whispering, "That dress looks stunning on you."

"I'm glad you like it."

"I'd like you in a potato sack," he murmured and then asked, "Are you having a good time?"

"I am now."

He kissed her again, his hands moving possessively over the smooth silk.

"As soon as I see the fireworks going off without a hitch, my responsibilities end." He nuzzled her neck, his tongue tasting the sensitive hollow of her throat.

"When do they start?"

"Twenty minutes."

"That seems like a long time," she replied, her hand reaching down to cup him through his trousers.

"It will be if you keep that up." She could almost see the sparkles in his warm eyes as he spoke.

"We better behave ourselves then. I've just missed you."

"I'm sorry. I was busy and I wanted the party to be perfect."

Lame. She knew it, but she couldn't confront him more than she already had.

He wrapped his arms around her waist and then ran his hands the length of her rib cage to cup her breasts. Leaning her head back against him, she relaxed. He was back and she would savor every moment. It had been a harsh lesson, having a taste of what it would feel like to lose him at the end of summer.

He draped his black suit coat, still warm from his body, over her shoulders.

"What's that for?"

"I felt you shiver."

"You felt me tremble…there's a difference." She'd trembled at the thought of losing him.

"Humor me," he said, quieting her with a kiss on the side of her neck, which sent fire through every nerve in her body.

When the first explosion lit the sky, he whispered, "How about we go make some fireworks of our own?" She was already anticipating how it would feel to be in his arms as she took the hand he held out to her. Turning their backs on the excitement, they made their way toward the cottage, but when they reached the fork in the path, he hesitated.

Wondering what was wrong, she looked up at him. Could he be having second thoughts already?

"Would you like to see my room?"

"Sure." She didn't think to tell him it was the room Kat had always given her when she visited with Leland.

Arriving at the main house, they walked up the marble steps together. He held the door for her and then took her hand once again. They were just starting up the main, winding staircase, when a familiar voice called out her name.

Still wearing Adam's coat, Laura hadn't noticed Kat standing just a few feet away when they walked in.

"Are you two kids having fun?" Kat asked with a mischievous grin as she held court among a group of admiring fans.

Laura glanced at Adam, who looked down at Kat and smiled. "We're about to," she said boldly and glanced to Adam.

Kat yelled back, "About damn time."

"Say goodnight, Kat." Adam instructed.

"Goodnight, Kat," Laura said and grabbed Adam's hand.

"Sweet dreams you two," Kat teased.

When they got to the top of the stairs, he turned to the left.

"Is this going to be a problem for you?" she asked.

"Why?"

"I'm sorry, maybe I shouldn't have said that to Kat…"

"I have a feeling she already knew," he replied with a sly smile and added, "Does it bother you?"

"No."

"Good, because the whole staff knows," he offered casually as he paused in front of a polished mahogany door and searched for his key.

"What? How?" she asked, her voice going an octave higher.

"Jackie, that evil secretary of Kat's. She guessed what was happening in the office that first time we almost…" his voice trailed off and then he finished his thought, "Really kissed…I'm not sure what that was besides crazy. Anyway, she talked. I don't give a damn, but my credibility with the female staff went down, whereas the men started listening to me and high fiving me in the hallways…I don't care…not like I'm getting paid, but it's no one's business but ours."

"You don't like her," Laura said a little too happily.

"After all I just told you…you narrow in on Jackie? She's not my type, but you don't need to sound so happy about it," he teased. "Where's my damn key?"

"What is your type?" she asked, purposefully distracting him as she fingered one of the buttons on his starched white shirt.

"You. You're my type," he said and gave her what was intended to be a quick kiss, but she leaned in and took control, pushing him against the door.

After a long minute, "Damn, now I really need the key!"

"We might have to go back to my place. Rough it on my satin sheets."

"I had satin sheets put on this bed this afternoon," he said with a rueful grin, holding up the key.

Adam switched on a couple of lamps in the large living room, which attached to an equally large bedroom, both decorated in mauve and taupe.

"I see Kat has done her best to make this room into a boudoir," she quipped.

"It was made for a woman," he agreed.

Laura noticed a large cluster of photos on a low table. She walked over to them, felt his eyes following her across the room. She was drawn to the largest, Adam and his wife on their wedding day. They were beaming with joy. It was a smile she'd never seen on his face in the time she'd known him. Maybe he was incapable of ever smiling that way again. His wife was beautiful. Laura didn't want to make comparisons, she could never compete with a dead woman, but looking at Melinda, the name she'd discovered thanks to Google and Kat, as she posed next to Adam, Laura was humbled.

Their son looked like Adam. Sadness started to well inside of her. She was looking at senseless loss, the destruction of a loving family at the hand of another.

"Is it okay if I look at these?" she asked, turning to see Adam watching her from the bedroom with a haunted expression on his face.

"I needed you to see them." He moved to the window, absently watching the fireworks.

The sadness got worse with each photo, yet she couldn't stop, not until she'd looked at each and every one. Moving into the bedroom, she noticed there weren't any photos on any of the tabletops and for a selfish moment, she was relieved. Had he removed them for her visit, planning all along to bring her here tonight?

He was quiet, staring at the flashes of light with no emotion. Then, breaking the spell, he said thoughtfully, "My photos are probably the most precious things in my life. Having you see them, well, maybe it helps you to understand me."

She stood next to him, but made no move to touch him, not wanting him to think she pitied him.

Turning to her, he leaned close, his lips barely touching her ear and whispered, "I'm sorry I've been distant. I haven't been exactly honest with you."

"In what way?" she asked quietly, focusing on the fireworks as a lump formed in her throat.

"When I told you I was with my parents last weekend, that wasn't the truth. I was with my wife's parents. They needed to talk and check in. It was a year ago last weekend that the accident happened. It was a hard weekend for all of us. They're having a rough time and wanted to be with me. I couldn't say no."

"You could have told me. I'd have understood." She brushed her hand softly along his cheek. She had no right to feel hurt or mad at him. She was sleeping with another woman's husband. Just because the other woman was dead didn't mean she wasn't a big part of his life.

"I just needed to get through it quietly. I needed to do it in my own way."

She nodded and thought carefully of her words before responding. "Is there anything I can do?"

"Stay with me. Let me hold you tonight."

Encircling her in his arms, they both fell silent as they watched the rest of the fireworks. After a few minutes, she sensed a subtle change in him. He kissed her once, twice, and then led her to the bed.

Without a word, he undressed her, the shyness she once felt having all but disappeared. She slipped between the cool sheets and watched him undress, his eyes never leaving her face. He joined her, switching off the lights before he got into bed. She wondered, fleetingly, if it was to allow the fireworks to illuminate the room or to enable him to forget who he was with.

He was never more tender or caring. And once the long fireworks display finished and they'd satisfied their passion, he switched the lamp on its lowest setting, casting a soft glow on the elaborately decorated room.

It was her cue to leave. He had asked her to stay, but somehow she knew he needed to be alone. If she suggested it, it would be easier for both of them. The last thing she wanted was for him to ask her to go.

"Thank you for tonight…" she murmured softly as she looked for her shoes.

"What are you doing?"

"I'm going to give you some space. I don't want to overstay my welcome."

"Don't leave," he announced, sitting up on his elbow to watch her.

"Are you sure?" she asked, hearing the desperation in her own voice.

"Absolutely. I've missed you…I want you to stay. Right here…" He smiled and patted the empty mattress next to him. Relieved, she dropped her shoe and climbed into his waiting arms.

That night, she slept nestled against him. When, sometime during the night, she felt him kissing his way down her body, she wondered if she was dreaming. Before long, her legs were resting on his shoulders and she was grabbing a pillow to stifle her screams as he pleasured her with his tongue. Keeping her legs high, he shifted his body and filled her, pushing until he was as deep as he could go. They coupled like two wild animals.

"Damn," he muttered sleepily.

"What?" she asked, her head on his chest listening to his heart.

"Why is it like this with us? Every damn time."

"The first time was very gentle."

"But I can't ever be gentle with you twice in a row. I have to pound into you. I have no control. Then, I worry that I've hurt you," he complained.

"Have I ever said I didn't like it?"

"No," he replied with a low chuckle, his hand gently moving to squeeze her breast.

"Then you should enjoy it. In fact, do you know what I'd enjoy right now?" she asked, reaching down to cup him.

"I think I might have an idea," he answered as she moved down his body to take him in her mouth. Within moments, he was breathing hard and murmuring her name as she continued to use her lips and tongue to make him forget everything in the world, except the pleasure she was bringing to him.

That morning, Laura awoke lazily and reached for Adam, but she was alone, and the shower was running. She moved slowly, stretching her muscles as she walked toward the open bathroom door. He was standing in the large, marbled shower, his eyes closed and a sweet smile on his lips as three showerheads bathed him in warm water. Sensing her arrival, he opened his eyes and then the shower door.

"Come here, beautiful."

She stepped inside and hugged him as warm, soapy hands drew patterns over her skin.

Leading her over to a little seat carved into the marble, he held out his arms and waited for her, his warm brown eyes mischievous. She straddled him, noticing he was already erect and ready for her. Slowly, she took him into her body, the warm water making their skin erotically slick. Gently slipping a finger between her legs, he began to rub her as she rode him to a fierce climax.

Later, as she towel-dried her hair, she stole glances at him shaving, the intimate morning ritual doing strange things to her head. She borrowed his comb and felt his gaze on her.

"Yes?"

"Nothing," he said with a rueful smile.

"I know I look terrible in the morning."

"You look pretty with your hair slicked back," he corrected and kissed her cheek. "But then, I always think you're pretty."

When they were dressed, they walked down the stairway together. Adam was casually dressed in jeans and a t-shirt, but Laura was still in the red dress from the night before, complete with matching sparkly shoes and garnet earrings.

At the bottom of the steps, he paused to ask, "Painting today?"

"Yes, I'm definitely in the mood. What's on tap for you? Gardening?"

"A little manual labor."

"Just like the day we met...you look very...sexy," she offered, feeling a bit shy.

With a wide grin, he pulled her into his arms and kissed her with the familiarity of long-time lovers. "Damn it. Sometimes I can't get enough of you..."

Despite everything they'd done to each other, she blushed.

"Part of me wants to drag you back upstairs and stay in bed all day."

"I like that part of you," she managed.

"I've got to go, but I'll see you later, if that is okay," he announced, turning, and walking in the general direction of the garage.

"See you tonight," she said, then she took one last glance over her shoulder before she rounded the corner and almost ran into her best friend. "Kat! Oh, I'm so sorry! I didn't see you..."

"Laura...*Laura*!" Kat declared, smiling, and nodding in approval.

Five minutes later, at Kat's insistence, they sat across from each other at one of the small café tables on her back deck overlooking the ocean. Kat was thrumming her fingers on the glass top table, her long red nails clicking nosily as she said impatiently, "I'm waiting."

"I don't know what you want me to say," Laura replied, feeling self-conscious in her red dress and damp hair.

Marco personally delivered two heaping plates of food, taking in Laura's appearance with a not too subtle smirk.

"Great, now he knows, too," Laura snipped as soon as he was out of earshot.

"Darling, everyone knows. Adam's frequent visits to your cottage are becoming old news," Kat said sweetly, taking a delicate bite of mango.

"How long have you known?"

"I was practically run over by people who wanted to tell me when we got back. Imagine my surprise! My best friend doesn't tell me about her passionate affair with my hunky houseguest. It involved a knock-down drag-out fight with her estranged ex-husband and I missed out on almost all of it."

Laura felt a headache starting, pounding in her temple, making her see splotches before her eyes. "You practically threw me at him."

"I didn't need to."

"Are you mad I didn't tell you?"

"I'm absolutely livid, but I guess anything or anyone that can distract you from your bastard of an ex is a good thing. You know I love Adam. And god knows he needs to get laid. Who started it?"

"You know he kissed me in your garden."

"That's not what I meant. The day it started. The first day you got naked. Who started it?"

"Why is this important?" Laura complained.

"Humor me..."

"He kissed me in his office. I went in angry, wanting to have a fight. We ended up...well, kissing, but he stopped it, and then he came to my cottage late that night and I basically seduced him."

"Damn it, I owe William a blow job."

"What?" Laura laughed, barely setting down her coffee cup.

"I bet him that you would start something. He said Adam would make the first move. We bet a blow job on it to make it interesting."

"When did you make this bet?"

"Before we left for Italy. We both sensed something would happen. Would it have killed you to make the first move?" she asked with a giggle.

"What am I going to do?"

"Keep fucking like bunnies," Kat said loudly, throwing up her hands for emphasis.

"You want to say it a little louder? I'm not sure Adam could hear you down at The Bay Shore."

Kat only laughed.

"I like him, Kat. I care for him."

"Take it one day at a time Laura. He's wounded and hurt. He reminds me a lot of someone else I know."

"Let me guess…me," Laura said, cradling her hand against her pounding temple. The smell of the food was making her nauseous.

"No, not even close…" Kat countered.

"Who then?"

"Scooter."

"My dog?"

"That wounded dog you rescued was the first love of your life."

"So, Adam's a dog?"

"Well, no, but before you rescue him, you might want to make sure he wants to be saved or someone else in this scenario might need to be rescued."

"Me," Laura replied with a dark foreboding.

Kat merely nodded and took a sip of coffee.

# Chapter Ten

K at and William left two days after the party, and despite Laura's sense of impending doom her affair with Adam continued and flourished.

"So how did you end up married to that guy?" Adam asked her one morning in mid-July as they made breakfast in her cottage.

Laura almost dropped the pancake she was flipping onto the floor.

"You're asking me about Leland?" she asked, turning down the heat on her pan.

"It just doesn't make sense to me," he said, watching her with those intense brown eyes. She wondered if it was disapproval she saw in them, or just curiosity.

"You really know how to surprise me," she said, thinking that this comment was from out of left field. Aside from their original discussion of Leland, and Adam throwing him out, he hadn't asked her a thing. In fact, he'd displayed no jealousy or curiosity about her past. Aside from comforting her, he didn't seem to care. It fit the parameters of their relationship.

"I'm sorry, I probably didn't pick the best time. It has been on my mind, and I didn't want to ask you last night when we were in bed," he said, setting down his cell phone and then reaching for his coffee.

"Thank you for that. It's fine, but how much time do you have? Because I can give you the long or the short story depending." Please say you don't have the time, she thought. That would give her time to decide how much she wanted to tell him.

"Start short, but I reserve the right to want the long."

Laura placed the pancakes on two plates and handed one to him. Her appetite took a dive and what had appeared so appealing a moment ago, had now totally lost its allure. In fact, she felt a little nauseous.

"You wouldn't have married an asshole, so he couldn't have always been like that," Adam said, his tone edgy, almost possessive. It could be her imagination, probably was. He wasn't possessive of her, hadn't he made that clear? No, it was just pure curiosity. Maybe if she shared a little, he would do the same. His wife had been a taboo subject, aside from seeing her photo.

"I was young and lonely. My parents had died, and I was still swimming in grief. That is the best way I can rationalize it. Leland was a lawyer in the firm handling my parents' estate. I'd see him strutting around the office each time I went in to talk to my parents' attorney. I was pretty vulnerable. You see, my parents each had a life insurance policy that I was the beneficiary of, but because they had died in a plane crash, neither policy would pay. It became a legal battle. My parents' attorney tried to go after the insurance companies. The thing was, I didn't want to fight it, but I was too meek or young or just in too much shock to put a stop to it. A large chunk of the remaining estate went to the legal battle and in the end, we lost."

"You were only twenty."

"Twenty-one," she corrected. "Young and naïve."

"And Leland swept in to offer comfort?"

"No, not yet. That came later. He was older and I was too young to catch his eye. I was also a client, not like it made any difference. His girlfriend, the one he cheated on me with, was one of his assistants. No, it took a few years back then. By the time I ran into him one day at a party, I was twenty-five and he didn't remember me. I introduced myself, reminded him of my parents and the lawsuit and it was like a switch flipped inside his head."

She paused, remembering the exact moment Leland had really looked at her. "After a few minutes, basking in the glow of his attention, something changed. I was wearing a turquoise silk dress and he told me that my eyes were the exact same shade."

"Your eyes are more of an aquamarine. And they sparkle like the stone. They aren't a flat color like turquoise."

"Thank you," she said and liked that he'd noticed.

"What had you done between twenty-one and twenty-five?"

"Went back to school, and then went on for a masters. After I sold my parents' home, and dealt with all their possessions, I had enough to get my degree and start teaching. I lived in a little apartment. I was finding my way. Lonely, but surviving."

"Then you met Leland again."

"Don't you have to get to The Bay Shore?" she asked, not liking to discuss her past with him.

"I'm kind of my own boss on this project and it can wait until I'm ready."

"Why do you want to know all this?"

"I just do. Humor me."

"We dated for about a year. He spoiled me. I was so distracted by the attention, I don't think I bothered to get to know him as well as I should."

"Did you love him?"

She hated this. "Yes, I did then, but sometimes I think the idea of love was actually loneliness. He proposed at the top of the Coit Tower. There was a harpist and champagne. It was very over the top."

"And you said yes immediately," Adam surmised.

"No, I let him work for it a bit," she said, smiling, remembering that she'd been too shocked to think when he'd proposed.

"Good."

Laura paused, dabbed a sparse amount of whipped butter on her two pancakes and then poured a small amount of syrup over the top. Adam watched this ritual and repeated it, using four times as much butter and syrup on his six pancakes, then raised an eyebrow at her.

"Then what happened?"

"What else do you want to know?"

"Wedding, ring, etc."

"Why do you want to know all this?" she asked.

"I like the distraction from my own crap. Now please, continue. I want to know about the ring."

"The ring was a solitaire, less than a carat because he didn't want people to think he made too much money. I can't say I liked that argument from a man who drove a very flashy Porsche, but I didn't argue at the time."

"A cheap, yet selfish bastard. Did you keep it?"

"No. He took it back, same with the plain gold wedding band. It was written into the pre-nup."

"It was in the prenup? Your ring? That's not cool. I don't like prenups anyway. Where was the wedding?"

"Leland was in the middle of a large case, so we went to a small justice of the peace in Carmel. Kat was filming in Hong Kong and William wasn't in the picture yet, but she would've been my maid of honor if she'd been here. She was really mad at me for getting married without her."

Adam shook his head and asked, "Honeymoon?"

"You are killing me. A couple of days in Carmel. Remember, he was in the middle of a large case."

"You mentioned that."

"Okay, so I should've demanded a real honeymoon. I didn't know any better," Laura admitted.

"Bingo. Now, when did it go south or were you ever happy?"

Laura set down her fork as she gave up on her breakfast. She thought about grabbing the bottle of champagne she had in the fridge and changing up her orange juice. A mimosa at breakfast didn't seem that out of line considering the breakfast table conversation, but the idea had her stomach roiling.

"I thought I was happy until Leland thought we should start having children. Because it was what you did after you'd been married for a while. I wasn't opposed; I was thrilled. I'd always wanted to be a mother. If fact, I found out that I wanted a baby more than anything else in the world. When I was thirty-two, we started trying to have a baby, but nothing happened. By the time, I was thirty-four, I started getting worried. My doctor, Dr. Mallory, referred me to one specialist after another. In the end, they decided that my uterus had a strange tip to it that surgery couldn't correct. This wasn't a conclusive answer. This is why they say doctors only 'practice' medicine. The end result never changed, and there was nothing I could do to get pregnant."

"Was your husband supportive?" Adam asked, scowling across the table at her uneaten pancakes.

"He was sure I could get it fixed if I just tried a little harder. I can't tell you how many fertility drugs I tried. Whenever a doctor told me of some new drug trial or treatment, Leland was all over it. The raging hormones, the shots, the tears…It was just all so horrible. I know I wasn't the best person to be around."

Adam added a large dollop of butter to Laura's pancakes, then a dose of syrup that had them swimming in amber goop.

Laura looked down at the plate and added, "Oh yes, how could I forget about the weight gain?"

Adam shook his head and said, "He wasn't there for you. He wasn't supportive. And then he cheated."

"Yes. You know about that and my body…"

"I've kissed every inch of your body," he said.

Smiling, despite herself, she shook her head. "I'm very aware of that."

Adam took her fork, cut a small triangle in the brown cake, and held it out to her.

"No," she said, shaking her head.

"Try it."

She leaned forward and let him feed her the gooey morsel. The salty butter and sweet syrup hit her taste buds. It was pure heaven in one bite.

Adam smiled at her and said, "Some morning I'm going to pour melted butter and syrup all over your body and lick it off."

Laura's body trembled involuntarily. She swallowed and watched as he cut another piece from the pancakes and held it to her lips. She ate the second piece and said, "Syrup and butter would ruin the very expensive satin sheets."

"I don't care. It would be worth it. Maybe I'll take you down on the beach so that the sun can melt the butter on your luscious body."

Laura shut her eyes and pictured it. His chair scraped on the hardwood floor and then he was kissing her, pulling her out of the chair and into his arms.

"You're going to be late," she said and playfully nuzzled his ear as he kissed her throat.

"I keep telling you, I'm the boss. No one will care."

"No one is waiting for you?"

A light bulb seemed to go on in Adam's head.

"Damn it! It's demolition day. I've got a crew coming in."

"I told you so. You're destroying something?" she asked.

He glanced at his watch and frowned. "Just some walls. How about you?"

"I'm painting Tranquility from the perspective of our beach wall."

"Nice. I look forward to seeing it later tonight."

"Should we pick this up later?" she asked, allowing her robe to fall open just enough to give him a view of her cleavage.

His hand reached down, his knuckles gently brushing the slope of her breast.

"Right from here," he said and kissed her.

As she showered, she went over the conversation again in her mind. Why was he so curious? Was it time for some of the walls to come down between them? If he'd asked her about her past, could she finally take the same liberty?

"Excuse me, lady, are you Laura?"

Laura turned away from her painting and looked in the direction of the voice, her gaze dropping to the small blonde-haired girl who stood awkwardly beside her. She was offering Laura a plate with a rustic-looking Italian sandwich next to a large salad laden with vegetables from the Tranquility garden.

"I am! Is that for me?" she asked as she smiled down at the little girl in a yellow gingham dress.

The little girl nodded and bit her lip in concentration. "I'm supposed to tell you that Aunt Kat wants you fed."

Laura set her paintbrush down and took the plate from the little girl.

"Thank you so much. What is your name?"

"Emily. Emily Johnston. That's Johnston with a T." The little girl offered with a shy smile.

Laura smiled, noticing the family resemblance, and asked, "Are you're related to Mrs. Johnston, who works with Chef Mario?"

"She's my Grandma. I'm supposed to ask if you'd like something to drink." The little girl placed her hands in the pockets of her yellow sundress.

"I have water but thank you. I really like your dress," Laura said. "I like the pockets."

"They have pineapples on them."

"I noticed. How old are you, Emily?"

"Six and a half." Serious blue-gray eyes looked up at her.

"I bet you are a big help to your Grandma."

The little girl shrugged and asked, "What are you painting?"

"I'm trying to paint the big yellow and white main house, but it doesn't look like I'm getting very far."

"I like to paint."

"What kind of things do you like to paint?"

"I like to paint pictures of my dog. She's got red fur."

"Do you use watercolor? I'm using watercolors."

"I use those too," she said, pointing to a palette of colored squares. Laura liked to use watercolor tubes as well as the traditional paints she'd had when she was a child.

"How often do you come with your grandma to Tranquility?"

"Only today and tomorrow. Mom and Dad had to go to Lost Wages for a conversation."

Laura nodded, thinking the adorable child meant Las Vegas for a convention, but she didn't have the heart to correct her.

"I wish Aunt Kat was here."

"Me too. We grew up together. I didn't know she would be gone all summer."

"She plays games with me, and we go to the beach when I come with Grandma."

"That sounds like fun."

"Aunt Kat is always fun."

The little girl looked up at her with pleading blue eyes and Laura felt the familiar tug of longing. It was so rare that she got to spend any time with a child that she had to make the most of any opportunity when it presented itself.

"Well, I'm not Aunt Kat, but since we've been friends for so long, I think I might be able to find something fun for us to do. Of course, you'd need to get your Grandma's permission."

"Could you teach me how to paint like you?"

"Hmm…" Laura murmured for dramatic effect. "It's taken me a long time to learn, but I think I could show you a few things if you'd like."

"Please!"

Laura picked up her sandwich with one hand and held out her other to the little girl. "Let's go find your Grandma and then we'll get you something to wear so you don't ruin your pretty dress."

Adam spent a long day at The Bay Shore with a sledgehammer knocking out walls. Sure, he could have paid someone to do it, but it was so much more satisfying to do it himself. Nonetheless, his once white t-shirt and spotless blue jeans were covered in plaster dust and grime.

He was coming out of the garage and walking the scenic path to the main house, hoping to find Laura and persuade her to have dinner with him. All day, she'd been on his mind. When he saw her, he stopped mid-stride to take in the scene before him.

Laura and a little girl were standing side-by-side painting on two different easels. They were both wearing matching oversized white t-shirts splattered with color. The t-shirt was more of a dress on the little girl. Laura wore cutoff jeans that molded to her butt in a way he admired.

Their hair was almost the same shade of blonde. Adam could see the content, carefree smile on Laura's face. She said something to the little girl and they both laughed. He felt a deep sadness that touched him to the core, and it was all for Laura. She would have made a great mother. To have her denied seemed beyond cruel.

Dropping his architectural plans on a table by the pool, he crossed the distance to where they stood, each painting a very different picture of Tranquility. He had to give the kid credit, the house wasn't half bad, but Laura's painting was almost photographic in detail. She was amazing.

Sensing that they were being watched, both blonde heads turned to look at him.

"Hi, sorry to interrupt."

"You're not interrupting. Emily and I were just admiring our work. Emily this is Mr. Stark. Adam, this is Emily Johnston. Mrs. Johnston's granddaughter."

Emily looked shyly at Adam, who bent down to talk to her. "Emily, it is nice to meet you. You can call me Adam if you like."

"Okay," she said, and shyly looked down at her painting.

"Well, what do you think?" Laura asked, pointing to their paintings.

"I'm impressed by both of them. Emily has a very good sense of color, and your work," he said, turning to Laura, "is all about the detail," winking at her.

Laura blushed and looked away. He saw the color rise and then radiate into a couple of rosy spots on her cheeks. After all the intimacies they'd shared, he could still make her blush.

"Is he your boyfriend?" the little girl asked Laura. The way she'd said it left little doubt that she thought the idea was downright repulsive. But now Laura was looking at him and the pause had been a little too long.

"I...um...yes," Laura said. "Adam is my friend."

"No, is he your boyfriend?" Emily asked, scrunching up her nose. "Do you kiss him and stuff?"

Laura bit her lip to keep from laughing and looked to him for help. "Adam, would you like to answer that question?"

He could think of nothing to say, meeting Laura's eyes that were now sparkling with mischief.

"I admit, I've kissed him and stuff," she said.

"That's really gross."

"Kid," Adam said, stepping closer to Laura and kissing her on the cheek although he longed to taste her mouth. "Don't knock it until you've tried it. How old are you?"

"Six and a half."

"Give it ten years and then you can tell me I was right all along."

Laura laughed. He loved the sound of her laugh and soon found himself joining in. He'd forgotten some of the things that kids said. They were always bluntly honest and true to a fault.

"There you are," Mrs. Johnston said from behind them.

The little girl lit up at the sound of the older woman's voice. "Grandma! Look what I painted for you!"

"Emily! Will you look at that? What a beautiful picture!"

Adam watched as the women showered the little girl with compliments and even added to the praise. He watched as her smile grew larger and brighter. How could he have forgotten the simple pleasures of children? What else had he forgotten?

Later, as he helped Laura carry the easels and painting supplies back to her cottage, he spoke without thinking.

"Why didn't you adopt? I mean your husband was an attorney."

Laura leaned the easel against the side of the cottage as she maneuvered the painting into her other hand and opened the door. But at his words she froze in place.

"At one time I wanted to," she said with a sigh. "I gathered all this information on the internet and met with an adoption facilitator. Although Leland was an attorney, no one in his firm handled adoption."

Inside, she opened the refrigerator and grabbed two bottles of water. She handed one to Adam as he sat at her kitchen table.

After she cracked the lid and took a long drink of the cold water, she continued, "But to be honest, when he found out what I was up to with the searching online and the facilitator, he had a fit. He refused to consider the idea because we wouldn't have a child that looked like us. At the time, I was shocked at his insistent refusal, but in retrospect, I should have left then. He was so offensive."

She shook her head and took the chair next to Adam. "Ironically, he became very interested in a surrogate at one point until he found out that in most modern adoptions the birth mother gets a certain amount of visitation."

"He really didn't have many redeeming qualities, did he?" Adam asked as he took a deep drink.

"No. None. In fact, I think he liked the idea of a surrogate because he liked the idea of impregnating a woman who was not his wife. Knowing him as I do, I wouldn't have been surprised if he'd have suggested planting the seed himself."

He had a feeling she was probably right. "Wow, and here I was thinking he couldn't be more of a sleazeball, but he found a way."

"Oh, there are depths he has yet to mine. It would have gotten worse with time."

"No doubt. You know, you could do it," he said.

She gave him a serious look. "Adopt? No. I don't make enough, and I'd be a single mother. Some countries won't let single women adopt. It is very sexist. I'm not sure that is fair for a child."

"You'd be a great mother. You should find a way to make it happen."

A brief hint of pain crossed her face and he realized he'd hurt her and felt like a complete jerk.

Placing his hand on the one she had resting on the table, holding her water bottle, he said, "I'm sorry. I didn't mean that to hurt you, I meant it as a compliment and I—"

"It's okay, I know what you meant."

She was looking down at the table, hadn't grasped the hand that covered hers.

"Laura, please look at me," he said, his voice pleading.

But when she did, tears leaked out of the corners of her eyes, her voice cracked as she said, "It's just that when you don't know what you're missing, it isn't quite as hard. When you get a taste, you want it all."

He pulled her hand free of the water bottle and held it tightly between his palms. "I know a lot about that."

Looking up at him, she said, "Now I'm the one who's sorry."

Shaking his head, he stood and pulled her out of the chair and into his arms. "Don't be. Sensitivity truce? And remember this morning, I thought we were going to pick up exactly where we left off?"

"I'd like that," she said weakly and leaned her head on his shoulder.

"You know what sounds really good?"

"Tell me please," she said, and he felt her relax in his arms.

"The Salty Dawg."

She pulled back to face him. "What is the Salty Dawg?"

"A little crab shack up the road. The food is supposed to be spectacular. The staff raves about the place." He kissed the tip of her red nose and smiled down at her. "What do you say? We could get showered, put on our finest shorts, and check out the Dawg?"

"Do you promise to take advantage of me later?"

"Definitely."

She smiled, her face relaxing as she said, "Bring it on."

An hour later, they were seated at a picnic table on a rickety wooden deck that looked over the Pacific, the outdoor seating area of the well-respected Salty Dawg. They had each ordered the Dawg Number Two and a pint of light beer.

The Dawg Number Two turned out to be a sampling of the establishment's finest fare, a platter of shrimp, clam strips, coleslaw, and French fries, which smelled and tasted equally delicious.

"You know what I see?" Adam asked, glancing toward the water.

"A great sunset in the making?"

"About four dozen, million-dollar condominium units with unobstructed ocean front views. The insides would have white-washed wood, possibly alder with light marble countertops. Granite is too dark for the look I'd want."

Laura shook her head and then shook a clam strip at him. "Why do I think you're so much more than just some handy-man-slash-concierge? Do you own The Bay Shore?"

"No, but my cousin does," he said casually.

"And he would be?"

"Alex Stark. Stark International Hotels."

"I knew you were related, but I didn't know you were that close. Alex Stark is your cousin? Wow. That's quite a family to come from."

He shrugged, seemed to pay a lot of attention to scrutinizing his plate. "All that money complicates things. I'm glad it is Alex's burden to bear. I'm very happy knocking out walls and seeing the potential in things."

"I didn't know they had anything as small as The Bay Shore in their fleet."

"They like interesting spaces."

"What did you do in New York before the accident?" she asked directly, thinking he'd avoided talking about his past at every opportunity.

"I worked for Alex in the accounting department, but after the accident, everything reminded me of what I'd lost. Even going to my office, working on the same things day after day with nothing waiting at home for me was torture. I needed a change and he suggested I come out here. He just wanted cheap labor. I'm cheap because I'm family."

She saw through his attempt at humor. He'd cornered her today and now it was his turn to take a little time on the hot seat.

"What will you do after the trial?"

"Maybe come back here, but I really don't know. Probably not. That is, what, three months away?"

He was living in the moment. She got that. She was in the same position, but damn wouldn't it be nice if they were both in a place to see where this might go? It was lovely, and it would hurt to walk away from him, but she would.

Speaking carefully, she tried to match his tone. "I'd be curious to see how my work had turned out. I'd have to see The Bay Shore in all her glory."

"You have to understand my cousin," Adam said, a smile curving his lips. "I'm sure he is assembling a list of other hotels for me to 'improve' in case I don't want to go back to New York. He already has a project after The Bay Shore picked out. He is always one step ahead of the game and his game is real world Monopoly. He owns all the red hotels."

"Remind me to never play Monopoly with him," Laura said with a laugh.

"He's ruthless at Monopoly, and I think he cheats."

"What did you do with your place in New York while you're here?" she asked.

"It's just a little townhouse. The mortgage is paid up and I think when I get back, I might sell it and find something else. It is too big for just me and if Alex does have plans for me, I will put everything in storage and live out of a couple of suitcases. It could be a good adventure for a couple of years."

It could be, but it was her experience that you couldn't keep running away from your problems. They followed you, even if the suitcases got lost along the way. And what if he asked her to go with him? Would she go? No. She loved teaching. She had her own career. Who was she kidding? If he asked her to go to the ends of the Earth she just might go. Of course, she would go.

As the days sped by, July waning into August, she stopped thinking about consequences. The way he held her, caressed her, and made love to her gave her hope for something more.

Each day, Adam found a new place or different element to add to their lovemaking. Laura became his most willing companion, no longer caring about how many more days they had together, just wanting to make the most of what they did have.

One night, Adam awoke her as he untangled himself and got out of the bed.

"Are you okay?" she asked sleepily.

"I'm fine, but I'm having this fantasy," he said, bending to nuzzle her ear.

"Are you going to tell me about it?"

"You'll see. Come on." In the full moonlight illuminating the cottage bedroom, she watched as he grabbed two large bath sheets from the bathroom, wrapping one of them around his middle and handing the other one to her. She followed him to the front door where he motioned for her to go ahead of him.

"We're going outside? We're naked."

"Exactly."

She followed him through the hot evening air to the pool.

"You want to skinny-dip?"

Instead of replying, he tossed his towel aside and jumped into the pool, the underwater lights illuminating his body. Swimming up to the edge, he said with a low chuckle, "The water is warm. Come in, beautiful."

She tossed her towel onto the nearest chaise and slipped in next to him. The water was bathwater warm. They danced around the pool, their arms locked around each other. She wrapped her legs around his waist and her arms around his neck, feeling his heart beat a little faster. He kissed the rivulets of water as they rolled down her breasts and before long the contact was too much, but not enough.

Laura led him out of the water and streaked across the lawn in the cool evening air.

"I've had a little fantasy of my own," she said.

"I've had it, too. Ever since I kissed you on that wild chaise lounge," he replied as they stepped into the private garden, lit with small perimeter lights. They dropped their towels and set the swing into motion.

# CHAPTER ELEVEN

Early morning sprinklers with their rhythmic pulsing gently brought Laura back to consciousness. Adam stirred, his hand gently cupping her breast. She pulled the bath towel higher, covering them in the cool morning air. Sudden realization of where they were had Adam jerking fully awake, making the chaise lounge chair move wildly. "Oh hell, we're on the damn chaise!"

Hearing Adam's outcry, Laura opened her eyes against the rising sun. Only a hedge separated them from the gardeners laughing a few feet away.

"Uh-oh," she whispered and started to laugh.

His expression relaxed and he joined her, chuckling at their predicament as he ran a finger down her cheek and whispered, "Good morning, beautiful."

She snuggled closer which elicited a kiss.

"Hey, you start that, and I am not responsible for what the gardeners might see or hear," he warned.

Kissing him again, she asked, "How are we going to get out of here?"

"The staff hasn't had any good gossip in a couple of weeks. How about wrapping up in the towels and taking a leisurely stroll back to my place?"

"Your place?"

"It's technically closer."

"Want to streak?" she asked touching his cheek.

"Sure, but I don't want anyone seeing you naked but me. Once we get inside my room, you can dance around naked to your heart's content," he replied as he brushed the back of his hand over the tip of a rosy nipple before dipping his head to take the tip in his mouth.

"Maybe you can join me," she said, leaning back and shutting her eyes.

"Maybe," he said, slipping his hands between her legs to touch her intimately.

"You're bad."

"You like me this way." She liked him a lot of different ways.

Eventually, they wrapped themselves in the large towels and left the safety of the hidden garden. Ignoring the leers and appreciative glances of the landscapers, they walked across the cool, damp lawn barefoot and made their way up the cold marble steps to the main house.

Adam held the door open for her as they stepped into the long hallway, smiling at each other as they made their way to the sweeping staircase.

"Adam?" a high-pitched feminine voice called from behind them.

A tall blonde woman, dressed in a lime-colored knit suit hugging every inch of her thin frame stood at the end of the corridor. Oversized pearls dripped from her neck and ears. She had the air of a spoiled child playing dress up in her mother's closet. Her heavily made-up face was a mask of surprise quickly turning to anger with each second that passed as realization took hold.

This was someone from Adam's past and she was not pleased to see him with Laura.

"Tess, this is a surprise," Adam replied, stepping toward the younger woman.

"I missed you. I decided if you weren't going to come to me, I'd come to you," Tess said, wrapping her arms possessively around Adam. He simultaneously dropped Laura's hand to embrace the other woman.

This woman, this little girl playing dress up in her mommy's clothing, pulled Adam close while giving Laura the snake eye over his bare shoulder.

"Tess," he repeated, trying to extricate himself from the woman. "I'm just really surprised to see you."

"I think I'm the one surprised, Adam," she chided, looking at Laura with contempt.

"Tess, this is my friend, Laura," he said and turned, not quite meeting Laura's eyes as he said, "Laura, this is my sister-in-law, Tess Radcliff."

"It is nice to meet you, Tess," Laura offered graciously, as she extended her hand.

Tess took the offered hand limply, causing Laura to wag it rather than shake it. Their eyes met in unspoken challenge. The woman had the same oval face and eyes as Adam's wife. The hair and smile were different—this woman's lips curved into a smile of cool indifference, lacking the sincerity Laura had noticed in his wife's smile.

It didn't take long for her to connect the dots. This woman had feelings for Adam and wanted to exert her possession. Was Laura his last fling before he settled down with his wife's sister? Laura knew she paled in comparison both in looks and sentimental past history to this Barbie doll. Tess was beautiful and looked the part of his other half. They were a much more likely couple than she and Adam.

"I should go," Laura announced, glancing at Adam. *Stop me*, she wanted to yell at him.

He shrugged, looking like he didn't know what to say, but Tess looked triumphant.

"Nice to have met you, Tess," she offered courteously, and turned, walking calmly to the nearest door where she let herself out into the warm, sunny morning.

Well, well, Adam had a few surprises of his own. And how dare that woman look at her that way?

Upset by the unexpected guest, Laura showered and dressed in shorts and a t-shirt and decided to walk down to the beach. She had no other choice but to lay low and wait to see what would unfold. Walking for several hours, she passed by home after elegant home, the doubts creeping in. Who was she kidding? She had no long-term chance with Adam. Not after she'd gotten a look at the competition. She kicked at the sand, her mind reliving the events of the night before.

Eyes-wide-open this was always meant to be a quick affair, *that's all.* That was the agreement from the start. She'd known in her heart he would move on after their summer fling. There would be someone else. She just didn't think she'd have to meet the woman.

And she should move on, too. Laura had responsibilities with school and navigating her own life and she didn't need commitments from anyone at this state. Okay, so the convenient affair had gotten out of hand. Someone had fallen in love or lust of whatever the hell this was. She was a big girl, she could handle it. Besides, it looked as though Adam's life was too messy just yet and Laura had enough messy with Leland for a lifetime.

What were they doing right now? Had she followed him to his bedroom? Were they making love? No. It was a baseless assertion, her imagination was running wild. Trying to get that horrible image out of her mind, she climbed the bluff, the majestic yellow and white main house coming into view. It looked so quiet, giving away none of its secrets. If she didn't know better, she'd have assumed no one was at home.

She spent the afternoon in her cottage putting together a budget for her new life. Hoping to be distracted, she had no idea it would further depress her. Leland's prenuptial had added insult to injury making her wonder why she signed the damn thing in the first place. She would have to carefully plan for every expense. The cushion she had enjoyed with his six-figure income was over.

Needing a break, she ventured out after the late summer sunset to watch the ocean and clear her mind. Familiar as she was with the sounds of the estate, everything seemed quieter, making her feel lonelier.

Tess was exactly the kind of woman Leland would go for, plastic and sugary. She was mad at Leland, but also really mad at Adam. What was that this morning? And was Tess still there? It was all bullshit.

When she heard a car, she stayed in the shadows of a palm tree, leaning up against the retaining wall that separated the pool from the beach below. She wasn't hiding, but also wasn't inviting company. Judging by the time, she predicted Adam and Tess must be coming back from dinner in town. How nice for them. As soon as they were back inside the main house, she would return to her cottage.

Despite the crashing waves, she was able to hear them as they walked the long way back to the main house past the pool.

"Just answer me, Adam. That's all I'm asking," Tess said, her voice hostile, cutting through the night.

"My answer isn't going to change. My life is my business," Adam replied in an equally sharp tone.

She smiled secretly. So, Adam wasn't as taken with the beautiful Tess as she'd originally surmised. Feeling a bit terrible for eavesdropping, she couldn't help but to listen more.

Tess stopped on the path, several yards from Laura's hiding place. "What would Melinda think of you having a fling with some older woman?"

Laura's breath caught in her throat.

"Melinda's not alive to give her opinion," Adam shot back. "And Laura is very close to my age unlike you."

"Think of what you are doing to her memory…to us…Adam…"

"There's no us, and there never will be, Tess." His voice dropped, sounding low and pained.

Tess countered, "You're only saying that because you're in the middle of this summer fling. She must really do something for you… Her and her round body…"

"That's out of line," Adam warned. "And, quite frankly, we make each other happy."

"Well, it's the truth, she looks old. You could do so much better."

"You're insulting someone I care about."

Laura, who had stopped breathing the instant Tess had mentioned her, could just make out the other woman's silhouette as she put her hands on her hips and said, "Come off it, Adam. We both know you can't be serious about her. She's just a fuck buddy to help you through your pain. When you come to your senses you'll come running to me. So, have your fun…get it out of your system now. I'll be ready for you when you finish sowing your wild oats with her, and it better be damn soon."

Adam's voice softened as he said, "You'll be waiting a long time, as in forever. I've told you over and over again, I will never have those kinds of feelings for you. You will always be my wife's little sister. And by default, my little sister. That's all."

"But you can have feelings for her? That old cow?"

Before Adam could respond, Laura kicked the nearest pool chair and sent its legs scraping across the concrete before it fell dramatically into the pool announcing her presence with a splash. Tess let out a little scream. Adam turned toward the noise and muttered a curse.

Laura took a deep breath. Then, she held her head high and walked past Adam and Tess, making a steady, yet controlled bee-line for her cottage.

"Laura," Adam called after her, his voice uneven. "Wait, I want to talk to you." But she didn't wait. She increased her pace even as his footsteps grew closer, her heels clicking on the brick path.

"Adam!" Tess called after him.

He stopped his pursuit of Laura and turned back to Tess. "You should have never come here. I want you gone by tomorrow morning."

"Adam! What the hell?" she asked, throwing up her arms with resignation. "Fine. That's just fine with me. I don't need to watch you make a fool of yourself with her. My parents will be disgusted when I tell them what you're up to. You could have had me. *Me*," she emphasized, and stalked off toward the main house.

Ignoring Tess's tirade, Adam closed the distance to Laura. He tried to grab her hand, but she twisted away and gave him a hard shove.

"No," Adam said, grabbing her firmly by the shoulders. "You're not going anywhere until we talk about this."

"Let go of me! You let her say all those things. Do you believe her? Is that why you didn't stop her?"

"Laura please, not here…let's go inside."

She pulled away, shaking her head. "Why? Everyone within a mile heard her. Maybe she's telling the truth. Maybe I'm too old for you, too fat and people see it. Maybe you see it, too."

"Damn it! Shut up!"

She took a step back. He'd never raised her voice with her. Never lost his temper.

"Aw hell, Laura, I'm sorry…" he said, rubbing his face with his hands. "Don't let her affect us. Please don't let her take away the only happiness I've felt in the last year."

"Us?" she asked meekly.

He stepped toward her and pulled her into his arms whispering in her ear, "Yes us…more to the point…you."

She looked up at him, not sure what to say.

"Will you please do something for me?"

"I think I need some time to myself."

He saw through her. "No way. Not until we've talked this out. I want you to go pack a bag."

"What?" she asked, wondering if he was asking her to leave.

"I want to show you something and we aren't coming back here until I'm sure Tess is gone. We're leaving as soon as you're ready."

"Why are you—"

"Laura, please do this for me."

Not quite believing him, she walked back to the cottage and packed a small bag. After all, he'd never agreed with anything Tess said, and hell, that's what you get for listening in on other's conversations…*hurt*. You get hurt. Well, toughen up, Laura, she scolded herself. Adam didn't need to defend her, because Laura could do that all by herself—and if she ever saw Tess again, she'd tell her just what she thought of her bony, smartass, childish threats, and Tess would learn that payback is a bitch.

Twenty minutes later, Adam walked in, not bothering to knock. He came into her bedroom carrying a bag in one hand and a covered picnic basket in the other.

She was holding up a black lace nightgown. It broke the tension like a hot knife through butter.

"That had better be coming with us," he said, with a weary smile.

"It is, but I'm not sure why," she answered, tossing it in bag, feeling his eyes on her. "Why am I going anywhere with you? Isn't this going to mess things up with your family? I don't want to come between you and them. But Tess is a serious bitch, and I wouldn't mind telling her to her face."

"She is a problem, and this has been a long time coming." He sighed and tried to explain, "Tess is not a bad person, but she's spoiled and presumptuous. I need you to know that I've given her no encouragement."

"And she's a complete bitch. How long does she intend on staying?"

She watched Adam try to hide his smile and it lifted her spirits considerably.

"The rest of the summer if I'd let her, which I wouldn't," he said as he sat on the edge of the bed. "Her parents started campaigning for this within two months of the accident. They want to marry me off as if Tess could ever replace Melinda. My wife wasn't at all like Tess. You're more like Melinda than she is."

Not knowing how to respond, she looked down and zipped the bag, fumbling her first attempt.

"I can only imagine how bad it would be if I was still in New York. You know I didn't invite her. She just showed up…"

"But you're going back," Laura said.

"I have to return for the trial," he replied, looking up at her with sad brown eyes.

She wanted to ask: Then what? But she didn't have the nerve. "I'm ready."

Adam gave her a tight grimace of a smile. "Good. Let's get out of here." Apparently, neither of them couldn't wait to get away.

Ten minutes later they pulled into the deserted parking lot of The Bay Shore in one of the Tranquility Escalades.

Perched on a high cliff above the crashing surf a few miles south of Tranquility, it was eerily quiet in the dark. Once it had been grand, but now it was in need of complete repair to return to its former glory. She could see that parts of the old relic were coming back to life, but it would take more time than a couple of months.

Adam parked under the large, curved breezeway.

"I've wanted to see what you do all day," she said, opening her car door.

He walked around and met her, his hands encircling her waist. "I've got the keys to the castle, so we can have the run of the place. Come on."

Unlocking massive glass doors, he held one open for her and said, "Wait for me, I'll get our things."

The lobby was like stepping back in time. It was original, ornate and grand in a cool 1960s kind of way. It was cocktail lounge and beach party themed and it worked. The walls had knotty pine paneling and there were conversation clusters of seafoam blue leather couches and low, amoeba-shaped coffee tables. On closer inspection, she noticed that the tables were made of tiny ground agates, which had been epoxied and formed in resin. A streamlined crystal chandelier hung from the ceiling, offering clear and light blue crystals.

Returning with their bags and the basket, he asked, "Have you had dinner?"

"I…I'm fine," she answered.

"I didn't know so I brought a few things."

"I kind of lost my appetite," she admitted.

"Maybe that will change after a bit. I raided the refrigerator and the cupboards at Tranquility."

"Didn't you have dinner with Tess?"

"It would seem I had no appetite sitting across from her."

Laura smiled, resisting the urge to say something else about the woman who she'd already called a bitch, but who was, after all, his sister-in-law.

He placed the basket on the front desk and took her hand in his. "Come on, I'll show you around and then to our room."

"We're going to stay here?" she asked, taking in the dust and piles of drywall and marble tiles.

"I put together a model suite to show our CEO. This place has great potential and I wanted to showcase it for him. We finished it yesterday. I wanted to surprise you with it today and get your opinion." He leaned close, his lips brushing against her cheek as he whispered, "My plan was to lure you here and get you naked. I wanted us to be the first people to make love in the room. Consummate it for good luck."

"Then Tess arrived," she said, causing him to pull back.

"Are you still thinking about her?" he asked, tension taking the smile from his lips.

Laura said simply, "Yes, and I will be for a while. She's in love with you. Probably has been since you were dating her sister."

"Yes, we thought it was a crush ten years ago. Even though it made me uncomfortable then, it is so much worse now."

"She appears a bit obsessed, and you aren't playing the game."

Adam walked toward the three-story-tall glass windows that overlooked a large, illuminated pool which seemed to disappear into the ocean below. After a long moment, he said, "It doesn't matter, because Tess isn't the kind of woman I could love."

"She is very pretty."

"It wears off after you get to know her. There's a hardness about her. Her looks don't quite mirror her personality."

"I wish I were younger...prettier..." she mused, looking out at the water. "She could tell immediately that I was older, not who she ever pictured you spending time with."

"This is a ridiculous conversation, so let me blunt. I like you the way you are. I think you're beautiful," he said, and squeezed her hand.

She tried to ignore the pain in her heart. This wasn't real. Everything he was saying wouldn't matter in a few weeks. They were living in the moment, trying to recover from something that had interrupted this temporary happiness. She tried to swallow down the lump in her throat and leaned against him, laying her head against his shoulder.

"I'm so sorry," he said, as he rubbed her back. "I shouldn't have let her say those things. She has a tendency to lash out. I've been on the receiving end of her attacks."

"Please don't apologize for her," she said, stopping him.

"She was a brat as a kid and grew up to be a bitch," he replied.

"Good. Now look, we've had a long day. I want to salvage this evening, so please tell me about the hotel, show me to the suite, and let's break in the bed."

The suite was like nothing Laura had ever seen. It was a corner, ocean-front suite with floor to ceiling windows. Decorated in aqua and sand colored silk, it was an extension of the ocean below. Even in the dark, Laura could see the iridescent waves.

"What do you think?" he asked, turning on several subtle lights as he set their luggage on a long, low coffee table in the sitting area.

"It's beautiful, and nothing is too overwhelming. That's a good thing. Understated is peaceful. The design is clean, but elegant. The colors complement the ocean view and yet the contemporary feel mimics the smooth beach below. I'm calm yet feel the romance of the space."

"Remind me to have you here when my boss sees the suite for the first time," he teased, wrapping her in his arms for a playful hug. "Or maybe you could write the copy for the brochure."

"Are there satin sheets on the bed?" she asked, whispering in his ear, and then kissing the smooth sensitive skin just below his lobe.

"Yes, I borrowed a set from Tranquility. They aren't standard, but I enjoy them with you."

Her stomach growled and he noticed. Walking over to the picnic basket, he opened it and extracted a bottle of champagne.

"I think guests who stay in this room should be given a bottle of champagne at check in." He quickly popped the cork and pulled out two glasses. Filling them both, he handed a glass to her and went back to the basket to remove a container of beautiful strawberries, several chunks of cheese, crackers, and grapes.

When the bottle was empty and they'd sated their appetites with the food, they fell on the bed, kissing and touching like a couple of horny teenagers.

Adam announced, "I think we're drunk."

"I think you're right. Good for us."

They laughed and held each other, the familiar passion fueling their fire once more. His mouth found hers and her hand went to the zipper on his trousers. Half undressed, they tore at each other wildly, their bodies needing release.

"I'm glad we're like this."

"Like animals?" Adam asked.

"Passionate," she corrected.

He cupped her face in his hands and kissed her. Managing to remove the remainder of their clothing, they snuggled in the satin sheets. Just before he drifted off to sleep, Adam murmured, "I love you, beautiful."

Laura knew he wasn't talking to her. He'd been thinking about his wife, ever since his sister-in-law had shown up. The suite, the wine, and even the way they'd made love were mere distractions to keep him from imploding. Knowing all these things didn't stop her from saying the truth in her heart, "I love you, too."

# Chapter Twelve

Arriving back at Tranquility, Adam and Laura found the estate free of Tess. The declarations of love from the previous night were left unmentioned, but Adam started spending every night at Laura's cottage in her bed. Their appetite for each other was insatiable. Every few days, a single white rose would appear, maybe on her pillow or her doorstep, but each time she found one waiting, it warmed her heart.

Laura continued to work on her watercolors as Adam encouraged her talent. Flattered by his comments, she began to paint a special painting for him, a special rendition of her guest cottage. It was a place she hoped he would look at with fond memories in the years to come and remember her. As she worked on the piece and thought of him, she tried to distract herself from what would happen at the end of August. Like an ominous shadow, it drew closer and closer, threatening the first real happiness she'd had in years.

His earlier words came back time and again to haunt her. They were just together for the physical pleasure they could bring to each other. She didn't want to believe it was all they were to each other. When he made love to her, the intensity she felt and also saw in his eyes could not be denied. Everything he had said over the last few weeks and during quiet moments when they were lost in each other were evidence to support that he did indeed care, possibly more than he ever meant to.

Despite the obstacles so obviously in front of them, Laura hoped their relationship would somehow find a way to continue even after she went back to San Francisco. She knew there was a Stark International Hotel San Francisco. She dreamed of suggesting that he take a job there so they could continue to see each other, but she thought he'd probably laugh at her and then sadly tell her he didn't feel as strongly as she did, despite what he murmured in his sleep.

On one particular morning, right before her world came crashing down, Adam awoke her with soft kisses traveling slowly along her spine.

"Good morning," he murmured in her ear and then he proceeded to make it a great morning for her.

The air was already warm, an indicator of a hot August day ahead. By the time he'd showered, she'd made them breakfast, a new domestic twist she found she thoroughly enjoyed.

"What are you doing today?" he asked.

"I'm going to finish my watercolor of the cottage and then start on the rose garden. But before it gets too hot, I'm coming back here and baking a peach pie."

"Baking? Pie?" he asked, a little surprised.

"I bake and I have a certain fondness for peach pie."

"What made you decide to do this?" he asked as he finished his orange juice and slipped into a pale khaki linen suit coat.

"I thought you might enjoy trying some of my pie," she said, as he pulled her into his lap.

"Can I spread it on your body and lick it off?"

"Sure, as long as you let it cool first," she offered with a Cheshire cat grin.

"You know you don't need pie to seduce me. You'll do just fine," he teased, grabbing the tie on her robe, expertly opening it, and running his hands from her bare hips up to cup her breasts.

"What would you like with your pie?" she asked, as she shut her eyes.

He kissed her and she knew all she had to do was push his suit coat off and he would stay, taking her back to the bedroom and making love to her again. She slid her hand between the jacket and starched white shirt, gently nudging the jacket off his shoulder.

"I think you're trying to tell me something," he whispered.

"Is it working?" she murmured, sucking on his lower lip.

"Yes," he said with a kiss, as he pushed her robe aside for better access to her breasts.

An hour later he left, promising to return in the early evening. Laura smiled as she stepped into the shower. What a perfect day. She would enjoy the beach, do a little painting, and then cook something wonderful.

She was headed out her front door with easel in hand when she saw Adam sprinting toward her, looking upset. She set down the easel as he reached for her.

"Adam, what's wrong?"

"I don't know how to say this…I have to leave tomorrow."

"What?" she asked, as the air left her lungs.

"The man who killed…my wife and son, the drunk who killed them, his trial starts day after tomorrow. Another case settled, so they moved up the calendar. They need me to come back and testify. I want to be there for the trial, I just didn't think it would be this soon."

"You have to be there…of course," Laura replied. He'd mentioned snippets of the upcoming trial, but never any details. She had made the incorrect assumption that it was in the fall.

"I fly to New York tomorrow morning."

She heard every word and felt her heart skip a beat. "That soon?"

"This isn't easy for me, either."

"I know." She thought they would have another couple of weeks together. She thought she would be the one to leave first.

"I wanted more time…I thought we'd have time," he said, tightening his hold on her as her world imploded.

As promised, Laura made the peach pie and a dinner that neither of them ate. They chatted, but the tension was thick between them. He asked her to spend the night with him in the main house. Still in shock that she was losing him so soon, she nodded, not trusting her own voice. She wanted to be honest, tell him she loved him, but it wasn't the right time. He'd already left her. He wore his grief on his face, renewed tragedy for his lost family.

She lay on his bed watching as he methodically emptied each and every drawer. Every item he folded brought their inevitable separation closer. She listened as he complained and worried about leaving The Bay Shore. Eventually, he talked about the trial and how awful it would be. He quietly told her he feared returning to the townhouse where he'd lived with his wife and son. He talked openly about his fears and sadness. He talked about everything, but them.

When he turned out the lights and pulled her close, she went into his arms eagerly. Vowing to enjoy their last few hours together, she committed every inch of him to memory, and most of all, tried to convey everything she felt for him as they quietly made love.

"You're leaving in two weeks yourself," he offered later as he spooned her.

"Yes," she replied meekly as if her leaving would make any difference.

"All those young minds waiting to be molded…I wish I'd had a math teacher who looked like you," he said, rubbing his hand slowly down her back.

"I'm known for being tough and a hard grader. I bet you were good at math."

"I was. You're not tough, you're passionate."

"My students wouldn't agree with that assessment," she said with a sad chuckle.

"Geometry was my favorite." Adam said.

"Mine, too," she replied and turned toward him, deciding to put her feelings on the line. "Have you thought about staying here? Maybe managing The Bay Shore? It's not anywhere close to being done."

"This has just been a break for me. My boss has already arranged for a replacement who will arrive next week. I haven't decided what I want to do," he answered.

She shut her eyes and felt pain to her very core. His coming back was the only thread of hope she had been clinging to for the last few hours.

"I ran away to escape, Laura. Maybe it's time I dealt with it, so I can move on."

"I think you've come a long way since I've known you."

"Some ways yes and some ways no." Adam was quiet for a moment and then said, "Is it acceptable that I can only be your friend and lover, but not your boyfriend? I want to be more to you Laura, but I can't right now. This is all I can give, and you deserve so much more."

The unexpected heartfelt declaration hit a raw nerve. "Let's give it some time, stay in touch every now and then," she replied, her heart hurting.

Ignoring her request, he said, "You have to promise me, that no matter what Leland does when you get back to San Francisco, you won't go back to him."

"I don't want to ever see Leland again. It's not like I'm going to go looking for him."

"You won't have to. He'll try to get back together with you. I can't think of you with him."

"I'm not changing my mind," she responded, a little surprised by his outburst.

"I hope not."

"I won't, Adam. After you, there can never be Leland."

The next morning, he finished up in his office and showed up at the guest cottage a little before noon to say goodbye to her. When she opened the door, she already had tears in her eyes. Without a word, he pulled her into his arms.

"Adam, no matter what happens, thank you for this summer. It was the best summer of my life and only because of you," she said, muffling a sob.

"I never meant to hurt you."

"You didn't hurt me. I just already miss my friend. I hope I see you again and I hope it is soon."

"I don't want to leave you like this," he said, his voice thick with pain.

"Life happens. And who knows? Someday our paths might cross again."

"I hope so," he said, and shut his eyes as he hugged her.

He was leaving her in much the way he'd first met her when she was crying over a broken heart.

Holding onto him until it became unbearable, she pushed away and smiled bravely, letting him know she would be all right. After kissing her one last time, he walked away.

Over the next couple of days, Laura told herself Adam's leaving was for the best. His departure had been quick and without ceremony. They had made no real promises. They had been summer lovers—nothing more, nothing less.

She walked on the beach each day feeling more and more alone. In the afternoons she tried to dabble with her watercolors, but quickly became restless and uninterested.

Each minute felt like five. Would he call her? Had he even taken her cell phone number with him? She had his cell, but she didn't think he'd welcome her intrusion, so she did the hardest thing she'd ever done. She didn't call him. And he didn't call her.

She didn't cry until the third day and when she started she wasn't sure if she'd ever stop. She cried for the loss of Adam, needing him more than she had ever needed anyone. She cried about losing her parents and how much she missed them every day. She cried out of the frustration at being left behind by everyone she loved. When she had arrived at Tranquility, she thought she had a broken heart. Now she understood why her marriage hadn't been worth saving. If she'd felt half as much for Leland as she did for Adam, she'd have fought like hell for her marriage. But she couldn't fight for Adam, not right now.

Wrapping herself into a ball on the bed she had shared so many times with Adam, where his familiar scent still lingered on the sheets, she wept, sobbing into her pillow. She had lost the love of her life. How had he come to mean so much to her? How had it happened so quickly?

Tranquility was suddenly too large and lonely, filled with ghosts from a happier time. There was no place she could go to escape her memories, and everything, even the sound of the ocean breaking on the rocks, reminded her of Adam.

She couldn't eat, and even the smell of food made her nauseous. It was hard to drink a bottle of wine by yourself when you vomited after the first glass.

After a few phone calls and some hastily made arrangements with her new landlord, Laura began to pack. Kat wouldn't be back for a week and a half. Laura couldn't wait. When she got settled, they'd talk, she'd explain it, and Kat would understand. Two hours after she'd rationalized all this, she was gone.

# CHAPTER THIRTEEN

The doorman at The Green, the luxury townhouse building where Adam had lived for the best nine years of his life, had changed little in the four months he'd been in California at Tranquility. The same could not be said for Adam. Straus, the English doorman, dashed out in the late summer rain the moment Adam's hired town car stopped at the curb.

"Good evening, Mr. Stark," he greeted, as he opened the back door with an umbrella to provide shelter from the misting rain. "It is so good to have you back home."

"Thank you, Straus," Adam replied and smiled sadly at the older man. "How are you?"

"Good, sir, and how are you, Mr. Stark?"

"Taking it day by day."

"Understandable, sir," he said as they walked together up the steps to the heavy front doors, adorned with ornate stained-glass windows the color of emerald crystals. Straus opened the door with an elegant flourish. Adam stepped ahead of him into the black and white marble floored lobby.

The warm rain and soft amber light of late summer had poured a little salt in his fresh wounds, reminding him of the day that he and Melinda had first stepped into The Green. They'd been new-lyweds, excited about starting their life together.

They'd bought a five-bedroom, four-bath townhouse on the sixth and seventh floor with a view of Central Park. It had taken almost two years to remodel and decorate it to get it to Melinda's satisfaction. It was her masterpiece.

In the first few years of his marriage, Adam had traveled extensively with Alex and Alex's cousin, Spencer, learning the family hotel business. When he was home, he and Melinda would scour art galleries and look at different designer showrooms. Her tastes ran toward the modern and Adam had gone along to keep the peace although he preferred more classic designs. It was easy. Making Melinda happy made him happy. So, he indulged her.

The budget she had was obscene and when their home was finished, Architectural Digest wanted to do a spread on the perfect use of color and space, a modern oasis among the rigid backdrop of a historical building. In the end, Adam had persuaded the magazine to do a spread on both his and Alex's loft just a few blocks away. That was before Alex moved to Portland to marry Daisy.

While Alex's loft was comfortably elegant, it provided the perfect contrast to that of Adam and Melinda's ultra-cool urban backdrop. The company website had seen a spike in traffic for the four weeks the issue was on the newsstand. Then Alex had blown it all up by moving, and Melinda had done much the same by dying. Life had moved on and Adam was left behind with his memories and a cold and empty home.

Adam rode the elevator to the sixth floor, thinking of how Adam, Jr. used to complain, "Daddy, why can't the elevator go faster? I want to see Mommy."

He slumped against the far wall of the elevator, let the soft hum of the motor that used to comfort him remind him of all he'd lost. Melinda wouldn't be waiting for him. A.J. wouldn't be listening for his key in the lock.

The doors opened and he stepped out of the elevator with two of his bags. Straus would bring up the rest of his luggage later.

He thought of his keys, remembered they were in his briefcase and fished for them as the front door to his apartment loomed up before him. 606. The brass numbers had once meant so much. Now, they seemed ominous in the subtle hall lights that were neither too bright, nor too dim.

Maybe he should have stayed at the family suite in his hotel. It wasn't too late. He could just get back in the elevator and leave. If he wanted, he never had to step inside the door of apartment 606 again. He could have everything put in storage. Sort it out later. Hell, he could tell Tess and Lillian to go through everything, but then he didn't want to spend any more time with Tess than absolutely necessary. And he didn't want her to even touch Melinda's things.

When he thought of what she'd said to Laura...

Laura.

He leaned against the door jam, keys in his hand.

The plaintive look on her face when he'd left had nearly broken his heart.

Laura.

Her lively blue eyes that earlier had looked so sorrowful...

"Damn," he muttered and took a long, deep breath and slowly let it out.

Laura had found a way to take away his pain. The moment he'd seen her at the top of Devil's Punchbowl, the pain had stopped. She was the perfect antidote, the perfect anti-depressant. The problem with antidotes was that sometimes they only worked for a while and then you built up a tolerance.

But, in truth, he hadn't grown tired of her. Growing tired of Laura wasn't possible. If it weren't for the trial, he'd still be at Tranquility with her.

Then what?

He wasn't a whole man and she deserved better than him. She deserved to be the only woman in a man's life, not the replacement. Not the second best always fighting a ghost of someone else. No, Laura deserved much, much more. He just didn't want to see it or know about it. That was a pain that might push him over the last ledge he was hanging onto so precariously.

If only he'd met her at a different time, when he was in a different place, it would be different for them. Because when he loved, he loved completely. And that was what Laura deserved. She didn't sign up to mend his broken heart, but she'd done it, hadn't she? She had done more for him than the grief counselors and the good old-fashioned manual labor of The Bay Shore. All of which were supposed to be healing and help him work out his "aggression." No, he hadn't worked out his aggression at The Bay Shore hammering nails and pouring concrete. He'd worked out his aggression pounding into Laura and pouring out his emotions every time they made love.

He'd been ruthless in their lovemaking from that first night in her cottage. With his wife and the few women who'd come before her, he'd been a gentle, considerate lover. He'd done things to Laura he'd never done with his wife or any other woman for that matter. Laura would always be special to him, indeed.

Would he contact her after everything settled? They had left it all open ended. He shouldn't, he knew that, but he wasn't going to cross out any options. Never say never. But hopefully as they'd left it, she'd find the right man for her—maybe fate would make him that guy...time would tell.

"Bastard," he said, and stuck the key in the lock.

The empty space smelled of cleaning supplies. Adam stepped inside remembering the sound of A.J.'s stocking feet on the hardwood floors as they pounded down the long hall to meet him, arms outstretched, smile on his face as he shouted, "Daddy, Daddy..."

A moment later, Melinda would step out of the kitchen, wiping her hands on a towel and give him "the look" which meant he was late, again. She hated it when he worked late, and he was always working late.

"That makes three nights this week. I want my husband home at night," she'd complain. Then she'd walk to him, usually wearing a silk blouse and pencil skirt, her "standard uniform" as she used to call it. Her heels clicked with each step on the hardwoods as she drew closer, her sable hair perfect, pearls dancing at her throat as she hugged him. Her perfume, Sacré, would linger in the air, always reminding him of a sunny, fall afternoon.

A.J. would grab onto his leg and hug tight, while Melinda would hug his other side.

"How's my beautiful wife and our nearly perfect child?" he'd ask, tongue-in-cheek.

Smiling up at him, A.J. would announce, "I was perfect today, Daddy!"

"That's a first!" Adam would announce and his wife would agree. "Day one!" she'd exclaim and then they'd all laugh.

They'd meander back into the space-age stainless steel and bottle-glass green kitchen where Adam would take off his jacket, loosen his tie, and then make a martini for his wife and himself. They would talk about their day and sip their cocktails as they finished getting dinner ready while A.J. played in the next room. Adam called it their "quiet time," but it was usually anything but quiet. He loved it nonetheless because it was their nightly ritual.

But this rainy August evening, thirteen months after he'd lost everything that ever mattered to him, the only thing that greeted him was the sound of traffic from the street below. Horns and sirens, the sound of rubber on wet road, noise that he'd never heard before and wished he'd never had cause to notice.

He walked from room to room, thinking it no longer looked like home. What did home look like? Laura's cottage was the first image that filled his mind. He shook his head and felt a different kind of pain give his heart a pinching squeeze. In less than twenty-four hours, the trial would start. He needed to do everything in his power to make sure that justice was carried out. He needed to be sharp and alert, not letting down his guard. What he didn't need was to be thinking about Laura and everything that happened in the last three months.

Laura's new apartment was close to the high school, and she could easily walk on nice days. In fact, the neighborhood, Buena Vista, was filled with small restaurants and shops. It was eclectic, traditional, modern, and gorgeous. There was even a flower shop just around the corner.

She had an apartment on the third floor of a Victorian brownstone that didn't have an elevator. She supposed it was considered a historic building, but she shuddered at the thought of what would happen if there was an earthquake.

The bay window in her living room had a view of the Coit Tower and at sunset cast a rosy hue, filling the room with warm, pink light.

It was the first thing she noticed as she stood in the empty living room with its cracked paint, chipped plaster, and worn hardwood floors. She felt the warm pink light on her face and wondered how long it would take for her to feel happy again. Some time, perhaps a lot of time would need to pass, she thought, but it would be possible. But in the intensity of finding your true love and then losing him, there were a lot of competing emotions. Happiness wasn't one of them.

On her first night, Laura treated herself to takeout Chinese food. Takeout was the ultimate perk of city life. She opened a bottle of white wine and sat on the floor next to her bay window, open white boxes spread around her. Aside from the street noise below, it was very quiet. Each noise she made, whether it be setting down her wine glass, or biting into a crunchy egg roll, echoed in the high-ceilinged space. This was what it was to be truly alone with yourself and your thoughts. The food didn't taste as wonderful as it usually did, but then her body had suffered a loss. This was grief. This was loneliness.

Stretching out on an air mattress that would be her bed until she had time to buy a real one, she tried to read a paperback she'd bought that afternoon under the light of the sale lamp she'd also purchased. When she couldn't get into the story, she tried to sleep in a strange place that didn't feel like home. Listening as she lay in the dark, she heard the city just beyond the windows. It was a very different noise from the ocean, which she had grown used to always hearing in the background at Tranquility. The ocean, she reasoned, should be lonelier, but it was the noise of the city that had her crying herself to sleep, missing Adam with a desperation she would not have thought possible.

Over the next few days, she worked hard to turn the apartment into some semblance of home. She bought a mattress, couch, and cheap dinette set for her kitchen, which all arrived one afternoon along with her boxes. She found a few decent gilded gold frames at a secondhand store and framed several of the watercolors she had painted at Tranquility.

As she placed her favorite painting of a huge white rose with subtle green leaves over her bed, she thought of all the white roses she'd been given over the summer. They had meant something and even if she never saw Adam again, she would never look at a white rose in the same way. Vowing not to cry, she got busy and made up her mattress to resemble a bed with the soft green-and-white-striped bed linens she had purchased. The final touch was to place her framed photo of Scooter on one of the green metal and glass top garden tables she had found at a garden store. Besides matching the room, the summer closeout items made for perfect nightstands. She'd look for a wicker headboard she could spray paint in the same shade of green to finish the room.

She stood back and admired her work. This small room was nothing like the expensive, dark bedroom she had shared with Leland or the light and beautiful room where she'd loved Adam. And the view, which was of the fire escape and the windowless red brick wall of another building with an alley in-between, wasn't exactly enchanting, but it was all hers. This room was to be her private oasis, friendly and inviting, filled with her favorite things. Well, almost all her favorite things.

Laura didn't frame any photos of herself with Adam. She did email the selfies she'd taken that summer to herself in case anything happened to her phone. Looking through them made her cry, so she didn't look. It was for the better, she reasoned. She didn't need the reminder. Heck, she'd never forget what he looked like, she would never forget a line in his face, a hair on his head.

She hung a half dozen of her other watercolors from Tranquility throughout the rental making it look less desolate. Her heels echoed as she walked on the hardwood floors from room to room. If Kat ever came to visit, she would have a fit. Laura knew that with just one phone call, she could have a fully furnished home, because Kat would consider it her mission to outfit Laura completely. Generous to a fault, Kat was a giver who never knew when to stop. Laura hoped by the time Kat saw her new home it would be furnished more satisfactorily. She'd have every weekend to scour garage sales, and the truth was that she didn't need much in the way of material things. There was only one thing she longed for and that was Adam.

Leaning against the doorframe to her living room, watching another pink sunset, she let thoughts of him wash over her. She wondered what he was doing at that very minute, how he was getting along in New York. Her mind was playing tricks on her and the night before she'd dreamed of him showing up on her doorstep and telling her he loved her. She knew better. Their affair had been one of the best and worst things that had ever happened to her. She had never meant to fall in love, but it had happened. He had handed her a silk handkerchief and she had surrendered her heart.

She returned to work the following week. Getting back into the routine should have helped, but her coworkers were curious about her divorce and had questions they weren't shy to ask. When they had seen her at the end of May, she had been married and appeared happy. Now they treated her with sympathy, assuming Leland had broken her heart. She couldn't very well tell them all her pain was reserved for Adam. She gave a performance that would have made Kat proud.

"What happened?" More than one asked.

"He cheated so I divorced him, the rat bastard."

"Good for you, honey."

Like clockwork, Laura received a call from Kat every Sunday afternoon, the day they had once agreed was the loneliest of the week. She had done her best to convince Kat that she was doing well, but Kat knew the truth.

"It's me," Kat offered, on the Sunday before Labor Day.

"How's Italy?" Laura asked, looking out her bay window and watching people walk by on the sidewalk below.

"Fabulous, but I miss my house and my bed. William is a few days behind schedule, so he is stressed. I can barely get the man to relax. Good thing he responds so well to physical affection!"

They both laughed and she sensed Kat was about to turn the tables.

"The real question is: How are you?"

"Some days are good, and some days are bad."

"Leland or Adam?"

"You have to ask?" Laura feigned mock surprise.

"Adam, of course," Kat replied with a chuckle.

"Adam. Only Adam. Always Adam. Leland could never compare to Adam," Laura offered more for her own benefit than for Kat's. "Never."

"I don't want to know, but I've got to know. Have you heard from him?" Laura asked.

"No honey, not since the day he left Tranquility and that was a very brief call thanking me for our hospitality."

"Do you think he'll ever call me?"

"Yes, eventually, but who knows when. He will call me to find out if the staff is behaving because he's a perfectionist. As for you...I think it will take some time. He has to forgive himself for caring about another woman. He came to Tranquility to find himself and let go of his wife and child. Instead, he found you."

"What if he doesn't?"

"Then he doesn't. You'll be fine. It just might take a while."

"Or maybe, I'll feel like this forever," Laura said, the pain leaking into her words.

"Three months from now, it won't hurt as much, but I'm guessing it will still sting," Kat said. "He's not thinking as much about you because he's wrapped up in the trial. You know that has got to be killing him."

"I would think reliving it must be the worst thing he could possibly do. I'm mad at myself for being so selfish and thinking of only my own feelings, when who knows what he is going through."

"You're entitled...so stop being hard on yourself."

Ignoring her friend's advice, she said, "I need to ask you something. Was he hurt in the accident? When I asked him, he told me a few scratches, but I didn't believe him, and I saw the scars on his leg."

"William said he got a pretty bad gash on his head. You can't see it because it's in his hairline."

"You can feel it," Laura said, remembering how he'd flinched when she had run her hand through his hair and felt the smooth line. "And when he gets tired or works too much, the femur he broke acts up."

"Poor man. We ran into his boss a couple of days ago. We're staying in one of his hotels in Rome. He wanted to check on us and Adam came up in conversation."

"And? Tell me what he said."

"He's not happy about Adam having to relive the details of the accident or having to be so close to his wife's family during the trial. I guess they haven't started to heal at all from the accident. Adam feels guilty for wanting to move on. You know all this..."

She did and she knew about Tess. She wondered if the other woman was still trying to sink her hooks into Adam and then, she decided, she probably didn't want to know.

Laura spent Labor Day on her couch, sick with a mild case of food poisoning. Several co-workers had invited her to holiday barbeques, which would have gotten her out of the house, even if she would have had to spew more details about Leland, but the very idea of food made her nauseous. She wished she could be anywhere but closed in her empty apartment, with nothing to do but think. Her conversation with Kat had stayed with her and the more she thought of it, the worse she felt for Adam.

September started warm and dry, with just a hint of fall in the air. Laura added some new plants to her home and found decent looking end tables and lamps for her living room courtesy of an estate sale.

Adam was the first thing she thought of every morning and the last thing she thought of at night before she went to sleep. Sometimes she dreamed of him holding her. When she would awaken and realize that she was alone, the tears would come. Should she text him? He hadn't texted her. This was the hard time, she just needed to get through it.

School started and she continued to feel nauseous. Her stomach was so touchy it was hard to keep anything down. Her stomach had always been the place she carried her stress, and she began to wonder if she was getting an ulcer. One morning, she took a good look in the mirror. The face looking back was pale and drawn with large dark circles under the eyes. She was exhausted and contemplated calling in sick, something she rarely did. By the second week, when she wasn't noticeably better, she made an appointment with her doctor.

Dr. Mallory, part medical doctor, part therapist, was a kindly gentleman with white hair and glasses. They had been through a lot together. He'd seen Laura at her best and worst. She trusted him to find out what was wrong with her. He took blood and ran a bunch of tests.

She had always sensed he didn't care for Leland, so it surprised her that after she told him about her divorce, he said, "I'm so very sorry to hear this."

"Thank you, but these things happen," she replied, giving the standard line she'd perfected over the last few weeks. She and Leland had spent a considerable amount of time and money with Dr. Mallory, hearing report after bad report on the state of her inability to bear children.

Today, she sat on the exam table and felt numb. This was the place she had sat many times and had her dreams shattered. It was almost a relief to know there wasn't much else he could say that could hurt her. So, when he came back into the exam room with a strange look on his face, she started to panic.

"Is there any chance you'll get back together with your husband?" he asked softly.

"None, he cheated, the rat bastard. Why do you ask?" Cancer, incurable diseases…he'd never taken her down those dark passages, but he had something to tell her and was having a hard time doing it.

"Did you have any menstrual cycles this summer?"

"Yes, they were minor, lasting a day or two, spotting mostly, but that's not unusual for me. My stomach has been a mess, but I thought it had to do with a few things that were happening, you know, butterflies. The way you are looking at me, you're scaring me, doctor."

"I just don't know how to tell you this," he said, spreading his hands wide.

"What?" she asked, thinking of all she'd gone through and the things she had yet to do before she died. Adam might be gone, but there was always hope that he'd come back. If something happened to her she might never see him again. Never know if he'd return to her, if they'd be together again one day.

"Laura, Laura…it's nothing bad…It's just that you're pregnant. Near as I can tell, about ten to eleven weeks along."

The room spun as she reached out to grab the edge of the exam table for support. Dr. Mallory stepped forward and offered his arm. She grabbed it, feeling strong hands holding her upright. The room didn't stop spinning. In fact, it whirled faster.

"Are you sure?" she asked, looking into the equally shocked face of her doctor.

"Yes. I ran the test twice. It was positive," he reported, surprise in his voice as he smiled brightly. "You're going to have a baby."

"You told me this couldn't happen."

"No, I told you if you were to become pregnant, you should consider it a miracle."

Laura looked helplessly at her doctor. Almost three months along with Adam's child. Adam, who was thinking about getting a vasectomy to prevent the possibility of ever becoming a father again.

"Mr. Daniels should be very pleased. I know how important children are to you and I sensed he wanted a baby, too. Maybe the idea of bringing a child into the world will help you both work out whatever issues you have. Make a fresh start," he offered.

"I suppose it could…if Leland was the father, but he isn't," Laura said, her voice seeming to echo in the silence that followed.

Dr. Mallory stepped back in surprise but pulled it together. "Well, that proves one of my theories."

"What theory?"

"I always had a feeling you and Mr. Daniels weren't compatible. I don't mean as husband and wife, but as reproductive partners. We ran tests but could never prove it. I just always had my doubts. And Mr. Daniels was never very enthusiastic about helping when it came to testing."

"You mean all along the problem might not have been me?"

"You've got your own set of challenges. We've been through all that. I just thought Mr. Daniels might have some issues as well but I could never run all the tests I wanted that would prove it conclusively."

As Laura's mind digested all that he was saying, he issued a stern warning, "Young lady, you're going to want to be very careful. I know how much this child means to you. Don't get too tired, don't overexert yourself, and don't stand all day, give some of your classes sitting down."

He gave her a long laundry list of dos and don'ts and in the end he smiled broadly and broke his cool persona by hugging her as he said, "What a great day! A wonderful day for a miracle."

Laura walked to her car in the early twilight. Adam's baby. She was pregnant with Adam's child. A part of him had never left her. And through some miracle, their lives would be forever intertwined, whether he wanted that to happen or not.

Would the baby look more like him or her, or be a blend of them both? Behind her joy, there was a forming wave of mounting fear and sadness. This baby was a pathway she'd never thought she'd travel down. For years, more than a dozen doctors had constantly told her that she wouldn't be able to have a baby and in a matter of moments all the past had been erased and the future forever changed, a life change in thirty seconds or less.

Laura got out of her old BMW and looked around. She was in the garage down the street from her brownstone. She couldn't remember the drive home. And when she thought about it, everything from the moment her doctor had given her the news to this moment was a blur, a faded whitewash of hue and tone.

Getting out of the car, she shut the door and then leaned against it for support before reaching down to feel her stomach. She wasn't showing yet, but something was definitely happening. Her clothing's waistband was a bit snugger. Her appetite was off and the thought of some of her favorite foods instantly nauseated her.

Her steps clicked rhythmically on the cement floor of the garage as she made her way to the stairs that would take her down to the street level. She smiled for the very reason that she was happy.

A few minutes later, she was inside her apartment, the sun just starting to drop below the skyline turning the sky to a rich apricot pink. Laura stared at the skyline framed in her bay window and knew what she had to do.

*Adam.* She had to get to Adam.

Picturing his face, she remembered the warm smile, the choc-olaty eyes, and the slight dimple that he had in his right cheek.

What would happen if she flew to New York to tell him the news?

She pictured the surprise register on his face if he opened the door to find her standing on the other side. Would he hug her? Or be upset that she'd suddenly shown up on his doorstep?

Once inside the home he'd shared with his wife and child, she would sit him down and break the news to him.

Then what?

Would he pull her into his arms and let her know that every-thing would be all right? Would he offer to marry her? Would he offer to pay for an abortion? Or would he simply turn cold and suggest she never contact him again?

He wouldn't want the baby.

Despite her usual optimism, this idea didn't feel like it would go well if she chose to carry it out, and a little of the happy bliss that had carried her home tarnished.

Turning on her computer, she was frustrated with how long it took the five-year-old dinosaur to come to life. It took long enough for her to start weighing her options.

She Googled the coverage of the trial and hit pay dirt.

The brief news coverage, six inches in The New York Times, focused on how the driver, who had never broken the law or been cited for drunk driving, was depressed from losing his job on the NYSE. It also mentioned that Adam's wife was a Radcliff of the Hampton Radcliffs and that Adam Stark had ties to the Stark International Hotel chain. It confirmed what she'd always believed, that Adam was more than he appeared to be. He said his cousin was the business. She hadn't believed it then and didn't believe it now, but it didn't matter. Someone had destroyed Adam's family and they should pay.

There was a slant to the coverage that she didn't like that inferred the driver was part victim. A victim where the true villain was the economy. It disgusted her.

Closing arguments were being heard this week. This was definitely not the right time to find Adam and tell him about the pregnancy.

If she wanted to talk to Adam, she could call him, but in her gut she felt it was the wrong thing to do. She needed to tell someone. She needed to call Kat and if she called Kat, she'd have to tell her about the baby. That might set wheels in motion that she couldn't stop. William would want to immediately call Adam, even if she didn't want him to. The only thing to do would be to keep the pregnancy a secret for just a little while until she could sort it out. After all, she was a high risk. She wasn't out of the woods yet and despite how much she wanted this child, there were no guarantees.

She would bide her time, and it would be the best for everyone concerned.

Maybe if she kept telling herself that, eventually even she might believe it.

# CHAPTER FOURTEEN

"This isn't going well. He is just too pathetic. The jury is sympathizing with his plight. We need to offer a plea," the assistant district attorney, Steve Vance, told Adam while they sat together during the lunch break the week of closing arguments.

"Are you kidding me?" Adam asked as he tried to keep a lid on his growing temper. "That reckless son of a bitch took my family. Fuck his pain. What about mine? What about the last moments of Melinda and A.J.'s life? Are you telling me that my story had no impact on the jury?"

"Mr. Stark, your testimony was very impactful. Unfortunately, we weren't dealt the best hand. That guy is everyone's fucked up friend that never gets a break. The defense is making the jury feel his pain."

For the last two and a half weeks, they'd heard from witnesses who confirmed that the man who killed Melinda and A.J. had been drinking and smoking weed the night of the accident to muffle his own pain. Coroners described in detail how each of Adam's family had died and offered insight with words that were so painful, Adam found new depths of his grief.

Friends of the defendant painted him as a dedicated family man who was down on his luck and facing an uncertain future. He had lost everything—his job, his house, and finally his family considering that his wife had just filed for divorce. He was to be pitied and shown compassion.

The defendant himself, a sweet looking baby-faced man with the innocuous name of Teddie Smith, took the stand and cried like a baby for two days. He felt guilty. He felt terrible. He wished he could trade places with Melinda and A.J. He had been prescribed anti-depressants, that he was suicidal with all he'd been through.

Adam watched as the man responsible for taking everything away from him told his story and painted himself as a victim.

"This is a complete outrage," Adam said. He felt his pulse quicken, his face was beet red, the heat and anger pouring from him.

"Mr. Stark, please," Vance said, using a placating tone Adam had grown to hate. "You have to understand that although we went into this with high hopes of making an example of Mr. Smith and having a conviction, his team has the upper hand. You must, for your own peace of mind, prepare for the worst."

"I've already had the worst thing happen to me. I lost my family."

"No one is trying to forget about Melinda and A.J., but the truth is that nothing can bring them back. Regardless of what happens in this trial, the day after it ends, you will wake up and have to face the rest of your life without them."

Adam stood and made a beeline for the door. He yanked open the handle and turned back to Vance. "Think of how you would feel if it was your family."

Without waiting for an answer, he let the door close behind him. He walked quickly to the nearest elevator with a watchful eye for Tess and her parents. The last thing he wanted was to run into the Radcliffs.

Each day, they would arrive and sit next to him in the front row behind the district attorney and his staff. Adam had thought that after their altercation at Tranquility that summer, Tess would be subdued and possibly embarrassed, but that proved not to be the case.

Tess and her mother, Lillian, looked like models from the Neiman Marcus catalogue in their flashy designer suits in an array of pastel colors and equally expensive jewelry. Brian just looked stuffy and pompous in his English-cut suits and vibrant ties that exhibited every crayon color in the large box of Crayolas. Not once in almost three weeks had any of the Radcliffs repeated an outfit, shoes, or handbag. After the first week, when they had arrived slightly late each day, the judge had to eventually chastise them. They emitted a superior attitude that illustrated that they were the privileged elite.

To his displeasure, Tess insisted that she sit with Adam. In fact, he found it hard to be civil to his young sister-in-law. After all she'd said to Laura, he wanted nothing to do with her. Once the trial was finished, he intended to never lay eyes on Tess again.

He pushed his way out the front door and into the sunlight. He wanted to run down the steps of the courthouse and keep running, until he was far away and so exhausted that he would sleep for days. Hell, he wanted to run to Tranquility and the safety of Laura's arms, but she wasn't there anymore.

He'd called two weeks earlier and discovered that she'd left. He might revisit Tranquility, but Laura wouldn't be there.

Four blocks from the courthouse, he took a deep breath and looked around. Sometime over the last few weeks, fall had arrived. The last time he remembered looking, all the leaves were green. Now hues of gold, orange, and scarlet clung to everything around him. He sat on a bench that was covered with bright yellow leaves, graceful as snow in winter.

Adam took the phone out of the breast pocket of his suit coat and looked at the screen. He had ten missed calls. As he scrolled through them, he looked for one number that would stand out from the others. It was stupid, he knew. He could just call Laura, but after leaving her like he had, could he really just call her?

He pictured Laura then, her honey blonde hair, beautiful sparkling aquamarine eyes, and kind smile. He missed her. He missed her terribly. Part of him wanted to run away to her, to find wherever she was and just be there.

But he owed his loyalty to Melinda and A.J. He owed them everything he had to give. Laura would distract him. He needed to focus, so he put his phone back in his pocket and put the lovely Laura out of his mind.

Laura went through the motions of teaching. She dealt with the morning sickness and smiled with each wave of nausea. She didn't have an ulcer. She wasn't sick and dying. She just had a little case of pregnancy!

Adam was constantly on her mind. Even though he was gone, a little part of him was growing inside of her. He had a right to know. But each time she started to consider how she would get in touch with him, she remembered his words. If she told him, he would think she had entrapped him and lied. After this, he'd never trust her, not to mention the financial obligation she would be causing him.

Further Google searching had proved that he wasn't the jack-of-all-trades, dressing in jeans one day and a suit the next as she'd assumed last summer. She got another large surprise. Adam had been the manager of the Stark International Hotel New York. Since the accident, he'd taken a leave of absence from his position.

She was an idiot for not thinking more of him. But regardless of what he did or how much he made, she didn't want to be a burden to him emotionally or financially.

What she needed was time. Time to think about her future and what would be the best for her baby. By late September, the morning sickness had started to taper off and she almost couldn't believe she had a baby growing inside of her. She was faithful to the diet and exercise plan Dr. Mallory recommended. She actually lost weight at first, then she started to gain it as the baby grew.

One Sunday afternoon in early October, she was entering the lobby of her brownstone when one of the other tenants, a good-looking man close to her age, opened the door for her and smiled.

"Thank you," she said in greeting and smiled back.

"I don't know how many times we've passed in the hall, but I'm Toby."

"Laura," she said, offering her hand.

"I've been meaning to stop by and invite you over for a glass of wine."

"I'm sorry, I've been a bit of a hermit since I moved in..." On impulse, she asked, "Would you like to come over now? I'm not drinking, because I'm pregnant, but I know I have a decent bottle of red somewhere..."

"You're pregnant?" he asked, his face lighting up with surprise.

"Yes," Laura smiled, "I am."

"Congratulations!"

"It's...well...complicated." She didn't know where to begin, couldn't believe she'd told a stranger about the baby.

Ten minutes later, they were sitting in her living room, enjoying a cup of tea.

"You know, I've watched you and wondered," he said.

"What have you wondered?"

"Why Gwyneth Paltrow was living in my building?"

Laura laughed. She looked nothing like Gwyneth Paltrow, the only thing they had in common was an ex-husband. "Bad divorce," she replied with a shrug. "My rat bastard ex cheated on me with his legal assistant."

"Is the baby your ex's?"

She smiled at the thought of her baby. "No, the baby is, well, this summer I had...it's my friend's baby for lack of a better word, my summer affair."

Over the next hour, she told Toby her story and waited for his reaction.

When she'd finished, he asked, "What are you going to do?"

"I have absolutely no idea," she answered. "Okay, enough about me and my drama, your turn."

"Honey, I can't compete with all that, but I'll try."

She learned that Toby was an unemployed model, who was up for a large contract with Abercrombie & Fitch. He had an older, semi-famous boyfriend who wanted to marry him, and he was trying to get up the nerve to tell his parents he was gay.

"And I thought my life was complicated," she replied, and they both laughed.

They chatted easily. Laura was happy to tell someone all the things that she'd been secretly holding inside. She caught Toby looking curiously at one of her watercolors.

"What do you think of it?" she asked, fearing what he might say.

"It's absolutely spectacular," he replied, cradling his cup.

"I've done much better. That was one of my first."

"You painted that?" he asked, setting the cup on the table, and moving closer to get a better look at the landscape of Tranquility.

"Yes, this summer."

"Do you have any more?"

"About twenty or so."

"Did I mention what my boyfriend does for a living?" he asked.

"No, you didn't," she said as little tingles danced along her spine. Something good was about to happen.

"Have you ever heard of Kevin Caplan?" Toby asked.

"Yes, I'm pretty sure everyone in the city knows him," she answered, thinking of all the Caplan galleries in San Francisco. "Does your boyfriend work for one of his galleries?"

"My boyfriend is Kevin Caplan and oh baby is he going to want to meet you!"

Alex poured four fingers of bourbon into the Baccarat crystal lowball glass and placed it on the art deco coffee table in front of Adam. Adam watched as he poured himself an equally generous glass. Then he sat across from Adam in one of a pair of abstract chairs Melinda had fallen in love with one rainy Sunday afternoon in Soho. She'd insisted they buy the black leather and chrome monstrosities. He'd never quite warmed to their harsh lines. The chair had been priced at $30,000. To his credit, he hadn't blinked when she'd asked for the pair. Odd, the things you remember. Even now he didn't mind the price, but he still didn't like the chairs.

Having Alex in the apartment made the space bearable, if only just. Few people understood him as well as his cousin, who was more of a brother in all respects.

"It's okay to drink up," Alex said. "I'm not driving and I'm not leaving you alone."

"That's good because I probably shouldn't be alone. But this," he said, holding up the glass, which caught a fading sunbeam and sparkled, "Won't change what happened."

"No, but it might soften the edges for a few hours."

Adam stared at the amber liquid in the glass hoping to make sense of the trial.

"I didn't know about Melinda," Alex said and took a sip of his whiskey.

"Neither did I, but I suspected. She was acting weird, but when the coroner gave his report," Adam said, closing his eyes as he remembered the way the coroner had hesitated on the stand, looked at Adam and then glanced away. A moment later, he told the court that Melinda had been about six weeks pregnant. They had been thinking about having another child, but the news hit like a battering ram. He wondered if Melinda knew. By the reactions of her parents and sister, he knew she hadn't told them. Had she been planning on surprising him? That was like her.

The jury had sentenced her killer to sixty-six months on manslaughter charges. Twenty-two months for each soul he killed. It was unprecedented, but they had considered the child Melinda carried when they gave their recommendation.

"Do you really think she knew?" Alex asked.

"Yeah, she'd been acting very happy. I remember her smiling a lot and not telling me why," Adam replied. "I think the news would have been my anniversary present the next week."

"A sweet surprise. That was very like her."

"Yes, very much so."

"I'm glad it mattered to the jury," Alex said.

Adam shook his head. The jury didn't care. "The jury could have given him twenty-five years."

"His life is over, one way or another," Alex said, his voice huskier from the bourbon.

"I would have preferred the twenty-five years. The whole trial was a cluster fuck from the beginning. It wasn't about Melinda and A.J. It was about the poor drunk driver and his pain. What led him to drive that night and his bad breaks in life and his suffering. The Radcliffs illustrated the differences between them and us in ways the jury might not have figured out. Melinda and I were painted as snobs. Poor, poor Teddie, just a guy down on his luck. Probably someone who resembled me, some rich guy in a suit fired him, and look what it made him do?"

"Melinda would want you to go on and live the best life you can," Alex said as he took a sip of his bourbon and settled back in his chair. "This trial didn't help take away your pain. In fact, I think it has brought it back for you. It seemed like when you were working in California at The Bay Shore this summer that you had some peaceful moments."

Alex knew him well and he was right. Laura had taken away his pain.

"The summer helped," Adam said. "Just being away."

"You didn't die with them, Adam."

"I never want to go through this again. I don't want to get married again or have another family. I won't open myself up for this kind of pain ever again. I'm done."

"You're speaking in absolutes. Give it some time."

"No. At least you have children, the next generation of Starks to run the business. I'm done. I will never, ever put myself through this again. I'll make sure I won't. Look at it this way, I'll make your kids even richer because they will inherit my estate when I die."

"Adam," Alex began and paused as he met Adam's eyes. "If I lost Daisy and Lexie, I don't know what I'd do, but I know you would be there for me and make sure I didn't do anything stupid, like never loving again. Just don't do anything stupid, please…"

"I know what I want."

"Wait. Just let things settle down. Years from now you might meet someone, and you might want to have a child with them. You won't be offending the memory of your wife and child."

Adam thought of Laura and her infertility issues. He'd felt sorry for her but pleased to know their affair wouldn't have any unwanted results. As much as his decision pained him, they would not have a future together. Fate played her hand, and he knew now he wasn't the one for Laura. No doubt, someone as special as her would find a true soulmate.

He couldn't think about this anymore. He wouldn't weaken on this either…that part of his life was over, and he would plod through his future a broken man.

"I'll think about what you said, but I won't change my mind." He picked up the tumbler of bourbon and took a healthy swig. It burned a warm path down his throat.

"You know—your parents, my mother, my wife, we are really worried about you. Your mother, my Aunt Sophie said she thinks you might be cracking up."

"Yes, I know. My mother lectured me just this afternoon about counseling," Adam said. "Grief is grief. No amount of counseling will take away my pain, unless I drug it away, which I do not intend to do, aside from this drink. At least now that the trial is over, Mom and Dad can go back to Bermuda or Bora Bora or wherever they like to go this time of the year, as happy retirees, drink a few cocktails, and forget about this."

"They asked me if I thought they should move in with you for a bit."

"Oh, hell no," Adam said, sitting up in his chair. They'd seen him every day of the trial, sitting behind Melinda's family. It had been a fight to get them to stay at the Stark International Hotel New York and not invade his home for the duration of their stay.

"I can hardly bear to even be in this place. It doesn't make me happy to remember my time with Melinda and A.J.; it reminds me of all I've lost. I need to leave or sell it."

"Sublet it. Get the hell out of here for a while."

"I want to go back to work. I need to be busy."

"I think that would be an excellent idea," Alex said, putting his hands together, all fingertips touching in strategic contemplation.

Noticing the posturing, Adam said, "Yeah, I thought you'd like that."

"You could go back to the New York property, but maybe a fresh start away from New York is a good idea. There are other places I need you."

Adam hadn't been to a meeting of the board in months. The company could be falling down around them, and he wouldn't know it. "Like where?"

"Cairo. The last guest leaves in three weeks. Then we've got to strip the hell out of that thing, if there is anything of value left. Then you just need to turn over the space to the new owners."

Adam was glad he hadn't suggested Dubai again. It was more than he thought he wanted to handle, but he needed to push Alex's buttons just like when they were kids. He said, "I thought you had someone for that, some other hotel manager from Europe you wanted to punish with a garage sale of epic proportion."

"Luis? He's too busy in France. But, while you are there overseeing the decommission, you can meet with the new buyers and make nice. Then, when you have a little time, you could look around Cairo and see if there is another opportunity."

Adam was pulled in like some trout on a hook. He liked the distraction and let himself get netted. "Now I get it, but I thought we all decided we were done with Cairo."

"Temporarily, yes, we are done. Eighteen months, maybe twenty-four, we let all the political action die down and then we go back in and reestablish the brand."

"What are my other options?" Adam asked.

Alex cocked his head and smiled. "Would you like to finish up at The Bay Shore?"

"No," Adam said. "I would prefer to avoid California for a while."

Adam saw the glint in Alex's eye. He should have known better.

"There was a woman, right?" Alex surmised. "July, when I talked to you in San Fran you were involved but wouldn't tell me about it. Still unfinished business?"

"Don't make me feel worse than I already do. It's finished. It's just a little awkward," he lied. "She is Kat Russell's best friend."

"Cousin, that was a really, really bad choice. William tells me that Kat holds a grudge," Alex said, and it bothered Adam. "I hope you didn't break her heart."

"No. Not a bad choice, but I think I hurt her. She deserves better than me. I can't be good enough for her. I won't further mess up her life by returning anytime soon."

"Well, you're probably right," Alex said, but Adam could tell he was a little too interested. "You know, when I asked my good friends the Russells to let you stay at their house, I didn't think you'd help yourself to all their amenities. She must be very special. Are you sure you don't want to go back and settle things?"

Adam ignored the comment. "How long would I be in Cairo?"

"Long enough. Two months, which is a good palate cleanser. When you get finished there we can discuss the next logical move."

Despite the way Toby had gushed over her watercolors the day they met, Laura had continuing doubts about her abilities. Maybe that was why she hadn't been able to give Adam the painting she'd planned for him to have. The day he'd left she could have asked for an address, even had a perfect excuse. "I painted this for you. Let me send it to you in New York." Yet, she hadn't been able to bring herself to even mention it to him. It was a complete chicken shit move on her part, and she still regretted it.

Now that very painting was in the hall closet of her San Francisco apartment gathering dust and reminding her of a time that was too bittersweet to recall. She still hadn't decided if she would show that painting to Toby's boyfriend.

She smoothed down her light lavender silk dress, a sheath that showed just the hint of baby bump and a matching lavender cashmere sweater. She'd drawn the line at her pearls. Instead, she'd added a necklace with chunky purple amethyst crystals. She thought the pretty stones made her look like more of an artist than a math teacher. However, the man she was about to meet would put any doubts to rest about whether she could ever call herself an artist. Kevin Caplan was coming to her apartment. She'd been following his career for the last ten years. His galleries were the places to have your work shown. If he liked you or thought you had talent, you were an artist.

"Stop sweating," she chided herself as she went to the window and looked down at the street. Of course she wouldn't see Toby and Kevin arriving, Toby's apartment was on the floor above her.

She walked off a little nervous energy by pacing her hardwood floors. For the tenth time, she checked out the platter she'd hurriedly put together with the most expensive cheeses she could afford along with baby vegetables she'd carefully blanched and artfully arranged. The small cocktail plates she'd been able to "steal" from her previous life with Leland were stacked neatly beside the platter and small linen napkins she'd ironed that morning were neatly folded beside them.

When there was a friendly, familiar knock she'd come to recognize on her door, she nearly jumped out of her skin.

What if he hated her work? What if he didn't think she had any talent?

"You asked for this," she muttered as she walked to the door and calmly pulled it open.

"There she is!" Toby exclaimed. He pulled Laura into a quick hug and then released her so she could meet his boyfriend, Kevin Caplan.

Laura quickly extended her hand, which Kevin shook, and then he pulled her into a quick hug, announcing, "I feel like I already know you! Toby has been bragging about your work for days. I can't wait to see it!"

Laura smiled and released the air tensely held in her lungs. They were off to a great start.

"Thank you," she said. "Please come in. I'm a huge fan of your galleries. It's an honor to meet you…"

But Kevin, a Greg Kinnear look-alike with a radiant, easy smile, was staring intently at the seascape she'd hung near the entryway. Laura couldn't tell if the expression that now obscured his face was that of appreciation or disgust. He moved closer, took out a pair of red framed reading glasses from the inside pocket of his chocolate suede jacket and scrutinized her work.

"Wow," he murmured as he moved to within an inch or two of the seascapes. "The brush artistry is sublime."

"And you say I can't spot talent," Toby said, looking past Kevin to wink at Laura.

Kevin reluctantly pulled his gaze away from the painting and looked at Laura, not in the friendly way he'd regarded her earlier. This time it was all business.

"This is your work?"

"Yes," she said.

"Where did you train?"

"I didn't. Painting has always been a hobby for me. It relaxes me."

He spotted another piece and moved toward it with graceful steps.

"Where is this?" he asked, his eyes never leaving the portrait of the yellow and white grand architecture.

"My friend Kat's house. It's called Tranquility."

"Tranquility? Tranquility…You mean Katherine Russell, the movie star?" he asked as he pulled off his glasses and looked at her.

"Yes, but I have a lot of paintings that aren't from there, so we can't say they are exclusively of Tranquility—"

"And how many of these do you have?"

"I have about twenty," she said. "Maybe another half dozen, which are in progress. I've started a series of San Francisco."

She tried to paint every day. But with her teaching, she could only get in a few hours here and there.

"I want to see everything you have," Kevin said as he tentatively stepped into her living room. She noticed then that he was scanning the walls, looking for more art. He moved quickly toward a painting of a little cove down on the beach. It was a beach where she and Adam made love after a picnic on a warm afternoon. For the last few days, she'd been thinking of removing the painting because even the sight of the sandy beach made her longing worse.

Toby helped himself to a carrot from the vegetable platter. Sitting on the couch, he crossed his legs and watched his boyfriend work the room with a satisfied look on his face. Laura wished she could feel as calm.

"I love this. I absolutely fucking LOVE this!" Kevin announced, looking at the painting of the little wrought iron table on the balcony where Kat and Laura had their fateful breakfast the morning after the 4th of July party. She had even painted in the fruit plate, croissant, and pitcher of orange juice as she remembered them.

"The bourgeois new money won't touch these, but the old money, the serious money will LOVE them!" he said, more to himself than to her or Toby.

Toby patted the cushion next to him and said, "It's going to be a while, you might as well sit down and try to relax."

Laura didn't want to move a muscle. Her heart was racing below her cashmere sweater, the amethyst crystal necklace threatening to choke her. He liked her work. He really, really liked it!

Kevin moved to her next painting. It was that of a woman lounging on the chaise in the secret garden. Laura had used her imagination. She intended on making the woman look like Kat, but she knew the woman looked more like her, a woman daydreaming about her lover.

"Did you use a model for this one?" Kevin asked.

"No," she admitted. "It is a little off."

"Yes, but not much. A prospective buyer won't notice unless they have a really good sense of spatial presence. I love it, just not as much as the others."

Laura didn't like the sound of that at all. What if it was downhill from here? He was only on her fourth painting.

"Delicious," Kevin murmured as he stepped toward another seascape. "Look at the sheer iridescence you captured as the wave crests, just ready to drop in on itself, the power of the journey at its height before a massive implosion."

"So, you like my work?" she asked.

"Like? No, I don't like it. I love it!" Kevin said, turning his full attention to her. "The vibrancy of the colors, the blues and greens you're able to coax out of the paint reminds me of Maxfield Parrish's blue. Even your style is from an earlier era. It has 1920s grace and deco with a fanciful twist. How long have you been painting?"

"On and off for the last twenty years when time has allowed," she said. "I started with art class in high school and have dabbled on and off since then."

"And now, you're a schoolteacher?" Kevin asked.

"High school math."

"What a waste," he said and moved to the next painting. "Girl, you need to work in acrylic or oils, too. Your ability with color will blow off the canvas!"

Toby laughed in the background and said, "Laura, I told you so…"

Later, after Kevin had scrutinized every painting she had and even looked at the one she had hidden in the closet and her works in progress, he sat cross-legged on the floor in front of her coffee table.

"Do you know how many young artists darken my door every day?"

"A lot?" Laura offered from her perch next to Toby on the couch.

"I had four today. You are the fifth artist. Unlike them, you are getting an offer from me. Would you like to have a show in one of my galleries?"

"There's even a question? Yes. Yes, Mr. Caplan, I'd love to have a show in one of your galleries," she said.

"Laura, it is time for you to call me Kevin. We are going to be very good friends."

# CHAPTER FIFTEEN

"How's our boy?" Alex Stark asked as Adam answered his phone on the second ring.

It had been a lousy day. The air temperature in Cairo was an unseasonably hot ninety-plus degrees outside. The hotel's air conditioning had shut off sometime in the middle of the night. The temperature inside the old hotel was well over a hundred degrees. Had he been paying more attention, he wouldn't have picked up the phone for his cousin. He wasn't in the mood for Alex's perpetual chipper demeanor.

"Tell me again how you ended up in Portland running the company and I'm halfway around the world in a godforsaken desert, pillaging what has to be the most dilapidated hotel in our chain?" Adam asked, hoping to push a few of Alex's buttons.

"You're not pillaging. You're removing viable assets before a large and profitable business transaction which will in turn stimulate the local economy."

"You're full of crap," Adam said, as he thought of the large sale they were planning on to completely rid the hotel of anything of value. Even the carp in the lobby pond had been evaluated and would be sold before the next hotel chain came in and purchased what would be a shell of its previous grandeur.

Alex got serious, his voice losing all of its humor. "Really, Adam, how are you?"

"I admit, I told you that I wanted to get away from everything. I just never considered that Cairo would be a different sort of prison. I can't wait to leave."

"By this time next month, Cairo will be just a memory."

"Great," Adam said, knowing that Alex would pick up on his total lack of enthusiasm.

"You should take a little time and visit the Pyramids of Giza, Valley of the Kings, Luxor…"

"I don't want to spend one minute longer than I have to in this place. Ripping apart one of our hotels is depressing and I was already having a hard time."

"What I have in mind for you can wait for a few weeks."

"I know I'm the dog token on your personal Monopoly board, but where do you want me to go next?"

"Adam, you can always turn me down, you own a big chunk of this company. I know you're doing me a favor right now. But no one could have done this Cairo thing better than you."

Adam paced in the ugly pharaoh-themed hotel room. The linens and curtains were printed with large black hieroglyphics on filthy sand colored fabric and the bed came complete with a King Tut headboard. The room was worn out, the brown carpet stained with undefined filth. The air conditioning never quite chilled the space enough to stop him from breaking into a sweat, even when it was working properly. Then again, he might have contracted one of the local viruses that would never quite leave his body and would remind him of his Cairo experience for years to come.

Time away in a faraway land kept him busy during the day, but his nights were brutal. Memories of his family, their screams, and the trial played over and over in his mind. The Radcliffs had taken to calling him each week and he made any excuse he could to not talk to them. The only light in his dreams was of his time in Tranquility. He'd hoped he'd be able to forget his luscious lover, his Laura, but she was as familiar to him as his own skin.

"Now you're just pissing me off and I want to tell you to do unpleasant things to yourself," Adam announced.

"Relax Runt, don't get your hackles up. I do have an offer for you. However, it is another exotic location and I'm concerned that you might consider it to be an equal or greater prison because of the similar climate."

"What? Do we have a hotel in Baghdad I missed? Let me guess, Afghanistan?"

"No, but it is pretty warm and sunny," Alex laughed.

Adam sighed and swore under his breath, recognition dawning. Then he said what he knew to be true. "Fuck, you want me for Dubai."

Enthusiasm back in his voice, Alex replied, "Bingo."

"Last I heard, you and Daisy were thinking of taking a break and running Dubai for the first couple of years."

"My lovely wife thinks it would be just the thing for you. She told me you need a complete distraction. Daisy, as you know, is a smart woman. In this case, I'm inclined to believe her, and since she is pregnant and hormonal, I want to keep her happy. Your being in Dubai, well, it makes her happy."

"Dubai," Adam said, hating that he both liked the idea of something so far off the map and felt homesick for some place that he couldn't quite identify.

"Truth be told, I can't think of anyone but myself who would be good in this position. You're a close second."

"Thanks. Remember, I own as much company stock as you do," Adam reminded him. Their rivalry had always been friendly. Adam had never begrudged his cousin. On the contrary, he was happy to take a role of less responsibility. He liked having a private life. At least he had, until the accident.

"I actually own one percent more than you do, Runt."

"Fuck off, you ogre."

Alex laughed, "Then I don't think I need to tell you how much this property set the family back and how much you personally have invested in its success. The contractors came in over budget. Everything from the concrete to the linens were much more expensive than anticipated. If we don't see profits within the first six months, the damage could be widespread. And by that I mean, you could feel the hit. Maybe we'd have to sell the plane or stop going to Milan for our suits."

Adam hadn't initially liked the idea of Dubai. Alex's enthusiasm had propelled the project forward. It was time to subtly remind him as to who had gotten them into this mess in the first place.

"I thought we agreed that if you passed on getting Dubai up and running that you were going to hire away a competitor from an existing hotelier. I thought you were going after some Westin guy and that it was 'in the bag.' Didn't you ask me to approve an enormous salary?" Adam enjoyed the silence that followed as his cousin tried to explain his way out of this detail.

"It got messy. The Westin countered and I refused to get into a bidding war, and I started to question his loyalty, playing us like that," Alex said. Adam had a feeling Alex had lost the bidding war early in the game but wasn't about to admit it.

"Great. Well, I don't know anything about the desert. I haven't studied the local customs. I don't know anyone. I have absolutely no connections in the business world. Why are you thinking of hiring me to manage this hotel? I've only been there twice, once to scout out a location with you and then again with you during construction. I've been a curious onlooker. It just doesn't make any sense. As a board member, I can't recommend or endorse myself as the manager."

"Give yourself some credit. This is right in your area of expertise. You'll be the onsite part owner. You'll hire other people who do have the connections we need. Money is power, Adam, don't ever forget that."

"Yeah, right. Listen, I'm going to need to think about this. I might want to take my position back in New York."

There was an uncomfortable pause. Adam wished he were facing Alex face-to-face.

"Unfortunately, we might have a small snag there."

Damn it. Alex was always doing crap like this to him. "Define snag, and for the record, you aren't supposed to make decisions like this without consulting me."

"Spencer will need another project after Rome and New York could use a facelift. You know, we discussed it when you left and asked for The Bay Shore project. A project, might I remind you, that I would have let Spencer handle."

Spencer had a knack for remodeling and improving the potential profitability of any property when they could get him off the ranch.

"How convenient. You're just about to open Dubai and need someone with a vested interest to run it, so you're going to have Spencer work on New York."

Alex said, "Now we are on the same page. Spencer has to want New York and he is just getting started on Rome."

"But he will want New York. We both know it. You took away New York to force my hand on Dubai."

"We all have our strengths. Spencer fixes them up, you take the brand and manage them into profitability, and I oversee the whole operation.

"Why not send Spencer to The Bay Shore now?"

"You did a great job, no need for anyone to step in, and he hasn't really started on Rome yet."

"I need time to think."

"Take a few weeks, then buy a dozen summer suits, because it gets hot in the desert despite the modern climate control. We'll need you to be looking your best if you're going to schmooze the locals and have a fantastic opening in just six weeks. It is going to be spectacular. If Daisy is feeling up to it, we are flying over for the grand opening party. We have Sultan Three reserved. That is my favorite suite at the property."

Daisy was pregnant with their second child. Adam was happy for them when Alex had told him after the trial, but he couldn't think too much about it. It painfully reminded him of all he'd lost. Adam Junior was the first grandchild born into the next generation of their family.

"Is Daisy okay?" Adam asked, genuinely concerned.

"Yes, she's great. I love that woman. And we think Lexie is getting a little sister," Alex said, and Adam could hear the tenderness in Alex's voice that he always reserved for his wife and daughter.

"I'm happy for you," Adam said, meaning it.

"Thank you. I'm going to be a Daddy to little girls, which should be okay until they are about sixteen. It's another reason Daisy wants to pass on Dubai. She wants to have family close with the baby. We could swing it if I could convince her mother to go with us, but that is a long shot and I'd need a big house to keep Daisy away from her mother or they'd kill each other. Bottom line, I want Daisy to be happy. Besides, this will be good for you. You'll love the night-life. Dubai is like Las Vegas on speed. Lots of beautiful women—"

Adam interrupted him. "Hey Alex, there is one thing you could do for me."

"Name it."

"You're in Portland?"

"Yeah, I'm in my office sitting at my desk."

"Good. I'll need you to go up to the rooftop garden."

"What for?" Alex asked.

"Would you please just do it?"

"If I really walked up there right now, you'd tell me to jump off, wouldn't you?"

Adam smiled. "Yes, I would." Then he hung up on his cousin.

He went over to his battered desk. At least the clutter that had accumulated made it look better by covering up the fake wood. Picking up a blue envelope from one of the piles, he stared down at the return address. It was from his father-in-law, an invitation to stay at their beach house in Aruba for as long as he wanted.

He could stay at any of the Stark International Hotels' for-ty-five properties any time he wanted, but none of them were actual houses. What he liked about Aruba was that he'd been involved in the negotiation and purchase for his mother and father-in-law. In fact, it might be a good opportunity to bury a few of his ghosts and say goodbye. He picked up the key that had been in the envelope and decided then and there that instead of visiting the pyramids as Alex had suggested, he would spend a couple of weeks recharging in the Caribbean.

Adam watched the translucent blue-green water break gently on the sugar sand beach. It was the same each day, sunny and perfect. For the last seven days he had sat on the beach and watched the water, trying to figure out how he would dig himself out of the hole he'd personally created and then jumped into.

Taking the Radcliffs up on their offer of the beach house in Aruba had to be one of the stupidest things he'd ever done, but after some of the worst homesickness he'd ever experienced, he was at a loss as to what to do with himself. After two months in Cairo, he hadn't wanted to go back to New York or Tranquility. Each place held too many memories. Aruba seemed like a good idea a week earlier. He was rapidly running out of places to hide from his pain.

Thoughts of Laura haunted him. He reasoned over and over that he'd disappeared with her best interest at heart. What he felt for her couldn't be love. Love didn't happen when you'd just lost the two people who meant more to you than anything else in the world. No, his feelings for Laura were complicated, fueled by physical passion and mutual need. If they'd met a few years from now, maybe they could be more, but for now he'd done her a favor and it was killing him.

He took a long sip on a local beer he'd pulled out of the ice bucket that sat next to him in the sand. Never in his life had Adam Stark ever felt restless and not known exactly what the future held.

He didn't hear her approach, but the moment he heard the voice, the invitation and the key made sense. He was truly an idiot not to have expected as much.

"Howdy, stranger," Tess purred.

Adam pulled off his sunglasses and looked at the perfect biki-ni-clad body standing just next to him, casting a shadow where there'd once been sun. On closer inspection, he noticed the lack of a bikini top. Two perfectly bouncy and completely fake tennis-ball-shaped breasts stood at attention.

"Mother and Father thought you might be lonely," Tess announced. "They asked me to come down and make sure you were relaxed."

"I'm leaving," Adam said, angrier than he'd ever been in his life as he quickly stood and gathered what could not be abandoned.

"What?"

"How dare you, little girl. I loved your sister for being every-thing you aren't. When you next talk to Mommy and Daddy, you can let them know that I will never see or speak to you or them again. We are done."

Walking past her and the shocked expression on her face, he felt better for the first time in months. His future was in Dubai. It certainly wasn't with the Radcliffs. They really were done. And he was leaving part of his grief behind.

# CHAPTER SIXTEEN

"I'm worried about you," Kat stated in her weekly call.

"Why? I'm fine," Laura replied.

"Something is up with you. Have you met someone?"

"I've met a very nice man named Toby. He lives in my building and is absolutely gorgeous. Last night, we had dinner with his friend, Kevin, who wants to feature my watercolors in his gallery."

"I knew it! I knew you'd meet someone. This is great news. And after all your hard work, your first gallery opening, how fabulous!"

Laura waited a beat and continued. "Kevin and Toby are a couple. I'm still in love with Adam."

"Damn it, Laura! I, well…shit."

"What is it, Kat? Have you talked to him?" Her hand went to her stomach, rubbing the slight bulge not yet too visible.

"He called William." After a pause, Kat said, "He's not coming back to The Bay Shore. I'm so sorry Laura…He's not coming back anytime soon."

"Why not? What did he say?" she asked. Having him come back was something she hoped for, despite the odds against it.

"He's not taking the outcome of the trial very well. They found the driver guilty of manslaughter. The man got only five or six years. He'll be eligible for probation way before his time is served. They were going for second-degree murder based on the driver's previous record. William said he could barely talk about it."

And he certainly hadn't called Laura to talk to her.

"I followed the trial. I heard about his wife being pregnant. I don't think he knew."

"He said he had a feeling," Kat said.

"It is too horrible for words, what is he going to do now?"

"He took another position with Stark International Hotels."

"What aren't you telling me?"

Kat hesitated, "I don't want to tell you something like this over the phone. I wish I was there with you."

"Damn it, Kat!"

"He took a position in Cairo."

"What?" Laura asked, the air leaving her lungs.

Kat continued, "Honey, you need to move on. He's made his decision, he's going overseas, now don't waste another minute on him, please."

After Laura hung up, she cried for an hour. She cried for herself and her baby, whose father was now half a world away. If he had thought anything of her, he would have called her. He should have called her. Kat had offered to fly home. Although touched by Kat's concern and her offer, Laura tried her best to reassure her that she would be all right. Laura had to deal with this on her own, in her own way.

By mid-November, Laura had decided not to tell Adam about the baby. She was angry with him for leaving and she didn't want him to regret anything that had happened between them. If she told him, everything would change.

"I'll be here for you," Toby said seriously, as he sat in a chair in her bay window one foggy Saturday afternoon.

"Thank you. That means more than you will ever know. I like the idea of the baby having a famous model for an uncle," she replied, dabbing color onto the watercolor paper sitting on her easel. She was painting his portrait, as suggested by her new beneficiary, Kevin Caplan. In two weeks, she would have her first show in his largest gallery. He wanted her to round out the landscapes with a few portraits and she'd gladly complied, needing as many distractions as possible.

Kat and William had returned to Tranquility several times during breaks in filming and each time they did, they pressured her to visit. They would be home for good in a week, arriving just in time to attend her opening, which was already causing her stress.

Trying to catch the highlights in Toby's hair just perfectly, she thought back to her last phone call with Kat.

Kat had been blunt. "What's up, Laura? You've been acting strange and secretive. I want to know what is going on. I thought it was because I'd introduced you to Adam, but now I think it is something more. Whatever it is, you can tell me."

"Meeting Adam was wonderful, Kat. You know I fell in love with him. In fact, I still love him."

"I know it has been hard, but darling, what is it? I know there is something wrong. I can feel it."

"Everything is fine." Laura stated, half believing it herself.

"Laura, if I were at Tranquility right now, I swear, I'd be getting in my car and heading toward you right now. Don't think I can't stop this production schedule and hop on a plane. What would the director do? Fire me? I'd stop sleeping with him! Now tell me, damn it!"

"Everything is fine," she repeated.

"Stop saying that! You're clearly not fine. I'd believe it more if you'd told me you were depressed. That makes sense, but this aloofness…is crap." Laura made an excuse to get off the phone and hung up abruptly. Kat was no doubt was still having a hissy fit.

"I think I'm finished," she said, giving her painting one last look and then smiling at Toby. "Come have a look."

He stood next to her, looking at the piece. "It's fantastic. It's like a photograph. I don't know how you do it…"

"I've gotten better with age," she said ruefully.

Just how many days could Adam sit on the beach and stare out at the water? Well, it had been six so far, not counting Aruba.

When Tess showed up, Adam had once and for all shattered any illusions she might have had that they'd be together one day. She'd cried and carried on as he hurriedly packed, but he didn't care. He owed nothing to her or her family. He had been a good husband to Melinda and father to A.J. He was done with her family, and he felt Melinda would have supported his decision. Hadn't she once called them parasites? The very night Tess arrived, he'd left and flown to nearby St. Bart's, and checked into the Stark International Hotels St. Bart's.

He thought he was good for at least another week or two of sugar sand beaches and cheeseburgers in paradise. The decision on Dubai, however, loomed over his head like a pending root canal.

A high-paying guest should be occupying the private cabana with its own pool and private beach at the Stark International Hotel St. Bart's, but since it was vacant and Adam was there, he didn't really care about the potential lost revenue. Hell, he might even reimburse them and pay the bill as if he were a paying guest. He felt like a hypocrite. He didn't care about the lush, extravagant accommodations. When he had the opportunity to get the best, it is what he did. It was how he was raised. Privilege from an early age had a way of dulling the senses. Although his parents had worked hard to instill in him a sense of purpose, money didn't matter to him. Life had taught him that lesson the hard way.

How ironic was it that everything he had ever really wanted wasn't for sale? At last count he was worth over a hundred million, but all that money hadn't saved his wife or his son. It hadn't taken away his grief. And it hadn't taken away the pain he'd felt when he left Laura.

What was she doing now? What would she do if he suddenly showed up on her doorstep? She should slam the door in his face, but what if she didn't? What if she invited him inside and forgave him for how he'd treated her?

He wondered if she'd followed the trial, what she'd thought— maybe she now realized why all of what happened to him left him with so much baggage. She probably realized that he'd be too much trouble.

Adam spread a blanket on the sand in the late afternoon sun, feeling the familiar frustration that always kicked in when the thought of the promises he'd made to himself with regard to Laura. The truth was, he still wasn't ready. It was cowardly, but the truth was still the truth. He was still in love with his wife.

He wouldn't go back to Laura until he was ready to make the commitment she deserved. Providing she'd be there…which he doubted she would. Sitting on the sand, he dusted the fine grains from his laptop. It was sacrilege to have a laptop at the beach, but then Adam couldn't fully disconnect, even when he desperately wanted to. Besides, doing work on his laptop might help him forget how the warm sand felt when you were making love to a woman whose eyes sparkled in the sunlight as she looked up at you…

Grabbing his new, favorite, beachside companion, a warm bottle of Carib, a local beer that had long ago lost its chill, he typed one-handed to open up his email. He practically choked when the email from Kat Russell popped up. The subject line has his heart pounding. *Laura.*

Hadn't he always said when you knew it was right, you just knew? It was too soon. His emotions were getting the best of him.

He dropped the forgotten bottle in the sand in his attempt hit the right key to open the document.

*Dear Adam,*

*I hope you're doing well. We followed the trial and were painfully disappointed by the outcome. You are in our thoughts and our hearts.*

*Everything is fine on this end. Our filming wrapped up in Italy and we are headed home in time for a very special opening. Our Laura is going to be famous! Turns out the Caplan Gallery has discovered what we always knew to be true, that she is fantastically talented! She has her first gallery opening in two weeks. If you're around, you should stop by. We'd love to see you! You'll certainly recognize the subject matter. Her show is entitled "Tranquility." Hope you're well, darling.*

*We miss you much. Know you always have a home with us…*

*Love, Kat*

Adam looked at his watch to see the date. He hadn't checked his email in a week and a half. Laura's gallery opening was in three days.

"Damn it!" he said, and then made the mistake of opening the attachment Kat had sent along. There was striking photo of Laura in a gauzy white blouse which hit him like a gut punch. She looked fantastic. Somewhere in his chest, his heart hurt as if it was being squeezed. And there were several photos of her paintings including their cove.

She was selling a painting of their cove. That idea had to sink in along with all the attached memories.

Adam stood and walked in slow circles around the twisted blanket and discarded laptop. Hands on hips, he moved aimlessly as his mind tried to bring order to the new information Kat had supplied. And why had she sent him an email? After he'd left, in the way that he had, he was sure he'd never hear from Kat again after how he'd treated her best friend. The email was an invitation. He knew that. Did that mean that Laura had asked her to send him an email? No, that wasn't Laura. She hadn't contacted him, and he knew she wouldn't.

He'd done everything in his power to forget last summer. The trial had reminded him that he'd lost his true happiness. So, what did that say about what he'd shared with Laura? Was she a fling? She had been there for him when he desperately needed someone. But they'd had an agreement, didn't they? Well, if not verbal their actions were of such. It was likely that if she hadn't been there, he'd have found comfort in the arms of another warm body, right? Then why, in the almost four months since he'd been with Laura, hadn't he moved on and found another woman?

Because he didn't want another woman, all he wanted was Laura.

Two days later, Adam was in front of the large photo of Laura that adorned one of the Caplan Gallery's front windows. She was smiling broadly. It was a rare smile he hadn't seen often, but when he did, his heart did funny fluttering things he didn't like. He didn't like that someone, some photographer, had been able to get her to smile that way.

He took in every detail. She wore a thin white linen shirt that was opened one button too far, just enough to display a hint of white lace from her bra. He'd always liked that she wore lace and silk for him, but he didn't like the world seeing it.

On the ring finger of her right hand, which she had casually cupping her chin as she smiled at the photographer, she had a pale amethyst ring he knew was her birthstone. The ring had been her grandmother's and he had looked at the delicate filigree at least half a dozen times as it was usually the only thing she wore when they made love.

She had on more makeup than he'd ever seen. Yet, it was subtle, and he couldn't say that it looked like she was wearing too much of anything. On the contrary, the subtle coloring enhanced her beauty from the natural lip-gloss to her inordinately long eyelashes, which seemed to flirt with him from even two dimensions.

Under the photo, a sign of minimalist excess read: Laura Hokensen. *Tranquility*. It was a little too pretentious in its unpretentiousness for Adam's taste and he wondered if Laura shared his opinion, but then for all he knew, she'd designed the sign and staged the photo.

With effort, he turned his attention to the two-story high, heavy glass doors of the Caplan Gallery, which had large, polished chrome handles. When Adam pulled on them, expecting them to open, he had another surprise. It took him a moment to understand the situation and the moment he did, he felt like an idiot. A small sign, no larger than a business card, dangled from one of the handles inside the glass. It announced, quite plainly, SHUT. Somebody must have thought that was a pretty cute way of saying CLOSED.

A moment later, he read the hours, 10:01a.m.–10:01p.m. They were being cute again. It didn't matter for it was almost ten o'clock and he could see Laura's paintings just beyond the glass doors.

Laura stood in the Caplan Gallery and stared at her name in large, black, sans serif letters just inside the entrance. It was happening and she couldn't believe it. Twenty of her pieces hung in the most famous gallery in San Francisco. She took a moment to enjoy the feeling and count her blessings. She only wished her parents could share this experience with her. At special times like this, the ache of their loss was a little sharper. Then her thoughts turned to Adam, and she thought she might lose her composure altogether, which she couldn't do because she was wearing makeup. If she looked like a raccoon, she wouldn't sell a thing.

"Congratulations," Kevin Caplan said, wrapping an arm around her. In the last few weeks, as he'd predicted, they'd become good friends. He still intimidated her, but she trusted his judgment and his impeccable taste. She'd done several of her best pieces in the last few weeks and he was encouraging her to move away from water-colors and into acrylics and oils. The idea excited her.

"Thank you for everything," she replied, and hugged him back.

"You earned it, and I have some good news. Did you happen to notice the little red dots on the labels next to six of your pieces?"

"No, I just got here. There are red dots? Does it mean what I think it means?"

"Teresa said a man appeared yesterday and bought them," he announced.

"The show hasn't even opened. What's his name? Please tell me it isn't William Russell."

"No, he is a private collector. We usually don't sell pieces before the show, but he was very insistent. Said that he had to have them and was leaving town before the opening. He offered triple the price, which we accepted. Teresa called me on my cell, and I said, honey, go for it. She works on commission and as of yesterday, she is now one of your biggest fans."

"Who would do that?" she asked, not understanding. "Did he really pay that much?"

"Yes, he most certainly did. Darlin', I don't question these things; I just get them shipped once we have an address. I will tell you this—I marked up each and every one of your paintings last night. I seriously underestimated your popularity."

Head spinning, Laura asked, "Where are they going? Cairo?"

"No, Teresa said it was an address in the Middle East. Abu Dhabi?"

"The Middle East? I don't know anyone in the Middle East."

Kevin shook his head. "You aren't supposed to. An admirer is an admirer, wherever they come from…"

"Do we have a name? I could at least send a thank you note."

"It is a corporation I've never heard of with a lot of vowels. Listen, we are just around the corner from a branch of the Bank of Saudi Arabia. Both the consulates of Yemen and Jordan aren't too far away. I made sure they were all on my mailing list. They got the glossy brochure for your show, which is part of my services. Just be happy."

Laura did the math in her head. "I'm very happy. This will help a lot."

He looked around to make sure they were alone, and conspiratorially whispered, "With the baby."

She walked around the gallery to scrutinize what her mystery buyer had purchased. Each piece was a landscape for Tranquility, two of the main house, the interior of the secret garden, her cottage, a view from the pool and a favorite she'd almost not parted with, a little cove where she and Adam once made love. She was glad she'd kept a couple of her favorites out of the show. It would be hard enough to part with these. Then, she thought of the extra money and felt elated. Those six paintings should just pay for some nursery furniture and half a year of daycare for the baby. She silently thanked the buyer, whoever he was, for easing her financial worries.

Voices flooded in around her as people arrived and scrutinized her work with glasses of champagne and appetizers in their hands. It made her a bit nauseous. Looking for a place to hide, she heard someone call her name.

Recognizing Kat's voice, she turned and was immediately engulfed in a hug, first from Kat, then from William.

"Laura, you're famous!" Kat yelled. "This is so wonderful!"

"I have to agree, this is fantastic!" William exclaimed.

"I've already sold a few pieces. I can't believe it! And now, my celebrity power couple has shown up! I've missed you both," Laura said, meeting Kat's alarmingly serious eyes. "What's the matter?"

"Oh my god, you're pregnant," Kat said, reaching out and placing her hand directly on Laura's stomach.

Laura couldn't believe it. She'd picked her outfit carefully. The empire waistline and dark color completely hid the slight bulge in her tummy, so she'd thought. She managed, "What? Me?"

"Don't even try that innocent bullshit with me. And don't forget that I'm the actress in this crowd. You're pregnant."

Resigned, Laura asked, "How can you tell?"

Confused, William looked between the two women and then asked his wife, "Laura's pregnant?"

Ignoring his question, Kat surmised, "You hate empire waistlines. You wouldn't be caught dead with one in your closet unless you had a good reason and all of the sudden you're wearing this... this outfit. Laura, do you think I'm that stupid?"

"No, I guess I just underestimated you, again."

"When are you due?"

"End of March. The week of Spring Break. I'll have the baby and then I'll finish out the school year. Everything will be fine."

"Oh fuck, how do you feel? Is everything okay?" Kat asked, her voice taking on a soft, concerned tone.

"I'm good, very healthy," she said, feeling stupid for thinking Kat wouldn't notice. Kat noticed everything.

"Oh, Laura, honey, come live with us. We will take care of you."

"Kat, I'm just having a baby."

"Just a baby? Oh please...you'll stay with us."

"I'm teaching until my delivery date."

"At least stay with us during your maternity leave and this summer."

"I'll definitely think about it," Laura said.

"Does Adam know?" William asked.

All eyes turned to Laura.

"I decided not to tell him."

Kat gave her husband a look and said, "William knows his family. He'll tell Alex, his cousin, won't you, darling?"

"Of course, tonight, I'll call him," William said.

"Kat, no. He was serious about not wanting to ever have another child. He'll think I did this on purpose. I don't want him to feel like he has to be a part of this or that he owes me anything. I can handle this without him."

"Laura—" she protested.

"No, not after what he's been through." She hesitated then thought better of it, "Adam and I talked about, well, things…just trust me on this Kat. I am sure he'd rather not be involved. I mean if he knew, yes, he'd be supportive, but if he doesn't know then it will all work out."

"Oh. My. God." Kat exclaimed, but her husband nudged her.

"Laura, it's your decision, but he should be told," William interjected, drawing both women's attention. "This isn't fair to Adam."

"Ok, well, please wait…I'll tell him in my own time. Promise me you won't call him. I want to do it my way." Her request was met with silence, the voices milling around them in the background.

Kat said, "You need to give him a chance to know what he might be missing."

"He'll do the right thing," William said. "Give him a chance."

Laura looked around, making sure she wasn't overheard when she said, "I know he had the trial, but he hasn't contacted me since our last day at Tranquility. The bottom line is that he walked away."

"He didn't expect to care as much as he did as soon as he did," Kat explained.

"If he cared, why did he move to Cairo?"

"He doesn't know what is waiting for him back home," William said.

"He knows I'm here," Laura said firmly. "And he knows I cared about him. He knows. This is my business, my story to tell, okay?"

"Okay, let's not ruin tonight," Kat said, trying to calm everyone down. "We will let you do this in your own time. But once the baby comes, please reconsider and know that William and I are always here for you."

She hugged them both and swallowed down the dread that she always felt when she thought of telling Adam about his baby. No one needed to know that she'd Googled him and gone so far as to call the hotel, only to be told he no longer worked at the Stark International Hotel Cairo. She'd even broken down and called him, but his number hadn't gone through. That told her all she needed to know. He was probably blocking her.

Laura worked the room, gave interviews to a couple of reporters, and watched the little red dots appear on each piece of her art. She moved to the front wall of windows and leaned back against the cool wall of glass, shutting her eyes, and savoring the moment. She might not have Adam, but she had this, her moment in the spotlight.

"Laura," a voice she knew, spoke softly next to her.

She slowly opened her eyes, smelling the large bouquet of blood-red roses before she saw them, and then looked into the eyes of the man who held them. *Leland.* This evening was just full of surprises.

"What are you doing here?" she asked.

"How could I miss it? I've been driving by this gallery on my way to the office for almost twenty years. When I saw your face, I almost had an accident," Leland said as he worked on being especially effusive. This was Leland in business connection mode. He would be pleasant and charming to everyone, especially her. People who didn't know their history would assume Leland was a great guy. They would second-guess every nasty and negative thing she'd ever said about him.

It was as if Angry Leland was wearing a Happy Leland mask. This was the charmer she'd married. This was the jerk who would turn on her the moment they got in the car after any event and criticized her all the way home.

She wondered how many extra business cards he'd brought along for the evening.

Adam sat in a dark sedan parked across the street from the gallery. Reaching into his pocket, he withdrew his cell phone. He had been waiting and watching for an hour, trying to get up his nerve to walk into the gallery and tell her he'd been a fool. The reunion he'd pictured a hundred times wasn't going to happen. Laura was back with her husband. How could she?

Leland Daniels hadn't left her side the whole time Adam had been watching her through the tall gallery windows. For the first time in years, he felt a bolt of jealousy. He wondered how long it had taken Leland to realize what a fool he'd been. Then Adam wanted to kick himself. He'd been a fool to leave and give Leland the opening.

Adam was very good at beating himself up for past events that had devastating consequences. If only he'd left the house with Melinda and A.J. a minute later. If only he'd decided to take their Range Rover instead of their sedan. If only he'd been in a different lane or paused to buy A.J. the ice cream he'd wanted before dinner.

As bad as Leland was for Laura, that was her decision—Adam asked her not to get back with Leland, but who was he to make that sort of request anyway. Leland was still probably better for Laura with Adam in this place in his life regardless.

He dialed a number and waited, watching Leland smile at something Laura said.

"Hey Adam, where you been, Runt?" Alex asked.

He got right to the point and didn't bother with any pleasantries, "I want to move forward on Dubai."

"Where are you? I've been trying to find you in St. Bart's."

"I'm in San Francisco."

"Ah, visiting the mystery lady?"

"No, that's been over since the end of summer. Listen," he said, changing his tone, trying to forget what he'd seen, "I just need to put everything in storage and get the New York townhouse on the market. Then, I'm free."

"This will be a great job for you. I know Cairo was a challenge, but you did a great job," Alex said. "The final paperwork on the sale should be signed next week."

"I never want to see Egypt again," Adam said, thinking of the heat and the city. "That hotel didn't fit our reputation. I'm glad you sold that piece of crap."

"You're reading my mind."

After Adam had looked at his fateful email from Kat, he'd flown to San Francisco the next day vacillating about whether or not to approach Laura. He missed her with every cell in his body, wanted to see her, but had no idea what he would say when he did. Parked in front of the gallery, the decision was made for him. How foolish and unpredictable he was being. He needed to move on.

"Listen," Alex said, "I don't want this to sound condescending, hell, if you'd been the older cousin, you'd be sitting at my desk, but what I want to say is that I'm proud of you."

"I'm not too proud of me right now," Adam said, watching Laura laugh at something Leland said.

"Adam, do you know how big this is? You're heading up the largest hotel in our company."

"I know. Listen, Alex, I don't want to sound ungrateful. It's just been one hell of a year," Adam replied sadly.

"I know, buddy. You've been to hell and back. Dubai is a fresh start. I'll move forward on the paperwork."

"Good. And Alex?"

"Yes?"

"Thank you for this."

"Try to feel a little excited. You're in charge of the largest hotel in the fleet. It's your baby to sink or swim. Have a good time with it but make us some money."

# CHAPTER SEVENTEEN

Christmas at Tranquility was a quiet, if not elegant affair. Kat and William sent all the staff home and cooked Christmas dinner themselves, Laura helping where she could. The beautiful, large estate was decorated to the hilt. Laura was given her choice of staying in the guest cottage or the main house and chose the latter. She asked for Adam's room, wanting to savor the memories she had shared with him in the same space.

She gave William and Kat a large watercolor of Tranquility she had painted over the summer with a frame she'd made and gilded with gold leaf herself. Kat loved it. Laura was especially touched when Kat decided to hang it over the fireplace in her sitting room. It was one of Laura's favorite pieces and one of her best that she'd kept out of her sold-out Caplan show. There was talk of a fall show and Kevin was hinting that she might consider painting as her full-time career. Flattered, she'd just shaken her head. The money from the show had done a lot to prepare for the expenses she knew she would incur with the baby, but she needed her teaching job and the health care benefits.

Kat and William's generosity showed no boundaries. For Christmas they gave her the gift of a completely outfitted nursery. And, ever interested in fashion, Kat insisted Laura be a very stylish pregnant woman and rounded out her wardrobe. Laura thought she must be the only high school teacher with couture maternity clothes.

By the end of the holiday and after much coercing, Kat managed to convince Laura to stay with them at Tranquility during her maternity leave.

Laura resumed her classes but by late January she was huge, her back aching if she stood or sat for too long.

Each doctor's appointment carried with it a sense of dread. She worried constantly that there was something wrong with the baby. Dr. Mallory ran the standard tests but skipped an amniocentesis. They both agreed the risk of miscarriage from the procedure was too high. Skipping the standard test for women of her age worried her, but every other test was completely normal.

Dr. Mallory was convinced that she was having a boy. The ultrasound wasn't conclusive, but Kat felt confident and started on the nursery picking tones of blue and soft butter yellow.

"That's a healthy little fella in there," Dr. Mallory told her when she was seven months into her pregnancy.

"If anything happened now and I went into premature labor, would the baby make it?"

"There is no reason to believe that you won't be carrying your baby to term. Everything is progressing as it should. But I can see that all that you've gone through has made you wary so let's talk about it. At this stage, it is most likely that your baby would survive with a bit of help. Each day he stays inside you raises the odds of his survival. So, get lots of rest. Don't push yourself and try to relax and enjoy this time. Because a few months from now, you won't be getting any rest."

Kat arrived and personally oversaw the installation of the nursery. Laura protested, but eventually gave in, allowing Kat to have fun and do whatever she wanted with the space. And in the end, Laura was delighted with the result. The nursery was the nicest room in her apartment. Kat had spared no expense and tried to move on to several other rooms before Laura stopped her.

Kat and Toby were both on call to be with her when she had the baby. By some sort of unspoken truce, they had stopped asking her when she was going to call Adam, because the very mention of his name made Laura cry and it took her a long time to stop.

Laura picked up the briefcase, which held the eighty geometry and calculus tests she had tortured several classes with on this cloudy Friday. At least the kids wouldn't have to worry about trapezoids and proofs over the weekend. In fact, she hadn't given them any homework, just told them to enjoy their weekend. With any luck, the grading would only take her four or five hours, unless she chose to write a lot of comments. If that were the case, the grading would take all day.

Sighing, she hefted the briefcase strap onto her right shoulder and her handbag on her left and started walking. The mild exercise wasn't difficult, but she got winded easily and by the time she got home, she just wanted to crawl into bed and fall asleep.

As was often the case with her after-school walks, the small fears that had incredible staying power flashed in her mind. As always, her thoughts first turned to Adam. She should make an effort to find him, but each time she got close to taking action, something he'd said from one of their first afternoons came back to haunt her. "Are you sure you can't get pregnant?"

He'd trusted her. She'd thought she was telling him the truth.

Kat and William, then Toby and Kevin, had each taken a turn at chastising her for not telling Adam about the baby. Their frustration was palpable. They thought she was being selfish and although they hadn't told her directly, she knew they thought she was enjoying being a martyr.

Nothing could be further from the truth. The real reason she didn't call Adam was that she knew what he would do: turn his back and walk away. None of them had seen the look in his eyes when he talked about his son. They hadn't seen the resoluteness that had haunted her when he'd said he didn't want to have more children. It wasn't as if he would open his arms to a new child and suddenly become the father she knew he had been to his first child. No, behind his words was a wall that he'd erected to ensure he would never love again. No amount of guilt or cajoling would ever change that.

Years from now, she would tell her child about Adam and let the child decide what they wanted to do. She would tell him or her about what their father had gone through and how if they decided to find Adam, he may or may not want to be a part of their life.

It would be a devastating conversation, she knew, but at least being a single parent, her child would know how much she wanted him or her. They would know that the best moment of her life had been when she discovered she was pregnant and that anyone who brought her such bliss couldn't be a mistake.

She continued along the sidewalk past her favorite flower shop. On impulse, she stopped. Sometimes when her thoughts got too far ahead of her she bought some flowers, knowing that by the time they had wilted that her fears would have done the same.

"Hello, Miz Hokensen. Did you have a good day at school?"

"Hi, Mack," she replied and reached for a ten-dollar bouquet of pink tulips. "Yes, but I'm glad it is Friday. How's business?"

"Good, lots of brides coming in and making arrangements for summer weddings. I'm cornering the market on pink peonies, sweet peas, and Pope John Paul II white roses."

Laura smiled and handed her tulips to the older man. She watched as he added another bunch of pink tulips to her bouquet and then wrapped them in green florist paper.

"Mack! You shouldn't do that!" she protested.

He tied a hemp string around the bouquet and held it out to her. "I had a very large shipment, and they won't last the weekend, so you're doing me a favor."

Shaking her head as she handed him money, she said, "You spoil me."

"Thank you for letting me dote on such a pretty lady," he said, handing her the change.

"Thank you, Mack."

"Take good care of yourself, little mama."

"Have a good weekend."

"You too, Miz H."

Laura continued toward home, her hand absently going to the cheap gold wedding ring she'd bought for her left hand. She didn't need to be married to have a baby, but a ring made everyone happier—the other teachers, the students, strangers on the street—so she wore it.

And who was the mysterious Mr. Hokensen? He simply did not exist. The other teachers knew she'd left Leland, they assumed she was having his baby, but Laura said nothing. That was the way she preferred to keep it.

Groundhog Day arrived, promising six more weeks of winter. Laura was erasing her chalkboard after her last class and thinking how nice it would be to put her feet up when she got home. Hearing footsteps on the highly polished floor behind her, she turned and dropped the eraser in surprise. "Leland?"

"Hi, Laura," he said sheepishly, his eyes resting on her swollen stomach.

"What are you doing here?" she asked, stepping toward him, not knowing what to say. She'd last seen him at the gallery opening when he'd suddenly appeared at her side and then gotten up the nerve to ask if he could see her again. She'd turned him down gently, not wanting to create a scene. He'd made several attempts since then to get together and each time, she'd made an excuse not to see him.

"I saw you out walking yesterday," he said softly, giving a sidelong glance at her stomach as he bent to pick up the forgotten eraser.

"This is a surprise," she said, touching the strand of pearls at her throat. They had been his first anniversary present to her and for a moment she wondered if he'd ask for them back.

"I thought you looked…um…pregnant."

"You're not the father," she said, suspicious of his agenda.

"It's that Adam guy's, right?" he asked, not quite meeting her eyes.

"Yes," Laura replied, surprised he had been able to guess the nature of her relationship with Adam.

"I saw the way he was looking at you or should I say trying not to look at you."

"Why are you here, Leland?"

"I just…it made me jealous. I didn't want anyone looking at you that way."

"Why?" she asked with a hint of sarcasm. "You didn't want me, but no one else can have me?"

"Look Laura, I was a stupid idiot to let you go," he said, his eyes rising to meet hers.

"But you did. You seem to like causing me pain."

"For what it is worth, I'm sorry, Laura."

"I'm sorry, too. I'm sorry I was such a disappointment," she added, rubbing the chalk dust from her fingers.

"You were never a disappointment. I was. I was a bad husband to you and a total jerk."

Laura, who had been tidying up her desk, abruptly dropped a heavy textbook with a thud on her desk and stared up at him. She agreed, he was a bad husband and a total jerk.

He continued, "I treated you badly and I want you to know, I miss you. I miss us. I haven't been able to stop thinking about you… not since that night at the gallery…"

"Why? What happened that night?"

"I was proud of you, really proud," he said, and paused. "Look Laura, I know this is short notice, but I'd like to take you to dinner and talk. Would you consider it?"

Gone was the slick lawyer who always was plotting for the advantage. Leland seemed contrite, almost apologetic.

"I'd consider it," she said, picking up her coat indicating she was ready to leave and end the conversation.

A smile broke out across his face. Then he said with enthusiasm she had once loved, "Wonderful!"

He looked almost giddy, and she wondered what had brought on his change of heart.

"How about tonight?"

Did she want to spend her evening with Leland? She knew the curiosity would eat away at her. If she had dinner, it would be over quickly. How could she have been married to him?

"I need to make it an early night. I'm tired, I've had a long week, and I want to be home by seven."

"I'll have you home by seven."

He helped her with her coat, and they left her classroom, walking side by side as they had done for so many years. Outside the school, Leland led her to a brand new Porsche, black with black interior instead of sand. It seemed in his grief over losing her, he'd bought yet another car. He opened the door and made sure she was tucked into the low bucket seat before taking his place beside her.

"Aqua? I've made reservations at several places, whatever you want," he said.

She didn't want to revisit the old memories of the special restaurant where they'd celebrated each wedding anniversary.

"I think that is a little more than I had in mind," she said, thinking it would be more memories, more emotions, and more pain from the past.

"I'll take you anywhere you want to go."

McDonalds would be an interesting choice, drive up window and all, but she knew such a suggestion would start a fight.

"I feel like fish and chips from McCormick's."

"Okay," he said, but she could tell it wasn't one of his top choices. The real reason she'd picked the fish house down by the wharf was that she could afford a reasonable entree and the cab fare home if Leland irritated her.

They sat in a dark booth. Leland nervously sipped a Bombay martini and looked uncomfortable, his eyes looking at everything and everyone, but her.

She sipped a soda through a straw, a habit he detested.

Laura enjoyed seeing him so unnerved and wondered if it was the pregnancy or the idea that she had survived without him.

"I think about us, wonder what might have happened," he said, breaking the uncomfortable silence.

"I don't think about us at all." She let her words sink in.

"I find that hard to believe, we were married ten years."

"Nine years, seven months, and five days until I learned of your betrayal. You know I hoped you'd take me to Paris for our tenth wedding anniversary. I was going to hint at it, but then I got the feeling that if you went to Paris that it wouldn't be with me."

"Laura." He didn't chide her, but he definitely wanted to stop this topic, so she dug her heels in and went for the jugular.

"No," she said, shaking her head and placing her hands soothingly on her stomach to calm her growing turmoil. "You invited me to come out with you, you get to hear this. You were cruel and mean to me. You said horrible things and yet I stayed. I don't know how I could have sunk so low to stay, but I did. Thankfully, I found my self-respect and did the only thing I should have done the moment you uttered your first cruel word to me. I left."

"I was an ass. I made one of the oldest mistakes in the books. Is that what you wanted to hear?"

"Yes," she replied, and nodded her head so there could be no denying her feelings on the matter.

"Laura, I don't want to fight. I didn't come here to fight."

"To what do I owe this sudden, if not predictably short-lived, interest in me, in us?"

"You have a right to be angry," he said.

"I am still a little mad at you, but I'm not sorry I left. You threw away the relationship. I accepted that and moved on. It wasn't easy, but I found happiness. For a few brief months this summer I was happier than I'd ever been. If you hadn't been such a jerk, I'd have never known I could be so happy. Then this wonderful thing happened. This miracle. I'm going to have a baby. With you, this would have never happened." She rubbed her belly for emphasis.

"That Adam guy," Leland said, his voice laced with anger.

"You don't have the right to be mad at him. Leland, we weren't good together. I couldn't give you what you wanted. I used to think if I was sexier or lost weight that I'd recapture what we somehow lost. But now I know that you couldn't give me what I wanted either."

"Laura, maybe it isn't too late."

She laughed, couldn't help it. And surprisingly, it didn't sound bitter, just surprised.

"You don't want that any more than I do. If this little evening is going to work at all, we've got to talk to each other as what we are, acquaintances who share a past."

"Are you kidding me?" he asked, genuinely surprised.

"Did you think because I'm pregnant I'd try to lure you in to being my husband and a father to my baby?"

"Is that an option?" He was serious.

A quiver of something she couldn't define slowly rolled along her skin, making her shiver. He didn't make her wait long.

"I miss you. I've been thinking a lot about this. We could have a fresh start. We could pretend that you were on an extended vacation. We could even tell everyone the baby is mine. I would raise it as if it were my own."

"Just pretend the last year of our lives never happened? Just rewind our lives?" she asked incredulously, the shiver becoming a chill.

"People split up and get back together all the time."

"What about all the other women? Notice, I used the plural form of the word because although I know about Amber, I'm pretty sure there were others."

Leland's face turned red, a sure sign she'd crossed some invisible line. "Let's have a reality check. You know how hard it was for me with all of that baby stuff. You weren't the woman I married. You were hyped up on hormones, you gained weight, and all you talked about was a baby. It was like you had tunnel vision. I was an afterthought. Our sex life was like taking out the garbage. It was a chore I didn't want to have to do. I hated you for ruining us."

She started to open her mouth to speak, but he cut her off.

"I'm not finished. Now you're a single, unwed mother who lives in a dumpy apartment. You make a teacher's salary and think you can raise a baby on your own. Time to grow up, Laura. I'm your best hope at a future. You should be begging me to take you back."

Laura was too stunned to be angry. The bile rose in her throat, threatening to gag her. The smell of the food on the other tables was making her nauseous. All of the seafood smelled rotten and old. It all was chum and she was on a swaying boat, getting more seasick by the second. Sweat had broken out on her forehead.

"What? Are you going to be sick?" Leland asked, his face scrunching up into a scowl. In that moment, she remembered every time he had scowled at her for making what he considered to be a mistake, or maybe he didn't like the outfit she was wearing, or how she had done her hair. Time to get away from this abusive prick once and for all.

"About to be. Excuse me," she said as she stood, grabbed her purse and made a quick beeline for the bathroom. Five minutes later, as she got her coat out of coat check, and then bribed the maître d' with a precious ten dollar bill to tell Leland she'd left. The caveat was that he had to wait for five minutes. To get the crying pregnant woman out of his restaurant entrance, he probably would have paid her. She didn't give him a chance, nor did she give Leland a chance to catch up with her.

There was a cab waiting at the curb in front of the restaurant and she grabbed it.

As she sat in the cab and watched the fare mount as they hit the tail end of rush hour traffic, she asked herself a question as she wiped her tears on the sleeve of her coat.

What have we learned today?

First, Leland painting an unflattering picture of her and yet offering to take her back so that he could raise Adam's baby made her sick to her stomach. Second, she had yet to feel the depths of pain that would come from his verbal assault. She was an over-thinker, and over the next few days Leland's painful words would only sink deeper and deeper into every cell of her body. And third, between the bribe to the maître d', the coat check, and the cab fare, she was out almost thirty bucks. Thirty dollars she really couldn't spare, because part of what Leland had said was true. She was ill prepared for her future. Thirty dollars bought diapers or helped pay for all the little extras she hadn't budgeted for.

Over the next few days, Laura felt the pain of Leland's words. Although she had long ago tried and convinced herself of every flaw and fault that had led to the demise of her marriage, Leland had touched on a couple of things she hadn't considered. Perhaps he had forgotten that he was the one who had pushed her to try everything she could to have a baby. He'd written checks to cover every procedure. He'd even once told her that all she needed to do was to show up for whatever doctor's appointment or procedure was next on the docket.

For Leland, love equated to money. Writing checks and buying things counted for love. When she'd left, he'd made her give back her engagement ring. Because once her love for him was gone, he'd retaliated the only way he'd known how; he'd taken things from her. If she went back to him, she had no doubt that her original ring and many other things would be waiting for her. But love, for her, could never be a thing.

Curiously, the pain didn't last or go quite as long or as deep as it once had. Thoughts of Adam and their baby and how they'd made their baby easily took her mind off Leland.

For Valentine's Day, Laura decided on a red dress Kat had given her. Looking in the mirror on the back of her bathroom door, she thought she looked like a big red barn. There was no denying it; she had gotten bigger in the last couple of weeks. Did she have feet? How, months earlier, could she have ever thought she had large ankles? Now, with the water retention, she really did have large ankles.

She slipped into a pair of black patent flats and checked her make-up. What would Adam say if he could see her now? Nothing good. She finally was the middle aged, overweight, dumpy school-teacher she'd always feared becoming.

The baby moved inside her, and she forgot the self-deprecating internal conversation. Her baby, Adam's baby, was hiccupping and it made her smile. She rubbed her stomach, gave the baby a pat for good measure and left for school.

Fifteen minutes later, she opened the door to her classroom and stopped, a familiar unease giving her pause. There was a huge bouquet of long-stemmed, dark red roses on her desk in a heavy crystal vase. She considered that the vase was probably worth more than the three-dozen blossoms. No doubt the crystal would turn out to be Waterford or Lalique.

She didn't want to look at the card, she knew whose name would be on it. The real question would be, would his secretary have filled out the card or would he have done it himself? Did she really care? No, she decided, and checked her feelings. Nothing. She was numb to the Leland effect. Numb was better than angry any day.

If the vase was valuable, she might be able to sell it on eBay and add to the stockpile of money she was setting aside for the baby's arrival. It would no doubt make up for the thirty dollars she'd lost almost two weeks earlier during her horrible evening with Leland.

Halfway to the roses, she could smell the heavy perfume coming off the blossoms. It was a different scent than the sweet and spicy blush white roses Adam had left on her doorstep. How odd, she thought, that she would be able to differentiate one scent of rose from another.

Like Leland himself, these roses had a fakeness bred into them. They were born with an unnatural charm, manipulated to resemble something that was genuine. They were hothouse roses, temperamental, easily irritated and not quite real.

Shaking her head, she picked up the card and separated it from its envelope.

*Laura,*

*I'm sorry we quarreled. I'm thinking about you today. Please call me so that we can finish the conversation about our future.*

*Regards, Leland.*

Laura ripped the card in half and then again and again until she had confetti pieces. She threw them in the garbage can. And here she'd thought she had finished with morning sickness. But the combination of the flowers and the note were enough to set her off. By the time the students filtered in, she was positively green.

By the end of first period, she couldn't take the scent any longer. She asked one of her students to move the roses to a table in the back corner of the room, as far away from her as they could get. Still, they were in her line of sight. The hypocrisy of Leland sending her flowers was laughable.

When the final bell rang, she quickly finished up at her desk and headed for home, giving the roses one last look. If she were lucky, someone would see them in her classroom and steal them.

Valentine's Day had always been her favorite holiday. Her parents used to give her sweet bouquets of small pink sweetheart roses from the time she was a little girl. After they died, she'd bought them for herself. When she married Leland, he had raised the ante, sending her three-dozen red roses. For her part, she would decorate their house with big red hearts and red streamers and cook something very special. It used to be one of her favorite nights of the year.

But last year, it was one of the worst.

Last year, she'd suspected Leland was cheating when she received the same flower arrangement as always, but this time there was a card that should have gone to someone else. *Baby, you're hot. Can't wait until Friday. —Leland.*

First, he hadn't told her she was hot in years. In fact, he'd done everything in his power to make sure she knew that he thought she was a frigid ice cube. And second, Friday was Leland's new poker night.

Laura had said nothing about the card. She'd waited patiently, done her research, and found the evidence she needed in the form of a credit card receipt. A week after Valentine's Day, she'd confronted him. That's when things turned nasty.

The unpleasant memories, which summed up the final days and weeks of her marriage, swirled in her mind as she walked on this windy evening toward home. Every store window she passed on the way back to her brownstone was filled with displays of red. Red flowers, red lingerie, red heart-shaped boxes filled with candy, and even red tablecloths and bouquets in restaurant windows.

Thoughts turned to Adam. Where was he today? Who was he sharing his day with? Sometime in the last few weeks, her fear of telling Adam about the baby had morphed to worrying that if she told him about the baby, he'd tell her he'd fallen in love with someone else.

Before she could go over this latest, dark scenario in her mind, she started up the steps to her brownstone and found Leland waiting at the top of the landing. He smiled as she looked up at him. She wondered how long it had taken for one of the firm detectives to discover where she lived.

"Hello, Laura, happy Valentine's Day."

Sighing, feeling annoyed more than anything else, she contemplated turning around and going back the way she'd come. Maybe she'd stop and have dinner at one of the small cafés because eating dinner alone in a public place on Valentine's Day was more appealing than interacting with Leland. But she was tired and needed to pee, but then, she always needed to pee these days.

Leland was in a black suit with a red silk tie. The red silk tie she'd bought him three years ago for Valentine's Day. When she'd given it to him, he'd thought it was too flashy, but obviously next to the new Porsche it paled in comparison.

"What are you doing here?" she asked.

He stood and walked carefully down the steps toward her. "You know we've spent the last twelve Valentine's Days together. It appears to be a habit I can't break."

She didn't move, just watched him. "Well, you know, I think the divorce broke the habit for me."

The words hit the mark, the tentative smile falling from his face.

"We can change that."

"You're certifiable," she said.

"Here I am offering to take care of you and all you can do is insult me."

"If you don't like it, feel free to leave."

"What will it take to get you to listen to reason? Laura, you can't do this on your own. You need me."

"Yes, I can do this," Laura said. "And for the record, I don't have to prove anything to you."

"You know something Laura, I've really had it with you," Leland said, stepping up to her, his face inches from hers. She could see and feel the rage that he had for her. Yet again, she wasn't doing what he wanted to do.

"You're too close, step back," she ordered.

"You don't tell me what to do. You're nothing without me," he said, stepping closer, the heat from his skin radiating onto her.

A door slammed shut as Toby appeared on the landing with Kevin right behind him.

Toby spoke first. "Is there a problem, Laura?"

"No," she said, stepping around Leland and walking up the stairs toward Toby and Kevin. "Leland was just leaving. And if he shows up again, I'm calling the police."

"How dare you threaten me," Leland warned.

"Why wait?" Kevin asked, pulling out his cell phone. "Let's call them now. I heard him threaten you."

"Is this the way you want it to be?" Leland asked, as his hands balled into fists. "Because if I walk away, you're on your own. I won't come back."

Laura looked down at him from her perch on the steps. "Is that a promise? No more abuse from you, wow, how will I ever be able to make it? I think I'll be just fine."

Toby and Kevin snickered.

Leland kicked the potted plant next to the stairway, turned, and stalked away.

Kevin and Toby circled around Laura to see if she was okay.

"Let's get you inside," Kevin offered.

"No, you guys are going out, I'll be fine."

"Our reservation isn't for an hour, we have the time," Toby said.

Reluctantly, Laura let them escort her into her apartment.

Once inside, she said, "You know the real irony? I never want to see Leland again and he keeps showing up. With Adam, I fear seeing him because of his reaction to the baby, but I want to see him. I want to see him more than anything. I'm really messed up."

"No," Kevin said, "You're just in love with Adam."

# CHAPTER EIGHTEEN

Two weeks before her due date in March, Laura stood before her fourth period geometry class, explaining how to proof a parallelogram, when the first contraction hit. She stopped mid-sentence as the excited murmurs of her student audience filled her classroom.

"It's okay, I'm okay, just something going on there," she replied, wanting to ignore what was happening. Then her water broke, a trickle that dribbled down her leg, but the fifteen-year-olds reacted with lightning speed. Chaos ensued as students gasped, groaned, and started to panic in unison.

One of the students pulled a cell phone from his jeans.

"Jake, is that a cell phone in my class?" she asked. "No photos posted online, got it?"

"Yes, Mrs. Hokensen," he said nervously.

"Good. Use it. Call 911. I'm going into labor," she said, as she groaned in pain. Another student helped her into a desk chair.

"Thank you, everybody," she said, as the paramedics arrived with the stretcher. "No homework tonight."

During the ride to the hospital, she began to panic. The baby was early. What if something was wrong?

The hospital was mass confusion, and her perspective from the gurney with everything flying by made it feel surreal. And in that moment, she not only wanted Adam at her side and chastised herself for not ensuring that he would be there, but she also missed her mother with a longing she hadn't felt in years. Every memory of her parents and how much they loved her played like a movie in her head. Would they be happy with the choices she'd made? What would they think of this baby? The idea that they would never know about her baby burned a place so deep, she couldn't reach it.

"She's a high-risk pregnancy."

She could hear Dr. Mallory conferring with another doctor in the hall outside her birthing suite and it scared her all the more. She wanted to yell, "I can hear you."

The door to her room opened and Toby and Kevin walked in.

"Little mama!" they both chimed in unison.

"I'm so glad you're here," she said and began to cry.

"No tears, darlin'," Kevin said. "You're about to be a mommy."

"I'm worried. I should have told Adam. If something happens…"

"Nothing will happen," Toby said.

"But if something happens, don't tell him. I don't want to add to his pain."

The men exchanged a look that included an eye roll.

Kevin said, "It's like a bad soap opera! Do you hear this?"

Toby nodded, "They must have her on some really good drugs."

"We're just lucky it was her friend who became the actress and not her. She doesn't have a flair for the dramatic."

"True that, honey."

"Both of you, shut up. I haven't had any damn drugs. Damn it, I'm serious!"

They laughed at her, and for reasons she couldn't explain, it was impossible to stay mad at them. Crossing her arms, she said, "Fine. Mock me."

They laughed harder.

The contractions continued for the next few hours. Laura's only satisfaction came from squeezing both Kevin and Toby's hands to the point they complained that she was breaking their bones.

At one point, they heard a commotion in the hallway and a minute later, Kat breezed into the birthing suite. Her long, black coat flowed around her like a cape over a bright red suit. She sized up the room and her audience quickly.

Removing her Chanel sunglasses, she looked at the very starstruck Kevin and Toby and narrowed her eyes.

"Kat, you made it!"

"Of course, darling," she said, leaning down to kiss Laura's cheek. "William is parking the car. He almost got a speeding ticket, the poor darling. When I explained to the nice young officer that I was giving my loving husband a blowjob while driving to relax him and that it distracted him instead and I was quite sorry, the man just could not write him a ticket. Not true about the blowjob this time, but he doesn't need to know that."

"I'm speechless," Toby said to Kevin.

Kevin nodded.

"Hello boys, so good to see you again."

"You know, in all the excitement of the gallery opening, we never got a chance to talk," Kevin said, his eyes glazing, a quality of star-struck behavior that Laura had witnessed before. This was all she needed.

"Down, boys. I'm Laura's best friend first, an Academy Award-winning actress second. If you boys don't get over it and remember to focus on Laura, I'll toss you out on your cute butts. Got it?"

They both nodded, awestruck.

Three hours later, despite Laura's worst fears, Samuel William Stark was born a healthy seven-pound, seven-ounce baby boy. He had a wisp of dark hair the color of his father's and bore a striking and undeniable resemblance to Adam.

Everyone cried. And then hugged.

"He's really beautiful," Kat said.

"And he is definitely Adam's son," William said.

"As if there were any doubt," Kat chided.

Kevin nodded and smiled, "Another great work of art, Laura."

Toby agreed, offering, "He'll be a heartbreaker."

Just like his father, Laura thought and smiled sadly, "Hear that Sam? Your Aunt Kat, Uncle William, Uncle Toby, and Uncle Kevin think you're beautiful."

The next day, William and Kat took Laura and the baby to Tranquility. For the next six weeks, they doted on Laura and Sam, hinting they might try for a baby of their own. Sam had a sweet disposition and enjoyed being the center of attention.

"Where do you think he went, Kat?" Laura asked one afternoon, as they sat in Kat's favorite sitting room and took turns holding the baby.

"What do you mean, isn't he in Cairo?"

"No, I tried to call in December, but he'd left. In fact, I found out that Stark International Hotels sold the hotel in early November. I don't know where he went from there."

"Why didn't you tell me earlier? William will find him," Kat said, as she smiled down at Sam.

Laura knew they had the resources and wherewithal to make it happen. "I have to tell him. I don't know how I'll handle it if he gets angry or doesn't want to see the baby."

"Well darling, you've got to ask the question to get the answer."

"Could I have messed up my life any more than this?"

"How can you look at this beautiful baby and say such a thing?" Kat asked, lifting up Sam, who smiled on cue.

"I don't regret him for a minute. But doesn't it seem ironic? Ten months ago, in this room, I was pouring out my problems to you and then Adam walked in."

"And handed you his handkerchief."

"And I handed him my heart," Laura said.

"Laura, it's going to be fine. We will find him." She put an arm around Laura and rocked her gently.

Later that evening, as they sat at dinner, William turned to Laura, who met his concerned gaze and waited. He reached out and patted her arm. "Kat filled me in. I'll give his cousin a call after dinner and ask him for Adam's number. Then you can decide what you want to do."

"That sounds simple enough," she said, and placed her fork on her plate, unable to eat.

An hour later, they found Laura rocking the baby to sleep in the new nursery, a room Kat had happily redone after finding out about Laura's pregnancy. She gone as far as to knock a hole in an existing wall and remodel the space to make sure the nursery was connected to what had once been Adam's room.

Laura put the baby in the crib and quietly shut the door.

She looked from William to Kat, two serious faces and asked, "My god, is he dead?"

"No darling, he's in Dubai," Kat said, putting a comforting arm around her.

"Dubai?"

"He's running the new Stark International Hotel Dubai," William answered.

Laura had read a Vanity Fair article about Dubai. It was the Las Vegas of the Middle East. It was chock full of wonderful career opportunities, and obviously he'd taken advantage of them. Since he'd left her, he'd lived in two different countries. Laura never felt further away from him than she did at this particular moment in time. Then she remembered her private benefactor in the Middle East and hoped it wasn't just a coincidence.

"Alex just told me he arrived in January and was helping to get the place up and running. It just opened."

"Dubai?" she asked again, not believing what she was hearing. "Did you get a number?"

"Yes. It's daytime there. You could call now," he said, handing her a slip of paper. "I got the country code, just pick up the phone and dial."

Before she lost her nerve, Laura walked across the room and picked up the phone. Over her shoulder she asked, "Please stay. I don't know how this is going to go."

"Sure honey," Kat replied, as William wrapped an arm around his wife.

Laura dialed the number and waited. A woman answered in perfectly accented English, "It is a lovely day at Stark International Hotel Dubai. How may I direct your call?"

"I need to speak to Adam Stark."

"One moment please…"

A long stretch of Arabian elevator music that sounded both exotic and other worldly began to play, which was interrupted by a feminine voice that could only be described as sensual, offering additional snippets about the hotel.

"The crown jewel of the Stark International Hotels, the Stark Dubai is a luxury experience for the senses…"

She was connected to another office.

"Mr. Stark's office," a pleasant voice answered.

"I need to speak with Mr. Stark."

"Whom shall I say is calling?"

"This is Laura Hokensen."

She was put back on hold for at least two of the longest minutes of her life as the Arabian elevator music continued and the sensual voice spoke of more amenities.

"Indulge your sensual side at the Spa Ocean, located on the twenty-second floor. The Spa Ocean uses actual filtered seawater from the Arabian Gulf that has been further enriched with natural occurring minerals…"

The pleasant voice returned. "I'm afraid Mr. Stark is unavailable."

"When will he be available?"

"May I ask the nature of your business with Mr. Stark?"

"It's personal," Laura said.

"I'm afraid Mr. Stark is extremely busy. I've been instructed to hold his calls."

"Would you please tell him Laura Hokensen called and he can reach me at Tranquility? It is important."

"Yes ma'am." Without another word the call was disconnected.

She turned to William and Kat and said, "He doesn't want to talk to me."

"You don't know that," Kat said.

"You don't know that he doesn't," Laura countered. "That woman couldn't wait to get me off the phone. It was like she knew not to let me through."

Kat hugged her. "You'll try again tomorrow. If that doesn't work William will call. I have an old email for him. We could try it."

"If we can't get through, I'll call his cousin again," William offered.

Laura tried to call Adam seven more times, only to be told the same message by the same woman time after time.

Frustrated, she decided to try a different approach. She wrote him a letter, working on draft after draft, second-guessing every word and phrase. Thinking it would be best to ease into the news, she found herself getting more direct with each rewrite. Picturing him opening the letter and reading the news, she cringed. Short of flying to Dubai, this was rapidly becoming her best option without involving a bunch of other people.

*Hello Adam,*

*I hope this letter finds you well. I've been calling you, but your secretary says that you are busy and not accepting calls. I've tried every day for a week and have had no luck, so I've decided to write you this letter.*

*I have news that I would prefer to be delivering in person. Please forgive me.*

*Last fall, after we'd been together at Tranquility, I discovered I was pregnant. You must understand, I wasn't supposed to be able to get pregnant. I was told that I was essentially barren. My doctor doesn't know how I was able to conceive, but he is now convinced that although I have fertility issues, my ex-husband must have been incompatible with me, which is why we weren't able to conceive. I know this is more information than you want to know, but it is important to me that you understand that getting pregnant came as much a surprise to me as it will come to you.*

*Four weeks ago, I gave birth to a baby boy. He weighed seven pounds, seven ounces. He is beautiful and I love him with all of my heart. I know that you owe me nothing and if you would prefer not to be a part of Sam's life, I will understand. But if a week from now or a year, or even five years, you want to know about your son, we will be here.*

*I'm staying at Tranquility for two more weeks and then I'll be going back to my job. I'm doing well. Sam and I will be fine. We have a nice place to live and lots of friends who are very supportive.*

*Again, I'm incredibly sorry to have to tell you about this in this way. I hope you can forgive me. Thank you for this wonderful gift. You will always have a place in my heart.*

*Love,*
*Laura*

When she was satisfied with the final draft, she drove the letter to the post office herself. Having used Tranquility stationary, she hoped marking it "Private" would get it directly to Adam. After she attached the airmail stamps, she gave the envelope a pat for luck and sent it off. She only hoped Adam would read the letter with compassion and not be too angry with her.

Returning to Tranquility, she found an unnaturally worried Kat waiting for her.

"What?" Laura asked, "Did he call?"

"No honey, I sent him an email yesterday. I didn't want to mention it to you until I heard back. I just asked him how he was doing. It bounced back this afternoon. The email was undeliverable."

"Or blocked," Laura said.

"I'm sure that Stark International Hotels has very strong firewalls and…with the move to Dubai, he probably has a new email."

But Laura immediately thought the worst. Adam obviously wanted to block out everything about last summer. It was her own damn fault for waiting too long to contact him.

Kat hugged her and said, "The letter will get to him, I know it. In the meantime, we will call his cousin and get a different email."

"No, I've waited this long, I can wait a little longer," Laura replied. "I want him to get the letter. I think it is more personal than an email."

Despite Kat and William's protests, Laura returned to San Francisco two weeks later in mid-May to finish out the school year. She needed to get back to her life and most of all she needed a distraction. Kat and William promised to give Adam her number if he called, but Laura knew he wouldn't. He'd moved on and didn't want to look back. She wasn't sure she could blame him.

She took Sam to the best daycare she could afford, the Duckyland. They treated Sam well and she could almost let go of the panic she felt every time she dropped him off each morning.

She began to fully realize the harsh reality of caring for a child as a single mother. Selling her paintings had eased some of the financial burden, but taking care of a newborn took its toll. Each day was filled from the moment she awoke to the moment her head hit the pillow. She looked and felt perpetually tired.

Every couple of days Toby and Kevin would arrive and spend a few hours, giving her a much-needed break. A couple of times a week, a deliveryman would arrive on her doorstep with dinner from one of the most expensive restaurants in town, courtesy of Kat and William.

Despite her hectic schedule, one thought loomed in the back of her mind. What had happened to her letter?

Wearing an Armani suit the color of crème caramel, which had been tailored to fit him perfectly in Rome, Adam looked out at the view from his office on the seventieth floor of the Stark International Hotel Dubai. Even through the tempered glass he could feel the late afternoon heat radiating against the building. The billion-dollar view, which included the Palm Islands, was mesmerizing. As far as he could see, large amounts of money were being spent to turn a lump of sand into a high-stakes business hub and ultimate resort destination. He was glad Alex had gambled and gotten them in on this highly profitable action.

He still couldn't believe the twists and turns his life had taken in the last couple of years. He'd been through so much, yet it had led him to this new life.

Walking over to one of the framed watercolors he'd bought from the gallery handling Laura's work, he smiled sadly. It was his favorite, the little beach cove he'd taken Laura to. They'd made love on a blanket under the warm sun. It had been one of the best days of his life. Looking at the painting now elicited a rush of bittersweet memories he had yet to begin to deal with. *Laura. Laura. Laura.* She must hate him by now.

He was an idiot. She meant so much more to him than he'd been able to admit last summer. Sometimes it was so simple. Sometimes timing didn't matter—when a person knew, they just knew. Love had its own timetable. What was he going to do about it? He had to try something, even if she was with Leland. He had to tell her how he felt. Let the chips fall where they may.

His overly officious assistant, Lily, a darkly exotic looking woman of Eurasian descent, who'd tried unsuccessfully to get his full attention since the moment he had arrived, entered his office, and placed his mail on the highly polished desk. Thanking her, but otherwise ignoring her and the mail, he went back to work on his month-end reports. Alex would be pleased. The Stark International Hotel Dubai was already proving to be a very profitable enterprise with endless possibilities. In the last three weeks alone, they'd seen an eighteen percent increase in their restaurant profits. Use of their private fleet of luxury cars had doubled and more guests were opting to arrive in style via helicopter to their fiftieth floor heliport. The twenty-story Waterfall of Iridescence, which dominated the lobby, had cost more than they had anticipated. However, hotel guests and tourists alike watched it from three different observation platforms twenty-four hours a day.

Their staff ratio of three-to-one was a little low, and he was thinking of expanding service in all areas. Some of their competitors had an eight-to-one ratio and he was feeling a little concerned that they might lose client loyalty for lack of service.

After he sent his report to Alex, he thought of how he would spend his evening, another lonely night in his luxury penthouse suite. Maybe his cousin was right. If he couldn't run to Laura and tell her how he felt, he had to let her go and finally move on. It might be time to start looking for distractions, not that he'd had any stomach for anything in the last few months. Well, except for Laura.

His cell rang. Alex. What new fresh hell was this? The reports were good. Very good, in fact. The family plane and their choice

227 of Milanese tailors were safe. And it was too early in Portland for

of Milanese tailors were safe. And it was too early in Portland for Alex to be calling unless something bad had happened.

"Alex, what is it?"

"Hi cousin, nice to hear your voice, too."

"I'm sorry, I'm just surprised you are calling me. Isn't it early in Portland?"

"Very, but not all of us are sleeping well. I just got an early morning call from my friend William Russell at Tranquility, you know, Kat's husband. He was kind of mad at you, upset in fact. Up early, not sleeping kind of mad. Couldn't wait another minute, had to tell me about it, damn the time, he had things to say."

"Is everything alright?" And by that, he meant with Laura.

"This Laura person you had a little something with last summer, was it serious?"

Adam felt the concern flood every nerve of his body. "Is she hurt? Is she okay?"

"I think she is fine, but she really wants to talk to you. William said that it was important and that you should call her, like, yesterday. She has been trying to call, but Lily, your assistant, won't let her through. A few weeks ago she even sent you a letter, but she doesn't know if you got it because she hasn't heard from you."

Alex glanced at the pile of stacked mail. "Oh shit, a rather large stack of mail was just put on my desk, hang on."

The last time he'd seen Laura was in front of the gallery with Leland. He had to wonder how that was going, did Leland finally realize how important Laura was? He should have gone into the gallery. It was a mistake he'd regret for years to come.

The postmark on the familiar Tranquility letter was almost three weeks old. He wondered how long it had been sitting on Lily's desk. No doubt she'd been wondering if she should open it herself. Whenever she saw anything marked personal, her curiosity was piqued. Her need to protect him from the outside world and be his personal gatekeeper was starting to get on his nerves. He'd discussed the issue with her once already and thought that if there was a second time, he might have to reassign her. Having her fired was out of the question, as her father was the head sommelier at their most profitable restaurant in the hotel, the Oasis.

The constant heat and sunshine in Dubai were also losing their charm. Not that either had any charm to begin with.

Pulling the envelope from the pile, Adam's hands stilled. Above the Tranquility logo, Laura had neatly penned her name.

"Oh shit, I just found it, hang on," he said dropping the phone noisily on his desk.

With a new urgency, he opened the large envelope and shook out the contents. A small watercolor, not much larger than the size of a postcard fell onto the desk. Laura had sent him a watercolor of the guest cottage. Their cottage, where he'd been happier than he'd ever thought possible. The rendition was good and knowing Laura sent it made his heart beat faster in his chest. How had she found out he was in Dubai? Was she still with Leland? If she was at Tranquility again, that meant she probably wasn't with Leland. Could she forgive him for the way he left? How could she forgive him when he hadn't forgiven himself?

Along with the watercolor was a heavy cream-colored envelope with his name written on the front. He carefully opened the envelope as if its contents were a prized possession, unfolded the sheet of paper, read the first couple of sentences, and had to sit to keep from falling.

"Alex, oh shit, holy hell, I've got to fly to San Francisco right now."

"What is it?" Alex asked.

Adam read the letter two more times, once out loud to Alex.

"Wow, what a surprise," Alex said, and then added, "Congratulations."

"I need to leave."

"Wait, let's talk this through."

"I'll call you back," Adam said, hanging up.

At the top of his lungs, he yelled, "LILY!"

Lily appeared, "If there is nothing else, I'm going to leave for the evening, Mr. Stark." She stood before him, posing like a cat ready to spring.

"Has Laura Hokensen from the United States tried to call?" he asked, barely controlling his anger.

She hesitated for a brief moment of strategic thought and then answered, "I've never heard the name before, Mr. Stark."

"Okay, let's try this again…has anyone called from a place called Tranquility?"

More hesitation, then she said, "Maybe."

"Damn it, this is not twenty questions! When?" he asked, wanting to jump over the desk and strangle her scrawny little neck.

"Today, I think…maybe earlier this week. Someone named William Russman."

"Russell. Why didn't you put him through?"

"Because I didn't know him. I only talk to people I know," she answered defensively.

"For the record, I do know him. Did he say what he wanted?"

"He said he needed to speak to you, but I told him I was afraid Mr. Stark was extremely busy. I'd been instructed to hold your calls," she said, with a casual shrug of her shoulders.

Adam put the baby news out of his mind. He immediately had an image of shoving Lily off of the Waterfall. Barely controlling his temper, he said, "Funny, Laura writes that's what you said to her, too. So, you lied earlier by chance, or did it slip your mind that she called?"

"I don't recall ever speaking to a woman by that name. You receive many calls each day, sir. I do my best to make sure you aren't bothered with unnecessary individuals who would undoubtedly waste your time."

"She called every day for a week almost a month ago. That must have stood out to you."

"I just don't recall, sir," Lily replied.

"Get out, you're fired," he ordered, he didn't care about her damn sommelier father, she had messed with Laura. He picked up his cell phone, wondering what time it was back in San Francisco. Phone in hand, he paused. He had to think this through.

At the bottom of the letter, Laura had given him her address and phone number. He recognized the phone number, he had it memorized. He glanced at his desk clock. It was eleven hours earlier in San Francisco, which would make it six in the morning. Was this the kind of conversation to have over the phone? No. Especially not when he was this upset. A conversation of this magnitude should be had in person, face to face. How could she not have told him? How could she have kept such a secret? How could those around her have done the same?

He punched in a number he knew by heart and waited.

Alex answered on the third ring with a muffled, "About time you called me back."

"We need to talk about this," Adam said.

"Hi, Adam," a sleepy Daisy said in the background. Adam felt bad for waking the pregnant woman.

"Tell Daisy I said hello and sorry for waking her."

"Adam is sorry for waking you, my darling," Alex said to his wife and then, "Let me guess, you want to fly to San Francisco to see this Laura and maybe your baby in person."

"What?" Daisy said in background, sounding more awake. "Did you say 'baby'? Did this Laura person have Adam's baby?"

"Her name is Laura. She isn't this Laura person. Got it? I need to see her."

"Now things are making sense," Alex said.

"What do you mean?"

"Before William's call this morning, he called about a month ago, wanted your number, and said it was important, but wouldn't say why. I thought it was something about their house from this summer. I didn't think about Kat's friend."

"You didn't think to tell me?" Adam asked, his anger finding a new direction.

"Well, I'm rather busy running the company and I didn't think it was a big deal. He did try me again last week."

"Great. Everyone knows about the baby but me."

"I didn't know. I'd have told you. Did I hear correctly, a little boy?" Alex asked.

"A boy named Sam."

"It's a blessing, Adam. Really. Sam Stark has a nice ring to it."

"Oh Adam, I'm so happy for you," Daisy said in the background. "I can't wait to meet Laura and baby Sam."

"I'm not sure of anything at the moment."

"Okay, I understand, you're in shock."

"I have to see Laura and make arrangements for her and the baby. She must hate me."

"Laura. Interesting. Is her name Laura Hokensen?"

"Yes? What? Why?" Adam asked feeling left behind, far away from everyone and everything.

"Wait, is she an artist?"

"Yes, and a schoolteacher, why?"

"I saw her paintings of Tranquility written up in a magazine. If I recall correctly and I think I do, she is a very beautiful woman. I showed the article to Daisy, now she wants a Laura Hokensen original. Do you think you could work some magic?"

Adam was speechless for a moment, then: "You're such a bastard. I have a child with her. I don't know if she will even speak to me. She could be married to someone else, like her fucking ex-husband. He could be raising my child."

Alex laughed. "I'll ignore that because life has punched you right in the kisser, but in a good way. I like this turn of events. Fun stuff. What kind of arrangements are you talking about with pretty Laura and the baby?"

Adam didn't like Alex acting so familiar and using Laura's name as if he knew her.

"I don't know," Adam said. "I thought she was back with her ex, but it doesn't sound like it. I fucking hope not. Hell, I haven't figured it all out."

"You love her, don't you?"

Adam didn't think, he just said, "Yes."

"Well, as you've always said, when you know, you know. Go do the right thing."

"I will because I do know. I'm leaving as soon as I can get on a plane."

"Wait a minute," Alex said, recognition dawning. "What about the media event you booked for later this week?"

"Who gives a shit? My press staff at the hotel can handle it."

Alex swore and then, "Do you think you could put off this reunion for a few days? This press thing has taken months to put together. You could probably use a cooling off period. I'll send the plane, so you don't have to fly commercial."

"No, I'll be on a commercial flight within the hour. I need to get to Laura," Adam said, suddenly mad at his cousin because he was available and had given him the perfect opportunity. "If you push me on this, I'll resign. In fact, why don't I save you the time? I quit."

"Shit. Adam would you just relax. Let's not get crazy here… take a deep breath."

"I don't want to be thinking about this hotel while I'm in San Francisco. I want to focus completely on Laura and the baby, no mistakes. No calls and no emails. I'm off the grid."

"How much time do you need?"

"I have no idea."

"Adam, please…let's talk in a week. I won't accept your resignation, just take some time and get this ironed out. Your hotel is doing really well."

"Don't call me, I'll call you."

"All right," Alex agreed, but Adam could hear the frustration in his voice.

"And Alex?"

"Yes?"

"Don't tell anyone about this."

"Too late, Daisy is smiling, no doubt planning your wedding or a family baby shower."

"Both!" Daisy yelled in the background.

# CHAPTER NINETEEN

aura walked slowly home from work with the baby in his carrier balanced in her hands. Sam was a sweet child, eight weeks old, and she was thankful every day for his easy disposition, but damn if he wasn't heavy. When she glanced down at him, he smiled back at her, warming her heart. He was going to have his father's warm brown eyes, she was sure of it. As it was, he was a mini-Adam.

It was Tuesday. A few more days and she would have the whole weekend to unwind and spend time with her baby. She had decided to accept Kat and William's invitation to spend the summer at Tranquility. Kat promised Laura she wouldn't be filming and would have a lot of time to spend with her and Sam. Toby and Kevin had promised to visit for a couple of weeks at Kat and William's invitation.

Laura couldn't wait. She only had one more week of school and then a week to clean up her classroom and then she and Sam could leave the city.

Kevin wanted to have another show in the fall bigger than before, and so she felt a new urgency to paint. Or maybe the urgency had more to do with distraction. It had been almost a month since she'd sent the letter. Either Adam hadn't gotten it, or he simply didn't care.

She walked by Mac's flower stand and saw a bouquet of white roses like Adam's white roses. They weren't quite as magnificent by any stretch, but they still triggered sweet memories.

"Hi, Mac," she said, picking up one of the roses, thinking it was absolutely perfect.

"How's the little man?" he asked, smiling down at Sam.

Sam looked at Mac with big eyes and smiled.

"We're having a good afternoon," Laura said, her heart filling with pride. At eight weeks old, Sam was a charmer and getting more animated with each day.

The friendly banter continued, until Laura handed Mac the single stem and said, "Just this perfect rose today."

"Secret Blush, just for you," he said, making Laura cringe at his words. She had a secret all right.

Laura wondered what Adam was doing at that exact moment. It was a new torture that had descended on her psyche after she'd mailed the letter. Whenever her cell phone rang, she raced to answer it, hoping to hear his voice. Whenever the doorbell rang, she ran to it with anticipation. It was emotionally and physically exhausting.

She looked down at the white rose and saw the hints of peach deep within the petals and felt the deep yearning. Last summer was the happiest of her life. The birth of Sam had been the happiest moment of her life. Adam had made it possible. Despite what he chose to do, even if that meant never meeting or acknowledging Sam, she would never, could never hate him. She didn't want to think about how much Adam might hate her at this moment thousands of miles away.

She tried to pay Mac for the rose, but he refused. She gave him a quick hug and after making sure the stem didn't have any thorns, she bent down and touched the rose's petals to Sam's pink cheek, tickling him.

"Your daddy used to bring me these," she said, and watched the baby smile.

Her next stop was the corner market, where she bought the oranges she'd been craving, a box of baby wipes, and few other necessities. Everyone she met said something sweet about Sam, warming her heart.

It would be a long evening ahead. She should do a load of laundry, but she hated going to the basement of the building. And Sam really didn't appreciate being carted up and down the stairs with a full basket of laundry.

"Sorry, kid," she murmured, looking down at a contemplative Sam who watched her with sparkling eyes. "It is laundry night."

Eventually, she rounded the corner to her street, feeling a tug at her heart the moment she noticed a man sitting on her front steps. At first, she assumed it was Toby. He often waited for them on the front steps so he could help Laura with the baby. But it wasn't Toby, Laura realized as the breath caught in her throat and she stopped walking.

Adam stood. He was dressed in a badly wrinkled buff colored linen suit, the collar of his shirt open. If there had been a tie, it had been discarded long ago. He was in need of a shave and looked thin. A small, sad smile formed on his lips as he said, "Hello, Laura."

She went weak in the knees, her head spinning as the ground raced up to meet her. The groceries hit first, the bag spilling its contents on the concrete. Adam crossed the distance to where Laura was wilting before him. He grabbed the baby carrier with one hand and her with the other before they all collapsed to the sidewalk.

"Laura!" he said, alarmed as he struggled to balance the baby and her in his arms.

"How did you…?" she broke off and looked up at him. "You finally got my letter."

Those deep brown eyes looked back at her, anger mixed with concern. Involuntarily, she shrunk back from him.

"Damn it!" Adam shouted as he placed the baby carrier on the sidewalk and put both of his hands on her shoulders to steady her, scolding, "Why didn't you tell me? I should have been there for you. Oh Laura, are you alright?"

"I tried to tell you, but you'd left Cairo then I couldn't find you. I didn't think you'd want to come because I knew how you felt about having more children. After reading about all that happened in the trial, I just…I —I didn't want to be a burden to you. I worried you'd think I entrapped you…I mean, I couldn't get pregnant, so I was told. How many more reasons do you need?" she asked, her voice cracking, tears coming steadily now as she stood on legs made of rubber helplessly looking up at him.

"Aw hell," he said, pulling her to him and wrapping his arms around her.

She let him pull her close, tears pouring from her eyes as she tried to speak, "I'm…s…sorry."

"Laura stop, please…I'm sorry. I just got off a plane, I haven't slept…hell, I've been a mess since I found your letter."

"I should've told you earlier…I know I should have…I just was scared, and everyone told me to call you, but I knew you'd be upset. I didn't want to upset you or be a burden."

"Shhh…it's going to be all right," he soothed, gently rocking her.

Feeling a bit ignored, the baby began to holler. Adam tentatively released his hold on her, asking, "Are you okay to stand?"

"Yes," she muttered.

Adam picked up the carrier nonchalantly, not looking at the baby as he asked over Sam's protests, "Can we talk inside?"

Laura nodded and began to pick up her spilled groceries.

"Leave them," he ordered gently.

"I cannot afford to leave them," she said, as she took a moment to compose herself as she carefully refilled the bag. How had she thought this might happen? Not like this. Adam was here, but he wasn't the same man. She could see it in the hard lines of his face. There were traces of gray at his temples. He looked as old as she felt. And if she had to guess, she'd bet his feelings for her had changed and not in a good way. She also noticed the slight limp. His mended femur was bothering him today.

What next? Would he pay her and Sam to go away?

She put her key in the lock and opened the door to the brownstone's lobby. A moment later, he quietly followed her up the steps to the third floor. Sam fussed, letting them both know that he was not happy. She opened the door to her apartment and stepped aside, waiting for Adam to enter. Putting the groceries on the kitchen counter, she asked, "Would you please just set him on the kitchen table?"

He did as she asked as if Sam were nothing more than another bag of groceries. Trying not to feel upset over Adam's cool demeanor toward his son, she went to the baby and picked him up. Once in her arms, Sam quickly relaxed and stopped fussing. Nervously, Adam picked up the rose and examined it, then set it down and looked out her kitchen window.

Laura waited for a full minute, the silence taking the oxygen from the room as she willed her heart to slow down. When she could take the silence no longer, she said, "Adam, there's a baby blue elephant in the room and he's a hell of a lot more interesting than that damn rose or the view out that damn window."

"I'm going to need some time. I lost my son, and I don't need a replacement. I just wanted to see you and make sure you're all right."

"You've seen me now, I'm fine, but if you don't want to talk to me or look at our beautiful baby, I'll understand, and you can leave." Each word hurt to speak. Posturing wasn't easy for her, especially when the stakes were so incredibly high.

He turned to her then, his emotions getting the better of him. "I'm tired. I haven't slept in two days, so give me a break. My emotions are a mess, I don't know what to say, what to do. I'm sorry, Laura, I'm doing my best. No ultimatums, ok? I'm not going anywhere."

"It's not Sam's fault that he was born. Blame me, don't blame him," she said, snuggling against Sam.

Ignoring the invitation to fight, he asked, "Is he healthy?"

"Very," she said with pride and let the silence stretch between them once again.

Adam sighed and leaned against her chipped linoleum countertop, the jetlag apparently catching up with him. "Was it a hard pregnancy with your issues?"

"No, but I was very worried something would happen. I was near paranoid. I wanted him so badly, you have no idea."

"And you're okay now?"

"I'm fine. I still have three pounds of baby weight to lose, and I feel dumpy because I look so tired. But I'm nursing so the three pounds should go away quickly. I had a checkup two weeks ago, six weeks after his birth and I'm healthy for a single mother who doesn't remember what it was like to sleep all night." She saw his eyes haze over and knew he still felt something for her. "I'm tired all the time, which I'm sure you can see."

"You look beautiful, Laura. Happy—motherhood looks good on you," he said, and she could almost believe him.

"I'm sorry I did this to you, I didn't mean for it to happen, but I'm so glad it did," she said and wished she hadn't said the words the moment they were out her mouth.

"Why did you name him Sam?" he asked, appearing not to have heard her as he met her eyes.

"I thought Samuel William Stark had a nice ring to it. Or Samuel William Hokensen, if that's the way it has to be."

"I see," he said, a trace of anger creeping into his curt response.

"Which name would you prefer?" she asked, feeling the ice form in her veins.

"He's a Stark."

"He's going by Hokensen for now."

"Oh, that's great," Adam said, glaring at her.

"I'm open to changing it, if we can work it out, satisfied?"

"Is my name on the birth certificate?" he asked.

"Yes, of course."

"Well, thanks for remembering me."

"I will never forget you. Listen, you traveled this far, wouldn't you like to at least take a look at him?" Laura asked.

"As I said, I came here for you. I wanted to see you. I've already had a son and…I just need some time." She could see his conflicting emotions. He was in shock, and asleep on his feet.

"Sam's an innocent baby. He will grow up missing an older brother he'll never know," she offered quietly. "Don't hold him responsible. Be mad at me. They told me I couldn't get pregnant. It's bad enough that he'll know that his father didn't want him. That isn't a conversation I look forward to having with him, but I will."

He flinched visibly.

"No Laura. I'm not mad at either one of you," he replied. "This is no one's fault. It's just an awful, awful mistake from my perspective."

"Sam is not a mistake. He's a miracle, Adam," Laura said, the anger making her words harsher than she intended causing the baby to fuss. "He's beautiful and means more to me than anything in the world. I love him with all my heart. If you can't even look at him, your own son, then you can leave, and we will be fine without you. You know about him. I've held up my end of the deal. I told you. That's all I wanted to do."

Arms extended in surrender, Adam sighed. "Laura, I'm sorry. This isn't how I wanted this to go." Something in her voice had gotten to him. Sadness mixed with shame. He looked into her eyes and slowly closed the distance to her. He touched her hand with his fingertips and murmured, "I'm sorry. I don't want to leave. Please don't throw me out. I'm…just…I'm in shock and that was a horrible thing for me to say. I want to be here and talk to you and work this out."

She nodded and looked down at Sam, knowing Adam was doing the same.

"He looks like you," she said, as Sam smiled on cue.

"The apple didn't fall far from the tree," he observed, reaching out to touch him, but before he made contact, he stopped and pulled back.

"You can touch him. You could even hold him," she said. "You should do both."

"I will, just not yet. Don't push me, Laura. I need a little time to get used to the idea. You knew my feelings on having a family after everything that happened and I just need to handle this in my own way. It's a little difficult right now."

"How long will you be here?" she asked.

"A few days if you'll have me or I could stay in a hotel and visit each evening."

"A few days? Tell me exactly what are your plans? How long are you in San Francisco?" she asked, thinking it was like asking some acquaintance how they were spending their vacation.

"That all depends on you," he said, looking forlornly at her.

"Could you spend the few days with us?"

"Yes, I can do that. I wanted to get a hotel and see you and work this out."

She had nothing to lose. If he wanted to work this out, as he said, there was hope for a future—unless she was reading into things. "You could forgo the hotel and stay with us if you want to.

I know it's a far cry from what you're probably used to. You can see, this place is well, needs work. I don't have any satin sheets, but I like to keep the place clean. Really, I'll understand if you don't want to stay here."

Adam shrugged, looking into her living room, taking in the space. She anticipated rejection. He wouldn't want to stay in her cheap little apartment. Now that she knew the kind of lifestyle he was used to, running a luxury hotel, he probably wouldn't be like the man she met who helped her with her tire on the side of the road.

"Your home feels nice. It feels like you, warm and loving. Do you have enough room for me?"

She felt the smile grace her lips as she replied, "I think we can manage."

The baby's fussing turned to need. "I'm sorry, but I need to nurse him. He's hungry. Come into the living room." Laura moved to the couch, unbuttoned her blouse, unfastened her bra, and began to feed Sam.

Appearing uncomfortable at the sight of her bare breast, Adam looked at the view from the bay window and said, "Would you mind if I got my luggage out of the rental?"

"Take my key, so you can get back in," she said and pointed to the kitchen table. Adam grabbed the key ring and left.

After a few minutes, during which she panicked and worried he'd left for good, he returned with his luggage, two large suitcases that boded well for a long stay. She smiled as she watched him carry the suitcases in and place them next to her living room wall. Then he turned to her and asked, "Where would you like me to put them, so they'll be out of the way?"

"If you want, you could put them in my bedroom. First door on the right."

Without another word, he moved his things to her room. She was happy that she'd made her bed that morning and straightened up out of habit. She finished nursing Sam and was patting his back when Adam reemerged.

"Are you hungry?"

"Yeah, I don't remember when I last ate. What I'd really like is a shower. Would you mind?" he asked.

"No, there are towels in the linen closet and it takes a moment or five for the hot water. What are you hungry for?"

Adam shrugged, "It doesn't matter."

"I'd planned on Chinese tonight, but I think I have some steaks in the freezer."

"Chinese sounds good."

She opened a drawer and pulled out a menu and handed it to him. "I like the Mongolian beef, the lemon chicken is tasty, and so are the lettuce wraps, but then I can't have spicy things because I'm nursing...I also like the lo mein...I'm sorry, I'm rambling."

"Order all of that, add some egg rolls and I'm good."

She nodded and grabbed her cell phone out of her purse. She had this particular Chinese restaurant on speed dial.

She heard the door to the linen closet open and then she heard the zipper on his luggage. After she placed the order and hung up, she heard the bathroom door shut and then the shower started. She needed to take it one minute at a time with the knowledge that he could change his mind and leave whenever he wanted.

Stepping into her bedroom, she stopped and stared at Adam's open luggage. He was really here and now he knew her secret. The relief she had anticipated was replaced with a different form of unease. She sat on the edge of the mattress and closed her eyes.

Adam was here and would be here for a few days. She hoped he would want to be a permanent part of Sam's life. She hoped he would want to be a permanent part of her life. She wondered if he could ever love Sam as he had his other child. Selfishly, she wondered if he could ever love her.

She had a couple of days if he kept up his end of the bargain. Never had she had a more important few days in her life.

After she changed into jeans and a loose knit top, she went back to the kitchen. The shower turned off as she picked up a drowsy Sam out of his carrier and moved to the couch. This was usually her favorite time of the day.

"A little later you'll have your bath, my handsome boy," she said, her voice low and soothing.

He looked at her with big brown eyes that seemed to say, "*Don't screw this up for us, Mommy.*"

"I'll do my best, I promise," she whispered.

Adam appeared a few minutes later, wearing a pair of khakis and a dark pullover. His hair was damp, and he was freshly shaven. She could just make out the familiar cologne that had lingered in her memory for weeks on end. Laura tried to ignore the pull in her stomach that had once signaled impending bliss. She needed to put any lustful thoughts on the back burner. He could have a girlfriend for all she knew.

"I've got some wine," she said. "I don't know if it's any good, or I could fix you a soft drink. I'm afraid I don't have anything very interesting, but we can go shopping tomorrow. The food should be here in five or ten minutes."

"I'm going to try some wine," he said softly, but when she started to get up to get it for him, he stopped her. "Just tell me where it is, I'll get it."

"It's chardonnay. In the fridge. I'm sorry it isn't something better, not like the wine at Tranquility."

Pulling the bottle from the fridge, he said, "It's fine. You know, I'm a little freaked out, too. I can be here a week. Let's just give it some time."

"I'm sorry—"

"We have time to talk about regrets later," he said, as he picked up a corkscrew and started on the wine.

"Damn it, I don't have any wine glasses. I meant to buy some, but all I have are lowball glasses." He could stay a week, she only hoped he would.

A moment later, he'd found the glasses. He poured them each a glass and placed one on the end table next to her.

"I should have told you I'm a bit of a teetotaler these days," she said too late.

"The breastfeeding, I get it. So, getting stinking drunk isn't an option?"

She laughed for the first time in months. "Afraid not."

"What would you like?" he asked.

"Ice water, but I can get it," she said.

"I'll get it," he replied.

The buzzer sounded. Again, she started to get up and he stopped her. "I've got it," he said and proceeded to the intercom where he talked to the deliveryman as Laura stayed on the couch with Sam.

A moment later the man was at the door and Adam handed him a credit card. Laura wished she'd thought to pay when she was on the phone placing the order.

Adam spread the food out on the coffee table. Arranging everything the way he always did, with perfection. Laura didn't want to think of what he'd seen in her bathroom, the nursing bras, the breast pump, the pads, the detritus of a new mother. It was amazing he hadn't gone screaming from her apartment.

She placed Sam in his carrier so she could watch him while they ate.

"What happens to him when you're teaching?"

"Sam is in daycare from seven-thirty to about four-thirty. I don't feel good about it, but they are the best I could afford. I checked them out pretty carefully and they are very nice to him. A couple nights a week, Toby comes over and helps."

"Toby?"

"My neighbor."

"Gay neighbor?" Adam asked.

"How did you know?"

"We met on the front steps. He told me it was about time I showed up," he said.

She cringed. "He's very protective."

"I picked up on that," he said, the inkling of a grin gone as he bit into an egg roll.

"He means well. Kevin, who handles my artwork, is his partner. That is something else that's new. I had my first show in November."

"I know. I'm proud of you," he said, his dimples showing for the first time.

"How did you find out?"

"Kat sent me an email with a link to the gallery. I bought six of your paintings. They're in my office…"

"In Dubai," she said, putting the puzzle pieces together. "You're my private collector."

"Made me feel closer to you, to have some of your things hanging on the walls…"

"Thank you," she said, putting down her chopsticks and wondering if he'd bought them in person. That would mean he'd been in San Francisco in November and hadn't tried to contact her. Then again, he wanted her paintings.

"Don't thank me, I haven't exactly been a saint," he said, and the dimples disappeared.

Several unpleasant thoughts went through her mind, but she didn't want him to elaborate because she didn't want to know.

"I'm far from it one myself," she said.

"Clean slate for tonight, okay?" he asked.

She nodded and changed the subject. "Please tell me about Dubai. What exactly do you do for the hotel? Your secretary wasn't very helpful."

"I got that impression from your letter. She has been dealt with. She considered herself my protector, similar to your Toby, but her not letting you through crossed the line."

"She's a gay man?" Laura chuckled, sensing the woman was more than just protective.

"She might as well be as far as I'm concerned. And in answer to your question, I'm a glorified concierge. I make sure the guests are happy and think of the Stark International Hotel Dubai as the most magnificent hotel in the world."

"No small task," she said, wondering why he didn't admit he was the manager of the hotel. She wasn't an idiot, and his photo was on the website. He was a very powerful man, and he was sitting on the floor, eating Chinese takeout in her little apartment where they may or may not have cable depending on if she could afford to pay the cable bill this month.

"Time consuming but manageable," he said, watching her, his chocolaty eyes melting into a smile.

"When did you get my letter?"

"Two days ago. Two horrible, long days. If I could have left the moment I finished reading it, I would have, but I had to explain things to my boss, pack, and get a flight."

"What did you tell him?"

"I told him that I have a son. He didn't need much more, he's my cousin. I'm taking some vacation time," Adam said.

His cousin, she remembered, was Alex Stark, the leader of the hotel empire that shares his name. Also, Kat and William's friend who helped them obtain Adam's location and number.

"I hope the last-minute plane fare didn't financially ruin you," she said, knowing it was nothing to this man whose estimated wealth was close to one hundred million. When would he tell her who he really was?

"Don't worry about it. It cost me nothing and even if it had, I would have dropped everything to see you after getting your letter."

"It's not every day you get a letter that tells you about a child," she said, her voice low and testing the water.

"No, and it makes you crazy with unanswered questions," he said, meeting her eyes. "It really, really tortured me."

"I'm sorry, but your Lily left me no choice. Now you can ask me anything, you're entitled." She took a sip of her ice water and waited for the firing squad.

"I'm a little jet lagged, but once I'm rested you might regret that offer. And just so we are clear, Lily was fired."

"Wow, so she isn't anyone I need to worry about."

"I was so mad that I fired her on the spot and no, you're the only woman in my life, there is no one you need to worry about."

Except his dead wife. She smiled to herself, at least she was the only living woman in his life. "Do you have any burning questions for tonight?"

"When did you find out and how?"

She told him about having the flu and deciding to see her doctor. Then she told him about her doctor's reaction to the news she was pregnant.

"When I told him Leland wasn't the father, I thought he'd have a coronary. We'd been to see him so many times…it was crazy," she said, able to smile at the memory.

"When was that? The date?" Adam asked tentatively, playing with his chopsticks, but intent on her every word.

"The week of closing arguments."

"My wife and son's trial? You knew that much?"

"I followed it," she said, looking down at her food, which was suddenly unappetizing. When she'd heard the bombshell about Adam's wife being pregnant it had been the deciding factor for her not to tell him.

"Did you think about calling me?"

"Of course," she said adamantly. "I thought about calling you right then, I actually had the cell phone in my hand, but the timing was terrible. I couldn't do that to you, not after everything that was disclosed at the trial. Not right after you'd found out about your wife and the baby. You didn't know, did you?"

"I didn't know, but I had a feeling something was up. I think she would've surprised me with the news a week later on our anniversary. She was big on surprises."

She nodded, didn't know how to respond, so she continued with her original thought. "I told myself I'd just wait a couple of weeks. Then it became easier to think that if you didn't know I'd be protecting you. I actually tried you a few times and the phone said you were unavailable and clicked off not giving me an option for leaving a message."

"My new cell phone from Dubai. A piece of shit."

"Agreed. Yes, I put a lot of thought into whether or not I should tell you. Kat and William were livid that I should. I thought about it all the time. Everything blurred together and well, I made a big mistake."

The silence stretched between them, and Adam topped off her ice water and his wine. He raised his hand and placed it on her cheek and said, "I know you weren't being malicious."

"No, I really was trying not to hurt you. I didn't want to bring you any more pain. I thought you'd been through enough," she said, a tear trickling down her cheek.

He touched the tear, wiped it away. "I did something really pretty stupid as I tried to avoid hurting you."

"Good. Make me feel better," she said, leaning into his hand and shutting her eyes to savor the feel of his touch.

"I came to San Francisco in November. I needed to see you. The day before your gallery opening, I went to the gallery and persuaded the salesperson to let me see your work and I bought the six paintings I couldn't live without. The next night, I parked outside the gallery and watched the opening, trying to get up the nerve to walk in."

"And?" she asked, remembering the night clearly.

"I saw you with Leland, thought you were back with him. I figured that pretty much told me what I needed to know."

"But you didn't get out of the car, walk in, and ask me?" She asked, exasperated.

"No, I made a big assumption. A big stupid assumption," he said, and took his hand away from her cheek to pick up his glass of wine. "I hate to admit, but I was feeling a bit insecure."

"Things would have been so different if only you'd gotten out of the car or if I'd called," Laura said, thinking of him watching her that night when he'd been so much on her mind. "That's the night Kat guessed I was pregnant. I thought my outfit hid it, but she knew."

"I wish I'd gone into the gallery. I think about that night often and my stupidity."

"It will haunt me too."

"I'd have figured it out, I think. That you were pregnant." He sighed, obviously frustrated with his decisions.

"You would have," she said. "Took Kat about five seconds."

"I'm here now and we have a week to sort this out." He reached over and took her hand in his. Their eyes met and in them Laura saw the passion she had missed in the last nine months.

Taking a lighter tone, but still holding her hand, he asked, "Tell me about your art. And tell me about your students, especially the ones with crushes on their math teacher."

She told him about meeting Toby and Kevin and how Kevin had a vision for her and wanted her to stop teaching and devote herself to her work. She talked about school and her students. When the sun started to dip and the sky turned apricot, the baby began to fuss and she said, "He's had a busy day. It's time for his bath."

She hoped Adam would volunteer to help, but somehow knew she'd be disappointed.

"I'll clean this up," he said as she picked up the baby and headed for the bathroom.

A half hour later, she put the baby down and returned to the living room. Adam stared out the window watching the lights sparkle over the city.

"Tired?" she asked, standing next to him.

"Exhausted like I've never been in my life. I wish I could stay awake and talk, but I'm falling asleep on my feet. Where am I bunking?"

Cautiously, she said, "You have a couple of options. The couch is what it is. It's new, but it was a bargain and now that you've sat on it, you know why. I could get you sheets and a blanket, which might help. Or, if you want, I have a queen-sized bed. If…if you want to bunk with me."

"That sounds good," he said causing her heart to skip a beat. "I want to be with you."

"Good, that's good," she said, wanting to jump for joy, even knowing they had things to say, hard conversations. "I always shower at night, so I'll just go take a shower then join you."

"Laura, you know I've really missed you," he said, a small, sad smile played on his lips.

"I've really missed you, too," she said, a tear sliding down her cheek.

Adam kissed the tear away, and then kissed her temple and whispered, "You look as tired as I feel."

"A baby will do that to you."

"You're a fantastic mother," he said.

"I'm still learning."

"You are doing great," he said as he walked with her back into the bedroom and stopped, indicating the painting over the bed of the white rose, "I love that."

"I was motivated. It reminded me of last summer," she said, grabbing the things she needed from her closet. "Make yourself at home."

"Thank you…for letting me stay," he said and started to pull off his shirt. It was all she could do not to stop and stare.

"Thank you for coming," she said and ducked into the bathroom quickly. They were circling each other cautiously, part old friends, part strangers, but mostly completely freaked out.

Under the spray of her lukewarm shower, her mind went places she didn't want to go. What must he think of her and this apartment? It couldn't compete with the luxury of his hotels or the elegance of the cottage at Tranquility. It just wasn't that nice. She'd done her best to make it cozy, but it wasn't the dream she had for herself or Sam. She wanted to tell Adam as much, but didn't know how to say it and with the future so vague, how could she make any guarantees about the life she could offer Sam? What happened in a week? Would he let Sam have his name, but go back to Dubai? Dubai. Half a world away. Maybe Adam would come back to see him once a year if Sam was lucky…if she was lucky. No, she didn't want that. It was all or nothing now for her and she needed to know by week's end which they were going to pursue.

He no doubt worked with many beautiful and exotic women. It was unlikely he had escaped their notice. She wasn't naïve enough to think he hadn't been with anyone in the months since they'd last made love. He'd basically told her there wasn't anyone else, but she knew he still loved Melinda. Had any space in his heart opened up for her?

In a few minutes she'd be joining him in her bed. Would they pick up where they left off? Would he continue to tell her it didn't mean anything if they could find a little mutual happiness in each other? That was fine last summer…Laura wasn't so sure now.

After her shower, Laura stood before the bathroom mirror in her nicest nightgown. The blush pink silk sheath was a birthday gift from Kat and draped pleasantly over her body. She was thinner now than she had been last summer, but her body was different.

The nightgown was totally impractical. She was a nursing mother. One slight accident and she would ruin the fine garment.

She took it off and hung it on a hook on the back of her bathroom door. She put on a pale pink cotton pajama top and a pair of lacy pink panties. It wasn't her best look, but it would have to do, she thought, as she added a little perfume for good measure. A hundred thoughts, both good and bad went through her mind, but she chose to shut out each and every one.

Standing in the doorway, she saw Adam lying on his side, facing her side of the bed. His eyes were shut, and he was snoring softly. His bare chest was tanned and as strong as she remembered. He'd turned back the covers on her side of the bed and the single white rose she had purchased earlier was resting on her pillow. The sight of it made her smile. She quietly got under the covers, trying not to disturb him, and switched off the light.

In the middle of the night, Sam's cries awakened her. She sat up and felt Adam stir next to her.

"What's going on?" he asked, sleepily.

"It's time for Sam's 2 a.m. feeding. I'll be back in a few minutes, go back to sleep." Laura whispered and kissed him gently on the cheek. It felt wonderful to touch him and then he reached for her, but she reluctantly moved out of his grasp eliciting a frustrated sigh that had her smiling in the dark. She wanted nothing more than to settle into his arms, but their child wouldn't be ignored.

# CHAPTER TWENTY

Adam slept well for the first time in months. He was dreaming that Laura was in his arms. Her body was curvy and lush, just the way he remembered it. Snuggling deeper against the warm body next to him, he felt content as he inhaled the familiar scent of lilacs and summer.

The ringing alarm pulled him from his dream and then to his delight, he found Laura nestled in his arms. But as quickly as he'd discovered her there, she was pulling away from him.

"Where are you going?"

"It's five. Time for me to get up," Laura said as she removed his hand, which was resting gently on her hip. "I wish I could stay."

"Why so early?" he complained, running his hand slowly along her bare thigh.

"I have to get to work. Sleep in. I'll leave you a key on the coffee table."

"Call in sick and come back here, please Laura, come back to bed."

"You don't know how much I wish I could, but I can't, I don't have any sick time left."

She patted him on the shoulder and then kissed his cheek. He grabbed her and pulled her to him, kissing her quickly on the lips.

"I'm so glad you came," she said.

"I am too. I'll miss you, today," he murmured.

"I'll miss you, too. See you in a few hours," she said, but he didn't hear her leave. When he woke up again, he reached for Laura and then remembered that she'd gone. His eyes quickly adjusted to the dim light as he stared up at the water-stained ceiling. He looked at the clock on the nightstand and blinked. It was a little before nine. Getting out of bed, he stood, stretched, and wondered what to do with his day until Laura came home.

All the way from Dubai to Atlanta and finally Atlanta to San Francisco, he wondered what he'd find when he arrived on Laura's doorstep. His emotions had tripped to the very edges of all extremes, anger that Laura hadn't told him about Sam, joy that she'd had a child and that it was his. Disappointment that he'd missed the pregnancy and birth, and finally, happiness that she wasn't with her ex-husband. He had no doubts that Laura would be a good mother, but he had no idea how she would be a single working mother without help.

His thoughts immediately went to Sam.

*Samuel Stark,* his son. Sam looked so much like A.J. at the same age. He didn't believe in reincarnation, but when he'd seen Sam for the first time yesterday, he couldn't deny the resemblance. He'd hurt Laura by not embracing their child. How could he explain to her or get her to appreciate how difficult it was for him to see a child who was almost a carbon copy of the one he'd lost? There was no way. She would never forgive him for calling Sam a mistake. He wasn't sure he could forgive himself. It had been a knee jerk reaction. He would have to do everything he could to make it up to both Laura and Sam.

It was unreal. The similarity between his two sons was incredible and he was having a hard time catching up. He walked carefully into the nursery, hoping he wouldn't wake up the sleeping child.

The crib was empty. The terror was momentary but had the desired impact. *Sam.* Then he realized that Laura had taken Sam to daycare and why wouldn't she? He wouldn't have left his child with anyone as unenthusiastic and uncaring as he'd been the day before.

The nursery was the nicest room in the apartment as well as the larger of the two bedrooms. There were no water stains or chipped paint. Even the hardwood floors had been carpeted with plush carpet the color of sand. The room, he realized, resembled the beach in front of Tranquility. The sky-blue ceiling flowed onto the walls and met the sandy beach landscape coming up from the floors.

The only window had the same view of the brick building next door, but the silk curtains with seashell tiebacks were the same color as the sky.

All the furniture, including the crib and the rocking chair, were smooth, whitewashed wicker, adorned with striped silk cushions in light blue, pink, and yellow.

Small details came into focus. The baby blanket had appliqués of seashells, starfish, and seahorses in pastels of blue, pink, and yellow. Laura had added her artistry to the walls in the form of sand dollars, starfish, and sandcastles. There were brightly-colored beach balls in one corner along with a plastic bucket and shovel.

The wicker dresser held pictures in whitewashed rustic wood frames. On closer inspection, Adam saw photos of Sam being held by all the different people that had known about his existence for months. Sam with William and Kat at Tranquility, Sam with Toby and the man who must be his partner, and finally, Sam in Laura's arms shortly after his birth. He took in every detail until it hurt.

Turning to leave, he saw that another mural covered the far wall. A large giraffe in a pink bikini sat on the sand next to a small giraffe in blue trunks. Above the giraffes it read: *Mommy & Sam.*

That familiar, invisible fist took hold of Adam's heart and tightened. He looked past how cute the painting was. He ignored the look of utter contentment on the pink bikinied giraffe's face or how with her big blue eyes and long lashes that she was an accurate caricature of Laura. No, Adam's first thought was that he hoped there would be enough room for another large giraffe to be added to the family scene on the other side of his baby, *his* baby.

Laura wouldn't require him to do anything for Sam. If he left right now and never returned, she would forgive him and blame herself. But he couldn't do that to her, to his child, or to himself. It was time to raise his hand and be counted. The knowledge that he was doing the right thing for all of them gave him a sense of peace that he hadn't felt in a very long time. He needed to prove to Laura that he was worthy of her, the strong woman, the great mother she'd become. She wouldn't settle for scraps of him, it was all or nothing and he knew what he needed to do because when you met the right person, you knew. He knew. He got ready quickly, pulling on a pair of jeans and a white oxford shirt with a pair of loafers.

Remembering the magnets on the refrigerator, he saw the one he needed and grabbed his cell phone. He had twenty-seven voicemails, which he ignored as he searched for an address and then directions.

On his way to get his son, he called William at Tranquility and asked for a special favor.

Laura heard her phone vibrating during her second period pre-calc class. She was explaining a difficult equation and wasn't able to break away and look at the caller ID. It was hard enough knowing that a mile away Adam was in her apartment sleeping in her bed.

When there were only ten minutes left in the period, the phone vibrated a second time.

"Excuse me a minute," she said to the class, picked up the phone and looked at her caller ID. She didn't allow cell phones in her class, but when you had a baby, you were allowed to break the rules.

Duckyland Daycare had called her twice. Panicking, she said to her students, "It is your lucky day. Take this next ten minutes to get started on your homework. See you tomorrow, same place, same time." There were a few smirks, but she knew they were happy to get sprung a little early.

She stepped into the hall to listen to her voicemail.

"Mrs. Hokensen, it's Miss Nancy from Duckyland. We have a bit of a situation here. A man who says he's Sam's daddy is in our lobby. The problem is, he's not Mr. Hokensen and he's not on your list of approved people. His name is Adam Stark, and he has a driver's license from New York state. He seems very polite, but should we be calling the police? We are a little concerned. Please call us back as soon as you get this."

Laura couldn't believe it. How had Adam found where Sam was and why, when he barely looked at him last night, had he gone to the daycare this morning?

The second message started playing.

"It's Miss Nancy again, Mrs. Hokensen. This Mr. Stark says he is staying with you and would like to take Sam home for the rest of the day if it is fine with you. Obviously, we are concerned because he's not on the approved list. He's just sitting in the lobby and waiting for us to speak to you. If we should be calling the police, well… please just call. And don't worry, Sam is fine. We'd never let anyone take him without your permission."

Laura hit the call back button and waited. She wasn't often pleasantly surprised. And this had to be a good sign, right? Adam wouldn't want to be with Sam if he wasn't bonded in some way to his child.

Miss Nancy, the gray-haired prim and proper headmistress at Duckyland, picked up on the first ring. "Hello, Mrs. Hokensen."

"Hi Miss Nancy. I'm sorry for all the trouble. Could I speak with Mr. Stark, please?"

"There's no trouble, really. We were just a bit taken by surprise."

The care provider wasn't going to let Laura off without sharing her own concerns. It reminded Laura of when she had missed curfew as a teenager and had to endure the lecture of all lectures from her parents.

"I'm sure you were. I'm sorry. He is Sam's father. May I speak to him?" she explained.

"Oh, I see. That's why we are confused. We thought Mr. Hokensen was Sam's father."

"No, Mr. Hokensen is my dad and if you'll notice he's not on the approved list either because he's dead."

"Oh, well, we've all wondered, but obviously it isn't our business."

Laura lost patience and decided to give the woman something to talk about. "Mr. Stark is my lover and Sam's father. May I speak to him?"

"Oh my!"

Laura heard a distressed Miss Nancy tell Adam that she wanted to speak to him. By the end of the day, every parent who took their child to Duckyland would know that her baby's daddy wasn't Mr. Hokensen.

"Good morning," Adam said, pleasantly.

"You're at Duckyland," she said unnecessarily.

"Yes. Will you please give your permission to what's her name so that I can free Sam from baby prison?"

"Her name is Miss Nancy, and she is very nice if you like judgmental old bats."

"She is nosy and annoying," he complained.

"And she can hear you. By the way, it's not a prison. They treat Sam very, very well. I wouldn't take Sam to people who wouldn't be kind to him," Laura said, feeling guiltier than she usually did that she couldn't be with her baby. It wasn't enough that for the first two weeks she'd cried every day after dropping him off.

"Of course, you wouldn't. And from what I can tell, it appears they do a pretty good job," he admitted, "but I'd like to spend the day with Sam."

"Are you sure you're up to it?"

"This might come as a surprise to you, but I can handle babies."

"Could have fooled me," she said coolly.

"Laura, I'm trying to spend some time with our son."

"That makes me very, very happy. I appreciate what you're trying to do. How did you know where to find him?"

"Fridge magnet. Please get me added to the approved list. I'm about to start trying to bribe them. What's a Duckyland worth anyway? Maybe I should just buy it."

He couldn't be serious about buying Duckyland, or could he? "You won't know his feeding schedule or—"

"Laura, I'll ask Grandma Nancy about his schedule. Enjoy your day. We will be waiting for you to get home."

"She is going to torture you for that comment. Okay, give me back to Miss Nancy."

"Thank you, we'll see you tonight."

Adam gave the phone back to Miss Nancy who sounded like she was gnawing on a rawhide bone as she asked, "Mrs. Hokensen do you really want this man to have your baby?"

"Well, actually I had his baby. You can add Mr. Stark to the list. As I told you, he's Sam's father. I give my permission for Mr. Stark to take Sam home today."

There was a long silence. Everyone, the teachers, the students, even the daycare had assumed Leland or the mysterious "Mr. Hokensen" was Sam's father, and she hadn't corrected them.

"If you're really sure, Mrs. Hokensen. Is there an issue we need to worry about? Is there a problem?"

"No issue or problem, everything is fine," she said, trying to add a smile to her voice. "Adam travels a lot. He's in town for a couple of weeks. Sam is safe with him," she said, but giving her baby to anyone wasn't easy, even the baby's father.

When the final bell rang, Laura could barely wait for her students to clear the door to the hall before she grabbed her handbag and followed suit. By the time she hit the sidewalk she was nearly running. In her mind, different images of the baby with Adam played in her mind. What would they have done today? Would Adam have fallen in love with sweet Sam? How could he not?

She hit the stairway in her building like a marathon runner. By the time she reached the third floor, she was panting.

Trying the knob, she found it unlocked. Her apartment smelled different. Something that smelled very good was on the stove in the kitchen, but she didn't register what it was. She couldn't stop staring at the sight before her, Adam and Sam.

Adam had moved the rocking chair out of the nursery and in front of the bay window. He gently rocked the sleeping baby in his arms. She looked from the baby to Adam. Their eyes met and held. His face was soft and peaceful as he raised a hand in silent greeting. His eyes were red rimmed and weary but filled with something she hadn't seen in them before. Sometime during the hours he'd spent with Sam, something had changed, something good.

The knowledge of this fact brought tears to Laura's eyes. Not understanding, Adam's expression grew tense with worry. She shook her head, smiled, and waved off his concern as she walked to her bedroom for a moment of composure.

Sitting on the edge of the bed, she smiled as the tears continued to make warm paths down her cheeks. Adam loved Sam. He loved his son, and he always would. She didn't know how it would happen, hadn't worked out all the details, but Adam would always be a part of Sam's life. She just knew it in her heart. Their bond couldn't be denied.

A few minutes later, Adam's frame filled the doorway.

She looked up at him and smiled.

"Welcome home, Mommy. We missed you today."

"Hi," she managed, her voice cracking.

Adam smiled, understanding what she couldn't articulate. "Sam's awake and I think he's hungry. I'm glad you're home because he wants the real thing. He's going to be a breast man when he grows up."

"Just like his daddy," she murmured.

The scene of pure domestic bliss ripped painfully at her heart. Adam was handsome in a pair of jeans and an untucked white button-down shirt. In his arms, Sam was contently cooing. Swallowing the welling emotion, she went to them, kissed Sam on the cheeks and then gave Adam a quick, tender kiss as she took the baby from his arms.

How had she been away from Adam for so long?

"I've got some things on the stove that need attention," he said with a wink. She followed him to the kitchen and stopped in the doorway. Italian food and lots of it filled every pot and pan she owned. She hadn't noticed all the cookware when she walked in the door, but the aroma couldn't be ignored. Now, the more she looked, the more she saw.

Most noticeable, Adam looked...happy. He strode confidently to the front of her stove and used tools that were foreign to her kitchen.

"How did it go today?" she asked.

"Great. He had a bottle at eleven and then at two. In between, we took a walk around the city. Sam's a very easy baby. Not at all like A.J. A.J. didn't want to do anything but cry the first three months of his life. He also didn't like to eat, and he spit up everything, but then Melinda didn't nurse him, because he didn't like to nurse. It was tough on her. I'm surprised Sam eats so well. It's amazing. What I really don't understand is how he can go from breast to bottle so easily."

Laura digested this information and realized it was the most he'd ever told her about his other child. "Sam is easy. He rarely cries. I'm lucky."

"We're lucky," he corrected.

She nodded, not quite believing his words, but wanting to believe them with all her heart. Changing the subject to prevent herself from getting any more emotional, she asked, "Did you do a little shopping by chance?"

"Earlier today, Sam and I took stock of your kitchen. We couldn't help but notice you didn't have a pot big enough for cooking pasta, so during our walk, we solved the problem," he offered casually.

"What else did you two do?"

"We went to the grocery store and a few other places. You have a lot of lettuce and rabbit food-like things in your fridge, but you were out of wine, beef, garlic, cheese, pasta...I don't know how you managed."

Enjoying the easy banter, she said, "I eat a lot of salad and takeout."

"Yeah, well, not on my watch," he said, and turned back to the stove.

She smiled down at Sam and winked at her baby. It was at that moment that she smelled something besides Italian food, something sweet.

In the center of the table was a bouquet of white roses that reminded her of Tranquility roses. She was embarrassed to admit that she'd missed them completely. "The roses are beautiful."

"Ah-ha, you noticed," he said, turning to smile at her.

"Of course, I noticed. They look like Tranquility roses. Where did you get them, from the florist around the corner, Mac? I buy flowers from him all the time."

"No," he said, "I got them from Tranquility."

"What? Why? How did you do that?" she asked.

"I called William, cursed him out for not telling me what was happening with you, he yelled back, and then I thanked him for being there for you. Then I told him I wanted some roses and he had Marco drive them over. Come here, I want you to try this sauce…"

"Ooo…kay," she murmured, and walked over as he pulled a spoon from the drawer and dipped it in the sauce for her to taste.

The sauce, like Adam, was perfect. But as she watched Adam pull the dinner together, her head spun. She was overwhelmed, high on a feeling of bliss that she'd only dreamed of until now.

"I think I need to sit down."

"Are you all right?" His brow wrinkled and she saw the worry on his face. It intensified her need to take a time out and digest everything she'd seen in the last half hour.

"I'm fine, just a little overwhelmed."

"Is it okay that I'm in your kitchen?"

"It's great," she said and meant it. "It isn't that."

"I'm sorry, I didn't ask even ask, how was your day?"

"Are you kidding me? I'm overwhelmed, but I think it's all good. Am I right? Is it good? Seriously, I need you to tell me, I don't trust myself," she admitted, sitting down on one of the kitchen chairs with Sam in her lap.

Adam bent down so that they were eye-to-eye, placing his hands on the hers as they held baby Sam. "It's much better than it was. It is good, darling. I'm coming to terms with everything. The shock is wearing off. He looks so much like A.J., it really affected me, but he is his own person, a part of me and a part of you, we created him through the passion we feel for each other, and that is good." Then he leaned in and kissed her, their first real kiss in almost ten months. His arms encircled her and the baby as the kiss grew. When at last he broke the connection, they were both a little breathless.

When she could find her voice again, she said, "That answered a few questions."

"I'm working through the pain I have and the pain I've caused," he said, kissing her again and then he went back to his dinner preparations. "I want us to work, the three of us." Adam added.

Dinner was homemade lasagna. It was the best thing Laura could remember eating. She'd watched him make the salad and then the dressing. Everything was delicious. But just having Adam there, she could be eating sand and she'd enjoy it. He and Sam were all she needed.

The candlelight from cream-colored candles and silver candlesticks that were new danced playfully between them as they sipped sparkling grape juice from newly purchased glasses. She was touched by Adam's thoughtfulness. He was making an effort and then some. They chatted lightly, but most of all, they looked at each other. When Adam reached across the table for her hand, Laura happily reached out to meet him halfway.

"You're frowning. What's wrong?" he asked, softly.

"You live half a world away," she said. "I missed you so much. How will I manage when you leave this time?"

"I'm working on it. I don't know what exactly will happen yet, but it will be okay. You're going to have to trust me. I can't be away from you and Sam, never again." Her heart skipped a beat, but she didn't answer, just picked up her wine glass and took a long sip of the sparkling juice. Adam had thoughtfully bought her something she could drink, and he was drinking it, too.

Adam smiled at her thoughtfully and gave her hand a squeeze, "I'm happy I came. This is the first time I've felt at home in months. Thank you for that."

She took a shower while Adam cleaned the kitchen and then, to her delight, he insisted on bathing Sam. She didn't argue, just watched from the doorway as he carefully bathed his son for the first time. Sam watched his father so lovingly, occasionally covering Adam with a good splash or two. It was obvious Adam knew what he was doing, not like she was at first, fumbling with Sam in the bath water.

Eventually, after Sam was put down, they met back in the living room. Before she knew what was happening, she was in his arms, his lips on hers as he pulled her to him. The need that always had fueled their desire in the past was there, made stronger by the long months apart. With very little motivation, Laura was ready to pull

Adam down onto the hardwood floor and make love the way they had the first time in the little cottage.

She reached for the buttons on his shirt and stopped herself. This was his dance to lead.

"You're beautiful," he said, reaching for the tie on her robe.

Somehow, they made it to her bedroom, dropping their clothes and kissing as they went. It had been nine months since they had last made love. The time and separation had done little to diminish their feelings for one another. Her fantasies and memories didn't do justice to the reality. She wanted him, now more than when they were together last summer. He was the father of her child, the man who'd made her dreams come true. He was the man she loved.

He kissed her, pushing the robe from her shoulders.

She wore a pink bra and matching panties. "My body isn't the same," she said. "I just had a baby, well two months ago."

His hands traced patterns over her skin, gliding over her curves, his gaze taking in all of her. Then he lifted his eyes to meet hers. "Your body carried my child. You're beautiful to me. You've always been beautiful to me, since day one."

His words sent shivers over her skin.

Leaning into him, she cupped his face in her hands and kissed him as if he belonged to her.

Pulling her down to the bed, he took his time lavishing attention on every inch of her exposed skin. When he got to her breasts, he opened the front latch of her bra, pushed it away from her body and gently massaged her tender nipples with the tip of his tongue. Kissing his way down her stomach, he got to the junction of her legs and gently lifted and spread her to kiss her intimately.

"Adam…" she murmured, feeling exposed and vulnerable.

"Shhh…relax. Let me have my fun remembering everything that I've missed."

A moment later, she didn't care what he did as long as he didn't stop. She moaned from the pleasure of it. He hadn't forgotten how to touch her or how to awaken her passion. Her breath came out in short bursts, needing him and wanting him inside of her as she whispered, "Adam, please…"

Kissing her cheek, he said, "Do we need to worry?"

"About what?" she asked, her body tensing, screaming for release.

"Getting pregnant. It's too soon for you to have another baby. You should wait at least a year," he said, as his fingers continued their intimate assault.

Laura punched the pillow next to her as Adam wrapped his arms around her, kissing her cheek and laughing. "Don't worry, I have what we need. I bought some condoms today."

"I'm glad you planned," she said.

"I wanted to make love last night, but I fell asleep."

"I wondered," she said as she reached down, and touched him intimately.

"Laura, I don't want you to ever wonder, I always want you, I crave you," he murmured, his voice thick and faltering, his lips close to her ear. "I missed this. I've missed you."

Releasing him, she said, "Then get the damn thing on and get inside me where you belong because it has been far too long."

Jumping up from the bed, she watched as he clumsily ripped the box open. Then he sheathed himself in a patterned condom and rejoined her on the bed.

Unable to stop herself, she laughed and asked, "Cheetah print?"

"The selection at the corner market wasn't great."

Aghast, she said, "I shop there!"

"I know because they recognized Sam. And now they know a little more about you."

While she was still laughing, he placed a hand under each of her knees, gently encouraging her to lift her legs and encircle his waist. He gently glided inside her in one easy thrust and sighed contently, resting his head on her shoulder. She opened her eyes and looked up at him as he smiled, their eyes locking as he began to move.

In the early hours of the morning, Laura awakened to a familiar cry as Adam spooned her in his warmth.

Before she could get out of bed and grab her robe, Adam was up and reaching for his. Switching on the light by her bed, she watched him as he tied the belt on his dark navy robe and smiled sleepily. He took three steps toward the door, stopped, crossed back to Laura, and kissed her.

A moment later, she heard the baby's cries die down as Adam spoke quietly to him. By the time Adam was back with Sam in his arms, the baby was cooing happily. With Adam's arm around her shoulder, she nursed the hungry baby and fought back the lump in her throat.

"Maybe I shouldn't say this, but not speaking my truth hasn't worked out too well. So, here it goes. Adam, being with you and Sam, I don't know if I've ever been this happy," Laura said, as she looked at Adam and noticed a contentment she'd never seen before.

"You make me very happy and I'm sorry it took me so long to figure it out. I just didn't think I was what you deserved, and I was so broken. Maybe I always will be, but I love you and I love this little man," he said, kissing her quickly and then brushing his fingers lightly over the baby's cheek.

"I love you, too," she whispered and snuggled against him.

Later, after the baby had gone back to his crib and they were lying together, facing each other on their sides, their faces close, she asked, "Why did you leave roses on my doorstep last summer?"

"That first morning after we'd been together in the cottage, I was walking back to the main house, and I saw them. They made me think of you."

"I remind you of roses?" she asked, running her hand lazily over his shoulder and down his arm.

"Yes."

"I like that."

Adam grabbed her hand and pulled it to his lips for a kiss. "You know, William planted them for Kat, because they reminded him of her."

"He's a hopeless romantic."

Adam placed several kisses on her cheeks and whispered, "When I found out the name, I thought they described us perfectly. That's when I realized that picking them out for you was no accident."

"What's the name?" she asked, enjoying the way his hand was tracing lazy circles on her back.

"Passion."

"You made that up," she said, rubbing against him.

"True story."

"So, what made you get them today?" she asked.

"I wanted you to know how I think about you," he said and silenced her with his lips.

On the last day of school, Laura walked slowly, thinking of the past six days and wondering how the evening would unfold. Tonight, when she got home, she and Adam were going to sit down and talk about their future. It was something they had both easily avoided for almost six days, playing house instead. They'd spent their time taking care of and marveling at the wonders of Sam. They'd cooked together and talked about everything from her former marriage to how hard it was for Adam to come to terms with the death of his wife and son. When they weren't talking or taking care of Sam, they were making love. Yet, they never talked about Adam leaving, and she hoped he never would.

After that second night, their appetite for each other was insatiable, just as it had been last summer. But this time, the stakes were much higher. For Laura, as much as she wanted to believe in happy endings, she couldn't be certain of how this story, their story, would end. Nor could she allow herself to believe that she could have everything that she'd ever wanted. He told her he loved her, but she didn't know if he was in love with her. There was a subtle difference in the wording that meant a world of difference in reality.

By three-thirty, she'd cleaned up her classroom and was on her way home. She was done early, happily able to get back to Adam and Sam sooner than expected.

Rounding the final corner that led to her street, she stopped mid-stride when she saw the large, black limo double-parked in front of her building with a license plate which read: STARK1. Had the Stark International Hotel sent a limo for Adam? Was he leaving today? He'd said a week. He couldn't leave her, and today was only day six. It immediately reminded her of how he'd left before. Panic raced through every nerve ending in her body. No, he could not do this to her, not again.

She hurried by the disinterested limo driver who was patiently reading a book in the front seat, and bounded up the stairs to her front door, her heart in her throat. She burst in ready to yell for Adam but was stopped short by the sight of Adam and another man in her living room making faces at Sam. Adam was facing her and smiling like a clown for the baby, the other man she didn't know, but felt she should. He looked strangely familiar and enough like Adam to be his brother.

"Mommy's home," Adam announced.

"Hi, what's going on?" she asked. "You're not leaving, not today? Adam?"

"No, darling, I'm here to stay as long as you'll have me," he said giving her a broad grin and moving toward her, his arms opening in welcome. He gave her a quick hug and then kissed her on the cheek as his arm tightened around her waist in reassurance.

"I saw the limo and I got worried."

"It's just him, I'm sorry darling, you don't need to worry," then turning to the other man, Adam said, "Laura, I want you to meet my cousin, Alex. He flew down from Portland this afternoon to see me and meet you and Sam. He double-parked the big, ugly limo in the street because he likes to make an entrance."

The tall, dark-haired man wore an expensive tailored dark navy suit and matching cream and blue striped silk tie. He resembled Adam not only in looks, but also demeanor. He held Sam in his arms and had to shift him slightly to extend his hand and introduced himself, "Laura, I've heard a lot of wonderful things about you. You are much prettier in person than even Adam described. My wife and I are both big fans of your work. And you can have a limo whenever you want."

She shook his hand and said, "Thank you. It's very nice to meet you."

The baby began to fuss. Laura held out her arms to take him from Alex. "You have a beautiful baby," he said. "Too bad he looks so much like his father."

"I hate to say this, but he looks a little like you, too," she said. "You and Adam could be brothers."

Adam laughed and said dismissively, "Alex has been a bully since he was a kid, just ignore him—especially if he calls me Runt."

Alex almost looked offended as he explained, "Runt is my pet name for him."

Laura rocked Sam gently and looked back and forth between the two men. "Why do I feel something is going on and you two are just waiting for me to figure it out? Why doesn't someone just tell me what's going on? I think we've all been through enough."

"Adam refuses to go back to Dubai. So, I've made him a job offer that's a little closer to home because I cannot afford to lose him," Alex explained.

"You're really not going back?" Laura asked, as Adam pulled her close.

"I never wanted to manage the Dubai property, so I quit," Adam said easily. "I actually quit a week ago before I got on the plane. I wanted to be able to focus on you and Sam."

"What? You quit?" she asked, knowing that she was missing the point.

"You didn't think I could go back to Dubai after spending a week with you and Sam?" When she just stared at him, he asked, "You do want me to stay, right?"

She looked into those warm brown eyes and whispered, "Of course. I want you to stay…forever."

Adam beamed with the largest, happiest smile Laura had ever seen and then he kissed her with enough passion that Alex whistled and said, "Easy Runt, there are children present. And uncomfortable relatives."

Alex's cell phone chirped, interrupting the moment. Looking down at the caller ID, he apologized for the interruption and walked into the hall to take his call.

"This last week," he began, and she could see that he was having a hard time with his emotions. "I'm happy." Adam leaned down and kissed the baby on his forehead and then kissed her again. "I haven't been able to say that in a very long time."

Laura started to speak, but the frog in her throat stopped her just as Alex returned.

"Hey kids…sorry to cut this short, but I've got to catch a plane back to Portland. My Daisy thinks she's in labor."

"Daisy?" Laura asked, regaining her composure.

"My beautiful bride," Alex said, with evident pride. "We are about to have our second daughter. Looks like Sam will have another cousin to play with at family get-togethers."

Adam stuck out his hand to Alex and offered, "Congratulations."

Alex shook it and then pulled Adam into a hard, masculine hug. "You, too. It's great to see you so happy. Laura is a miracle worker." He looked at Laura over Adam's shoulder and winked.

Adam said, "Take good care of Daisy. Maybe try for a boy next time."

Alex muttered a curse and said, "I'll make sure to place my order with my wife."

"She'll hurt you," Laura said with a smile.

Then Alex turned to Laura, "I'm sorry to leave like this, I'd like to stay and get acquainted, but there will be other times." He kissed her cheek, adding, "Welcome to the family. Daisy's going to love you. I hope you keep this one in line. He needs a lot of containment." He inclined his head toward Adam and offered her a cocky grin.

"Thank you, I'd love to meet your Daisy," she said, surprised, and added, "I hope you make it in time."

"It is a priority. Daisy is very excited to meet you. Okay, the jet is waiting. Good job on this little one," Alex said and held out his finger for Sam to squeeze. Turning back to Adam, he said, "Because I care, I'll pay to have your things shipped from Dubai and I'll make sure they are careful with the paintings. Welcome back to the company…again."

"I never left my own company, you jerk."

Alex laughed, then he and his big black limo were gone.

They put Sam down for his afternoon nap and Adam followed Laura into the bedroom so she could change out of her school clothes.

Her mind sought to digest everything that had happened in the last few minutes as Adam put his arm around her and offered tenderly, "I love you, Laura. I want to make you happy."

When she only stared at him, the smile dropped from his face as he asked, "Do you love me?"

She nodded and managed to whisper, "Yes, I love you. I've loved you for a very long time."

"We have a lot to talk about. And it's all good."

He sat on the bed watching as she shakily kicked off her heels and unzipped her skirt.

Grinning down at him, she said, "I'm listening."

"It's hard for me to concentrate when you're getting undressed."

She paused and looked at him. "Try."

"Fine," he said, reaching out to run his hand over the curve of her hip. "Alex came here to see what it would take to get me to go back, but I told him I'm done. I want to be stateside with you. He came up with the offer to accommodate us because I told him that we're a package deal."

She smiled as she put her skirt on a hanger and hung it carefully in her closet.

Pulling a raspberry-colored silk summer dress from a hanger, she held it to her chest, and asked, "What's the job offer?"

Then she laid the dress on the bed near Adam and unbuttoned her pink linen blouse, happy for the distraction of changing clothes as she waited for his answer.

"Well, he wants a bit of a trade, but it's up to you. If you don't want to do it, I'll get something else within the company. I can do that."

"What kind of trade?" she asked, her hands nervously smoothing the lace edge of her white silk slip.

"How do you feel about living in Portland?"

"Portland, Oregon?"

"A few years ago, it became the headquarters for Stark International Hotels. Alex would like me to trade jobs with him for a couple of years. It seems Daisy has always wanted to travel, and he thinks a couple of years in Dubai would be an adventure for her. They would like to try it, but he needs me to run the daily workings of the company. We've always worked very closely with each other. We've basically run the company with Spencer, who is Alex's cousin through his mother's side. He's an honorary Stark."

Laura sat on the edge of the bed and fell backward, her hands stretching out above her head. Adam stretched out next to her and asked, "Is that a no? It's okay if it is. I want you to be happy."

She looked up at him and smiled. "You'd be running the company?"

He nodded. "I'd work as closely with Alex as we do now."

"Thank you for finally telling me the truth about your family, but I already knew."

"Kat and William told you?" He looked sheepish and continued, "It wasn't that I was trying to hide anything from you, Laura. I was trying to run away from my life, from New York, and the less I reflected on reality helped me get through it all."

"Oh Adam, Kat and William didn't need to tell me, I figured it out at Tranquility," she said, shaking her head.

"I'm sorry that I wasn't entirely truthful about my position," he admitted, running his hands soothingly over her silk slip.

Their faces just inches apart, she asked, "You oversaw the renovation of The Bay Shore, but now you'll be running the company. I think that's wonderful, Adam."

"The Bay Shore was merely a small vacation for me to clear my head. To get away from it all."

"And that's why you told me you were a glorified concierge, to not have to remember it all," Laura surmised, grabbing his wandering hand so it would stop distracting her.

"I don't know. I guess I liked that you thought I was a lawn service guy when we first met." Adam smiled as she smirked at his comment, "There was something kind of relaxed and easy about it."

"I believe I originally thought you were a landscape architect," she corrected with a grin.

He pulled her to him and kissed her, easing down the straps of her slip to get better access to her skin. "I'll be whatever you want me to be. The real key to my recovery was falling in love with you.

You saved me. I'm yours. If you want me to be a stay-at-home dad for our children, I'll do it."

"I can't think when you're seducing me. And I have a lot to think about. You just told me that you've fallen in love with me."

"I've been telling you I loved you at every opportunity over the last week."

"You didn't say you had fallen in love with me."

"Then let me be clear. I'm hopelessly, passionately in love with you, Laura."

"I'm hopelessly, passionately in love with you, too," she said as tears ran down her cheeks.

He whispered between kisses. "When exactly? When did you know?"

"The bluff at Devil's Punchbowl when you held me. How about you?"

Without hesitation, he said, "I'd say, about five seconds after I saw you standing on that bluff. Especially when you went into that colorful rant about your flat tire, I saw your strength and knew you were the woman for me." He stopped, then added, "I just needed some time to recover and act on it. I've been so afraid I'd lost you."

She couldn't help but smile. "Do you want to take the job in Portland?"

"Alex said it will be about six months or so before Daisy will want to go. In the meantime, I told him that I'd like to oversee The Bay Shore's first summer after renovation. Then, if you are up for it, we will head to Portland. We are a package deal. I'm not going anywhere that you don't want to go. And really, we can go almost anywhere we want in the world. Alex and I own forty-four hotels, forty-five if you count his recent new Cairo purchase. By the way, I refuse to go back to Cairo."

"Forty-five hotels?" she asked.

"Yes, travel for us will be very easy. When we come to town, we get treated really well."

Laura thought of her apartment and how it must look to him. "I want Sam to have everything. I've worried a lot about that."

"I think he already does. You're doing a wonderful job. Sam is happy and loved. What else could I ask for my child?"

"For him to have a father," she said.

He smiled and said, "He does. I need to tell you something. You and Sam bring me joy. I never thought I'd feel happiness again. I owe you so much. I owe you my life, my future," he said, smiling as he took her hand and put it on his heart. "Thank you for saving me."

Shyly, she met his eyes and smiled. What could she say to this man? She looked up at him and said, "You and Sam, you are my world. You are my everything."

"Everything that is mine will be yours, starting with this." He reached into his pocket and pulled out a red Cartier box, which he held out to her. But Laura's mind was still mulling over his words and hadn't yet focused on the box in his outstretched hand.

"This looked like you, but if you don't like it, we can get something else," he said. She watched, mesmerized, as he gently opened the box. A ray of sunlight caught the largest diamond she'd ever seen, momentarily blinding her.

It was a stunning Asscher cut diamond, set in a platinum band of diamonds, that burst with flashes of light.

"It's beautiful and blinding," she said with a laugh, pulling her eyes off the sparkling ring to look at the man she loved. He loved her right back.

"It's big so that people will know you're taken. You are mine."

"I like being taken," she said in their playful way.

"I know you do. I also have an offer to make of my own," he said, taking the ring as he slid off the bed and kneeled next to her. He slipped the ring onto the third finger of her left hand. Pausing, as he appeared to collect his thoughts, he then looked up at her with warm, passion-filled eyes. Her lip trembled as she waited. She gave him a timid smile, which was the exact encouragement he needed.

A single tear leaked from the corner of his left eye as he said, "Laura, I'm sorry it took me so long to come back to you. I didn't think I deserved to find happiness twice in one lifetime. I don't want to miss one more day, one more minute of being with you and our son. Will you marry me?" She threw her arms around his neck and leapt into his arms, knocking them both to the floor.

"I take it that means yes?" he said with a relieved laugh.

"Yes!" she replied and kissed him.

He cupped her chin and smiled. "And just for the record, there will be no prenuptials, no conditions. I'm not marrying you because of Sam. I'm marrying you because I can't bear to live without you. These last few months without you were hell I never want to live through again."

Running a finger along his cheek, she wiped away the tear that had fallen. "I love you, Adam."

His eyes slowly, purposefully, traveled the length of her body before he flicked one of the silk straps off her shoulder.

"I think you're starting something," she whispered.

"Our lifetime, our story," he replied and flicked off the other strap.

# CHAPTER TWENTY-ONE

4TH of July Wedding / Tranquility
        The bride wore a pale cream lace dress picked out by her best friend that looked like it was made of five thousand rose petals. The famous and flashy Hollywood star felt it showed the appropriate amount of cleavage and leg to satisfy her high standards. The groom wore a black suit and complementary silk tie that exactly matched his bride's dress. The bride carried a large bouquet of Passion roses and a smile more brilliant than any of the Fourth of July fireworks that would follow.

They were married on the beach in front of Tranquility with their family and friends in attendance. Adam's cousin, Alex Stark and his wife, Daisy, had arrived from Portland with their two daughters. Kevin and Toby, Sam's unofficial uncles, entertained him during the ceremony. Adam's parents happily met their daughter-in-law, and marveled at sweet Sam. Even Scooter 2, Laura's wedding present from her husband, a new rescue dog of mixed heritage, sat politely next to them at the altar.

William and Kat thought it was the best Fourth of July party they had ever given. Kat was Laura's matron of honor, wearing a gown that concealed her own baby bump, and Alex served as Adam's best man.

Laura thought back to the previous Fourth of July and how far they had come. Not only did they have Sam, they were starting a new adventure. They were spending the summer at Tranquility while Adam managed The Bay Shore, and then they were moving to Portland in the fall after a two-week Parisian honeymoon. They had already bought a house and were going to decorate it together, putting in a large artist studio for Laura, who was preparing for a second fall show at Kevin's gallery. Sam's beach-themed nursery was being recreated with the addition of a tall giraffe wearing black and white polka dot trunks and a bright smile to the wall mural. The caption above all three would now read: *Daddy, Mommy, & Sam.*

Later that evening, after the festivities and fireworks had died down, Mr. and Mrs. Adam Stark slipped away to their honeymoon suite at The Bay Shore. Sam spent his first night away from them with his grandparents and his extended family under the Tranquility roof.

As they lay in the large bed, which had a breathtaking view of the ocean, Adam's hands roamed seductively from Laura's bare hip to her tousled blonde hair as he kissed her until she was dizzy with love for her husband. Reaching out to touch the shiny new band of platinum on Adam's finger, Laura smiled. He was officially her husband.

Laura looked down at her own sparkling band and smiled.

"What's that for?" Adam asked sleepily.

"Can't I smile?"

"That wasn't a smile. That was a Cheshire cat grin," he murmured, reaching out to touch her cheek.

"I'm in love and happy; happy for the first time in my life."

"I didn't think I'd ever be this happy again, but then I met you and damned if I couldn't stop myself from falling in love."

"And you became my friend and my lover."

"And we created a miracle," he whispered, softly touching her cheek. "Do you think we'll be able to do it again? I think I want a couple more if you are up for it."

"I think I want three or maybe four," she said hesitantly, as she shyly looked at her husband.

"Really? Well, you may have as many as you want," he said. "I don't mind giving them to you and practicing until we get it right."

"That's a relief. We will have to be very diligent about trying to get that many, lots of this continued baby-making activity."

"Maybe a little girl next time," he suggested.

"I'll do my best, but that is kind of up to you," she teased.

"I think I'm up for my end of the job," he said confidently, pulling her into his arms, almost certain there would be a little blue line that was going to prove that practice had made perfect over these past couple of weeks.

"Um," Laura said, and quickly kissed him.

"Um? What?" he asked.

"I have something to tell you," She said, burying her face in the crook of his shoulder.

"Tell me, no secrets between us," he said, his hands roaming over her.

"Your wedding present. I'll be right back," she said, and hopped out of bed. She ran into the bathroom and came back with a pregnancy stick in her hand. "I know you said we should wait a year, but when it comes to you, I'm kind of a fertile myrtle."

Adam smiled, then he said, with the softest kindest voice she had ever heard him use, "We're having a baby? Sam is going to be a big brother."

She nodded and smiled. "It appears that those cheetah condoms were just for show."

"Good," he said and held out his arms to her. "I love you, Laura Stark, now come here and let me show you just how much you mean to me."

Out of the worst tragedy imaginable, Adam had found love again. Before he saw Laura kicking her car on the top of Devil's Punchbowl, there had been dark moments, moments that he could now look back on with a shudder of fear. His life, the one that had once been unbearable, now had love again. He would protect and love Laura and their children as if each day was their last because as he knew from experience, precious gifts needed to be celebrated every day. His love for Laura and Sam would get stronger and more precious each and every day.

THE END.

# OTHER BOOKS BY MARY

Don't miss any of Mary Oldham's exceptional stories:

*The Silver Linings Wedding Dress Auction*
(stand-alone) October 2021

## The Hotel Baron's Series:

*A Paris Affair*, November 2021
*A Summer Affair*, December 2021
*A Roma Affair*, 2022
*A London Affair*, 2022

# About the Author

Mary Oldham is a multi-award-winning author, and three-time Golden Heart Finalist with the Romance Writers of America in the areas of Contemporary Romance and Romantic Suspense. Mary resides in Portland, Oregon when she is not writing by the Pacific Ocean in scenic Yachats, The Gem of the Oregon Coast.

# ACKNOWLEDGEMENTS

Originally titled: *Laura Takes a Lover*, this was the first book I wrote and it finaled in the first contest I entered, the Maggies. A few months later it went on to be my first Golden Heart finalist with the Romance Writers of America. Now titled, *A Summer Affair* it follows *A Paris Affair* and is book two in The Hotel Baron's series.

I've taken some liberties. Devil's Punchbowl and the Salty Dawg are places around Yachats, Oregon. The Bay Shore and Tranquility are figments of my imagination.

I couldn't have done this without a strong team behind me, Sue Grimshaw, my dream editor, thank you for loving this story. To Lynn Andreozzi, who designed another beautiful cover, you understand me. To the Deliberate Page, Tamara Cribley for making my baby shine and Chris Knight for flawless grammatical editing, thank you.

To my friends Catherine, Leslie, Lorinda, MarySue, Suzie, Tanith, Trudy, and Valerie who have encouraged and supported me, given me pep talks at midnight, thank you!

Thank you to Dr. Cynthia Aks, my yoga instructor and friend. Thank you for all of your encouragement and the generosity of your teachings.

A special thank you to my friend Valerie Thorne for all your marketing advice and help to promote my books.